The En...

Justin Scott is the ...
Who Loved the Normandie, *A ...*
and *The Cossack's Bride*. Born in New York City in
1944, he now lives in Connecticut with his actress
wife, Gloria Hoye.

JUSTIN SCOTT

THE EMPTY EYE OF THE SEA

HarperCollins*Publishers*

HarperCollins*Publishers*
77–85 Fulham Palace Road,
Hammersmith, London W6 8JB

This paperback edition 1994
1 3 5 7 9 8 6 4 2

First published in Great Britain by
HarperCollins*Publishers* 1993

Copyright © Justin Scott 1993

The Author asserts the moral right to
be identified as the author of this work

ISBN 0 586 21227 2

Set in Linotron Meridien by
Rowland Phototypesetting Ltd
Bury St Edmunds, Suffolk

Printed in Great Britain by
HarperCollinsManufacturing Glasgow

For Michael Donald Patrick,
My stepson, comrade and barbecue pal;
And for his mother,
Gloria Hoye,
My love, my beauty, my friend.

For their generous hospitality and abundant good talk,
I am indebted to Captain Whit Petrie,
Captain Kevin O'Conner, Captain Brian McAllister,
and Chief Engineer Ed Dougherty.

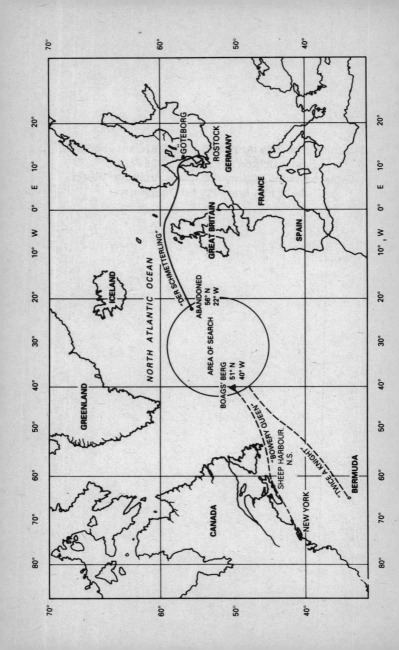

PART ONE

ONE

Mid-ocean in the high latitudes, far from any shore, the North Atlantic rolled before the wind. A winter sky hung low, black in the east where night loomed, grey where the pale sun descended from jumbled clouds. Snow squalls raced, bunched hard and dark as prairie stampedes, tore on and were lost upon a million miles of salt water as infinite and remote as space.

A ship crawled between the horizons. The sun settled below clouds and the sea was suddenly aglimmer in slanting yellow light that lit its tops. Slabsided, stacked high with steel containers, it split the rollers and sent them tumbling like avalanches of cream. The wind shredded its smoke and the sea swallowed its wake.

Hilda Krueger, the ship's stewardess, huddled in the lee of a container on the main deck near the bow, draining a bottle of Johnny Walker Red and mourning that the disappearing wake and darkening sky made it seem as if neither she nor the ship even existed. She pressed the icy bottle to her cheek where her boyfriend, the bosun, had slapped her, and took a slug for courage and another for hope. Four days to New York. She would jump ship, find a man, and become an American. Screw the new Germany. Enough unification, enough superior *Wessies* and whining *Ossies*.

A snow squall hit with a shriek. The temperature dropped twenty degrees. In half a minute, decks, cargo, and cranes were crusted white. Numbed, Hilda crawled around for her hat, then lit a Marlboro, expertly cupping the match from the wind.

Water dripped cold on her face and doused her cigarette. She cursed and looked up. Snow was melting from the

11

container she was propped against. Puzzled, because it was still bitter cold and everywhere else the snow was frozen, she rose to investigate.

From the bow all the way back to the house, some four hundred feet astern, the containers were stacked three high and seven wide. The front row, however, was only two high and four wide. She stepped from her shelter and pushed forward against the wall of wind, doubting they could see her from the bridge, if anyone was even watching. The container looked identical to the other five hundred on the ship — a steel box twenty feet long, eight feet high and eight wide — except that it was emblazoned with the international danger sign, test tubes dripping acid: CORROSIVE.

The door was neither locked nor sealed. Curious, Johnny Walker singing in her brain, she stuffed her bottle safely inside her quilted jacket. The handle lifted easily. Something told her she should report these oddities to the bosun.

The ship rolled and wrenched the door from her hands. Warm air poured out of the dark. The dying sunlight flooded a row of narrow cylinders, wrapped in plastic and secured upright like a set of organ pipes. Hilda stepped in for a closer look. A gloved hand closed around her throat, clamping off air, blood, and her astonished scream.

TWO

Kevin Patrick, captain of the tugboat *Bowery Queen*, sailed from Staten Island bound for Nova Scotia, with a big barge on a short wire and sympathy for Captain Ahab. They had owners in common, lingering owners. The *Pequod*'s had hassled Ahab dispensing pickles, spare Bibles, and last-minute orders. The *Bowery Queen*'s was in a panic about superstructure icing: 'Now remember, Kid,' Mike Fulton warned for the fourth time, 'if she starts icing, you head for the beach and anchor up. No heroics.'

'I'm not a hero, Mike.'

Mary Fulton, Mike's daughter, had a sack of Dunkin' Donuts for the crew, and a brisk sermon on the rising price of diesel fuel for their captain. Mary had even invited a guest, Mr Takashi of Okimitsu Diesel, the Japanese company that owned the barge.

Captain Mike wanted to drive, which was fine with Kevin. He could learn more watching the old man thread a ten-thousand-ton barge through the Kill van Kull than in two years at King's Point. And once they reached the open Upper Bay and headed for the bridge, it gave him a chance to run down to the towing deck to help the chief mate beat some rust out of a frozen Norman pin.

It was a bitter cold morning, with smoke stacks steaming on the Brooklyn shore and broken river ice riding the tide. He got back to the wheelhouse red-faced and shivering. Mike, who didn't get out on the boats much any more, was still having a ball, except that he kept reaching for the ashtray beside the steering sticks where a cigarette would be smouldering if Mary weren't standing guard.

Kevin said, 'Hey, Mary? I told Roberto you'd explain why he can't have a new fridge.'

13

Mary Fulton ran below to terrorize the cook, trailed by the wide-eyed Mr Takashi, and Kevin passed Mike a Marlboro he had bummed from the chief mate.

'Thanks, Kid . . . Where's yours?'

'I'm quitting.'

'Yeah.' Mike puffed happily. He was busy watching ships and tugs ahead, talking to their captains on the radio, and glancing back at the *Okimitsu Enterprise*, which loomed over the *Bowery Queen* like a four-storey building. Suddenly he lowered a window to yell at a deckhand: 'Sanborn, get your ass off the towing deck. If the tow wire parts, it'll cut you in half.

'How many fingers,' he growled to Kevin, 'does that asshole have to lose to get heads up?'

'I'll talk to him.'

The accident-prone Sanborn, a sort of *Exxon Valdez* and SS *Titanic* rolled into one, should have been fired years ago. But Mike had a soft spot for losers. He was also aware that outfits that couldn't guarantee deckhands steady work got the dregs. Kevin liked him. Sanborn was a reader, so they always had books to talk about.

'Now remember, Kid, if she ices up head for the beach.'

The *Bowery Queen* had a handsome, sea-keeping bow, but like most New York tugboats, her long, low towing deck offered less freeboard than a canoe. Coat her with ice, get a list on her, and over she would go, sucking seas into her stacks and ventilators. With a pair of locomotive engines shoehorned into her steel hull, she would sink faster than the crew could open her watertight doors.

Kevin showed Mike the chart. He had circled a dozen harbours where the *Queen* could shelter. The old tug had been built big and strong, a real brute in her day at a hundred and forty feet and six thousand horsepower. But a big tugboat was a very small ship, and winter turned hellacious up the Atlantic coast where forty-knot gales, fifteen-foot seas, and witches-tits' air temps united in freezing spray.

Mary came running up from the galley, looking confident that little Roberto would think twice before requisitioning new Brillo pads. She shot a suspicious look at the cigarette Kevin sailed out the window, but Takashi was right behind and she said only, 'Look, Mr Takashi brought a present for the *Queen*.'

She was flushed with excitement, her heart-shaped face all strawberries and cream, her eyes sparkling in the winter light. The Nova Scotia run was a big deal for Fulton Towing, and she, Kevin suspected, rather than her father, had swung it, even though Takashi kept bowing to 'Cap'an Furton'.

She unwrapped an elaborate paper box and removed a lacquer tray with a picture of Mount Fuji seen through a curling sea. Two boats scudded through the curl, their fate uncertain.

'"The Breaking Wave off Kanagawa",' said Kevin. 'Right, Mr Takashi?'

'Very right,' Takashi beamed. 'Woodblock print by Hokusai.'

'Yeah, well it's gonna break them canoes into chopsticks,' growled Mike, who blamed the Japanese for America's economy.

Mary, who wasn't often surprised, looked surprised and even a little respectful that Kevin knew the name of the woodcut. Kevin shrugged: 'I knew a girl, had it hanging in her kitchen.'

'Figures,' said Mike.

'Thank you, Mr Takashi. We'll hang it in the galley.'

Takashi obviously wanted it hung in the wheelhouse, but it was short on wall space, being mostly windows. Besides, the wave conjured memories of a grim blue-water voyage Kevin was still trying to forget. 'The galley's the heart of the boat, sir. We all go there when we're not on watch.'

'Mr Takashi was wondering what you were doing down on the deck before,' Mary said, with a glance Kevin interpreted as, 'Help me with this client who's going to be

15

paying both our salaries, before my father starts another round of World War Two.'

'I was servicing the Norman pin,' Kevin replied, which was one way to describe hammering rust out of neglected gear. The Okimitsu representative wanted to know what a Norman pin was. Kevin explained that vertical steel cylinders were raised hydraulically from the bulwark on either quarter of the stern to prevent the tow wire from sliding forward. He could have added that the wheelhouse controls had long ago died, so someone had rigged a Rube Goldberg contraption to pump the *Queen*'s Norman pins manually – great fun in a rolling sea.

'What is bulwark?'

Kevin and Mary hid smiles. At least he knew the stern was in back. The rest was easy; below decks was 'downstairs', and 'port' and 'starboard' were often as not referred to as 'left' and 'right'.

'Bulwarks are the rim around the deck,' Kevin explained, 'the sides. They keep us in and the waves out.'

Takashi remarked at the spray flying from his barge, which the *Queen* was pulling at an effortless six knots. 'Very strong motor.'

'Two motors. Twin screws in Kort nozzles.' And then, because the little guy looked genuinely interested, and Kevin really liked the lacquer tray he'd brought, and Mary was nodding encouragement, he drew a picture of the propellers spinning inside their tunnel-like sleeves. Takashi said, 'Efficient.'

'Forty per cent more.' Figuring they were on a roll, he drew him the rudders. 'Two sets of rudders. Okay? Rudders behind the nozzles for steering forward. And flanking rudders ahead of the nozzles for steering backward.'

'Very manoeuvrable, yes?'

Kevin hesitated. 'Yes and no . . . You can walk her sideways with the flanking rudders, but she takes about fifteen seconds to reverse propellers, so you have to sort of plan your moves ahead.'

Takashi asked for the sketches and folded them reverently in his notebook. Then he brought out a camera, took Kevin's picture and another of Mary and Mike, to whom he said, 'Wise captain, but so young. Very much school?'

'School?' Mike snorted. 'The Kid came up the hawsepipe.'

'Hawsepipe?'

'The hawsepipe is a hole for the anchor chain,' Mary explained. 'Captain Fulton means Captain Patrick worked his way up from deckhand.'

Translating manfully, Takashi arrived, Kevin guessed by his expression, at a fairly accurate image of a rat boarding at night. 'Is usual?'

'It is in this outfit,' Mike asserted proudly. 'Tugging's what you might call a contact sport. A man who's never seen carnage on deck ain't worth shit in the wheelhouse.'

Takashi glanced fearfully at his new and as-yet-undented barge. '. . . And now, with your permission Captain, I take pictures outside.'

'Go right ahead,' Kevin told him. 'Just please don't go down on the towing deck.' Mary showed him out the door on to the abbreviated deck behind the wheelhouse, and beamed her thanks. 'That was really great.' And then, with Takashi safely outside snapping his barge and the New York skyline, she gave her father a significant nod. More nods — flurries of fine dark hair as black and shiny as onyx — and Mike finally got it.

'The other thing, Kid, Mary says we need a list of any shit needs fixing. Right, Mary?'

'As soon as you can, Kevin. If this Canada run turns out regular like we hope, we've got to get the boat in better shape.'

'I know a good cheap yard in Halifax.'

'Halifax?' The Fultons looked at him, both with their frank and knowing blue-eyed gaze. 'I'll bet you do,' Mike snorted. 'Probably got some gal there, figuring to shack up on company time.'

Mary laughed. One of the mysteries of the New York waterfront was how petite, finely-featured Mary Fulton had inherited her father's foghorn laugh. The two of them going at him together threatened to blow out the wheelhouse windows. 'Maybe she's a port engineer. You dating a port engineer, Kevin?'

'You want a discount?'

'Anytime. We can't afford to be proud. Jesus, maybe *I* should date a port engineer.'

'I doubt you'd find one clean enough.'

He had spoken more sharply than he had intended. Mary's expressive mouth could be full with Mike's big smile and laugh, or taut as a stretched hawser when something pissed her off. Kevin got the taut one, now, and a fiery blue glance as she hunched down in her big duffle coat and oversized sweater, demanding, What was his problem?

Mike intervened: 'This repair list is Mary's idea. The boat feels fine to me.' He jiggled the steering stick to demonstrate. This time Kevin laughed. There was so much play in the linkage that the boat didn't swerve an inch; the shorter stick for the flanking rudders was worse.

'What?' Mike growled, furrowing his scarred brow.

'Nothing, Mike.'

Run 'em till they break was Mike's motto. Fulton Towing had been a fair-sized outfit until well after the Second World War, when containers destroyed the barge business, and Mike had been born with the fleet-owner's loathing of spending a buck on maintenance. Mary was having a hell of a time convincing her father to take care of the few boats they had left. Kevin caught her eye and nodded below, down toward the engine room. Mary returned a co-conspirator's smile.

'Dad? Why don't we ask Kevin's J.D. character what work he thinks the engines need?'

Mike growled reluctant assent. Kevin cranked the communicator. 'J.D., you got a moment?' He had set three conditions when Mike asked him to take the old tug on the Nova Scotia run: a new radar, a decent radio, and J.D. Doughtery in her engine room.

J.D., a three-hundred-pound giant with arms as big around as Kevin's waist, clumped up the half-circle of stairs and squeezed into the wheelhouse. Squinting through thick eyeglasses, he touched the peak of his Coonesville, Mississippi, Volunteer Fire Department cap, and drawled through a drooping walrus moustache, 'Morning, Miss Mary. Morning, Captain Fulton.'

Kevin said, 'Mike wants us to write a repairs list so Mary can schedule some dry dock time.'

'Whoa, whoa, whoa, nobody said dry dock time. Just write the list.'

'List?' J.D. pulled a big red bandanna from his overalls, removed his eyeglasses, and wiped them slowly. 'Why don't we start with that vibration in the port tail shaft.'

'Just a bent wheel,' Mike said hastily. 'We'll pull it one of these days and straighten it out.'

'Well, yessir, I believe the propeller *is* bent, but the stern tube gland's leaking, and that's a pretty fair indication the shaft's bent, too. Kev and I had her out yesterday and she shook something fierce over seven-fifty. So what I recommend is we pull the port tail shaft, straighten the wheel, straighten the shaft and seal the gland all the same time.'

'Yard time's expensive. How long?'

Before Kevin could stop him, J.D. answered, in all innocence, 'I wouldn't be surprised we run into a few other problems. Figure two weeks, tops.'

'*Weeks?*' both Fultons chorused, reminding Kevin that Mary was not a totally stalwart ally in this campaign to put the *Queen* in shape. Mary was still an owner at heart, genetically disinclined to spend money. She said to J.D., 'My Uncle Ed used a trick on a leaky gland where he cut a gasket, slipped it over the shaft, and then heat-sealed it.'

'I know how to nigger-rig it,' J.D. scoffed. 'It don't have to go on your list.'

Mary bridled. 'Now wait. I know the *Queen*. Dad and I lived on her. She's vibrated over seven-fifty, portside, since I was in high school.'

'Not like this, or you would not have celebrated your Sweet Sixteen.'

Mike picked up the binoculars and focused on two tankers and a multiple tug and barge tow converging on the Verrazano Bridge. Kevin had been watching them for several minutes. Mike slowed the *Queen* to let them through first.

'Let's let her earn some money first, then we'll see what we can do.'

'Kev knows a yard in Halifax.'

'We heard about her . . . Dad, we got to get back to the office.' She pulled the VHF microphone down from the ceiling to call *Mary Fulton* alongside. The little harbour tug had pushed the rear end of the barge through the tight turns of the Kill van Kull, then trailed to take her and her father and Mr Takashi off when Kevin put to sea.

'Wait a second, Hon,' Mike protested. 'Can't we stay till Kevin pays out the wire? Okay, Kevin?'

'Stay as long as you like, Cap.'

They cleared the Verrazano Narrows and descended the Lower Bay by the Ambrose Channel. Kevin took over and had J.D. winch out a couple of hundred feet more tow wire until it sagged into the water. He was just about to call little *Mary* alongside, when Mike Fulton's favourite saying — 'No two tows are ever the same' — came true with a vengeance.

The *Okimitsu Enterprise* had been trailing fairly docilely for an empty deckhouse barge in a strong wind. Suddenly it sheered to the right, overtaking the tug, riding hard alongside on ten thousand tons of momentum. The wire scythed up out of the water, taut as an iron bar.

Little *Mary Fulton* steamed to the rescue, slipping bravely between the barge and the edge of the channel. But her main engine, a notorious Fairbanks-Morse that had long ago turned her captain's hair white, chose that moment to quit dead. *Mary* clanged against the Number 11 channel buoy, driven by the wake of the barge, which, accelerating malevolently, threatened to catch up and drag the taut tow wire over the *Bowery Queen*'s right side. Kevin had raised her Norman pins to prevent that because pulling sideways on a tug was another way to sink it.

'The Norman pin is going down,' Mary announced calmly. And indeed the starboard pin was receding into the bulwark like a weary erection, thanks, he cursed, to a hydraulic leak he and the chief mate must have started while hammering the rust. Jimmy Sanborn charged out, taking his life in his hands to pump the pin, but he was way too late. The wire had already slid ahead of it. The tug heeled; coffee mugs, pencils and dividers, and Mr Takashi went flying.

Mike asked, once, very softly, 'Need help, Kid?'

'I got it.'

He couldn't outrun the barge. Going faster would only make it sheer more, right out of the channel. Fortunately, J.D. was ready at the winch controls, his walkie-talkie clipped to his parka. Kevin told him to let out more wire. As soon as the chief engineer had cut him a few hundred feet of slack, he steered the *Bowery Queen* left, across the narrow channel, and got the wire lined up behind the tugboat where it belonged.

'The barge is aground,' Mary announced in a voice a little less calm than when she had reported the Norman pin. 'Goddammit to hell.'

'There's sixteen feet of water there!'

'Not today, there isn't.'

A cruise ship behind them blew five short and rapid whistle blasts — the 'IN-DOUBT' signal — followed immediately by three short blasts to indicate 'I AM OPERATING ASTERN PROPULSION', which struck Kevin, caught with his wire across the channel, as an excellent idea.

Tankers, container ships and car carriers behind the cruise liner echoed the three blasts. Traffic backed up to the Verrazano. And when the cruise liner's Sandy Hook pilot finally got his ship stopped, he called on Channel 16, '*How long you intending to sit there, Cap? . . .*'

After the tide had finally helped float the barge, and

a three-hundred-dollar-an-hour diver confirmed minimal damage to its bottom, Kevin off-loaded the Fultons and a sombre Mr Takashi on to the revived *Mary*.

Mike was philosophical. 'Shit happens,' he said. 'At least nobody got hurt.'

Kevin said nothing. More shit happened when boats were neglected. But he worried he might have let out too much wire, or waited too long to turn. Mike patted his shoulder with a scarred, wrinkled hand. 'Hey, you're still the best boat handler your age in New York.'

Mary stewed in silence and Kevin couldn't meet her eye. Fulton Towing had blocked a main channel of the Port of New York for an entire afternoon, which was lousy advertising for an outfit that already had trouble getting work. Nor had his own reputation soared. That night, as the *Queen* pounded along Fire Island, still within VHF range, any number of tug captains radioed to ask whether the best boat handler his age in New York had seen himself on TV.

He had, while grabbing a quick bite of what J.D. had happily pronounced 'Roberto's fine grub'. Channel 9 News had sent a helicopter to tape the traffic jam in the harbour. The *Bowery Queen* had received star billing, streaming long white trails of prop wash as she tried to haul the barge off the sand. While her captain, leaning out the wheelhouse window, gesturing to his deckhands, appeared to be giving the camera the finger.

THREE

Der Schmetterling's crew were rousted into the cold to search for their missing stewardess. Muffled to the eyes against the cutting squalls still pounding the ship, they stumbled through the labyrinth of stacked containers until a seaman, less drunk than his shipmates, noticed water dripping from one container while all the others wore a coat of fresh snow. To his horror, it was plastered with the black and white CORROSIVE dangerous cargo labels.

Fire, he thought, a chemical fire, raging inside, melting the ice and threatening to ignite the entire ship and cargo. He yelled for the bosun on the walkie-talkie. The bosun arrived with the rest of the crew wielding pry bars, axes, and fire extinguishers, and cautiously opened the door.

A big man in a ski mask burst out of the container, waving a machine pistol in each hand. The bosun raised his walkie-talkie to alert the bridge. A weapon cracked, and the bosun went down with a bullet through his shoulder.

Suddenly there were no more heroes.

Which was fortunate for Manfred Echtheit, who was alone. Hurling the bosun's walkie-talkie overboard, he ordered the sailors to lie prone, then ran four hundred feet to the house. Inside he took the elevator to the bridge deck, burst into the peaceful, almost silent room of windows and started shooting.

He blasted the VHF radios hanging from the ceiling, then ran past the watch officer and seaman who had thrown themselves to the deck, and found the chart room, and the radio room behind it. He riddled the long-range radios and shot the weather fax, before he realized it wasn't a radio, and barely stopped himself in time from smashing the Loran. A satellite phone caught his eye and he shot the handset.

Shouting at the men cowering on the deck not to move, he circled the bridge, investigating radar, depth finder, internal ship phones. He shot an emergency distress radio. Then he remembered the captain, below in his cabin. He jerked an officer to his feet and ordered him to lead him there, which proved unnecessary, because the captain was lurking on the companionway with an old revolver in his hand; he dropped it hastily when he saw Manfred.

The two men locked eyes a moment, and when the captain looked away it was a tacit agreement that he saw no profit in admitting what he knew. 'Is there a radio in your cabin?' Manfred asked.

'No.'

Herding both men ahead of him, and smoothly reloading both weapons while their backs were to him, Manfred went down to the cabin and checked for himself. There was a satellite phone, which he shot without delay. Then he drove them back up to the bridge, and took stock. He had the captain, an officer and a seaman. At the bow, the bosun was bleeding. Nine more men were either with him or working their way back to the house. There must be cooks in the galley. Engineers in the motor room. But no stewardess, he thought with a grim smile. The bitch who started all this.

The men on the deck were watching him, gauging . . .

'How many crew do you have, Captain?'

'Fourteen – we had fifteen, but the stewardess is missing.' The captain searched his face.

Fifteen including the captain. Three he could kill. Four he could kill. Fifteen reeked of slaughter. But it was his life or theirs.

The world, as he saw it, was made up of two kinds: slaves and masters. One only had to look east to Slav Europe to know how badly things went wrong when the slaves got the bit in their teeth.

'All Germans?'

'*Jawohl!*' the captain replied hastily. 'All Germans.'

'Order them to the lifeboat.'

'What?'

'Every man to the boat, Captain. Abandon ship.'

And there it went wrong again. He couldn't blame himself, no more than he could blame the stove he had needed to keep warm for melting the snow on his container. If the woman had only — too many things to think of at once. Fifteen men, frightened, angry, huddled on the boat deck, shambling through the motions of launching the boat. The problem was he couldn't see them all at once. They were all over, working on the davits, unfastening gripe lines, entering the enclosed lifeboat and disappearing inside.

'*Wait!*'

A bearded sailor froze, terrorized, in the entry hatch.

'Leave the emergency beacon.' He had almost forgotten. After unification, West Germany had equipped the old East German merchant fleets with the modern Search and Rescue Satellite Aided Tracking System. He had already shot one on the bridge, but the lifeboat was sure to have one, too. Its beam, bounced off a satellite, would draw rescuers like whores to a Party Congress. With a hopeless expression, the sailor laid the metre-long cylinder on the deck. Manfred rolled it along by shooting holes in it.

Suddenly, while he was watching the last of the crew climb in the entryway, one of the hatches that studded the canopy banged open. The youngest sailor, a big fellow with the ferret eyes of a Berlin street fighter, popped out, head and shoulders and then a hand training a huge pistol straight at him.

He had a split second to realize his only advantage: the sailor was too big to move freely in the hatch. Manfred threw himself sideways as the gun gave a loud pop. A signal flare sailed past, missing his head by a foot and exploding in a shower of white phosphorus against the steel wall of the house.

Still in motion, still moving by sheer instinct, Manfred

snapped a shot from his left hand that creased the sailor's head with a bright red line and dropped him through the hatch like a puppet on a trap door.

The captain, last to enter the boat, stood frozen, his face a mask of horror. 'You killed him.'

'I think not,' said Manfred in his coldest voice, rising to his feet in a single fluid motion, both guns ready. 'Get aboard, Captain.'

In that instant, they were alone and the captain whispered, 'Where is the woman?'

'Overboard.'

'I wish we had never met. You used me for a fool.'

'I paid you like a prince. Get in the boat.'

'You're sending fifteen men to their death. We're in mid-ocean. We will die out here.'

Manfred shook his head. 'You have food, water, and protection. The boat is seaworthy. Someone will find you.'

The captain gestured at the water tearing past the hull. 'You'll have to slow the ship. We can't release at speed.'

Manfred hesitated. Recovering from panic, he had begun to conceive his next move. The ship was fully automated. One man could control course and speed from the bridge. He would run it himself, leave it on autopilot and try to figure out what tending was needed in the engine room. All he had to do was maintain course and speed for three more days.

'We must slow the ship or you will drown us all,' the captain pleaded.

The captain was right. She was making fifteen knots. But to reduce speed someone had to ascend eight decks in the house to the bridge. Manfred weighed the danger of leaving the crew in the boat, while he went to the bridge, against sending the captain, who could wreak God-knew-what sabotage. The choice was clear.

'Go!' Manfred raised both machine pistols and levelled them at the captain's chest. He knew nothing about ships, but a lot about small boats. 'What you must do is release

26

the after fall first, when you're just above the water. At two metres height.'

The captain was staring in disbelief, but Manfred was well into the problem now, breaking it down into compartments.

'You must be quick. But not too quick. The stern will drop and the ship will tow you bow on. Don't try to fend off the hull, you'll just injure your men. As soon as the stern hits the water, release the bow falls.'

'She'll capsize.'

Manfred considered this. 'Perhaps, if you're clumsy. But she's self-righting. Make sure the men are wearing their seat belts. She'll roll back around.'

'Dragging her upside down at that speed might tear off the canopy.'

'That's a chance we'll have to take, Captain. Lower away. And don't forget to close the hatch that bastard tried to shoot me from.'

The captain ducked through the entry door. His face was a pale, frightened blur as he dogged it shut.

They started the engine, a little diesel that rattled the fibreglass hull, and, upon the release of the gravity davits by a control wire within, the boat began to descend down the high wall of the hull.

Manfred, thinking he was safe now that they were encased in the boat, turned to race to the bridge and slow the ship, unaware that her momentum would carry her along at a brisk clip for many miles. In that instant, he spotted a radio antenna, a thin, flexible wire emerging near the back of the lifeboat and secured along the length of the canopy. There was a hinge at the exit point and it appeared designed to be raised upright to broadcast. Another radio. Probably an old one, but what if it were working?

The boat was beyond his reach, below the main deck, and descending fast. Pocketing one of his pistols, he gripped the other with two hands, changed to single shot, and fired at the hinge. A black dot appeared beside it in

27

the fibreglass and cries of alarm rose from the canopy. He fired again, missed again, and tried once more with no success. The boat was swinging in the davits, out over the water, then banging against the hull.

Another miss. More cries. He imagined them scrambling about the cramped space, desperately trying to unhook their seat belts. Fuck them. He was not about to trade his life for theirs. He switched pistols, switched the fresh one to full automatic, and sprayed the area around the hinge, obliterating it and tearing an apple-sized hole in the canopy.

Three metres above the rushing water, they released the stern fall and the back of the boat plunged into the sea, the bow too high. The little boat skidded on its stern, twisting violently, and spraying a rooster tail of water. Suddenly the bow wire let go, and the lifeboat dropped hard with a loud boom and a cloud of spray. Rolling and pitching, tossed like a feather in the wind, it careened so sharply that Manfred glimpsed the handrails moulded to the bottom of its hull. Then it swung back, buried its portside gunwales, and banged the side of the rushing ship. The ship raced past and enveloped it in its wake.

Hull trail and sea combined in a steep wave that caught the sharply careened boat and flipped it on its back. The orange canopy vanished under water. The white hull gleamed like the ragged whitecaps. Manfred watched her propeller spinning in the air; he was rid of witnesses.

Another rolling sea broke over the upside-down hull and suddenly it righted, springing up to land in the trough between two waves. And there it floated, orange and wet in the sun, a triumphant little speck on the sea, mocking him.

What if they had kept the old emergency beacon, as well as the old radio?

Crazed, he ran into the house and took the elevator up to the bridge, intending to turn the ship around, go back, and run down the lifeboat. He was reaching for the stick that would override the autopilot and return the ship to manual control, when it occurred to him that he didn't really know how to set her back on course for that invisible point in the ocean where Hans and Alison were waiting.

He ran out on the bridge wing. The lifeboat was so far behind that even eighty feet above the sea he needed binoculars to find the bright orange speck. And moments later the glasses themselves proved inadequate and he and the ship were alone on the sea.

Der Schmetterling's controls looked fairly simple. First he checked her course; it was precisely what the captain had promised, the same 260° WSW he had last reported to Alison with his own radio in the freight container. He left the autopilot alone. But when he found the dial that displayed the engine's revolutions per minute, he nudged the stick that controlled speed.

The deck throbbed as she picked up knots. The knot counter crept towards twenty and when it passed twenty she began to pitch rather more sharply, rising and falling in quickening rhythm. Manfred opened the throttle further, excited by the way she seemed to grow from steel and oil to flesh and blood. Four hundred feet ahead of the bridge her broad bow slammed into the seas. Huge spumes of white water crashed boiling to her sides.

Wondering why the captain had run her at the slower fifteen knots, he decided he was saving fuel. But if Manfred knew Alison Knight, she'd make the rendezvous ahead of time. You could set your clock early by her. A pleasurable smile softened his hard, sensual mouth; she even came early: getting a leg up, she called it. He had had good luck in his short life, and bad, plenty of bad. But she was his good luck; and Fate had been kind, because, for whatever reasons, however she was fuelled, Alison Knight needed him, and she knew it. Manfred smiled again. It made for a loyal woman.

After he had increased her speed to twenty-two knots – which seemed to be her limit – he decided to take advantage of his new situation. The captain's cabin was directly below the bridge, and luxurious by the standards of a man who had lived the past two weeks in a freight container with a chemical toilet, a kerosene heater, and bottled water. He took a long, hot shower, soaping and rinsing repeatedly, and turned the water so hot it was like a sauna. Emerging at last, he found a warm, clean robe, cashmere socks, and slippers in which he padded down the central stairwell investigating open doors until he found the galley. Suddenly homesick for Germany, he made an enormous sandwich of Black Forest ham on freshly baked rye, and washed it down with a cool Dortmunder beer and two cups of excellent coffee still fresh in the pot. The cook had baked a plum cake and he wolfed half of it before returning to the bridge, where he stood in the captain's robe and watched the sun set with a very brief yellow glow.

It was bitter cold outside but he thought he should check that no lights shone on the speeding ship. Whoever got in his way would have to get out of his way, though it was hard to imagine another living being in the desolation that spread to every horizon. When he went below and emerged on the main deck, he spotted several lighted windows in the bridge house and went in and located the cabins where men had left lamps burning. Satisfied that *Der Schmetterling* was dark, he returned to the bridge. He sat in the comfortable captain's chair and thought he might as well be on a spaceship hurtling through the night.

Sleepy with food, he dozed and awakened content in two hours. His contentment turned quickly to anxiety. The ship seemed to be pitching harder than before. He went out on the bridge wing and stood with the frigid wind slapping the robe, studying the sea, which had begun to change. Luminescent as their tops broke, the waves were higher and spread farther apart. And the ship was smashing into them harder as she dropped in their troughs. Reluctantly he throttled back to twenty knots, and then an hour later to eighteen, when again she had begun to ride too hard.

He couldn't get over the sense of power the speeding ship gave him. Four hundred and eighty feet long, twenty thousand tons, she flew at his bidding. He dozed again, and awakened to the disturbing thought that she was racing across the planet with him the merest barnacle clinging to her hull. He dressed and made his way out through the long corridors that led to his freight container. He had to talk to Alison.

But the radio couldn't reach her tonight. If she was sleeping the alarm should awaken her. Maybe on deck, changing sails. Or swept overboard, leaving poor Hans on a boat he couldn't sail. The seas *Der Schmetterling* was butting into at sixteen knots would be monsters to their little boat. He went back to the bridge. The empty house was too big and too empty — a playground for ghosts. He retreated to his freight container and tried to sleep.

The ship's plunging motion was greatly exaggerated at the bow. He lay in his hammock, feeling the ship pivot from the stern, dropping, down and down and down, shuddering into the sea, then rising, higher and higher and higher . . . plunging. Anticipating each descent, he began to feel queasy. Tasting the coffee and the ham in the back of his throat, he got up angrily. He had never been seasick in his life. He was an Olympic sailor, for God's sake. He dressed warmly and walked back through the rows of containers. The motion was easier in the house. He sat in the captain's chair and waited for the dawn, which came grudgingly in the high latitudes. Wide awake, he worried about radios in the lifeboat.

What if they repaired the radio antenna? Maybe they had an old beacon, the short-range type that beamed up to transatlantic jetliners . . . Maybe his ship was off course, the autopilot broken and lying. He prowled among the electronic instruments, found the satellite navigator, and located the readout on the Atlantic chart. Then he found the last entry on the chart, about twenty minutes before he had taken control. Measuring carefully with dividers, he reckoned he and his ship had averaged twenty knots in the last twenty-four hours, for a distance travelled of four hundred and eighty nautical miles.

His spirits rose. It felt like a marvellous accomplishment. Measuring ahead, he saw he was only five hundred miles from Alison. One more day! In that magnificent moment, the main engine alarms started shrieking.

FOUR

The Fulton Towing Company's office in the old ship-owner's building at 17 Battery Place was an extravagance for an outfit whose fleet had diminished to three elderly tugboats, one of which was often out of service. But whenever Mary broached the subject of moving to a barge at the company's last dock on the Kill van Kull her father, who in failing health deferred to his only heir in most things, argued that Mary had already reduced the expense by renting two of their four rooms to the Chang Brothers, late of Hong Kong. Ship agents who drove new Ferraris, the Changs were often behind with the rent but made amends by tossing work Fulton's way, for which Mary was grateful.

The front room where she worked looked like a combination harbour museum and botanical garden, crowded with a fleet of tugboat models in glass cases that had decorated the rooms they had rented, and a host of angelwing begonias Mary had driven across the country from California. Here she kept the books, manned the radio, answered the telephone when Hazel, their receptionist-typist, was out, hunted ship-assist and towing work, and staved off creditors.

Her father had kept the corner office, with its spectacular views of the Narrows, Upper New York Bay, the Statue of Liberty, and the abandoned Jersey railheads across the river. She found him on the telephone the morning after Kevin sailed, dickering with one of his old pals to buy a used EMD — a General Motors Electro-Motive Division locomotive engine convertible to tugboat use — for the *Mary*.

'Gotta go. The kid's here . . . Yeah, she's doing a hell of

a job –' he winked at Mary '– the rate she's going we'll buy out McAllister Brothers.' He laughed, which was a mistake, because it started him coughing. Doubled over, he choked goodbye to his friend, and dropped the telephone. Mary cradled it, brought him a cup from the water cooler, waited for what seemed like hours while he caught his breath.

'Thanks, Hon. Goddammit. This goddam winter . . . I got cold on the boat yesterday.'

'Why not go to Florida for a few weeks?' she asked, as she had repeatedly since before Christmas.

'Can't afford the time.' He glanced at the clock. '*Queen* call in?'

'Kevin says he'll make the Cape Cod Canal at sixteen-thirty . . . He also says that he's going to enter in the log that he strongly recommends the port tail shaft be repaired. His exact words. I think J.D. put him up to it.'

The tug's log was a legal document and she took it as a serious threat, but Mike Fulton snorted amiably. 'Covering his ass like a lawyer. The thanks I get for sending a dock rat to maritime college.'

'At least he didn't graduate.'

'Tell you what,' Mike grinned. 'When Kev calls in at sixteen hundred tell him I said to maintain equal revolutions on both engines.'

'What is that supposed to mean?'

'More bullshit for his log.'

'Dad, I've been thinking. Mr Takashi was a little vague on the phone last night. Sounds like a week or so delay in loading the barge. Maybe we *should* put her into dry dock.'

'Dry dock?' Fifty years ago a parting hawser had split his brow to the bone; now, scars and wrinkles gathered in a red scowl. 'I thought we been through this already.'

'Dad, if she dies on us and we lose the contract, we're in worse trouble than when I got home . . .'

Her father did what he usually did when he didn't want to talk about something. He swivelled his chair around, picked up his old binoculars, and scanned the harbour.

The dwindling band of cronies Mike Fulton tapped for jobs were retiring from the ship and barge business and most of the work these days went to aggressive outfits like McAllister and Moran that surrendered family control to international corporations. The Okimitsu contract was a fluke. Thanks to the Changs tipping Mary off early about a joint venture between the Canadian Province of Nova Scotia and the Japanese diesel engine manufacturer, she had managed to underbid the big fleets to tow assembled generators to Port Elizabeth, New Jersey. It would be the first steady money that the *Bowery Queen* or any other Fulton boat had seen in years. Her next step was to find a cargo to tow back to Nova Scotia in the light barge.

'Dad?'

'Yeah?' He was trying to focus on a big car carrier a tug was shepherding out of Brooklyn.

'I compared prices in Staten Island, Boston, and Halifax. Kevin was right. The Nova Scotia yard is really a bargain, and I think we could do even better in Pictou, up on the north-east coast.'

'Who's sailing that ship?'

Mary glanced down the harbour. Four miles south, below the Bay Ridge Flats, a blue speck nudged the stern quarter of a great black hull. 'Bouchard.'

Mike wiped his eyes. 'Damned binoculars are screwed up . . . Let me tell you something, Hon. It is the nature of tugboat captains to always want to put into dry dock. I used to pull the same shit driving my old man's boats.'

'J.D.'s supposed to be one of the best engineers on the Gulf.'

'Chief engineers enjoy dry dock even more than captains. They get to meet other chief engineers – the only people in the world they care to talk to – discuss engines, and drink beer on salary.'

'What's worrying me is we've got no offshore backup.'

Mary Fulton was too small to leave the harbour in the

winter, with or without the Fairbanks-Morse, and the single-engine *Sally Fulton* had no business outside, either. If the *Bowery Queen* broke down, Fulton Towing could lose their contract to the first seagoing tug to come along.

'Relax, the boat's got plenty more jobs in her. They don't make 'em any tougher than the *Queen*.'

Mary reached for an antique brass spyglass on the window sill, extended it to its full twenty-four inches, and peered through it. The water glinted malevolently in the pale morning sun. She shivered. Her years in California had thinned her blood.

'I'm going to meet her at Cape Cod, Dad. I'll go aboard with the Canal pilot.'

'What the hell for?'

'I'll ride along and see for myself.'

'Toot! Toot!'

Mary focused on Staten Island, sharp-edged and blue. 'That wasn't funny when I was a kid and it's not funny now.'

Mike trained his glasses on the harbour again. 'Still want to be a tugboat captain?'

'Too late . . .'

The barge and tug business had changed in every way but one: it was still so totally a man's preserve that a quarter-century into the women's movement, the United States Navy was the only outfit in the harbour where a woman could get a job driving a tug. She sometimes wished she had tried harder; with her contacts, she might have been the first.

'I better get going.' She had to pack warm clothes, cancel lunch with a ship agent, water her plants and straighten out Hazel.

At that moment Hazel plodded in to tell Mary she had a long-distance telephone call. But when she saw the Fultons behind telescope and binoculars, she backed silently away and told the caller that Mary Fulton was in conference.

'You're like a dog with a bone, Mary. You're like your

mother is what, always worrying. Right up to the day she died, she was still putting money aside for more insurance.' His mouth worked uncertainly, but it wasn't until he started coughing that Mary guessed that he was afraid to be alone without her. She got him water again and was about to assure him that she wouldn't go, when Hazel stuck her head in the door. 'That guy called from Los Angeles, again.'

'Tell him —'

'He said since you won't return his calls, he's coming to New York.'

'Tell him I've gone to Nova Scotia.'

Her father caught his breath. 'Poor son of a bitch seems to think you were going to marry him. What happened?'

'He started telling me things I already knew.'

Mike Fulton chuckled, but didn't smile. 'Better to find that out before you have kids, I guess . . . Hon, you don't have to ride to Nova Scotia.'

'Daddy, I promise I'll call in twice a day. I'll be back the end of the week. Okay? . . . Hey, you have my old radio at home. Leave it on and I'll call you in the evening, too. Okay?'

He rose unsteadily from his chair and hitched up his pants. 'I'll go.'

'I wish you could,' she said, gently, going around his desk and persuading him down with a hug. 'But I don't think it's a good idea, just now. Wait till the cough is better.'

'They're calling forty-knot gales. You'll have ten-foot seas. You'll be puking your guts out and cursing the day I let you go.'

'I'll get an earpatch.'

'There's five guys on the boat. Where you going to pee?'

'I'll knock first.'

He picked up his binoculars again. 'Where you going to bunk?'

'I'll borrow Kevin's cabin. He can hot bunk with J.D. and the chief mate. It's only two or three nights.'

37

'Look out that black Irish devil don't talk you into hot bunking with him.'

'Yeah, right.'

'What's wrong with Kevin?'

Mary swept the brass spyglass over Liberty Island.

'I said, "What's wrong with Kevin?" '

'Start with incest. He's practically your son.'

'He is not.'

'He *lived* with us after Mom died.'

'The kid had nowhere to go. I found him sleeping on a barge.'

'You did the decent thing . . .'

Mike rubbed his scarred brow. He and his daughter had started talking on the phone in the year before she came home. It was still a slow process, but they were getting used to the idea. 'You make me feel guilty, sometimes. You sound so jealous of him.'

'I'm not jealous. Not any more. It's past . . .'

'What's past?'

'I didn't want a boy moving in when Mom died . . . forget it. Let's just say he's not my kind of guy.'

'You haven't seen the kid in years. How do you know he isn't your kind of guy?'

'Have you ever seen the women who show up at the dock looking for him?'

'I seen 'em,' Mike chuckled. 'The kid grew up rough. What do you expect?'

'I'd expect you'd want better for me.'

She glanced sidelong at him, then back into the spyglass.

'Wait a minute. He's a decent kid. He's come real far from that whore of a mother. Real far.'

'From what I saw the other day at the dock, whore is the word. Lounge Lizette, if you want to be polite — I just don't think that a man who hangs around with women like that feels any self worth. Kevin expects women will be as awful as his mother and the ones he hangs out with keep proving his expectations.'

'Sounds like you put some thought into it.'

'Have you ever seen him stay with a woman for more than a month?'

'He's changing. He's getting older. Listen, Hon, I'm not saying Kev's a guy you wouldn't want to wear a — well, you know. And if you got serious, you'd want tests.'

'That applies to anybody and that's not what I'm talking about.'

'Well, don't worry. I've made damned sure he's careful about that stuff. He's no dummy and he's got no death wish.'

She lowered the glass, looked her father in the face, and said, 'Dad, I don't want to be a notch on the guy's belt.'

'I always thought you two would click . . . In fact, when you came home last spring —'

'When I came home the son of a bitch quit and left us in a lurch.'

'Mary, Mary, Mary, he was back in six months . . . He always comes back . . . All I can say is, he's not my son, but he'd make a hell of a son-in-*law*.'

She kissed his cheek. 'Just what I always wanted. Another man in the tugboat business. If you want a son-in-law find me one with clean fingernails who bunks at home.'

Her father's smile slid from his face. 'You're going to sell when I die, aren't you?'

'Sell what?'

'The outfit.'

'First of all you're not going to die. Second, who would buy it?'

He wasn't fooled. 'For Crissake, Mary, if you don't care why'd you come home?'

She couldn't tell him that she had come home because he was dying — perhaps she should report the burst of pride she had felt yesterday on the deck of the *Mary* at the sight of the *Bowery Queen* thundering to sea. Or that for one crazy second she had imagined the birth of a Fulton

39

offshore fleet. That would make him happy, but she wasn't feeling that generous.

Because earlier, while the barge was aground, and the *Mary*'s crew was struggling to repair their engine, what had filled her mind was the simpler fantasy she had been nursing for months. In it, she would whip the remains of the business into shape to sell it for enough to buy a house in the country. She would support herself as a freelance bookkeeper and then one day turn her business skills and green thumb talents to a small business, like a plant shop or nursery. Hidden somewhere in her desk was a course catalogue from the New York Botanical Garden.

'Tell you the truth, I always thought you'd leave it to Kevin.'

'Are you nuts? I like the Kid, but you're my daughter – even if you did run away . . . This is all we have. My old man left it to me and it's all I got to leave to you.'

FIVE

Der Schmetterling drifted clumsily on the swell, driven sideways by the wind that pushed its slabsided hull, deckhouse and silvery stacks of freight containers like a giant sail.

In the engine room, where men had sweated in swimming trunks, the air was frigid. Acrid smoke swirled in the dark. Compressed air sighed to death through burnt seals and ruptured tubing. From outside beat the rhythm of the lifeboat falls slapping the hull.

In the empty wheelhouse the helm staggered left and right, jogged by the rudder loose in the sea. A breaking wave slushed past, excavating the water beneath the hull, dropping it into a trough. The ship heeled violently. A coffee mug smashed on the grate where the helmsman had stood, and, deep in the hold, a fifty-ton bulldozer tested the chains that kept it from bursting through the side.

The wind probed, whistling and moaning.

Manfred Echtheit, colder than he had ever been in his life, had retreated to his container on the bow. It was warm inside. His kerosene lantern, swinging with the roll of the ship, cast a golden glow about the interior of the twenty-foot-long, eight-foot-wide, eight-foot-high box.

He had a hammock to sleep in and he lay in it now, his only escape from the abysmal rolling.

He had food and water for weeks and an oxyacetylene torch to cut his way out in case the container was loaded on the wrong ship with the door blocked, or the ship held unexpectedly in port. Neither had happened. The reality was worse.

He had warm clothing and a survival suit laid out in one corner like a mummy; and he had his canopied life raft, stowed in a white canister eighteen inches round and four feet long. He had his radio, his link to Alison and Hans, and a little Japanese generator to power it if the batteries went dead. He had a satellite navigation machine to tell them exactly where he was at the moment of rendez-vous, and a short-range beacon to guide her sailboat to the raft.

He had his little kerosene stove, on which he cooked his meals and which kept him warm. A kettle bubbled on it for tea and coffee — Indian green, and fresh ground Viennese roast — held down by a spring cord, because the dead ship was rolling in vast, frightening arcs.

He had an arsenal: his regular issue sidearm, plus two machine pistols and an assault rifle — all from the Staat-sicherheit armoury on Normannenstrasse — and a superb Soviet grenade launcher. These had not been standard issue by the East German secret police, but he had had access to them, along with almost anything else he wanted, as Stasi liaison to the Russian army. Alison had been quite impressed when he attained that post at such a young age; Manfred had taken it for granted as just another privilege enjoyed by what he had come to look back upon, wryly, as the Socialist aristocracy, into which he had been born the third generation.

He swung back and forth in the hammock, moodily recalling the moment the ship broke down.

Startled and confused, he had taken a long time to read the source of trouble. The flashing lights indicated the engine room. He ran to the elevator and pressed the bottom button. The elevator descended with maddening deliberation. Halfway down, he thought he felt the ship slowing, but who was to know, locked in a car in a shaft inside the ship?

When it had stopped at last and the doors opened, Manfred was assailed by a volcanic roar — a thundering rampart of sound pierced by the banshee-shrieking sirens. He had to push his body out of the elevator into a second barrier of searing heat. His battered senses, hunting an escape, were yanked upward as if by a noose and when he looked up, he saw a vast, open space that soared a hundred feet. Vertical piping lined the walls and stood in the centre, interlaced with tubes and wire. The pipework loomed like a forest in the fog, for the air was thick with the acrid smoke that had tripped the alarms.

He had pressed the ship too hard. With no one to tend her engine, something had finally broken. As the realization came crashing down on him, he supposed he should be grateful for his four hundred and eighty miles. Alison, ever the optimist, would have been, but all he felt was profound dismay at the five hundred still ahead.

The engine room was brightly lit with fluorescents. A sharper, bright orange light danced in the distance. Manfred, still forcing himself to enter the hellish noise, rounded the three-storey engine block and found a blazing fire.

Flames had engulfed a row of tanks – the purpose of which, and their contents, Manfred could only guess. The fire was intense at the centre, spewing from a ruptured pipe. He seized a fire extinguisher, puzzled out the controls, and sprayed rich white foam at the base of the flames.

Knocking the fire down, he saw that the deck was awash in thick oil that started burning again as soon as he stopped spraying. He emptied the fire extinguisher. Flames jumped again. He traced the pipe to a valve and threw his full weight against the handwheel. Gradually the oil had stopped spilling out. Then he found a fresh extinguisher and doused the flames again. Gasping for breath, he had leaned on a bulkhead, only to jerk back with an angry cry. The steel was so hot it had penetrated his heavy wool shirt.

Something had changed. Something was different.

The sound. The sound was fading and with it the rumble in the deck. The ship's engine was slowing, rapidly. He stood, staring about the labyrinth of pipes and tubes and tanks in disbelief. The valve he had closed. But if he opened it again, the oil would pour out again, and ignite.

The motion was different. The ship had stopped butting

the waves. She was rolling, adrift, and he hadn't the vaguest idea how to get her started again.

But that was absurd. There had to be some way to shunt fuel around the broken pipe. Even a man who had never been in a ship's engine room before could figure that out. Somewhere were operating manuals. Somewhere the engineers had instruction books. He cursed himself for not keeping the engineers aboard. He had panicked.

He would figure this out. He would find a way to shunt around the pipe or repair it. Only then had he finally got a close look at what had burned. Not only tanks, but electrical consoles. He saw broken glass and charred wire and finally the truth: the fire had destroyed the main engine controls, burned up pumps, switches, relays. An instrument array — a full wall of gauges that monitored the flow of fuel to the engine, oil and coolant — had turned to a face of blackened eyes. When he saw that, Manfred had sagged against the bulkhead, burned his hand on the smouldering paint, and screamed in pain and despair.

He shoved through the debris, back into the elevator. Halfway up the shaft the lights went out and it stopped. The last generator had failed and the rolling ship was dead inside. Flung about the pitch black car, Manfred had seen himself as if from another planet: trapped in the black car, in the black shaft, in the black hold of the ship, on the black ocean under the darkest sky.

The ship rolled harder.

He felt a deep rumble somewhere, as if an enormous animal were wandering around the hold. He was stricken by a numbing dread; for all he knew the ship was sinking, had already tumbled under the waves and was plunging to the bottom of the ocean as the water surged through her hull, filling the spaces and finally finding the elevator shaft.

He clawed in his clothes for his flashlight. The weak beam flickered on the ceiling hatch. He hauled himself up and climbed on to the roof, where, standing on a crossbeam, he probed the dark, located doors to the deck above and tried to prise them open with his burned hand. He got his fingers between them and pulled with all his strength, but it was useless. There was a fire axe in the brackets in the car. He went for it and finally prised open the split door and escaped into the house. He fled up the stairs to the dark bridge and out on the wing in the bitter wind . . .

. . . Now all he had left was Alison Knight fighting winter gales on a sailboat, somewhere five hundred miles to the west-south-west.

'Come in R-O-O-K. Come in R-O-O-K. Romeo-Oscar-Oscar-Kilo.'

Alison signalled the '*Go Ahead*' by switching the transmitter on and off.

'I am stopped.'

'*I'm afraid I don't copy*,' she radioed back. 'I am stopped' did not fit their code to confirm the point and time of rendezvous.

'Stopped!' Manfred snapped back. 'Stopped dead in the water in the middle of the ocean.'

'*Where?*'

Manfred radioed his position beside the northernmost, least-used Great Circle Route, adding ten degrees to his latitude and forty-five to his longitude. To anyone eavesdropping on the open channel, he was hard aground in the mountains above Oslo, Norway.

'*For how long are you stopped?*' she radioed back.

'Until you get here.'

SIX

'What's this "*Mayday*"?'

Three days after Mary had joined the tow at Cape Cod, tug and barge were making a comparatively smooth eight knots in the lee of Nova Scotia. The coast had finally checked the north-west wind that had kicked the Gulf of Maine into ten-foot seas.

'Exactly what the log says,' Kevin answered, 'a radio distress call.'

'No call sign? No position?'

'Just *Mayday*. I called the Canadian Coast Guard. They hadn't heard it. Maybe a lobster boat or a trawler lost his engine.'

He was standing the eight-to-twelve morning watch in battered Nikes, wool slacks and an old sweater. Running a slow, appraising glance down her jeans, he flashed his brightest 'black-Irish-devil' grin.

'Coffee in the thermos.'

Mary's stomach flip-flopped, and Kevin winked across the wheelhouse at J.D., lounging on the port steering stool.

'Good morning, Mary,' J.D. drawled. 'I was just correcting Kevin's misconception that you were seasick. He had forgotten the custom of New York tugwomen to conduct regular and close inspections of the sanitary integrity of the commode.'

'Good morning, J.D.'

Rushing to meet the pilot boat she had not had time to get a prescription earpatch, and over-the-counter pills had not worked. This morning she felt sufficiently recovered to venture up to the wheelhouse to read the log.

Each watch had recorded the tow's position, course by gyro and magnetic compass, speed in knots – which had

increased as the sea went down — wave heights, v
barometer, the revolutions per minute of the port an
board main engines. Each watch ended with the nan
the relief and the salutation, 'All is well.' Here and th
were added remarks: 'Passenger, Mary Fulton, the
Owner's daughter,' Kevin had entered in his crabbed,
little-boy's hand, 'Aboard with C.W.P.', a reminder,
couched in ancient language, of who was master and who
was a guest with the 'Captain's Willing Permission'.

Mary inspected him briefly in the backglow of the
shielded chart light. His thick, curly black hair was tousled
boyishly, his blue eyes were piercing, and his white teeth
laser-perfect. All that saved him from looking vacuously
handsome was a broken nose. A shackle pin flying across
the *Bowery Queen*'s towing deck like a cannonball, failing
to knock his head off, had stamped his face with an appearance of character.

'Kinda weird, that Mayday,' said J.D. 'It was like some
little feller living inside the radio just called out, "Mayday",
and went back to sleep. Good machine you bought, Mary.
Clear night like this, could of caught a skip signal a couple
of thousand miles off.'

It was still more dark than light — daybreak late so far
north — but off to the east a breathtakingly pure blue line
swelled on the horizon where the new sky met the darker
sea. Mary watched a string of gulls forge through it and
head landward, their wings labouring as if they were
towing the weight of the dawn.

The temperature had dropped. The *Bowery Queen*'s foredeck was slick with frozen spray and her rails and bulwarks
glinted under a thin white coat of ice. Overhead, the sky
was black, scattered with fading stars. The sea was empty,
and they were alone except for the birds and dim clusters
of lights on the sparsely populated Canadian coast. Two
thousand feet astern, a red light and a green light marked
the barge at the end of the wire.

Mary dabbed into the cup of oatmeal Roberto had
coaxed her to take to the wheelhouse when she fled the

fried egg odours of the galley. Thankfully, Kevin and J.D. were locked in a joint cigarette-stopping campaign and neither had backslid, though Kevin had started chewing on a horrible-looking cold cigar.

There was a stillness in the wheelhouse now that the boat had stopped rolling, a quiet broken only by the distant whine of the turbochargers, the occasional hiss of the air-assisted steering sticks as Kevin made small adjustments to their course, and soft static from the long-range single-sideband radio, a rhythmic sound like a sleeping dog. Overhead, a red eye marked the short-range VHF radio, suspended from the ceiling; a green glow emanated from the radar screen, in the middle of the dark between the port and starboard steering stations; the Loran navigator glowed green on the chart table in the back of the small cabin.

'Okay, Mary, come clean,' Kevin said. 'The old man sent you to spy on us, didn't he? Afraid me and J.D.'ll organize a new union?'

J.D. snorted in the dark. Powerful tugmen's unions were as dead as the Confederacy, since losing a strike in 1988. In New York, the older men had retired, opening the job market to Gulf Coast men like J.D. who had learned their trade running supply boats to offshore oil wells.

Mary swallowed a spoonful of oatmeal, liked it, and dipped for another. 'We heard you guys were trying to sell our boat.'

'For what, scrap?' Kevin nudged the port throttle and shone a flashlight on the rpm counter. As the needle staggered from 750 to 850, a tremor began to rattle the boat. It came from the left side. Down on the towing deck, as Mary had confirmed during a desperate hunt for fresh air, the vibrations were pronounced.

J.D. cried, 'Stop that, Kevin, 'less you want to sink us.'

They had been double-teaming her since she came aboard. It was the engineer's turn to carry the ball. 'Well, the trouble is, Mary, the boat's like a dog with tumour.

You just don't know how long . . . And now you got this towing contract your daddy's gonna be runnin' her balls to the wall.'

'We've had some lame engineers since the strike,' Mary admitted freely. 'The old hands retired. But now we've discovered you fine fellows from the oil fields.'

'Well, hell, Mary,' J.D. rumbled from the depths of his enormous chest. 'He'd a found us a whole lot faster if he'd told us we'd get a pretty girl aboard.' This statement fitted the tacit parameters they had worked out since Mary joined the boat. J.D. was married – and at thirty-eight, a grandfather several times over. In girth and steel-edged humour, he reminded her of her favourite uncle, her mother's brother Ed McKay.

'Fact is,' he continued, 'EMDs will put up with a lot of abuse.'

'God knows these have,' said Kevin.

'But a bent tail shaft is something else. Hell, Mary, we're only talkin' about a week in the yard.'

Mary shook her head. Her father was right: the *Bowery Queen* was not the foundering wreck her crew suggested. 'We're going to complete a few runs first, and get some cash flowing. Then, when we get a hole in the schedule, we'll put her in.'

Kevin recognized the signs that her mind was made up. 'There's Sheep Rock Light, J.D.; why don't we take in a thousand feet?'

The lighthouse was winking on an island half a mile off Sheep Harbour. Kevin cranked the communicator and called the seamen from the galley. Leo, the Filipino chief mate, came up to the wheelhouse, eyes widening at the sight of the ice that coated the boat. 'We'll take up a thousand feet now, and shorten some more after we round the buoy,' Kevin told him.

J.D. shrugged into a parka big enough to shelter a family.

Mary said, 'By the way, I'm still waiting on your fix-it lists.'

'Start by buying insulated sea boots for the little guys. They've never seen ice before, have you Leo?'

The mate was a squarely built, mature man in his forties, his shiny black hair tied up in what looked like a Sumo wrestler's knot, his skin smooth as a man's half his age. He had a solemn smile and a soft, deep voice.

'Only in Coca-Cola, Kevin.'

Mayday. Mayday. Mayday' suddenly sounded on the open distress channel, 2182, thin as a cry from the bottom of a well. *'Mayday. Mayday. Mayday.'*

Mary raised the volume and switched on the shielded chart light to write the sender's call letters and position. Instead, silence stretched.

'Same guy as before,' Kevin whispered. 'Sounds German.'

'Definitely German,' Mary agreed. 'That's no lobster-man. That's someone on the high seas.' She worked the receiver, delicately probing the ranges around the distress frequency. Silence.

J.D. had paused on the steps. 'Apparently,' he rumbled, 'they're attempting to rig an antenna, and not enjoying success at it.'

'Or some jerk kid screwing around in science class,' Kevin growled. 'You want to log him in if he comes on again, Mary? I gotta steer. J.D., let's grab that thousand.'

He turned on the work lights, illuminating the back of the boat and the sea around it. The long, red, oval-ended towing deck was low to the water and bisected by the tow wire that passed over the stern and dipped into the boiling wake. Leo moved cautiously on to it, bearing a yard-long wrench and trailed by Boags, a young Filipino seaman with an eager puppy-dog grin and a hard lean body like a cat.

J.D. emerged on the fiddley deck, one level down, and went to the winch controls, where he could watch the seamen on the towing deck, the wire, and the big winch drum that reeled it up. He winched in fifty feet so that the seamen could loosen the chafing gear, a six-foot-long, rubber-lined steel sleeve that protected the wire from rubbing where it dipped over the stern.

Leo and Boags approached it warily, shooting glances over their shoulders as they worked. The towline was two-and-a-quarter-inch plough steel wire wrapped around an oiled rope, and taut as an iron bar. If it hung up, then suddenly freed itself as the boat or the barge shifted on the swell, it could crush a skull, lop off a leg, or fling a man overboard into the path of the barge.

Jimmy Sanborn came out of the house and hovered, close enough to get mangled – or inadvertently block the other men's escape path – if the wire jumped. Kevin spoke into the walkie-talkie, and Leo motioned Sanborn into the lee of the house. Just last summer Jimmy had caught his fingers in the towing winch, and the way Kevin had heard it, had been lucky he kept his arm. After lecturing the deckhand on the dangers of the boat, he suspected that it was less ignorance of the explosive forces coiled within the weight and momentum of marine machinery that made Sanborn take crazy chances, than a pernicious variety of mid-life-crisis bravado.

Leo and Boags attacked the bolts that locked the chafing gear, gripping their tools with both hands and throwing their full weight against the wrench handles. The Filipinos were awfully small and light for tugmen, Mary thought, and, indeed, the lithe young Boags twice put down his own wrench to double up with Leo on a particularly stiff bolt. Teamwork delighted him: big smiles split his face and he slapped the older mate on his back as if cheering their bodies on against rust and steel.

'Little Boagsie is something else,' said Kevin.

Mary was reminded again of her adolescent dream to be a tug captain like her father. Decking – working your way up handling the heavy six-inch hawsers used in ship docking – was the only way to start, he had insisted. How else could a captain really understand the forces at play? But New York deckhands tended to weigh in at over 160, whereas it had been clear already that even a diet of Sarah

Lee and chocolate malteds would never fatten Mary Fulton much past 120. Eventually she had let him convince her he needed her more in the office, keeping the books and answering the telephone, as her mother had. In return, he did teach her to drive the *Queen*. She had picked up many of the finer points of ship-assisting in the harbour, but out here, corking around on ten-foot swells, was a whole new story.

Leo and Boags loosened the sleeve and connected it to a holddown cable, so the tow wire could move freely through it, then stepped back out of the way for J.D. to start winching. The wire ground slowly on to the winch drum, snapping and crackling from the strain and throwing little sparks like fireflies. Yard by yard, the barge caught up with the tug, halving the distance between the two vessels while the engineer watched for damaged strands.

The *Bowery Queen* rounded Sheep Rock as the sun spread over the ocean. In the fresh light, land formed up clearly on both sides of the channel, a sprinkling of little islands at first, then long forested arms of the shore. Green fir trees, deep in snow, grew down to beaches stacked with ice. Kevin ordered the cable shortened to three hundred feet. Slowly the dip of wire between tug and barge straightened, until it sprang from the water, slicing the surface like a cutlass.

The little harbour was a narrow, fjord-like finger of the sea. Mary saw a steep-roofed church on one side and a concrete wharf on the other. A heap of ice marked a reef below the church. 'Handy,' said Kevin. 'Run aground and jump ashore to pray.'

'*Mayday. Mayday. Mayday. This is lifeboat Vhiskey-Oscar-Mike-Romeo. Vhiskey-Oscar-Mike-Romeo.*'

'*Lifeboat?*' Mary and Kevin looked at each other.

Mary wrote *WOMR*, and waited for his position. The caller sounded German all right, pronouncing Whiskey with a V.

'*Abandon ship. Abandon ship.*'

'*Where*, for Crissake?' said Kevin, eyes busy with the barge aft and the wharf ahead.

'*Position: latitude fifty-six degrees North; longitude —*'

The radio buzzed for a second and the signal died. It buzzed again, like the lowest note from a bass guitar, went silent and after a moment resumed the breathing noise of a sleeping dog. Mary switched on the transmitter: 'WOMR. WOMR. WOMR. This is the *Bowery Queen*, Sheep Harbour, Nova Scotia. Can you come back on twenty-one-eighty-two?' She switched to receive, waited, and tried again.

She reached past Kevin for the short-range VHF hanging from the ceiling and radioed the Canadian Coast Guard on Channel 16: 'This is the tug *Bowery Queen*, Echo-Lima-Mike-X-ray, heading into Sheep Harbour.'

'*Come back on eighteen, Bowery Queen.*'

Mary stabbed the tuner to 18: 'Good morning, we just caught an abandon ship distress call on twenty-one-eighty-two. Whiskey Oscar Mike Romeo. Latitude fifty-six degrees North.'

'*Thank you, Bowery Queen. We copied.*'

'Did you get the rest of his position?'

'*Negative.*'

Mary looked at Kevin, who said, 'The middle of the middle of nowhere, somewhere between Scotland and Labrador.'

'Those poor people — maybe they're in a shipping lane . . .'

Cold comfort, both knew. The so-called Great Circle Routes between Europe and North America, the shortest courses across the empty ocean that shipmasters followed more or less closely depending upon ice and weather, were not heavily trafficked. They themselves had not encountered a single ship crossing the Gulf of Maine, which was merely the slightest dimple in the vast Atlantic. A lifeboat in a winter sea might as well be sixty miles away as six if a passing ship's radar was unattended, which was common in mid-ocean.

The wharf was close now. Mary had flown to Halifax and

driven out here last month to look it over. This morning something seemed odd about the big blue assembly plant up on the hillside where the Japanese engines were mated to the Canadian generators. Nearly 10 AM, and no cars in the parking lot.

Kevin was conversing by walkie-talkie with Leo on the towing deck and J.D. at the winch. Docking the barge would take a while. Keeping out of Kevin's way as he shuttled between the port and starboard controls and the back windows, she radioed the Coast Guard again. 'This is *Bowery Queen*. Have you gotten a position from Whiskey-Oscar-Mike-Romeo?'

'*No further transmission.*'

'What ship is the boat from?'

'*Former East German container ship* Der Schmetterling. *ETA Port Elizabeth, New Jersey, the day after tomorrow.*'

'Spell that, please.'

'*. . . German for ''Butterfly''.*'

'How many crew?'

'*Anything from ten to thirty,*' came the dry reply. '*They're cutting crews since they've gone capitalist.*'

She signed off, promising to report any new signals, and hovered near the radio while Kevin manoeuvred the barge alongside the loading end of the brand new government-built wharf. In less than twenty minutes, the seamen were wrestling frozen stiff hawsers on to the pier. Then Kevin gentled the *Queen* to her own rest around the corner from the barge, and told J.D. he was done with the engines.

'Very nice,' Mary said.

'Thanks, Boss . . . I'm going to catch some sleep. Okay if I use my bunk? J.D.'s going to want to crash, too.'

'I'll be busy all day with our Japanese friends.'

'If we're still here tonight, I thought I'd take the little guys up to the Canadian Legion Hall for a beer.'

'I'll give you an idea as soon as I can when we'll leave.'

He left her alone in the wheelhouse, where she lingered by the radio, wondering whether their brittle exchange had rung as stiffly in Kevin's ears as it had in hers. Finally, she went below, reached into his darkened cabin, and pulled out a parka. Out on the main deck, the cold was stunning. She climbed over the bulwark, across the big truck tyres chained to the hull, on to a log roped to the wharf and on up to the windswept dock itself. The assembly plant lay a quarter-mile up the cleared slope with the forest streaming down on either side. It looked deserted.

She had started walking up the ploughed road, when a Royal Canadian Mounted Police car came bouncing down it from town. It passed her and stopped beside the barge. Mary went back to investigate.

An officer in a bulky uniform parka and broad-brimmed hat nodded sternly, and scrambled over logs and tyres on to the barge. He pulled a piece of paper from his coat and Scotch-taped it securely to the barge's raised gangway, taping all four sides so the wind couldn't blow it away.

'What is that?' called Mary.

'Court order.'

'What for?'

'The barge is impounded.'

'Impounded!' she echoed in disbelief. 'It belongs to Okimitsu Diesel. I just towed it up from New York.'

'Thank you. We'll have a devil of a time running down their assets.'

'What?'

He pointed an accusatory finger at the deserted blue building. 'Belly up.'

'Bankrupt? That's crazy, Japanese don't go bankrupt.'

'Folks around here don't know whether they're madder at Okimitsu or the bureaucrats in Ottawa.'

'But I have a contract to tow their generators to Port Elizabeth.'

The Mountie dug out a business card. 'My barracks will have the lawyer's telephone number.' His eyes hardened on the *Bowery Queen*. 'Whose boat is that?'

'*Mine!*'

'All yours, Miss?' The Mountie broke into a condescending smile.

'She belongs to Fulton Towing of New York. I'm Mary Fulton. You want documents?'

'No . . . that's all right. I only have orders for the barge, anyway.'

He drove away, leaving Mary standing by the *Bowery Queen* at a deserted pier. Kevin poked his head out the galley hatch. She turned her face to hide the tears searing her eyes.

'Sounds like you're out of a job, Boss.'

'Where do you think that leaves you, fella?'

'Same place I've always been.'

'*What* is your problem? You've been taking potshots at me ever since my father gave you your job back.'

'Your father *asked* me back.'

'So what's your problem?'

'No problem,' said Kevin, backing into the galley and behind the eight ball where he usually ended up when he tangled with her. No problem. Except that until she came home last spring, Kevin had been enjoying the privileges of Mike's senior captain and favourite 'Kid'. Not to mention nearing an agreement, or at least a sort of understanding, that when Mike retired he would make it possible for Kevin to buy the *Bowery Queen*. Then suddenly Mary was home, after running out on them eight years ago. Mike immediately appointed her general manager – boss of all his captains, including Kevin Patrick – leaving no doubts who was heiress to Fulton Towing, including the *Bowery Queen*, which left Kevin stuck as a hired hand.

Mary spent the afternoon radio-telephoning agents in New York, St John's, and Halifax, but failed to find even one barge or dead ship to tow down the coast. The *Bowery Queen* was doomed to return to New York light, burning nearly six thousand dollars' worth of fuel – six thousand she had no prospect of earning, since Okimitsu's Canadian venture had gone belly up. And once back in New York the big tug would be reduced to begging around the harbour for day work when the fleets contracted to the shipowners were temporarily short of a boat.

The crew ate supper in silence; Fulton Towing was too small an outfit to cloak its troubles in a corporate cloud, and they feared for their jobs. Mary volunteered to stand anchor watch so that Kevin could take them all drinking at the Canadian Legion Hall, the only bar in Sheep Harbour.

She tried to cheer herself up by washing her hair in a long, hot shower. Running out of hot water first, she returned to the wheelhouse and tried to raise her father on the single-sideband. He had a 150-watt Heathkit at home, which Mary's Uncle Ed, a McAllister port engineer, had helped her assemble for her ninth grade science project. If conditions were good, direct radio-to-radio communication was a lot cheaper than long-distance telephone. The atmospherics *were* good tonight, and she heard him clearly. His voice was round and full and he sounded ebullient, thanks, Mary suspected, to an absolutely forbidden Seven & Seven. She had a horrible feeling he was smoking a cigarette.

'How's the weather?'

'They say snow. Daddy, I had no luck at all getting a tow. No one's doing a damned thing up here. How'd you do?'

'Something'll turn up,' he promised, hurling her thoughts back to her teen years when, having switched to a commercial course in high school to learn to keep the books, she had begun to see the disaster looming. Containers had replaced barges in the port of New York and only the companies rich enough and quick enough to go international into the oil fields and ocean towing would survive. They had owned sixteen boats when Grandpa died, eight when Mary took up the jobs her mother had done in the office, six when she fled to California. But Mike Fulton had never lost his optimism.

Too down all of a sudden to spare his feelings, she said, gloomily, 'I hope you're right, because we're not going to make it, otherwise. We owe too much money.'

Ice cubes clinked against glass. *'Sure we are,'* he said, his voice trailing off as if he had finally grasped the situation: without regular work they couldn't keep the *Queen* going; and without their strongest tug it would be impossible to maintain the fiction that Fulton Towing still existed.

'Anything new on *Der Schmetterling?'* The last she had heard was the Mayday this morning, which felt like a year ago.

'Yeah,' he lunged at the change of subject. *'I talked to Bob Moore; he was talking to Bud Lowe, the ship's agent. The guy's tearing his hair out. Hasn't heard from the ship in four days. Doesn't know where the hell she is, can't raise her on the radio.'*

That was not particularly unusual. Mary knew it could take days to make a high seas radio-telephone connection, depending on the atmospheric conditions. Satellite phones were expensive, and even if the ship had one, it might not be working.

'Does Lowe think she sank?'

'Why the hell else would they abandon ship? . . . Poor bastards, what a place in winter . . .'

'Did Lowe mention her cargo?'

Lowe had been talkative. Bob Moore had reported in detail to her father. It sounded as if *Der Schmetterling* was on an especially profitable voyage. Embarking from Rostock with several hundred containers, some cars and farm machinery, she had picked up more containers in the Swedish port of Göteborg, along with some bulldozers and trucks.

'What's it insured for?' Mary asked.

'Twenty million.'

'Dad? . . . What if we went looking for the ship?'

'Huh? What are you talking about? Salvage?'

'Well, I mean go out and . . . well, yeah, I guess . . . salvage.'

'On spec? Forget it. What if she sank? Who'd pay for your fuel?'

'Ouch! . . . How much do you get for salvage?'

58

'The award's set by an arbitrator. Depends on the value of vessel and cargo, and the effort the salvor puts into salving it.'

'Let's say the ship and cargo are worth twenty million dollars.'

'Depends. Tow her in from Sandy Hook on a summer morning, you'll get tug time.'

'Let's say you towed her two thousand miles on a winter night.'

'The way I hear it, the fees average around five-six per cent. But if you really bust ass, risk your equipment, spend your own money going out on spec, the arbitrator could go ten per cent.'

'Ten per cent . . . That's *two million dollars*.'

'Peanuts from Lloyd's of London's point of view. Two million salvage fee is a lot less than twenty million insurance if the ship is lost.'

Mary stared at the radio in slack-jawed astonishment. Two million dollars? From the point of view of a woman scrambling to keep three tugboats afloat, a salvage fee of two million dollars was all the answers to all the problems she could conceive.

They signed off after Mike promised not to pour a second drink. Mary opened the door to sniff the air and think about two million dollars.

Night had fallen bitter cold and the little harbour was pitch black except for the carbon arc lights blazing on the wharf, and the slowly-whirling beam of Sheep Rock Light. The wind, which had shifted northerly, smelled of fish and salt and snow. A storm was coming. The wind carried a sullen boom and it took her a minute to realize that the sound she heard was surf pounding the outer islands that shielded the harbour mouth.

'Mayday' jumped out of the radio. She dived for a pencil. The signal was thin as an echo, the English halting, the German accent thick.

'Mayday. Mayday. Mayday. Vhiskey-Oscar-Mike-Romeo.

Vhiskey-Oscar-Mike-Romeo. Lifeboat Der Schmetterling. *Latitude fifty-six North. Longitude twenty-two degrees thirty minutes Vest. Fifteen man. Lifeboat. Ship steam —'*

The transmission ended abruptly in a hail of pops, hollow thunder, drumbeats and whistles; Mary tried to pull it back, fingers flying on the digital tuner, as she scanned the micro-edges of the distress channel.

'Latitude fifty-six degrees North. Longitude twenty-two degrees thirty minutes Vest.' She glanced at the coastal chart. It didn't go that far out. *'Fifteen man. Lifeboat. Heavy sea. Two man wounded. Ship steam vest . . .'*

The signal faded again. There was no pop this time, no hollow thunder, as if the frantic caller's transmitter had gone down for good. She switched hers on and for ten minutes tried to raise them. Finally she radioed Yarmouth Coast Guard on Channel 16. *'Der Schmetterling's* lifeboat again. Did you copy?'

'We got some.' They traded notes. The Canadians weren't as sure as Mary was of the longitude, and were running their tapes through the computer to enhance the recording. On the other hand, they had picked up the information that the men had been four days in the lifeboat.

'Could you tell me what this steaming west is, Bowery Queen?'

'His last words were something like "Ship steaming west." ' She scanned her hasty notes. 'He said it twice. First he said, "Ship steaming." Later he ended, "Ship steaming west", I think.'

'We have: "Two men wounded" – they mean injured – "Ship abandoned. Life vest." ' '

'No, no. I think he said, "Steaming west". Or maybe "speeding".'

'I'm afraid that makes no sense, Bowery Queen. *Maybe he meant steamship.'*

'Is *Der Schmetterling* a steamship or a motor vessel?'

'Motor vessel.'

'I think he said, "Steaming".' The phrase was used

commonly. The *Queen* was said to steam, though in fact she was powered by internal combustion diesel engines.

She signed off and radioed for a taxi. Then she radiophoned *Der Schmetterling*'s New York agent.

Bud Lowe, who answered the telephone as if he was expecting the worst, had a voice like a man who enjoyed gravel for breakfast. He had no idea where the ship was or what had happened to the crew.

Mary related what she and the Canadian Coast Guard had heard on the radio. Then she took a deep breath and plunged: 'We're positioned to search. We've got the biggest tug this far up the coast, four days closer than New York. Six thousand horsepower, bunkered, crewed, and provisioned.'

'I'm not paying anybody to go joy riding around the ocean before I find out what's going on.'

Mary could not wait. At twelve knots top speed, the *Queen* was much slower than the fast European salvage tugs. To beat them to the ship she had to sail immediately.

'Then would you sign a Lloyd's Open Form? No cure, no pay. Costs you nothing unless we find her.'

'Salvage? Sure, sweetheart. Soon as you get a line aboard.'

The taxi she had called pulled on to the wharf, blowing its horn.

'As I understand it, once I get a line aboard, I don't *need* a Lloyd's agreement. And a voluntary speculative salvage effort will enhance the award.'

Lowe tried to mollify her with a magnanimous growl. *'Tell you what. I'll talk to the insurers and get back to you tomorrow. Where you going to be?'*

'Out there. We're going now. On spec.'

'Who are you?'

'Mary Fulton. Mike Fulton's daughter?'

'Oh yeah . . . ''The Kid''. Didn't you go to California?'

'I'm back.'

'Your dad used to run the old Bowery Queen, *right?'*

'She'll put to sea in an hour.'

There was a short silence while Lowe added up the years. *'How'd you get her to Nova Scotia? Flatbed truck?'*

SEVEN

Sheep Harbour's Canadian Legion Hall was an abandoned oil storage tank in which the veterans had cut holes for windows and doors and a chimney. Music thumped through the steel walls. The parking lot, ploughed out of the snow that blanketed the two-gas-station, one-motel town, was packed with pickup trucks and rusty Japanese compacts.

The taxi driver, who claimed to be a retired seaman and had been drinking like one, promised to wait at the bar.

Mary signed into the club, which welcomed sailors as guests, 'Mary Fulton, Tug *Bowery Queen*, New York', grabbed a bottle of beer and went looking for her crew. Credence Clearwater blared in the dark. As her eyes slowly adjusted, she saw people dancing — holding tight and moving much slower than the beat. Others sat in clusters, drinking from bottles.

Suddenly, in the middle of 'Proud Mary', the music stopped and a woman's voice roared from the loudspeaker: 'It's hot dog time!'

Lights blazed, turning the cavern bright as a landing field, and revealing what had to be every resident of the town from toddlers to grandparents. Couples disengaged and drinkers rose carefully to their feet and all trooped towards a long table where enormous women were forking hot dogs from steaming cauldrons and slapping them into rolls clasped by eager hands.

Mary spotted the great bulk of J.D. Doughtery propped against a wall with a hot dog and a half-empty half-gallon bottle of rum labelled 'Screech'. He was watching a big fisherman who was glowering at Kevin Patrick, who was hitting on a large-breasted blonde under the guise of a beer-chugging contest. The Filipinos stood by, wide-eyed, draining bottles of Keith ale like men in a desert.

Kevin greeted her with an owlish grin. 'Welcome to Sheep Harbour's Winterfest. May I introduce Miss — Miss —'

'Deidre.'

'And that there's Mr Deidre.' J.D. exhaled Screech in Mary's ear. 'Fixin' to nuke a skull or two if our captain gets careless where he lays his paws.'

'How soon can the tug put to sea?'

'Tug's ready right now,' said Kevin. 'Right, J.D.?'

'Tug's ready,' J.D. agreed. 'Seventy-seven thousand gallons of diesel, sufficient power packs to change out as our more elderly cylinder heads blow up, and plenty of grub — includin' an ample supply of pretzels in the port tail shaft. We could sail her to Europe and back, although I would feel most confident towing a drydock. On the other hand, I may not be the man for winching out a barge this evening, having made considerable inroads upon the local spirit supply.'

'No barge,' said Mary. 'Can we sail tonight, Kevin?'

'And as you've likely observed,' J.D. went on, 'even Old Kev's fallen prey to the fate afflicting many of his lot, indulging a seaman's classic predisposition towards intoxication while ashore.'

'Kevin?'

'What's the rush?'

She glanced at Leo. The chief mate was wearing a grin like the grille of an Oldsmobile, and Mary wondered whether she was going to have to steer the boat herself. Sanborn lurched up, hot dog in hand, mustard on his shirt.

'I'll tell you in the taxi. What do you say we round up the little guys?'

They trailed her reluctantly to the taxi. J.D. and Boags sat in front with the driver. Mary, Kevin, Leo, Roberto, and Sanborn rode in the back, Mary sharing Kevin and Leo's knees. The car smelled like a distillery and bottomed every other bump. The old salt driving was too ripped to notice.

'We caught another Mayday from that German lifeboat. Latitude fifty-six North, longitude twenty-two degrees thirty minutes West.'

'That's got to be eighteen hundred miles from here, Mary. There's plenty of European ships closer and faster.'

'They'll be looking for the lifeboat. We're looking for the ship.'

'I thought it sank.'

'I think the ship kept going – J.D., how long could a motor vessel keep going, untended?'

'Well . . . assuming a fire or some disaster panicked the crew overboard but didn't wreck her engine room, and assuming the autopilot's still working, and assuming the air or hydraulics moving the rudder are still working . . . hell, about all that would stop her would be running out of juice in her day tanks. So depending when they last transferred fuel and water to her day tanks, she could run for an hour or maybe even a day – we talkin' salvage?'

'No way,' said Kevin Patrick, 'you could pay me enough to take that broken-down, overgrown harbour tug into mid-Atlantic in the winter. We're not salvors, Mary. I worked a couple of months for the Australians down in the South Pacific, and Leo, you told me you did a job once in Indonesia, but that's about it. In both cases mine were strandings, not deep sea stuff, and all I was doing, I was driving a work boat.'

'I'll go with you,' Sanborn blurted. 'Hell, this is the kind of thing guys tell stories about. Let's do it.'

'Thanks, Jim. I'm glad you're coming. Kevin? Are you saying you're not capable of running the tug out to a ship, getting a line on board, and towing it back?'

'Mary, for Crissake, it's a little more complicated than that. The fucking ship's two thousand miles from here.'

'A moment ago it was eighteen hundred . . . If it steamed west a day – five hundred miles – then it's only thirteen hundred. You know how to find it. You know how to get a line aboard. And you know how to tow it. What's complicated?'

'Leo? Tell her!'

'Very hard,' answered the chief mate. 'Not enough men. Too little boat. Bad bad weather. We can do it.'

'You hear that, Kevin?'

'I heard "Very hard, not enough men, too little boat, bad bad weather".'

'Oh shit, I wish to hell I had my master's ticket — now look, everybody.' She twisted round, trying to see their faces in the dark. 'Fulton Towing is offering shares in the enterprise. Ten per cent of the salvage fee for captain and chief. Five per cent each for crew.'

Kevin said, 'You're nuts. And if Mike said that, you're both nuts.'

'What's her cargo?' J.D. asked.

'Ship and cargo are insured for twenty million dollars.'

There was a speculative silence as each man tried to guess a likely salvage fee and calculate his share. Then the straining taxi crested the last hill. The harbour was a speckle of lights. The black of the Atlantic spread beyond.

The silence deepened. Her crew could see the *Bowery Queen* in the wharf lights, her jaunty plume of generator exhaust shredded by the wind. The wind shook the car, and when Sheep Rock Light slid across the sea, they saw row upon row of combers charging the shore. Dwarfed by the impounded barge, the tugboat nestled against the wharf like a little red toy.

'How we going to find her?' asked J.D.

'Eventually,' said Mary, 'she'll be spotted from the air. Our job is to be near there first.'

'Hey,' said the taxi driver, 'you call yourselves sailors? What's the difference between a fairy tale and a sea story?'

No one but Sanborn wanted to know. 'You got me there, Cap. What's the difference?'

'A fairy tale starts, "Once upon a time . . ." A sea story starts, "No shit, this really happened . . ."'

*

'Snowing like a bastard.'

Kevin paced the narrow confines of the wheelhouse, swilling coffee, shooting black looks at the towing deck where the seamen were wrestling a big nylon messenger line into the house. Mary, he eyed warily. She had already ransacked the bookshelves in the galley and was now rummaging through the chart drawers.

Mary had him in a bind. He did not really want to go looking for *Der Schmetterling*. The *Bowery Queen* was a big tug but a mighty small ship, and blue-water salvage was asking too much of her short-handed, untried crew; most of the guys had never worked together, while only he and Sanborn knew the *Queen*'s many idiosyncrasies. But if he lost his job for refusing to go, it would be tough to get another. He was exceptionally young to be captain. Besides, owners preferred to poach working captains from their competitors, on the theory that an out-of-work tug master might be unemployed for good reason. Short of an unlikely oil boom off the Carolina coast, new tugging jobs were few in these hard times. If he lost his, he'd be looking at the grim prospect of a year on the beach, or signing as mate under some old rummy on a coastal tanker.

What he couldn't seem to explain to Mary was that offshore was a lot different from harbour and coast. 'It's not like you can anchor up for the night,' he tried again. 'If the sea makes up —'

'You can run before the wind, right?'

Kevin sighed and ran a hand through his thick hair. The boat was nearly silent, her generator a distant vibration. J.D. was below, prelubing the turbochargers before starting the main engines. 'Mary, I don't have to tell you of all people what a tugboat is. She's got about as much reserve buoyancy as a rowboat with a Mack truck engine.'

'When I was thirteen my father towed a humongous floating drydock to Bermuda with the *Queen*.'

'I'll bet he didn't bring you and your mom along.'

'My mother was too sick by then.'

'I'm sorry, I didn't think. But you know what I mean.'

'The point is, the *Queen* has already proven she's sea-worthy — Here we go!'

Mary spread a ten-year-old small-scale chart, the North Atlantic Ocean Northern Sheet, and pinned the curling edges with the shot-weighted ashtrays that littered the wheelhouse. The chart covered the enormous field of water framed by the coasts of North America and Europe and ranged from Cape Hatteras and Gibraltar in the south to lower Greenland and Norway in the north. Depths were marked in six-foot fathoms, latitude and longitude in five-degree squares; it had latitude scales for measuring distances, and compass roses and lines of magnetic variation to steer by.

'Terrific!' She unfolded a second find, last year's North Atlantic Pilot Chart for the month of January, which displayed in minute detail observed wind speeds and directions, currents, air temperature, wave heights, iceberg and icing limits, visibility, and the Great Circle Routes between Europe and America. 'And here's an old *Sailing Directions* I found in the galley.'

Kevin took the dog-eared planning guide for the North Atlantic. 'Leif Ericsson's?'

Mary studied the pilot chart over Kevin's shoulder. In the region of 56°N 22°W, eight hundred miles east of Greenland and five hundred miles south of Iceland, the blue feathered roses that indicated percentages of wind speed and direction showed unceasing westerly gales. Half the days of the month waves were expected to exceed twelve feet.

'The middle of the middle of nowhere,' Kevin repeated gloomily. If Fulton Towing went bankrupt, he would be on the beach same as if Mary fired him tonight.

'So we won't have a lot of competition.'

'It's a needle in a haystack.'

'Needle in a haystack' was the last thing Mary wanted to hear. Dreading the fuel costs of an extended search, she ran the numbers on the calculator. The *Queen* burned 160 gallons an hour. That was $1920 a day. Close to $14,000 for the week it would take to reach and search the area. And, if they found nothing, another $15,000 to sail home to New York, emptyhanded.

'Jesus. Twenty-nine thousand dollars.'

Nor did 'a needle in a haystack' convey the immensity of the ocean. More like looking for one dim star in the Milky Way, she thought, or a single Chevy parked somewhere in America.

'Ever been out there?' she asked, tapping the chart with her last fingernail to survive mad grabs at greasy railings as the boat had rock-and-rolled across the Gulf of Maine.

Kevin's grin faded. 'Last fall,' he muttered, hunching over the Loran navigator, which was a brick-sized instrument with a numerical keypad and a liquid crystal screen.

Mary waited for further explanation, but suddenly Kevin was very busy, frenetically punching the lifeboat's position into the Loran to calculate bearing from the *Bowery Queen* and a course from Sheep Harbour. He kept hitting the wrong numbers and clearing the screen. The economy of motion Mary had admired in his boat handling seemed to have deserted him. The Loran beeped protest. He cleared it again, muttered under his breath, 'Come on, you cunt.'

'Was it a tow?' Mary asked.

'What?'

'Was it a tow?'

'What? Yeah. I was chief mate, towing a broken-down tug from Belgium. We made it as far as St John's, Newfoundland, and I swore "Never again", and took a plane home.'

'What do you mean, never again? What happened?'

'Three weeks of fifty-foot seas is what happened. It was the worst October in seventy years.' He returned to the Loran.

'*Fifty*-foot seas? How big a tug?'

'Bigger than this one.'

'So what do you mean, never again? Kevin, what are

you doing? I can't do this without you.' She thought he was putting her on – he seemed half-drunk still – until he glanced off into an invisible place and mused, 'It wasn't so much the seas – though after weeks of them you just feel beaten to death. It was one wave – came from a totally different direction as the rest of the shit, moving at about fifteen, twenty knots. It looked like a block of brownstones. That tall and that square. You could see water coming over the top of it, as if it were solid, you know, like a huge river pouring over a cliff.' He looked at her, misinterpreted her speculative expression, and said, 'No shit. I really saw it. If you don't believe me, ask J.D.'

She was thinking that she believed his story, but didn't believe that was what was bothering him. 'So what happened?'

'It broke over us and we were a submarine for about an hour, it seemed. She was a North Sea boat, so her stacks were pretty well protected – not like this sieve – and we had her vents dogged down as tight as we could. It still flooded the engine room and shut down both motors and the generator. Only reason she didn't sink, she was an anchor handler – you know, no bulwark aft? – open stern right down to the water, so the towing deck emptied before the next wave hit. A closed stern boat like the *Queen* would have sunk like an anvil . . . Anyway, J.D. got the second generator going so we could operate the pumps.'

'What happened to the tow?'

'Rolled over, snapped the towline, and sank.'

'You're lucky the wire broke or it would have dragged you down with it . . .'

'There were two guys on the riding crew.'

'Jesus, Kevin.'

'So you see why I'm not interested in blue-water salvage. See, I got real, real lucky. I don't deserve to be alive. I can't count on that kind of luck again.'

'Yeah, but fifty-foot seas are –'

'Maybe we won't run into fifty-foot seas, if we're lucky, but what really worries me is ice. Mary, if she ices up, we're in real trouble. I can hold her ass-end to really big seas if I have to, and we can batten down and maybe survive, but if it gets cold, with a high wind, I can't run away from the ice.'

'J.D.'s coming.'

'J.D. lives in a trailer with a dozen kids. He could use the cash. Same thing with the little guys. You're paying 'em twenty-five bucks a day on a ten-month contract.'

'We're paying Leo and Boags and Roberto what we can afford,' Mary retorted hastily.

She had always been torn on the ethics of labour. While the Fultons had been owners since their first barge in 1843, the McKays had not, and her mother had been quick to defend labour's right to a decent living. These arguments around the kitchen table had usually started with a Fulton pointing out that for two hundred years the American merchant marine had thrived on cheap labour from the South Seas. Bread from the mouths of working men, a McKay would retort.

'I'm just telling you that with the salvage share you promised, they could live at home. Boags and Roberto could marry and buy farms. Leo worries about his kid growing up without a father. So you just might want to consider why these people are taking your risk.'

The hollow shriek of a compressed air starter announced that three decks below J.D. was cranking over a main engine.

'Please think it over,' said Mary. 'I'm going to go talk to J.D.'

Descending from the wheelhouse to the fiddley deck to the main deck, she looped a pair of earmuff hearing protectors around her neck, opened a door, and stepped on to the catwalk over the engine room, which was lighted bright as day by clusters of fluorescent work lamps.

The *Bowery Queen*'s V-16 diesels lay side by side like a pair of double-parked stretch limousines. They were painted grey, and J.D. had them gleaming as they hadn't in years. Mary had ventured below one night in the Gulf of Maine seeking a low-down spot in the boat that didn't roll so much, and had discovered the giant wandering about in a sort of reverie, swabbing the thundering monsters with a mop.

Behind the main engines were two electrical generators, and aft of them stood four compressed air tanks to power the winches, clutches and rudders. The port generator was running with a high-pitched roar not quite loud enough to demand ear protection.

In front of the main engines were throttles, alarms, a blackboard, and gauges for water temperature, oil pressure, fuel and rpms. J.D. had chalked a reminder on the blackboard: 'Taking Fuel From No. 11 to Day Tank.' Mary went down the steel steps and joined him there.

'How long?'

'Twenty minutes.'

'Come up to the galley when you can.'

J.D. cranked the port engine, filling the steel cavern with another wild shriek. Then he circled the engine, screwing shut the compression testers he had just opened. Mary was impressed. Not everyone did that any more, although in her uncle's day it had been routine, before starting an engine, to blow out any fuel or water that might have accumulated in the cylinders. J.D. sounded an alarm and hit the starter again. There was another scream. A shudder, and the port engine rumbled to life with a gentle *chug-chuff-chuff-chuff*, clouding the air with exhaust fumes, turbocharger whistling, gears and belts squeaking and squealing.

J.D. belched Screech, blew the alarm again, and started the starboard engine. The noise was almost tangible with both main engines and the generator running. Mary retreated, motioning for J.D. to join her in the galley.

She found Leo, Boags and Roberto watching *Body Heat* on the VCR and finishing a big, flat chocolate cake Roberto had baked for supper. Sanborn was wedged in the corner of the banquette, nose in a book. Kevin was staring into a coffee mug.

'Boags, you want to turn that down a minute? Mary's got something to say.'

She almost flinched as the Filipinos turned golden brown faces to her that blossomed with trust. Little Boags and Roberto, the cook, were boys struggling to grow the wispiest of moustaches. All three were fastidiously neat, changing into clean clothes after every watch. She had hired them on the international labour market for the offshore Okimitsu contract. Only Poles worked for less, but the Filipinos were known to be great seamen, and, in their agent's words, 'Don't all think they're Lech Walesa.'

On the TV screen between their trusting smiles, Kathleen Turner was hustling William Hurt, who looked glad of it. J.D. wandered in and squeezed on to the banquette, reaching for a piece of cake and passing the tray to Sanborn, who dug in with his maimed hand. Mary took the extra moment to banish her doubts.

'In all fairness, I have to say right now, "All ashore that's going ashore." The company will put you up in the Sheep Harbour Motel until we get back; or, if you want to break your contract, we'll pay you off through tonight and issue your plane ticket home from Halifax.'

'What if we find the freighter?' asked Boags.

J.D. answered for her. 'Then you go home to the sunny Philippines, amigo, and buy a fuck-bigger farm than I'm gonna buy in Mississippi — standards of living enjoying the differential they do in our native lands.'

The Filipinos smiled.

J.D. said, 'Pardon my French, Mary, it's the liquor talkin'.'

'No problem, J.D. . . . Again, in fairness, this is not going to be easy. We don't even know if the ship is afloat. With luck it will be spotted from the air by the time we get near, and with any luck we'll get there first. The weather reports are lousy, and Kevin tells me they get worse real fast this time of year. At best, we're going to be extremely uncomfortable.'

73

'Starting tonight,' Kevin added.'They're calling forty knots.'

'Maybe you shouldn't come,' Leo said to Mary. 'Maybe better on the beach.'

'*I'm* coming,' said Mary. 'We're talking about you guys.'

Boags looked hurt. 'Don't you want us?'

'Of course I want you. But I just want you to know that it's going to be rough, with no guarantee of success.'

'*Bakit siya sasama?*' Boags said softly to Leo.

'What did he say?'

'Tagalog.'

'But what did he say?'

'He say, "Why you coming?"'

'I'm coming along, Boags, to share watches and to write a salvage log more specific than "I was relieved at 1200. All's well."'

Leo nodded. 'Very important. I was on a tug that salvaged a burning gas carrier off Surabaya. The lawyers said it was a piece of cake. We got nothing but tug time.'

. A worried silence greeted Leo's story. Boags and Roberto began fidgeting. Finally J.D. said, 'Leo, I wonder if I might bum a Marlboro?'

'Traitor,' said Kevin.

'You'll be firing up that stinkweed you're suckin' on before we cross the Newfoundland Banks.'

Leo snicked out a cigarette and gave the engineer a light. J.D. tugged an oily rag from his back pocket and spread it on the table for an ashtray. 'Your engines are panting, Mary. Thirty-two cylinders rarin' to go.' He cocked his ear towards the rumbling whine that shook the galley deck. 'Well, thirty-one or so, give or take a busted cylinder head.'

'Let's do it,' said Sanborn.

'Captain?' said Mary to Kevin, who still hadn't said he'd do it.

Kevin sat silent for a long moment. Then he addressed his crew in the engaging manner tugmen took for leadership in the port of New York: 'Why not cast off, Leo? Maybe bow line first.'

The temperature had plummeted, freezing the little harbour, since they had come back from the Legion Hall. As Kevin swung the *Bowery Queen* away from the lighted wharf, and the seamen gathered her stiff mooring lines, she sent shards skidding on the snow-covered ice. Mary glanced back. The black channel in their wake was strewn with broken ice, and the wharf was already a darkening point of light. The ice ahead ended where the wind and ground swell stirred the water.

The VHF crackled weather from the Yarmouth station: blizzard conditions, forty-knot winds; fifteen-foot seas by morning, twenty beyond the lee of the coast. 'Sloppy,' said Kevin, as the *Queen*'s bluff bow rose to the ground swell.

'Great for the log. We'll look like major heroes going out on spec.'

'Just hope snow means it'll get warmer.'

Kevin pulled down the VHF microphone and made his *Sécurité* broadcast in the unlikely event that there were any boats nearby: 'Security call. Security call. This is the tug *Bowery Queen*, Echo-Lima-Mike-X-ray, from Sheep Harbour, steering east at twelve knots.'

He switched on the big spotlight and manipulated a wheel in the ceiling to scan the ice-strewn islands. Snow streamed in from the sea, reflecting the light back at them. He turned it off, and steered for the whirling lighthouse beam.

'Mary, you want to log passing Sheep Rock at 2311?'

'Sheep Rock 2311.'

He opened the throttle. 'And pop that Wagner tape into the stereo. The *Tannhäuser*.'

He loosed a long blast on the airhorn, and the *Bowery Queen* butted into the Atlantic.

By midnight the tugboat was plunging violently in heavy seas, and the lighthouse had dwindled to a tiny glow on the bottom of the radar. An hour later it and the coast were indistinguishable from the wave and snow clutter that speckled the picture. Kevin activated the clutter suppressor, rendering the screen as empty as the ocean ahead.

Mary was braced on a stool behind the port steering sticks, hanging on to the wooden dashboard and staring past the windshield wipers. Snow and spray rattled the glass. Breaking crests glowed in the dark.

'Isn't this fantastic!'

'Mary, you ought to get some sleep.'

Kevin was standing across from her, steering by the starboard controls. Everyone else had gone to bed.

'I'm fine. Too excited to sleep.'

'I want you "fine" to stand watch in the morning so my crew isn't half-dead by the time we put a wire aboard that ship.'

'Give me a break, Captain Bligh.'

Cold water dripped from the spotlight handle. Mary wrapped it with a rag. She felt wonderful, wide awake and dying to talk. But Kevin had wrapped himself in a chilly silence. When she found his eyes reflecting towards her in the glass, he glanced aside.

'Kev?'

Kevin looked back, studied her for a while. 'What?'

'I appreciate your doing this.'

'No problem.'

'What turned you around, Cap?'

'. . . Maybe I'm not getting any younger or richer. Maybe I need the money, too.'

'Do you mind my asking what for?'

'Ask your father.'

'Why are you jerking me around? We're not kids any more, but you still fight me.'

'Forget it.'

'Kev, we're going for a long voyage on a small boat. Let's clear the air. What's your problem?'

'No problem.'

'I am not going to bed until you tell me what your problem is.'

'Your father was supposed to sell me the *Queen* when he retired. Till you came home.'

'Oh God — I didn't know . . . Did he promise?'

'I thought we had an understanding.'

'Jeez, I'm sorry . . . You know, Dad has a way of saying what people want to hear.'

'Well, he sure knew what I wanted to hear.'

'He doesn't mean to lie, he just wants people to feel good. Maybe —' she started to say, but there was nothing more to say.

'Forget it. I shouldn't have said anything. If we get lucky, I'll buy my own tugboat.'

'A harbour tug, presumably?'

His faint reflection brightened with a smile. Turning from the glass he faced her directly. Mary turned up the dimmer switch on the radar to see more of his face. Kevin laughed.

'You didn't tell your old man, did you?'

'Tell him what?'

'I'll bet Mike thinks we're still anchored up in Sheep Harbour.'

'Hey, how I handle my father is none of your business.'

'Excuuuuse me. Now who's Captain Bligh? Or should I say Boss Bligh?' He snapped a hand to his brow in a crisp salute. 'Yes, Ma'am, Ms Owner. No, Ma'am, Ms Owner. No problem, Ms — Ow! Wait! Before you abuse the help, let me switch on the autopilot.'

Mary had leaned across the radar and poked him in the ribs. Now, as he engaged the steering gear, she jumped off her stool and poked him harder. Kevin caught her wrist in his big, scarred fingers.

'Am I right about your father?'

'He's probably guessed by now.' She moved towards him as the boat heeled. Or as he tugged her gently closer.

'You jerk all your guys' chains like your dad's?'

'When they have chains to jerk,' she replied, fencing

out of long habit, holding him at bay even as she allowed herself to devour him with her eyes.

'What are you looking at?'

'You.'

He had always been a terrific-looking man, but never more so than tonight. Fully aware she was crossing a line drawn many years ago, she took back her hand, reached up, and caressed his cheek. He stood still, his eyes on hers. His cheek was smooth. He had spruced up, singing in the shower, before setting out for the Legion Hall. She traced the line of his nose, the jagged break. She tore her eyes from his and stared at the black glass, her hand still on his face. She had never felt so at risk in her life. Try and keep a leopard for a pet . . . Maybe for a night.

'I feel like the last two people on the ocean.'

'The last two dumb enough –'

'Shhh!' She ran her fingers across his lips, slid her hand behind his head, and pulled him to her mouth.

Great mouth. Great, beautiful mouth. He tasted right and felt right. Hardly a surprise. And definitely not disappointing. Like a thick, warm malted she could drink and eat at the same time, magical food that shot straight to her heart and set it pounding and squeezed her lungs so she couldn't breathe.

He reached down and tucked her closer and she pressed her body hard against his, suddenly sure she would be safe for ever if only she could surround him. She found his back hot under his loose sweater. Under hers, he opened her bra with one hand and she gasped 'Oh!' as he cupped her breast with fingers rough and calloused and light as silk. Kevin closed his other hand around the firm curve of Mary's behind. Heart hammering, breath short, he inhaled the perfume in her hair and felt himself reeling with the raw sensuality of the taste and feel of her. Her body was an astonishing combination of hard and pliant, soft and strong as braided nylon. His last rational thought was that he had to let go of some delicious part long enough to find a zipper. Eyes wide, locked on his, she licked his lips, cocked her leg around him, and tugged his belt.

Motion, bright in the tail of her eye. Kevin saw it, too. But neither let go and in that fatal instant a bone-white cross-sea rushed out of the dark and slammed the *Bowery Queen*'s starboard bow. The tug fell off her course and slid sideways to the oncoming waves. The impact crashed Mary into the curved rail of the stairs.

Kevin seized the steering stick to turn the boat's head back into the waves. But the *Queen* wallowed where she was, heeling at a steeper and steeper angle, the entire length of her 140-foot hull exposed to the force of the ocean.

Before Mary realized what had gone wrong, Kevin had hauled back on the port engine throttle, powered the starboard engine, and was madly cranking the communicator: 'J.D.! J.D.! I lost my steering.'

Kevin's hands had flown automatically from the dead steering stick to the throttles. But it still took the *Queen*'s clutches fifteen long seconds to transmit a change of direction to her propellers. And in that eternity, out of the darkness came another darker wave.

It loomed over the tug, even as the starboard engine began to push her nose around to meet it, and thundered against the wheelhouse. Mary felt the tug going over, felt the port propeller finally bite hard in reverse, felt the *Queen* fight back. Then the sea blew out a window and roared into the wheelhouse.

A wall of icy water knocked Mary flat on her back. Flung about in swirling darkness, unable to breathe, she thought the *Queen* had sunk. She flailed her arms as if to swim. Her hand closed on the handrail that rimmed the dashboard.

'Get something to plug that window,' Kevin yelled. He had both hands on the throttles as the boat rose sluggishly to the next sea. Where the aftmost starboard window had been was a gaping three-foot hole. Wind and spray, diesel smoke and snow stormed through it.

'You okay?'

Mary's teeth were chattering with cold and fear.

'Move!' Kevin yelled. 'Grab a flashlight.'

Mary ripped one from its charger and stumbled below. Leo was stepping into the sea boots that sat outside his cabin. 'What happened?'

'We lost the steering and a window.'

'Boags,' the mate yelled, heading up the stairs two at a time. 'Go with Mary. Find wood and bring it up to the wheelhouse.'

Boags ran into J.D., who was pounding up the engine room stairs with a toolbox. 'Linkage musta busted up top. She's okay downstairs. Boags. Let's go, amigo. Gangway, Mary.'

Mary ran to the bosun store and rummaged through the vast and orderly collection of lines and pulleys, tools and spare parts. The tug was lurching from sea to sea. She found a square of canvas, hammer and a pocketful of short nails, and ran back to the wheelhouse.

J.D. was lying on his back with his head under the wooden dashboard while Boags and Leo held a light and passed tools. Kevin had turned the boat's stern to the seas and was running before them, steering by speeding and slowing the engines.

Mary hammered nails through the canvas into the splintered wooden rim around the empty window. She secured the top first, then worked her way down the sides as the spray and snow drummed against the cloth.

J.D. called, 'Try that, Kevin.'

The steering sticks hissed, the rudder responded, and the *Queen* circled cautiously back on course.

The engineer hauled himself out from under the dash, stood ponderously and, glancing accusingly at Mary, said, 'First time I ever saw a tugboat's steering gear made of Froot Loops and Spaghetti-Os.'

'Will she hold?'

'Guaranteed for ten nautical miles or one hour, whichever comes first.' J.D. clumped down the stairs, nodding at the canvas Mary had nailed over the broken window. 'I'll rustle up a piece of glass when the sea goes down some.' Leo and Boags trooped after him, leaving her and Kevin alone again.

Both were soaked and shivering. Mary said, 'That was nice going, Cap.'

'Helluva start.'

'Helluva interruption, too.'

'You want to steer while I find some dry clothes?'

When he came back, he said, 'Your turn.'

'I'm going to sleep.'

'Shall I wake you when I get into bed?'

'Wake J.D. when you get into his bed. I think I'd rather put everything on hold till we hit the beach. Good night, Captain.'

She started down the stairs.

'Hey! Where'd you learn to kiss like that?'

'UCLA night course.'

Kevin laughed. 'Sweet dreams, Boss.'

Mary changed into dry clothes and burrowed into the blankets of her borrowed bunk. She tried wedging in with lifejackets and pillows, but the *Bowery Queen* was throwing herself all over the ocean and sleep had to be claimed in a half-conscious state between falling and grabbing hold. Sensitive to the boat she had known her whole life, she was aware every time Kevin altered engine speed, or moved the rudders in futile attempts to find a smoother course.

What had finally happened, after all her teenage years of flushed longing at a distance? Could she chalk it up to the excitement of putting to sea? Everybody said danger made it hot. Very hot. If that wave had come along a minute later they wouldn't even have noticed drowning.

At three o'clock she popped wide awake. The pumps were grinding. Seconds later the crew communicator rang. Shadows in sea boots clumped by her curtained doorway. Leo's orders, repeated in English for Sanborn, indicated they were trying to rig canvas over the ventilators to keep breaking seas out of the engine room.

A scream sat her up straight, wondering for a wild second where she was. Engines rumbled. Pumps ground. The bunk tilted sharply. The *Queen* shuddered as if she had hit a wall, stumbled to a near stop and ploughed on. Men shouted in the galley. Mary jumped into her shoes and ran down the steps.

Jimmy Sanborn was sprawled on his back on the galley table, white-faced, biting his lips, and moaning. There was blood on the table and on the deck, bright red in the fluorescent glare. Still half-asleep, Mary thought for a moment that Roberto was serving raspberries or tomato sauce. But Roberto had backed against the range, his soft brown eyes wide with horror.

The blood was pouring from the mangled flesh of Sanborn's left hand, the one with the dragon tattoo that had been until a minute ago his good hand. He was holding it clamped to his chest, fighting Leo, who was trying to get a look at it.

'What happened?'

'Caught it in the fucking hatch,' Sanborn gasped.

The watertight doors between the house and the main deck were solid steel and weighed a ton. Sanborn kept fighting Leo.

Mary nudged the chief mate aside. 'I'll do it . . . Roberto. Get ice and water in a bucket. Can I see it, Jimmy?'

Sanborn forced a grin. 'Tell me you studied medicine in California.'

'Better. I worked for a marina. Sunday sailors and power tools.'

'You got morphine in the first aid kit?'

'Let's get it in ice and water, first. Roberto!'

'Here, Miss Mary.'

She took the bucket. 'Okay, Jimmy. In the water.' The boat heeled and she spilled half. Roberto ran for more. Jimmy lifted the hurt hand with his maimed hand and immersed it slowly. '*Ahhh!* Son of a *bitch!*'

Peering through the bloody water, she concentrated on his tattooed dragon, gathering courage to count his fingers. 'I'm going to pick it up a little, Jim.' She inspected it carefully. Blood was oozing from a thick blue-black line that ran from the base of his little finger to his wrist. The door had crushed the fleshy part of the hand and pinched a piece off.

'Can you move your fingers?'

Sanborn tried, tentatively. 'Yeah, but I don't want to.'

'You won't be throwing lines for a while, but I don't think anything's broken.'

'Anything missing?'

'A lot of skin.'

'Can we keep going? I mean, do I have to go back for a doctor?'

Mary glanced at Leo. Tough call. Leo said, 'We got to clean it and keep it clean. There's stuff in the kit. Penicillin.' Neither he nor Mary voiced the fact that while Sanborn would survive his injury without a doctor, the deckhand would be useless for days.

'Last time I took penicillin,' Sanborn said, 'the original reason felt a lot better than this.'

Mary and Leo dressed the wound, following the directions in the medical kit. Sanborn still wanted morphine, but settled for Tylenol with codeine.

At five o'clock Mary climbed back into a cold bunk. The *Queen* was rolling heavily, the pumps were still grinding, and every few minutes the wind felt like it would tear the house off the deck. She tried to sleep, but couldn't shake off the thought that in the first fifty miles her short-handed crew had already lost the services of a deckhand.

EIGHT

Der Schmetterling wallowed.

To Manfred Echtheit, clinging to the handrails on the bridge, it appeared that every molecule of water in the ocean had aligned in identical, evenly-spaced rows of sharp crests and broad troughs. Like torture, they rolled the ship in giant arcs relentless and predictable as a pendulum.

But the sky was worse than torture. After shrouding him for days in gale-blown clouds, snow and rain, the sky had suddenly turned so blue and the air so clear that the sea sprawled in an infinite circle. Smack in the middle, *Der Schmetterling* gleamed like a silver bull's-eye.

The drunkest, blindest lookout on the worst-manned ship could see him thirty miles away; a hundred miles for an airline pilot with his hand up the stewardess's skirt. From the radio traffic on his HF scanner, he knew a search was on for the lifeboat, led by the British Royal Navy and assisted by the Dutch salvage tug *Noorde Titan*, which, it was reasonable to assume, also had designs on the missing *Der Schmetterling*. And an American vessel was steaming from Nova Scotia. God knew who else. He should have killed the entire crew. Manfred lashed out suddenly, punched the back of the captain's chair with all his strength. The high stool was welded to the deck; the padded backrest broke off and flew twenty feet.

He went outside on the bridge wing again, and turned another slow, desperate circle in the cold. Was the western sky finally greying? He closed his eyes and opened them again, daring to hope. Yes. A faint haze. And above it, feathery banners of jet stream cirrus spreading high in the atmosphere. Already the wind was dropping and, as he stared and hoped in the next hour, it began to back round, south-west, south, south-east. The clouds were banding and thickening so quickly now that the jet stream must be blowing a hundred and fifty knots. A few hours would bring rain and maybe snow on gale force winds. Hans and Alison were doubtless getting pummelled already. His wallowing ship was next and he was in for a beating. Worth it to be invisible.

A faint sound, a distant buzzing, brought his head around sharply. A high-pitched summer sound, like a mosquito, it seemed to come from the east, where the sky was still as clear as a sapphire. He saw nothing but empty sea and sky, but he whirled and ran in to the bridge and down six flights of stairs, running as hard as he could, smashing into the bulkheads as the ship lurched. Outside on the main deck, where the wind whistled down the long corridors between the stacked containers, he ran harder, stumbling, tripping on chains, cursing, forward to the front stack of containers, which he scaled.

The buzzing was louder. Clawing open his container door, he saw it in the east – a pinprick glint of sunlight two thousand feet above the water. Then the *thud-thud* of rotors chopping the air. He yanked a sheath knife from his belt and slashed the heavy plastic from the nearest cylinder.

From the *Noorde Titan*'s long-range search helicopter, the North Atlantic looked like royal blue corduroy. Until recently, in this sector the wind had blown steadily from the west, rolling the seas into stately ridges. It was a sight, infinite and featureless, that riveted one eye to the fuel gauge.

'Captain calling again,' said the copilot.

'Fuck him,' said the pilot. 'Greedy bastard.'

The law of the sea – the remote and endless sea two thousand feet below their rotors – said that you searched for lost sailors until you found them, or knew for certain they were dead. It was not a law to weasel out of, the way the captain was doing. To the pilot the law was clear: lives first; booty second. But when the weather had turned too ferocious to fly in the lifeboat search sector, Captain van Pelt had ordered the helicopter west where the weather was clear to track the abandoned container ship, which might have kept going.

The law of the sea said they should wait poised to dart into breaks in the weather, to hunt for the lifeboat, and not waste the helicopter whose side-looking radar and capacious fuel tanks increased the *Noorde Titan*'s search range tenfold. He hated the captain's greed and hated himself for obeying. But jobs were scarce, so he mollified his conscience by switching off the radio.

His copilot was encased within mouthpiece and headset, but a sharp glance said that breaking radio connection was a risky business in mid-ocean. Fuck him too. If the helicopter went down, they'd be long dead of exposure before the *Noorde Titan*, a full day's steaming east, reached these ranks of twenty-foot seas. Radio or no radio.

'Target!'

He looked at the radar. Another big ship. Dead ahead.

'Try to raise him,' said the pilot, and the copilot switched on the short-range VHF. Neither man held much hope it was *Der Schmetterling*.

Earlier, two hundred miles back, they had buzzed the American express freighter *Katherine Hart*, out of Baltimore, bound for Bremerhaven. The *Katherine Hart* had radioed back that she had seen nothing of *Der Schmetterling*, and had reminded the Dutch pilot that the Atlantic was a big ocean.

'Not under power,' said the copilot. The radar indicated a two-knot passage on a northerly course, which was probably wind drift. Despite himself, the pilot felt the first glimmering of excitement. 'Maybe,' he said. 'Maybe.'

'There!'

And there she lay, a big grey container ship, abeam the wind and wallowing on the swell, her stack cold — no smoke — her radar scanners still. They swooped lower to confirm. Ships broke down, after all. It could be a fully crewed vessel making repairs.

'Shit!' said the copilot. 'There's a guy waving.'

A lonely figure stood atop the forward containers, and the pilot's heart sank. Even if the stricken ship needed a tow, the profit in assisting a manned ship was nothing compared to salvaging the abandoned *Der Schmetterling*.

The pilot veered toward the bow. 'What's he waving — Jesus Christ!' A white flash enveloped the figure's arms. 'He's shooting —'

To his disbelief, the pilot saw a short black missile rising lazily toward the helicopter. He jinked left, dodging it like a thrown rock. But it was coming faster than it looked, and tracked him easily. The copilot gave a strangled shriek, cut off abruptly as the missile burst through the plastic bubble that enclosed the cockpit.

A split second later the pilot realized he was still alive; the missile hadn't exploded. Bitter cold air swirled through the shattered bubble. The missile had struck the copilot and pinned him to his seat. It was sticking out of his shoulder like a third arm.

Assuming that the copilot's body had miraculously absorbed the impact which would have detonated the warhead, the pilot reached to open the rescue bay in the floor of the aircraft. If he could somehow gently extract the missile from his partner's shoulder, he might drop it into the sea before it exploded.

A blue-green fog poured out of the missile. The helicopter started falling and it was then, when he tried to correct, that the pilot realized he couldn't move his hands and feet.

The ship came angling swiftly into his field of vision. His brain screamed to fly. He could see and think, but his hands lay on the sticks as if glued to them. His feet were locked to the pedals. He couldn't breathe. His heart stopped beating. His bowels let go. The helicopter hit the water hard beside the ship, the impact driving dead air from the pilot's chest. Still aware, he saw the hull tower on the swell. Then it crashed down, and drove him under.

Manfred lowered the empty Tannenberg launcher with a growl of disgust, and tossed the spent cylinder over the side. What a waste. Like dropping an H-bomb on a Volkswagen.

One of only twenty such weapons in the world. Nineteen left. Painstakingly assembled by Stasi technicians, the Tannenberg was a deadly *ménage à trois* of Russian rocketry, the latest German chemistry, and elegant American electronics captured from Afghan rebels.

The East German revolution of 1989 had wrecked Stasi plans to supply it to the terrorist units it armed and bankrolled. Manfred's colleagues had fled the revolt with gold, jewels and stolen art, and secrets to sell, but he and his brother Hans had scooped up all twenty Tannenberg rockets and stashed them for a better day. Easily smuggled in a length of six-inch PVC pipe, and simple enough to be fired by a monkey, the Tannenberg was the ultimate terrorist weapon: maximum kills for minimal skills.

The helicopter had vanished under the ship, but the super-dense gas, still spewing from the warhead and turning to liquid in the sea water, was fanning upwind of the ship like a sickly green bloom of algae. There was little point in putting on a mask. If the stuff got him, which was unlikely as he stood one hundred and ten feet above the water, not even a full chemical warfare suit could save him.

Presumably sea water would neutralize it, though how fast only the scientists who had packed an astonishing quantity into the little warhead would know. They had claimed that death was absolutely painless: first you couldn't move and shortly you suffocated. There had been some debate about whether you stopped thinking before you stopped breathing, as the dog and cat tests had been inconclusive.

Something grey and shiny broke surface within the

spreading bloom, a porpoise thrashing on its side. Another bobbed up beside it, flapping, then a third, and Manfred realized that a school had blundered along. A fourth nosed in to investigate from beyond the bloom, swimming hard, until it went as rigid as if flash-frozen.

Manfred watched a dozen mammals die, trailing out behind the drifting ship, watched a shark tear into one of the bodies and die too. He was still annoyed he had had to waste a valuable missile on the helicopter, and worried they might have radioed their find. But there was nothing to be done about that. As for wasting the missile, he consoled himself with the thought that at least he knew the weapons still worked after years in storage. It had been a successful field test, and now when some hook-nosed Palestinian or slant-eyed Chinese drug lord pestered him for details, he could assure Hans's posturing clients that the poison worked nicely under water, too — though always at its best wind-borne in a crowded city.

NINE

Jim Sanborn marked his place in *The Mind of the Middle Ages* with his dirty bandage, and announced to the galley, 'I've been thinking – if God set up Heaven for the faithful, flat-out, pedal-to-the-metal, balls-to-the-wall believers, then the twentieth-century section must be empty.'

'That's a pretty safe bet,' said Kevin, with a smile for Mary over the top of *her* book, the North Atlantic *Sailing Directions*.

'Where you think you're going?' J.D. asked Sanborn.

The deckhand gazed a moment at Mr Takashi's breaking wave, then out of the galley porthole. Beyond the glass, which was alternately caked with snow and washed by spray, jagged waves reached from a black sea to claw the white sky. Mary shivered, but Sanborn smiled like a man with a secret. 'I've made a study of it and I honestly can't imagine all this happening any other way. I'm in like Flynn.'

The discussion threatened to continue, so Mary took her *Sailing Directions* to the wheelhouse. Leo was standing watch. A hundred feet ahead of the bow, snow and water joined as if the sea stopped at a frozen cliff.

She settled at the chart table. Kevin had underlined passages on superstructure icing, but in the column beside it, she noticed an article on optical phenomena:

'A mirage is caused by refraction of light rays in a layer of air having rapidly increasing or decreasing density near the surface . . .'

'. . . Objects below the horizon may actually be brought into view . . . common . . . in the higher latitudes.'

More to the point, however, as far as the *Bowery Queen* was concerned, superstructure icing could:

'. . . lead to capsizing of the vessel. The dangerous conditions are those in which gale-force winds last for several days in association with air temperatures of 28° or lower . . . normally when the wind comes from the northern quadrants.'

The wind, which had turned west yesterday, had been shifting north all morning. The temperature was dropping and the barometer was rising. But still it snowed, as it had for two days, slashing down in long pelting flakes that caked the *Bowery Queen*'s aft and port windows and streaked the view ahead. The tugboat was all white, except for where spray and breaking seas washed the red towing deck and dark gunwales.

Kevin came up and relieved Leo, and Mary radioed her father. The snow so strained the signal that even connected through the directional antennas of the AT&T High Seas station in New Jersey, Mike Fulton sounded as if he had his telephone in the shower.

'How's the weather?'

'Still snowing, and cold as a stepmother's kiss.'

She was bundled up in two sweaters, flannel-lined jeans, boots and a knitted watchcap. The wheelhouse radiator had stopped working again, and J.D. was banging pipes a deck below. She reported their position from the Loran — 460 miles east-north-east of Nova Scotia, approaching the Newfoundland Grand Banks — and fuel, which J.D. estimated at around seventy thousand gallons.

'You want to put Kevin on?'

Kevin heard him on the loudspeaker. He reached for the handset. Mary surrendered it reluctantly, and stared out at the bow rising and falling in the snow.

'How's the boat, Kev?'

'Rockin' and rollin'.'

The tug had been, in fact, riding fairly smoothly in following seas, but was beginning to wallow as the waves shifted north with the wind.

'Icing?'

'It's not that cold, yet . . . Barometer's rising. And the temperature's going down . . .'

The radio had a squelch device, which eliminated noise when no one was speaking. For a long moment the only sound in the wheelhouse was the distant whine of the turbochargers. The radiator transmitted another clang from J.D. Finally, Mike Fulton said, *'Maybe the two of you are nuts.'*

'She's nuts. I'm just following orders.'

'I woke up thinking you're out where you shouldn't be.'

Mary took back the handset. 'Dad, I don't want to discuss our finances on an open channel, but that ship is a gift from heaven. All we have to do is collect it and we're home free — Anything new for us?'

'Good news, bad news and weird news. What do you want first?'

'Good news.'

'Lowe gave me an update on her cargo. Der Schmetterling's carrying five hundred and thirty containers, plus a whole shit load of tractors and Mercedes Benzes in her hold. That's 'cause her owners get special preferential treatment from the German government for being a breakaway outfit from a former East German state company.'

'What about the Lloyd's Open Form?'

'They sign with whoever gets there first.'

'And the bad news,' murmured Kevin, 'is we're not alone.'

Mary shot a look at the radar, but the screen was empty. She pressed the transmit switch in the handset.

'What's the bad news?'

'None of the rescue satellites have picked up any signals, but yesterday a KLM pilot reported an EPIRB distress signal at fifty-six degrees North, twenty-two degrees thirty minutes West — which is great for the lifeboat, but lousy for us, because a Dutch salvage tug has gone to investigate.'

'Which boat?' asked Kevin.

'Which boat, Dad?'

'Noorde Titan.'

'We're fucked.'

'What's the *Noorde Titan*?' asked Mary, though it hardly mattered which Dutch boat was hunting. Smit and Bugsier and Noorde were the kings of ocean salvage.

'She's a twenty-six-thousand-horsepower, twenty-knot supertug,' Kevin growled, moving to the chart. 'She'd tow Staten Island if you paid her enough.'

He measured the distance with the dividers. 'She'll find the lifeboat with her helicopter, trace the freighter's line of drift, and get a wire aboard. They'll be scoffing pea soup in Rotterdam while we're still rockin' and rollin'.'

He took the radio receiver from Mary. 'Mike? Who's her captain — van Pelt?'

'*Yeah, you know him?*'

'His daughter,' said Kevin.

Mike laughed. '*Figures.*'

'The old man told me to take a hike. He has bigger plans for his daughter than an American tug driver.'

'*Take it from a father, Kid, he just didn't want her knocked up.*'

Kevin grinned at Mary, who gave him the finger. 'Anyway, Mike, we don't have a chance against the *Titan*.'

'*Maybe not, Kid. They lost their 'copter.*'

Mary snatched back the handset. 'Is that the weird news?'

'*No. It's weirder, but three days ago the captain of an eastbound Mersk Line car carrier reported passing a ship that looked like* Der Schmetterling.'

'Why didn't he stop?'

'*Der Schmetterling was tearing west-south-west at twenty knots.*'

'Yes!'

'*My buddy at the Coast Guard thinks the guy was seeing things. But Mersk captains are pretty good.*'

'Where?'

'*Fifty-two degrees twenty minutes North, thirty-three degrees seven minutes West.*'

'Four hundred and fifty miles from the lifeboat?'

'*Maybe you were right, Mary. Maybe she kept going.*'

Kevin was already measuring the distance from the *Bowery Queen*. 'Eight hundred miles.'

'Three days?'

'If we can maintain eleven-twelve knots.'

'But where's the ship now?'

'If she kept doing twenty knots? Let's see, that's four hundred and eighty miles a day . . .' He measured 480 from the scale on the side of the chart and walked the dividers across the ocean. 'Three hundred miles behind us,' he grinned. 'Due in New York tomorrow.'

'But the ship couldn't do twenty knots for three days. J.D. figured one day tops.' She took the dividers. 'The Mersk ship probably saw him while he was at the end of his rope. Let's say he kept going another half-day. So he's here. We're here, less than three days south-south-east of him.'

'*You still there?*' said her father.

Kevin started to answer. Mary stopped him. 'Careful. It's an open channel. Let's not give it away. Dad, we'll talk to you later. Keep checking for anyone else who spotted her since the Mersk ship.'

'Hey, Cap,' Kevin asked. 'Who else is looking? Who's in Newfoundland?'

'*McAllister has a six-thousand-horsepower tug in St John's, but she's in dry dock. They're trying to float her, and you can be damned sure they're combing the whorehouses for the crew, but so far it's just you and the* Noorde Titan.'

'Just?'

Mary signed off and thanked the AT&T High Seas operator. 'Right! The *Noorde Titan* has to make for the lifeboat first. We're too far away to help. So the ship is ours.'

'But where?' Kevin turned back to the chart and circled a million square miles of water with his finger. 'Stopped, she'd drift east . . . We could make for her last position and follow her drift line with a ladder search. Only we don't know when she stopped.'

A pencil was rolling as the *Bowery Queen* pitched. Mary

94

picked it up and sketched a line from the lifeboat position to the Mersk sighting to Virgin Rocks where the Great Circle Routes from Northern Europe to North America converged below the Newfoundland Banks.

'I still say *Der Schmetterling* will eventually be sighted again, from an airplane, or a satellite, or a passing ship. At worst, this line will get us close enough to be the first salvage tug to get a wire aboard.'

Kevin shrugged. 'We've only got thirty miles radar range – at best – in the second or two we crest a big wave. And soon as the ship's position is known, *Noorde Titan* will be steaming there gangbusters.'

'Kevin, all I'm doing is making a plan we can follow. We're better off working from a plan. This will get us close. Once we get within that half-day she might still have been steaming, we'll move to leeward of the line to match her drift.'

'It's your fuel.'

'If you've got a better plan . . .'

'We're three and a half days from New York. We could go home.'

Mary measured the distance between the *Bowery Queen* and *Der Schmetterling*, then divided that by the 288 miles per day she hoped to get out of the tug. '*Less* than three days from the ship.'

'Like I say, it's your fuel.'

'I don't want to go home. Are you with me?'

'It's your boat.' He went to the rudder controls and stared out of the front windows. 'Snow's stopping.'

The snow lifted quickly and the air turned bitter cold and so clear they could see five or six miles when the tug crested the waves. The cloud cover thinned, horizons firmed up, and the light brightened and took on a metallic glow until the water gleamed like aluminium.

The wind quickened and hit the *Bowery Queen* hard on the port side. Spray began to fly over the bulwarks, dripping from the handrails and speckling the wheelhouse windows. Down on the foredeck the H-bitt began to take on the aluminium colour of the water as it glazed with ice.

Mary was standing the afternoon twelve to four watch, driving the tug at ten knots through broken seas, when Kevin angrily bounded up the wheelhouse stairs. He rubbed the sleep from his eyes and glared out at the ice that coated the decks and railings.

'Why the hell didn't you call me?'

'It's not that much worse.'

'The hell it isn't. We're listing five degrees.' He tapped the inclinometer, which she had been steadfastly ignoring, and quickly cranked the intercom. 'J.D. You want to come up here? . . . Jesus, Mary, shape up — here, I got it.' He shouldered her aside and knocked fifty rpms off the engines. The steering sticks hissed a change of course.

'Where are you going?'

'Downwind so we stop heaving spray.'

'But you're heading south. The freighter's east.'

The *Bowery Queen* shuddered through the turn, rolling ponderously under the weight of the ice, and settled down on the smoother new course with the seas coming from behind and slipping by a little less riotously. J.D. clumped up the steps. 'I was wondering whether someone up here was going to come to her senses.'

'What do you say we do something about this list?'

'I hope you're not asking me to go out and chop ice with a fire axe. That deck looks slicker than a pre-owned condom — Beg your pardon, Mary. Forgot you was still here.'

'I was thinking maybe we could shift some fuel to the left side.'

'Then can we get back on course?' Mary demanded.

Kevin ignored her. 'Why don't you do that, J.D.?'

J.D. lumbered down to the engine room. Kevin turned on Mary. 'Listen, I don't care if I just went to sleep two seconds ago, you call me whenever you're in doubt.'

'Sorry. I wasn't in doubt.'

'Then you need your head examined . . . And while

96

we're at it, don't increase speed without my permission. Okay?'

Mary retreated sullenly to the chart table and logged the new course, noting the abysmal sea conditions, the falling barometer, four-eighths cloud cover, and the twenty-knot wind.

'Heavy icing. Five degree list. Captain ordered fuel shifted to empty port tanks to correct list,' she concluded the entry.

Below decks, pumps rumbled. Slowly the tug stood a little straighter, and the long lazy arcs she had been rolling seemed to shorten up slightly. Kevin maintained a dogged grip on the steering sticks.

'So can we get back on course?' Mary asked.

'All we've done is sink a little deeper. She'll still ship spray, which will freeze into more ice. And we'll be right back where we were, only lower in the water.'

They ran south for an hour, farther and farther off the track of the freighter. Twice Mary protested. Twice Kevin ignored her. When he poured his fourth cup of coffee from the thermos, she said, 'You'll be a wreck if you drink that.'

'What is it with women and coffee? I've never met one yet who didn't get on a guy's case about coffee.'

'I meant, you need to sleep. You can't stand every watch. But now that you mention it, caffeine *is* terrible for you.'

Kevin regarded her over the rim of his cup. 'It's an aphrodisiac. I'd be lost without it.'

Mary shrouded herself in chilly silence and watched the chaotic seas. Finally, she ventured another observation: 'Is it just me, or do you notice there's more ice on the main deck? The seas were washing it off the bulwarks before. Now it's sticking.'

'There's less frozen spray higher up,' Kevin answered with so little conviction that Mary guessed he had noticed it too. He downed another coffee in a single, defiant gulp. A minute later he seized the steering stick.

The compass floated back to 90. Immediately, a wave

angled hard against the *Bowery Queen*'s port side and exploded into a sheet of spray. Kevin winced and throttled the engines back two hundred revolutions. The tug slowed to six knots. Subsequent waves licked the rim of the bulwark and slid quietly past. Now he increased speed, until every third or fourth wave broke over the bulwarks and washed the deck. After a while the warmer sea water melted the ice that had formed low down on the boat.

'Take her,' said Kevin. 'Increase speed one rpm and I'll throw you overboard.'

'Thanks, Captain.' Mary stepped to the console and gave him a grateful smile, but Kevin just shambled past her, his eyes dark with exhaustion.

Leo's trick started at four.

1600: relieved by chief mate . . . Temperature dropping, ice increasing. Four degree list.

'Not good,' said Leo.

It was pitch dark by five o'clock. Mary went down to the galley, ate a spicy Philippine lamb stew Roberto called *caldereta*, and, too anxious to sleep, took her coffee back to the wheelhouse. The tugboat was rolling long, lazy arcs again and Leo kept shooting glances at the inclinometer. Two hours into his watch, he cranked the intercom.

'Captain Kevin, you better come up.'

Kevin entered the dark wheelhouse thirty seconds later and glided to the windows like a shadow. 'Want to turn on the lights?'

Leo switched on the work lights. '*Madre,*' he whispered. Mary swallowed hard. Kevin said, 'Looks like a goddamned wedding cake.'

Every surface above the main deck was crusted in white ice. Handrails had thickened into six-inch cylinders and fat icicles hung like fangs from the dented visor that topped the wheelhouse windows. Mary leaned forward over the control console to see the bow. The seas were still washing ice off the bulwarks, but the H-bitt down on the foredeck wore a thick coat that nearly doubled its bulk.

Aft, ice glazed the hoisting crane's boom and cables, J.D.'s towing engine controls, railings, ladders and the baffles on the engine room intakes. Kevin tried the door at the back of the wheelhouse. It was frozen shut. He threw his weight hard against the steel.

'Leo. Let's get this hatch freed up, like right now.'

Mary turned from the ice and tried to read his face in the back-glow of the worklights. He sounded scared.

He took the rudder controls. 'After you get the hatch open, why don't you try chopping some ice off topside — But tell your guys to go easy around the antennas. That fibreglass'll snap like twigs. And tell them not to beat on the insulators. Bust them and we got no radio.'

Mary thought it an uncharacteristically detailed command to the competent chief mate, who hurried below. 'How we doing, Cap?' she asked.

'Terrific.' Kevin snapped on the searchlight. The hard white beam skipped across a violent sea of steep crests; he tried to steer a gentler course, more downwind, to throw less spray. But it had little effect because the gale was whipping the tops off waves, constantly dousing the tug.

Leo and Boags appeared in heavy foul-weather gear outside the back windows, having climbed up from the fiddley deck. With safety lines around their waists and mallets and rust chippers in hand, they attacked the ice blocking the door.

Finally it swung open on the quick thunder of engine exhaust. Wind and diesel smoke swirled through the wheelhouse. Kevin relaxed.

The Filipino seamen started chopping ice from the railings to reduce the weight the *Bowery Queen* carried topside. Roberto joined them, struggling to keep his balance on the rolling, icy deck as he scattered rock salt underfoot. It was vital, Mary knew, but the bookkeeper in her brain thought of rust.

'Poor Roberto,' Kevin chuckled, 'his last job was cooking for some rich Arab in — Shit!' He sprang to the door. *'Sanborn! Get in here.'*

Jim Sanborn picked up the mallet he had dropped and came into the wheelhouse with a sheepish grin. Kevin fought the door shut and turned on him, angrily. 'What in hell are you doing out there? You can't hold a tool, much less grab on if you fall.'

'I pull my own weight.'

The seaman looked at Mary for approval. She looked away. This was Kevin's bailiwick. Besides, he was absolutely right.

'You heal your hand up, you pull your weight. Till then, stay off the deck.'

'Come on, Kev. I can —'

'You want to work, there's plenty to do inside the boat — wait a minute. Where's your safety rope?'

'I couldn't tie it with one hand.'

'That's great, Jim. That's wonderful. You know how long you live in this water? Try three minutes.'

'I'm just trying to help.'

Kevin looked around. His eyes brushed Mary's with a helpless expression and her heart flew to him. He was as decisive as any ship's master had to be — but he was not tough. Her father would have kicked Jimmy down the stairs. But Kevin was prey to the neediness of a lost soul like Sanborn.

'I know you're trying to help. But you're risking your life and the guys around you . . . Why don't you go give J.D. a hand?'

Sanborn retreated, glowering unhappily. When he was gone, Mary said, 'I'll help them.'

'Stay out of it. There's enough tools flying around to brain somebody.'

'I'll sweep the ice overboard.'

Kevin shrugged. 'Go ahead.' He cranked the communicator. 'J.D.? You wanna find "Miss Contrary" a shovel — Hey, Mary, don't forget to tie on to something.'

100

Mary hurried below, wishing already she hadn't volunteered. The tug was plunging hard each time it pitched forward. Reeling about the little cabin, she struggled into boots, insulated slicker and thick gloves, and headed back to the fiddley deck door. J.D. waited, grinning, a coal shovel like a spoon in his enormous hand.

'Sure you want to do this?'

'What do you think?' She took the shovel. It weighed a ton.

'*I* think that if *my* daddy owned a tugboat, I'd a gone to college.' He looped a length of half-inch nylon line around her waist. 'In which event, I'd preside right now over the shiny engine room of a gigantic steam-powered vessel and dispatch eager assistants on errands of my choosing – Mind you hold tight, now.'

As he leaned close to attach the line, Mary caught the sweet whiff of rum on his breath.

'J.D.'

'Yeah, Mary.'

'There's a company notice on the bulkhead in the galley. Read it.'

'Beg pardon?'

'No booze or drugs. Dump it overboard.' The notice said, in fact, as it did on every tug in the world, that violators would be fired.

J.D. slid his hand under his moustache and rubbed his mouth, hard. 'I can't do that, Mary.'

'You're going to hurt yourself or one of us.'

'It don't get in my way,' he muttered through his fingers. Then he addressed the deck at their feet in measured, earnest tones.

'I been drinking since I was fourteen. I made my living since then too. I raised my family. I got kids and grandkids. My wife don't want for food money. She's got a car to get around. One of the kids needs something, we can usually scare it up. I do my job, I don't screw up, and what I do on my own time is my business.'

'On this boat it's my business, J.D. My living and my

father's. We don't allow it. And Kevin shouldn't allow it either.'

'Kevin don't know.'

'I don't believe that.'

J.D. looked up, his face hard. 'I do have one problem sailing with a woman, Mary.'

'What's your problem?'

'You see, if a feller calls me a liar to my face, I have every right to defend my good name. I can't do that with you.'

'Well, J.D., I'm glad you feel that gentle to women.'

'So please don't take advantage. I told you Kevin don't know and I meant Kevin don't know.'

'We're getting far from the subject, which is breaking company rules about drinking on the boat. You made an agreement when you signed on, J.D. So drinking is a kind of lying. You're lying to me and your shipmates.'

'I want you to understand two things. It don't get in my way. And it's the only thing I've ever lied about in my life.'

'I believe the second. But reality tells me the first isn't true. You can't handle yourself as well with booze. No one can. I don't care how many families you raised and how many jobs you've held. You're going to get hurt one of these days, or hurt somebody around you. Dump it!'

'I can't.' He braced himself and swung open the heavy steel door, admitting a roar of sea and engines and a floodlit view of their boiling wake. He held the door for her, his head bowed so she couldn't see his face. Mary hesitated, weighing the dangers of a drunk at sea against the stark fact that she could not hire another chief engineer in the middle of the Atlantic.

He spoke, and she barely heard him over the noise of the *Queen*'s stacks.

'Don't blame Kev. He don't know.'

Still doubting that, she stepped over the coaming without another word and tied the bitter end of her lifeline to an ice-coated rail. The steel door slammed shut behind her.

She moved out of the lee of the house and the wind was almost as loud as the engines; reaching for the ladder to the wheelhouse deck, Mary looked up. The *Bowery Queen*'s crooked mast was triple-thick in ice. The wind tore her hood from her face. Spray slashed her cheek like flying nails. She tugged her hood tighter and worked her way up the ladder which Boags and Leo had chipped clear.

She found them beating ice from the railings and she started scooping the shattered pieces off the narrow wheelhouse deck. Flinging the shovel sidearm, she managed to hurl some of the broken ice into the ocean, though most of it fell on the main deck where breaking seas washed it out through the scuppers.

The *Queen* threw her about the deck, banging her against the wheelhouse and the railings. The wind caught her shovel blade, threatening to tear it out of her hands. She held on tight and it felt for a second as if it might take her with it.

The seamen cleared the rails of the wheelhouse deck and the fat icicles hanging from the visor. Boags scrambled on to the monkey island, the railed deck on top of the wheelhouse roof, and banged away at the mast, scattering brick-sized shards. Leo joined them and pounded the roof with a heavy mallet. Mary shovelled the chunks that fell around her. Then they went down to the fiddley deck, which Roberto scattered with rock salt, and pounded away at the rails, vent baffles, winch controls and the deck crane. Mary shovelled until her back ached and her hands were too cold to close her fingers. All the while, the wind kept ripping the wavetops and spraying the tug with freezing water. Every surface and every projection grew its coat of ice. The hood of Mary's slicker froze like a shell around her face, rubbing her skin raw. Before they had cleared the fiddley deck, the handrails on the wheelhouse deck were thick again.

Leo ordered everyone inside to warm up. Timing the pitching of the boat, he and Boags heaved the fiddley hatch open and tumbled in after Mary and Roberto. Blessed heat poured up from the engine room. Mary sagged against a bulkhead and pulled her hands out of her gloves. Boags stood his frozen-solid slicker on the deck to coax a laugh out of the frightened Roberto.

Sanborn brought mugs of coffee and a gigantic package of Oreos. He was still wearing boots and slicker and Mary had a feeling that if she weren't there and hadn't witnessed Kevin's order he would have sneaked out on deck.

The *Bowery Queen* rolled in long, lazy arcs; Mary held her breath at their extremes and counted the seconds until the tug picked herself up again and swayed the other way. Leo donned his slicker. Boags and Roberto jumped up. Mary put on her own gear while still sitting, husbanding her strength.

Out on deck it was colder than before. She thought at first the wind had dropped, but that delusion was swept away when the tugboat climbed out of a trough on to the crest of the huge wave that had sheltered it. There, high on top of the sea, the wind shrieked like a gale on a mountain. A gust lifted her off the ladder. She lost her grip. Leo seized her slicker and dragged her back.

The wind tore her 'Thanks' from her lips. Then the tug accelerated down a sea slope into the next trough where the full force of the wind was blocked. The price of that respite was drenching spray that rained down from a towering wave; it seemed to freeze the instant it doused the upper decks. They were falling behind, the ice freezing faster than they could knock it off. The *Bowery Queen's* increasingly sluggish motion spoke their failure.

Frantically, they attacked the ice, smashing and shovelling, forced to duck and hold every time the tug met the wind at the top of another wave. Boags, lithe and bold, was first up to do battle again, the last to hunker down. He raced along the rail, swinging his mallet as if he were defending a castle with a sword. Mary couldn't keep up with the shovel. Boags returned, smacking the lower rails. She ducked from the wind. Boags kept going. The wind reached around the wheelhouse deck like a hand and plucked him off the deck.

The boy flew past her in a tangle of arms and legs, skidded on the ice and tumbled over the railing. Mary lunged for him and missed. His lifeline fetched up, then started to slide along the rail, back in the direction where it was tied. Leo got both hands on it, breaking Boags's fall. He and Roberto heaved on the line until a white-faced Boags was able to scramble over the rail. Roberto hugged him. Boags grinned, a little shakily, and waved in triumph the mallet he had never let go, unaware that he was splashing blood on the ice.

Leo hustled him into the house. Only inside, when he pulled his hood off, did Boags see the blood. Leo pressed a towel to his scalp. Boags pulled back. Leo scolded him in Tagalog. Boags answered with a shy smile. The chief mate scolded some more, Boags was adamant. Leo turned to Mary.

'What's wrong?' she asked.

'He wants you to do it.'

'Huh?'

'You bandaged Jimmy.'

'Boags, Leo can do a much better job than me. I'm sure he's been patching up guys since before you were born.'

Boags looked hurt.

'Okay, okay. Sit down. I'll get the kit.'

Sanborn was attempting to brew fresh coffee in the pitching galley. Mary pulled the first-aid kit from its locker.

'Who's hurt?'

'Boags, who thinks I'm Florence Nightingale.'

'Should I cover for him?'

'Ask the captain.'

Leo had gone back to the ice, and Boags was sitting on the deck, luxuriating in the warmth from below. He smiled at Mary and seemed monumentally unconcerned by the deep gash in his skull which still welled blood when she removed the towel. She spread his hair out of it and wiped it dry. 'This might hurt.'

Boags gazed a moment into the middle distance, slowed his breathing, and said, 'Okay, Mary.'

She cleaned and disinfected the wound and pressed a gauze on it and taped it down. Throughout the operation, Boags sat still as a tree trunk, his eyes dreamy.

'You okay?'

'Fine, Mary.'

'You don't feel a thing, do you?'

'Send it away. Come back later.'

'How?'

The boy shrugged. 'Kick-box master teach me. Okay?' He jumped up, just as Leo and Roberto staggered in to warm up. 'Hey. Look. Look what Mary did,' Boags said, bending his head to show them.

Leo went up to report to Kevin. He came back, looking grave, and issued orders to Roberto in rapid Tagalog. The cook ran off.

'What's up?' asked Mary.

'Captain says lay out the survival suits.'

Mary exchanged a look with Sanborn. Nobody was saying it, but they hadn't a hope in hell of getting out if the tug rolled over. And who would abandon ship before, knowing that even in a survival suit, a life in the water would not last? She did as ordered, however, hauling the heavy rubber gear back to the fiddley deck hatch and laying it out like an empty mummy. The boat listed sharply to port, where the ice was heaviest from the north-wind spray.

'Ready?' she asked Leo.

For the first time the chief mate showed his age. Exhaustion had dug lines under his eyes. 'Take it easy,' he said. 'Five more minutes' rest.'

Mary went up to the wheelhouse. Kevin was on the radio, concluding a position broadcast to the Canadian Coast Guard. The back-glow of the searchlight showed his face to be as placid as a pool of oil. 'I thought we might get some help, but a trawler's sinking about sixty miles north of here. Coast Guard's searching . . . You may want

106

to try to raise your dad,' he added, indicating the radio.

'What for?'

'Just to say whatever you want to say.'

Mary looked at him, envying his self-control. Her own hands were shaking and she felt her cheek was jumping with a nervous tic. 'You're awfully calm.'

'I'm just trying to steer.'

'Can't we do anything?'

'I'm doing it, running before the wind. Otherwise, pray it gets warmer.'

'There must be something.'

'Mary, I'm sorry. Every time you go out to chop ice you get a little weaker and a little slower. Same time, we're taking on more ice. The math is easy. We got a few hours.'

Mary looked at the compass. They were heading south again, far off course, at a bare four knots. The warmer waters of the Gulf Stream were many hours away. She went to the pilot chart. East lay the shallow Newfoundland Grand Banks fishing grounds where the icy Labrador Current and the warm Gulf Stream converged like giant rivers.

'What's the weather report on the Grand Banks?'

'Fog —' Kevin looked at her. 'Jesus Christ. Fog melts ice.'

They pored over the chart. 'Four or five hours.'

'Never make it.'

'What do we have to lose?' It was a race. South to warmer water, east to fog. The freighter lay east. 'East,' she said.

Kevin nodded. 'Run for the banks. Pray for fog . . . You drive and me and J.D.'ll chop ice so the little guys can rest. Can you handle it? Want Leo to drive?'

'I'll tell you when I can't.'

Kevin scanned the sea with the searchlight. Mary followed the beam, trying to learn the water she'd have to contend with. The boat she knew, better than most people knew the family car, but these seas were unique.

Kevin waited until they had crested a big sea; then, in

107

the relative calm of the trough, he slowly turned ninety degrees to port and put the *Queen* on an easterly course. The tug started to heel as the next big wave came at her from the left side. Kevin held his breath. The *Queen* heeled further, rising reluctantly on the approaching wave. Just as it felt as if she would roll over, the wave passed her under and the tug lumbered on.

He moved aside to let Mary take the steering stick. 'You'll do fine. You got a nice touch. I'll send your survival suit up with Boags.'

Mary drove for two hours, and in that time every ragged roller that loomed from the north felt like the one to tumble the *Queen*. On deck, the crew attacked the ice, gaining for a few minutes, then losing all the ground won when cold and exhaustion drove them inside. Exhaustion took its toll on Mary, too, limiting how long she could control the boat with precision. Kevin sent Leo up to take over with strict orders for Mary to hit her bunk for an hour.

When she came up again Kevin had relieved Leo. Mary went on deck with a shovel, working behind J.D., who flailed away like Paul Bunyan, ice scattering from his blows. They worked until frozen to the bone. Hot coffee, cookies, and out again, the entire complement led by Leo.

Sanborn tied a heavy mallet to his wrist and demonstrated how he could swing it like a mace. Leo had one look at the wildly flying tool and ordered him inside. The others concentrated on the wheelhouse and the roof as the *Bowery Queen* lurched east.

The clear, cold dawn found the *Bowery Queen* listing seven degrees to port, shambling among the crests of the gale-blown sea. Her crew moved as wearily, beating at the ice with such diminished strength that their tools glanced and skidded sideways as if the ice were steel.

Five hours had become six had stretched to ten, and still the Atlantic rolled before them, under a cold and leaden sky without a wisp of fog. They could see for miles. The barometer held steady. The wind backed east past north, but the visibility remained clear even after they were on to the Banks. Sharp seas pummelled the ice-laden boat.

Mary scanned the empty water for fishing boats, hoping if they did capsize they would have a chance of being picked up, but the storm had emptied the waters and the short-range VHF ship-to-ship radio provoked no replies. Braced against the *Queen*'s steepening list, she scanned the way ahead with the binoculars, bleary-eyed and faint with exhaustion.

When at first she grew aware of a softening on the horizon she attributed it to eyestrain or hallucination. But the line between sea and sky seemed to melt. She lowered the glasses and stared, rubbed her eyes, and stared again.

'Fog!'

A bank of fog towered skyward. The *Bowery Queen* lurched towards it, charging a solid grey wall that expanded side to side and sea to sky. Tendrils began wisping past. Their cold, damp breath permeated the wheelhouse. And then, quite suddenly, the tugboat was inside the fog bank, in fog so deep that her bow was almost invisible and her stern deck disappeared. An opaque mist blanketed the windows, overwhelming the wipers.

Mary went out on deck again and relieved an exhausted Roberto of his shovel. Leo and Boags were still beating the ice, lunging in weary slow motion like deranged robots. The ice was rotting, dripping water, dropping from the rails as if Spring had swept the *Bowery Queen* and the sun would rise on daffodils.

TEN

'Where's Sanborn?'

Kevin leaned wearily against the galley door. Mary, Leo, Boags and Roberto were slumped over victory mugs of milky hot chocolate before falling into their bunks.

'Sleeping,' said Mary.

'He's not in his bunk.'

'Down in the engine room?'

'J.D. just called me to send him down. He's not in the engine room.'

Roberto said, 'Maybe in the head, Captain Kevin. You want I check?'

'First place I looked.'

Kevin's cheek started twitching. 'Anybody seen him on deck?'

'No one's on deck, Captain. I just made the round.' Leo, Mary had observed, checked the boat top to bottom before he turned in after his watch.

The crew rose, exchanging baffled looks, and searched the boat. He wasn't in anyone else's cabin, nor in the store, nor the bosun locker, nor the shower beside the head. Mary followed Kevin out on deck. The fog filled her lungs like wet sand. Kevin circled the house on the main deck. Halfway round, he started muttering, 'Oh Christ, oh Christ, oh Christ.'

He dashed up the fiddley deck ladder and slid down again. 'No.'

Mary knelt under the giant winch drum, which was, she knew, the last place to look where a man's body might have been washed under by intense seas. She remained on her knees, head bowed, staring into the empty, rusted space, then emerged with a mallet tied to a length of twine.

Kevin was watching her; afraid to meet his eye, afraid he would accuse her by a look of having started the events that killed a man, she showed him what she had found.

'Goddammit.'

Kevin closed his eyes, leaned over the winch, and pressed his forehead to the tightly wound reel of towing wire. 'Goddammit,' he whispered again, screwing his eyes shut and slowly beating his fist on the rough strands of wire. Mary went to comfort him. He whirled away from her, raising his bare hand high, and smashed it down on the reel.

He cried out, a low, guttural cry of pain. Blood laced his knuckles. He swung again.

'Stop!'

The rough strands tore flesh. Kevin yelled again, and swung again.

'Stop!' She was horrified, but frightened by the violence in him. She tried to grab his arm.

The heavy blow tore through her hands and into her breast, hurling her against the winch drum. Kevin jerked his hand back. 'Jesus! What are you doing?'

'Don't,' she pleaded, hunched in pain.

'I didn't mean —'

'I know, I know, I know. Please. Please don't hurt yourself.' She tried to pin his arms. He pulled away, his voice ablaze with helpless anger.

'That stupid dickhead. He musta gone out beating ice.'

'You told him not to, Kevin. It's not your fault. If it's anyone's fault it's mine, for getting us out here.'

'It's my job to keep them alive.'

He turned his back and climbed the ladder to the fiddley deck. Mary followed, her breast aching. Kevin was staring back at the *Bowery Queen*'s flat wake. On all the windblown sea, which stretched endlessly beyond their shroud of fog, of all the jagged heaps of moving water, the single place the *Queen* dominated was the hundred feet of smoothness her deepset propellers flung astern. Mary imagined

111

Sanborn, breaking surface in it after he fell and swimming until the sea tumbled after him.

'I guess that's it,' Kevin said at last.

'What do you mean?'

'Gotta give it up.'

'No.'

'We lost a man, Mary. Don't you feel anything?'

'I feel horrible. He was becoming a friend. I liked talking to him about stuff. And he was also the guy who kept telling me "Go for it." So I'll miss him, a lot. But giving up the ship doesn't make Jimmy alive again. It's not like he's clinging to an iceberg waiting for us to pick him up.'

Down on the towing deck, Leo and Roberto and Boags and J.D. ventured out to stare at the wake. Then, one by one, they turned round and looked up at Mary and Kevin. 'They want to know if we're going back,' he said.

'We're not, if I have anything to say about it.'

'I don't know if I can do this. There's something about going after a pot of money after a guy's been killed that bothers me a lot.'

'Forget the money, Kevin.'

'So what are we going for?'

'*I'm* going for the money. If we can pull this off, my share of the salvage fee will buy me time to keep Fulton Towing going as long as my father is alive and then whatever I want afterwards. I don't have any doubts about that, Kevin. This is my lucky shot and I want it. And it's the same for your crew. You told me. It'll change every one of their lives. So if you don't think you deserve this break, how about the rest of us?'

'Probably would have been better if *I* went overboard.'

'We need you. We don't need a chief engineer, we don't need a chief mate, we don't need seamen and we certainly don't need another owner. But we sure as hell need a boat handler — a real hotshot your crew can believe in.'

He met her eye with a thin smile. 'Is that an appeal to my altruism or my ego?'

Mary wanted to take his bleeding hand, but the whole crew were watching, staring up at them in the fog. Funny guy, she was beginning to realize. Clawed his way so fast to his master's ticket, then just stopped, as if the ambition that must have driven him had drained away. 'Maybe it wouldn't hurt to salvage your ego.'

The North Atlantic disintegrated into chaos on the fishing grounds of the Grand Banks of Newfoundland. Undermined by a shallow sea bottom, blown asunder by shifting winds, battered in the collision of icy Labrador Current and torrid Gulf Stream, the majestic structure of ocean crests and plains collapsed. Steep cross-seas scattered to every point of the compass.

Driving hard at her full twelve knots, the *Bowery Queen* plunged and twisted like a motorized cork. And for all the human activity aboard, she might have been a cork. Her exhausted crew slept round the clock – wedged into their bunks with pillows and life preservers – rose like robots for their four-hour stints in the wheelhouse, then shambled back to sleep again, trusting the watch, the sonar, the collision alarm radar to warn of fishing boats, factory ships, rocks and icebergs in the fog.

Mary, awakening stiff and sore for her third watch since they shed the ice, found the galley deserted and reeking of burnt coffee. She dumped it, cleaned the carafe, made fresh. While it was brewing, she locked her legs against the big aluminium sink and splashed cold water on her face. She dried it with a paper towel, chewed some saltines, and stared at the corner of the banquette where Sanborn used to wedge himself to read a book. There were shelves in the bulkhead. He would sit down, reach back without looking and pore through what his hand had fallen on first. She took the thermos to the wheelhouse.

Leo was sitting at the autopilot with a close eye on the radar. He accepted coffee, tasted it warily, and smiled, 'New.'

'J.D.'s lubing the turbos with the old.'

A loud noise exploded underfoot and the tug shook hard.

Mary whirled around, expecting to see a chunk of pack ice in the wake.

Black smoke was gushing from the left stack. Engine alarms shrieked.

'Ohhhhhh, shit!'

She thought they had slammed drift ice through the Kort nozzle and bent the propeller. The engine driving hard and going nowhere would explain the smoke.

Leo hauled back the port throttle, back to neutral, and eased the starboard motor to half speed. He corrected with the rudders to keep the boat on course. Mary bolted for the engine room.

J.D. was ahead of her, stomping down the fiddley deck corridor in sweats and stocking feet, fumbling his glasses over a face creased with sleep. Mary followed him through the engine room hatch and watched from the catwalk while the engineer scrutinized the control panel. He threw some switches and the alarms stopped shrieking.

'What happened?' Mary yelled down. 'She was throwing black smoke.'

J.D. could not hear her over the roar of the starboard engine and the generator. He pored over the port engine gauges again, then commenced a slow circle of the huge engine. Squeezing through the narrow spaces, he paused at the front end, patting it absentmindedly like a sleeping dog. Then he polished his glasses on the fold of his sweatshirt, lumbered back for another look at the control panel, and laboured up the steel steps, shaking his head.

'Blew a cylinder head,' he told Mary.

Bad as that was, her heart soared. At least the trouble was inside the boat, not a bent propeller blade. 'How long to fix it?'

'Fix it?' J.D. looked away. 'It's Number Sixteen. Toughest sumbitch to get to.' He pointed at the foremost cylinder on the inboard side of the V-16 engine, snugged hard against the forward bulkhead.

'How long, J.D.?'

'I can't change it out while they're moving up and down.'

'I know that,' Mary shot back. 'We'll stop the engine. You've got spare power packs, right? I paid for three last week.'

When something broke down inside a cylinder, it was faster and therefore more economical to exchange the entire power assembly and send the old one back to General Motors to be rebuilt in the factory. The spares were chained to the bulkhead just inside the hatch. Shifting heavily with the motion of the boat, they looked like fire hydrants wrapped in black plastic.

'You can change it, right?'

'I think I'll report to the captain, if you don't mind, Mary.'

Kevin had slipped in behind her. He looked like he hadn't slept in a year.

'How we doing, J.D.?'

'Blew a head.'

'Shit.'

'He can change it,' said Mary. 'We'll keep running on the starboard.'

'You want to?' asked Kevin.

J.D. shrugged. 'It's a job for a port engineer. I've changed the 'suckers out at dockside, but even sitting still it's taken me twice as long as a feller's got the tools and helpers.'

'I'll help,' said Mary. 'I can pass tools. I used to help my uncle. I know a little —'

'Mary, will you chill out? You're asking the man to hump a ton of steel across a rolling deck.'

'I know, but —' Both men were staring at her. 'Okay, what are our options? Can we keep going?'

Kevin and J.D. exchanged a long look. Finally, Kevin said, 'Sure. Till we blow another one or the fucker burns up . . .'

'Can we tow the ship?'

After another silence, Kevin said, 'Twenty thousand tons? We'll barely make headway at *full* power if the wind's blowing.'

'I think we can count on the wind blowing.'

'Yeah.'

'So we have to replace the power pack, now. Otherwise we head home, right?'

Kevin shook his head. 'It's up to J.D.'

It was hot on the catwalk above the wounded engine. J.D. tugged a fold of his sweatshirt and wiped his brow, exposing a grey undershirt and a mound of hairy belly. Then he wiped his glasses again and stared at the mini-machine shop on the workbench. He spoke past Mary's head as if he were addressing the power grinder.

'If we go back to Nova Scotia, Boags and Roberto don't get to buy no farm, nor raise no little piggies. Leo's little boy falls in with the wrong crowd and grows up a Communist terrorist. Captain Kev, here, can't buy his tugboat, and you, Mary, lose your Daddy's towing outfit to the feller with the twirly moustache . . . On the other hand, if I do try to change out that power pack and she gets loose on me and rolls over my fingers, I can retire on disability and live like a king the rest of my life, sitting round the house watching the kids grow — "Hey, Granpa, show my friend Beauregard here your flat hand." . . . "Do it hurt, Mr Doughtery?" . . . "Only when I flip griddle cakes."'

Kevin laughed.

Mary, feeling the sting of his laughter directed at her, retorted in a whisper that only J.D. could hear. 'I'd be scared, too, if I couldn't trust my reflexes.'

J.D. flushed.

Kevin looked at the engineer, looked at Mary, and back at him. 'Am I missing something?' A hint of suspicion crossed his face, and with it, anger. 'What's going on, J.D.?'

Mary figured he had to guess that J.D. was drinking. And J.D. apparently did, too; he lifted his huge, round shoulders in a pathetic shrug. 'Okay, I'll shut her down . . . Let her cool off a couple of hours. I'll catch me some sleep. Meanwhile, run the starboard motor at seven-fifty.'

'I'll pass tools,' said Mary.

J.D. gave her a look, equal parts disgust and disdain. Kevin said, 'I think your watch started about five minutes ago.'

They turned their backs on her and Mary retreated up to the wheelhouse to relieve Leo. The chief mate said, 'No problem,' to her apology for being late, told her the tug was easily making twelve knots on the one engine, which was to be expected running light. He showed her a few targets representing fishing boats on the radar, and made sure she knew how to fiddle the autopilot to correct the one-sided push of the single engine, before he went below.

Four hours later, when Boags relieved her, Mary found the engine room a snakes' nest of air hoses and electric cables. J.D. and Kevin had removed the valve cover from the forward half of the inboard bank of the V-16 diesel — exposing the rocker arms, which gleamed like rows of teeth. They had already unbolted the top assembly of the Number Sixteen cylinder, and J.D. had screwed a pulling device into the top of the piston to lift it out. Neither man took notice of Mary watching from the catwalk.

Having prepared the top of the cylinder, J.D. knelt down in the narrow space between the cold port engine and the thundering starboard and opened several manholes in the side. Black oil spilled out. Kevin crouched beside him, swabbing with a cloth. J.D. wiped a socket wrench and touched it lightly to Kevin's shoulder. He moved out of the way and the big engineer lowered himself ponderously to the deck grating. Squeezing one way, then the other, he finally managed to lie down on his back and reach through a manhole with the socket wrench.

He worked by feel, gazing vacantly up at Mary, the fluorescent lights glinting on his glasses, eyes flickering beneath the lenses as if he were imagining himself inside the engine with a clear view of its innards. After a while, he extracted a fat nut. He wiped it with a cloth until it shone, inspected it carefully, then handed it up to Kevin,

117

who put it in a bucket. J.D. reached inside and again removed an array of nuts, bolts and lugs, each of which he wiped, inspected, and set aside.

Then he worked for a long time without result, straining, shifting his bulk on the deck. Kevin leaned over him, signalling with his hands. J.D. shook his head. Finally, though, he climbed painfully to his feet and gestured in disgust, as if to say, 'All right, you try it.'

Kevin lay on his belly and reached through the manhole. Then he tried it on his back, with no better result. Staring up at the catwalk, he noticed Mary for the first time. She leaned over, expecting him to ask her to try to reach whatever was inside, but instead he shook his head at J.D. and mouthed, 'Coffee.'

They washed their hands in diesel fuel.

Mary headed for her bunk, then decided she would not be intimidated on her own boat, went to the galley and planted herself in a corner of the banquette. Roberto was frying chicken on one burner and simmering a pungent marinated beef stew on another. He was chatting with Boags, who quickly explained his absence from the wheelhouse by saying Leo had relieved him with orders to eat supper.

J.D. came in and sank to the banquette. Roberto brought him coffee. The engineer bummed a cigarette from Boags, lit up and spread a rag for an ashtray.

'How's it going?' Mary asked.

'Dropped my socket wrench.'

She waited for more. J.D. stirred sugar into his coffee, then drank it silently, in small, almost delicate sips between drags on his cigarette.

'Where?' Mary asked patiently.

'Inside . . .' he trailed off again, embarrassed. '. . . Your tugboat, she's got a funny roll, first this way, then that, then suddenly she'll sling you against the bulkhead. Well, she slung me when I weren't expecting it and I dropped that wrench and now I can't reach the 'sucker for the life of me. Old Kev couldn't either.'

Mary closed her eyes; they had not even lifted the old cylinder out yet and that was the hard part. She let her mind drift to a fantasy of a glass house on the edge of the woods where fresh water trickled between still pools and the sky was hemmed by rich green trees. She had never seen this place, though she knew it well. It lay upland, far from the coast, clean and quiet. The only machinery was a pickup to run into town, for food she did not grow, or to collect a visitor at the train station, or stop at a bar for a beer and music on Saturday night. The only salt would be in a shaker stashed in the tomato rows, and the nearest thing to grease would be hand cream after gardening.

'Amigo,' J.D. called to Roberto at the range, 'I need a little feller I can insert into that motor through a manhole. He's got to be strong and he can't mind getting greasy.'

Roberto grinned nervously, not sure J.D. was putting him on. But the engineer was not. 'I wouldn't ask if it weren't important, Roberto, but I simply cannot reach that tool . . . And in a way, you're responsible.'

'Me?' Roberto looked to Boags for assurance.

'You,' J.D. went on, 'seeing as how I've put on a few pounds eating your very fine grub . . . I am thinking of your chocolate cake in particular.'

Roberto looked terrified.

'Why don't I take a shot at it?' Mary asked.

'You'd do fine, Mare, up to the vicinity of your bosoms, where you'd likely get stuck. And even if we managed, somehow, to cinch them in, we would almost certainly encounter further difficulty in your nether regions, which I can't help notice are a mite rounded — though not in a displeasing manner.'

Mary felt a ridiculous amount of relief that J.D. wasn't so angry he wouldn't tease.

'If I talked to her that way,' Kevin remarked from the doorway, 'she'd fire me. How do you do it, J.D.? What's the secret?'

'Gals have a fine ear for the difference between loose talk and loose trousers. Thanks, Mare, but I'm afraid it's

Roberto. He's built skinnier than a water moccasin. What do you say, amigo? Nobody gettin' no farm before we fix that motor.'

Roberto found a ladle and plumbed the depths of his stew. J.Đ. sat smoking silently. Boags played with his hands.

'Do you have any farm animals at home?' Mary asked him, seeking to jumpstart the discussion.

'My mother has a goat.'

'How about you, J.D.? Do you have any animals at home?'

'Only my old lady . . . What do you say, amigo?'

Roberto looked again to Boags. The young seaman asked, 'Can I hold Roberto's legs?'

'I would recommend it. Hate to lose such a fine cook, and frankly I'm not sure that motor would run so hot with him inside.'

Roberto nodded. 'Okay, J.D.'

'Good man. Let's do it.'

He led Roberto and Boags away. Kevin sat down across from Mary, shaking his head. 'The little guys treat J.D. like they tamed a polar bear . . . What's got into you?'

Mary downed her coffee and started to get up. 'I better go down for moral support.'

'J.D.'s got plenty of moral support. What's got into you?'

'Nothing's got into me.'

Kevin turned a little smirk into a look of appraisal. 'I mean,' he said to Mary, who was staring at the bottom of her cup, 'what's driving you?'

She said nothing.

'Mary, you're pulling a Captain Ahab. You're a little weird on the subject of that ship. What are you looking for?'

'A fat salvage fee.'

'I never heard you hot for money.'

'I'm hot for what money can do for me and my father. I told you before, I want to straighten the boats out and pay Fulton Towing's debts.'

120

'You going to extremes, pushing J.D. like that. The man could get hurt.'

'I'm extremely in debt.'

'There's something more. You're pushing me and my crew and this sorry old boat. You didn't give a damn about your father's business when you ran off to California. What's different now?'

'My father is dying. I'd like to see him still owning his outfit when he dies.'

'He's not dying.'

'Grow up, Kevin. He's got emphysema and an enlarged heart. He's dying.'

Kevin shook his head and swallowed hard. 'He'll be fine. He's got years left. You watch. He's strong.'

'Right. I'll watch.' And then, because she saw him scrambling within himself to forge some new denial he could believe in, Mary took pity. 'Maybe you're right, Kevin. He *is* strong. He might have a few years — all the more reason for me to put his company on an even footing. I couldn't stand to see him lose it.'

'What about you? Do you care?'

Mary hesitated.

Kevin said, 'You know, the trouble with you is you take all this for granted. You don't know how lucky you are.'

'You're right, I'm not ambitious. I'm not a self-starter. I never have been. Give me a job and I'll do it, but I'm not a — a Captain,' she concluded with a smile.

'You ran a humongous marina in California.'

'Did my father tell you that? Jesus, Kevin, you know how he exaggerates. I didn't run the business, I was just the bookkeeper-office manager.'

'So you ran it,' Kevin persisted. It seemed important to him to perceive her as weightier than she was. She had never understood her father's impulse to embellish her achievements, and now Kevin was doing it too.

'I ran the details,' she explained. 'I didn't make decisions. When yachts ran aground, I reminded the owners it was time to deepen the slips. But they decided

121

whether to hire the dredge . . . And put it off too long.'

'Why'd they give you the job? How old were you then, eighteen?'

'Seventeen.'

By eighteen, she had begun to realize what she had sensed in New York: that small and medium-sized businesses usually functioned on the back of some dedicated woman – be she wife or daughter or employee – with no other life but to run down the details and pinch the pennies and stay hours after the others had gone home.

'So how'd you get the job?'

'I guess they figured anyone who could keep track of tugboats could keep track of sailboats. I don't know, Kevin, I just applied for the job and got it.'

'Bookkeeper to salvage master,' he mused. 'Quite a leap.'

Mary threw her head back and smiled, suddenly happy. 'I feel wonderful. I'm no salvage master, yet, but for the first time since my mother died, I'm not picking up someone else's pieces. I'm out here because I want to be.'

Kevin stood, bracing his legs against the table top as the *Queen* crashed into a trough. 'They've probably rescued that socket wrench by now. Now comes the fun part.' He leaned down and kissed her lightly on the mouth.

Mary looked to see if they were still alone, and combed her fingers through his thick hair and held him. 'Thanks for the talk.'

'Coming?'

'Right behind you.' She savoured a moment alone, tasting him on her mouth, and wondering whether she could retreat to her usual private places while making love with Kevin Patrick.

She jumped up and hurried down to the engine room. A black and greasy Roberto was cradling the socket wrench he had rescued like the awed father of a new-born baby. Kevin, J.D. and Boags were rigging the chain hoist from a steel rail attached to the ceiling above the engine.

Dangling from the chain hoist, which looked like a

partially flattened beach ball, were an endless loop of chain and a sturdy hook. Kevin slid it along the ceiling rail until the hook was positioned over the pulling device J.D. had screwed into Number Sixteen's power pack. Then he pulled down on the chain loop, hand over hand. The links rained through the hoist, lowering the hook an inch for every yard.

As the chain grew longer, the hook began to sway with the tug's roll, clinking against the loop in ever-increasing arcs. Twice Kevin had to stop and untangle it. J.D. watched grim-faced until it had descended low enough for him to secure it to the puller.

Kevin headed for the wheelhouse to drive the tug on the smoothest possible path through the tangled seas, and J.D. manned the hoist, hauling up the slack in the chain, pulling hard, hand over hand, when it grew taut. Slowly as the hands of a clock, the massive power pack rose from its cylinder, caked with blackened, unburnt oil.

When it had emerged halfway, with some eighteen inches standing above the engine, the engineer ceased lifting, to inspect it with a work light. He picked at the thick carbon coat, his lips moving inaudibly, as if he were mumbling secrets with a spy who had come out of hiding. He detached the piston ring, scrutinized it in the light. Round and round he turned it in his big hands, polishing it like a wine glass until it shone.

He resumed pulling on the chain hoist and when the power pack was nearly out, beckoned to Boags and Roberto. Mary ran down the stairs to help, but J.D. shooed her up to the catwalk with an imperious wave of his oily rag. Boags secured a pair of belaying lines between the power pack and stanchions fore and aft.

J.D. draped one line over his shoulder. Roberto squeezed behind Boags and grabbed the other, braced to haul forward if the power pack swung back, while J.D. would haul back if the motion of the boat caused it to swing forward. From her vantage on the catwalk, Mary could see that it was absolutely vital that the ton of steel not be allowed to swing freely, for the three men wedged into the aisle between the engines had no room to get out of its way.

J.D. nodded to Boags and Robert and resumed lifting.

The power pack cleared the engine, leaving a gaping hole in which the piston shaft leaned drunkenly. J.D. immediately walked it sternwards, the hoist rolling heavily on its overhead track. The *Bowery Queen* careened port, then starboard and the load began to arc. Suddenly the tug snapped hard to starboard — J.D.'s 'sling-you-against-the-bulkhead' manoeuvre — and the thick shaft of steel took ponderous flight.

Boags moved fast, threw a lightning second wrap of the line they were fighting to control around the stanchion, and put Roberto on the end while he pulled on the length between the stanchion and the power pack. The new tension, closer to the pack, narrowed its arc enough for J.D. to roll it to the end of the hoist track. There, they hoisted the piece up to the catwalk level and against the bulkhead where the new power packs were stored. They transferred some small parts, screwed in the puller, and began the process of lowering the replacement and trundling it forward, stayed again with belaying lines.

The *Queen* again rolled hard. Boags threw what little weight he possessed against the taut belaying line, which fetched up and hurled him head first against the starboard engine. The boy staggered backward with a silly grin and his eyes glazing over, leaving Roberto to battle the belaying line alone.

J.D.'s bellow was lost in the roar of the starboard engine. The *Queen* pitched, bow plunging, and the new power pack got away from him, rolling along the chain hoist track straight at Roberto's head like a grey and silver cannon.

It knocked Roberto flat and crashed into the forward bulkhead with a *clang* that shook the boat. J.D. brushed past the dazed Boags, leaped Roberto's body, wrapped a belaying line around the first solid bit of steel that met his eye, and waved frantically for Mary to help him.

Mary could not move from the catwalk. She was transfixed by the red smear where Roberto's face had been.

She thought he was dead, until he started screaming.

It was a high-pitched wail of pain and fear that Mary could hear distinctly over the roar of the starboard engine. Boags knelt over him, and recoiled. Mary clung to the catwalk railing. There was nothing left of the boy's face but his screaming mouth and the tip of his nose.

Screams were crowding her own throat, driven hard by the contents of her stomach. She clamped both hands over her mouth and started fearfully down the stairs, knowing she had to do something, if only hold Roberto's hand. Boags was still leaning over his friend, paralysed like stone.

J.D. shouldered him aside and knelt over the screaming cook, adjusted his eyeglasses and reached down. The red smear, Mary saw now, extended from Roberto's hairline to his wispy moustache. She gaped in sickened disbelief as J.D. reached gently, picked it up, and folded Roberto's torn brow back in place, revealing nose, cheeks, and pain-darkened eyes astonished to discover they weren't blind.

The boy blinked. His voice trailed off to a moan.

J.D. eased one big arm under him and worked his hand around to hold the flap of skin and flesh in place, cradled him to his chest, and carried him slowly past the engine and up the steps. Mary ran ahead, clearing the galley table. J.D. laid him on it. Boags ran in with blankets and bundled him up to his chin.

Roberto was crying. The engineer patted his shoulder. 'You done real good, amigo. Man to ride the river with.'

Kevin, who had run in behind Mary, hovered, his face working. 'How bad, J.D.?'

J.D. turned his head so Roberto couldn't hear him. 'Damned if I know.'

'How'd you know to pick up his face?'

'Saw something similar with a feller scrappin' in a honky-tonk. Dude who punched his lights out told me it happens on occasion to boxers. Tell you one thing, though,

Roberto's one lucky son of a gun. Power pack musta just grazed him or we'd be mailing him home in an envelope.'

'Yeah, but what do we do? You can't stand there holding his face on all night.'

J.D. glanced at Mary. 'As I recall, the honkytonk proprietor sent for an ambulance.'

Kevin looked at her, too. 'Sorry, Mary. J.D., secure that damned engine and we'll run for St John's.' He leaned over the table, 'Don't worry, Roberto, we'll get you into the hospital in a couple of days. We're heading there, now.' He started out the door.

Mary caught up with him at the top of the wheelhouse stairs and grabbed his arm. 'Wait.'

'For what? He needs a doctor.' Kevin bent over the chart table, plotting a course for the Newfoundland coast, two hundred and fifty miles behind them. Leo was working the helm, trying to keep the boat steady.

'He's cut, but he's not unconscious,' Mary protested. 'There's nothing broken, is there?'

'He's conscious,' Kevin agreed. 'But he's got hamburger for a face.'

'We can't stop now. We're so close.'

'I don't want to stop. No one wants to stop. But we gotta.'

'We're so close. We've gone through so much already. We can't stop.'

'Mary. It's not like there's anybody waiting to be rescued on that ship. I won't be part of risking a guy's life for money.'

'Not if it's not life-threatening.'

Kevin pencilled a line on the chart. 'You want to sew him up?'

'Sew him up?'

'You know how to sew, don't you?'

'Yeah, I can sew.'

'Well, Roberto's brow fell over his eyes. Makes it hard to cook when you can't see. Tough throwing lines, too. So if you want to keep going, you're going to have to sew

126

him up – and do a good enough job so he doesn't look like Frankenstein.'

'I don't know if I can.'

'There's Novocain spray in the first aid kit.'

'Morphine?'

'Not a good idea with a head wound. We don't know how badly his brains are scrambled. Maybe you can ice him down with the spray. And pump him full of penicillin so he doesn't get infected.'

'Jesus.'

'But first, Roberto's gotta agree to it.'

'I know that . . . I'll go talk to him.'

Kevin grabbed her arm, hard. 'Don't bully him.'

Mary jerked free. 'Is that what you think of me?'

'We've already killed one guy. We just now almost killed a second.'

'I didn't force them to come. They came because they wanted to.'

'They came because they *need* to.'

'Is there any better reason to do something? Leo, did I force anybody?'

'Leave me out of this.'

Kevin said, 'I'm just saying that Roberto is a timid little guy. Don't take advantage.'

'Come with me, then. You're his captain. Protect him from the ruthless owner.'

They went back to the galley. J.D. was struggling to stand still while holding Roberto's brow in place. Boags was talking to him, softly. Kevin said, 'Go relieve Leo, Boagsie. Tell him I want him down here.'

Mary bent over Roberto. 'How you feeling?'

'Okay, Mary.'

'I'm so sorry you got hurt.'

'Not your fault, Mary.'

'Well, listen, Roberto. We've got to . . . patch you up.'

'Yes, Mary.'

'Roberto,' Kevin called from the door. 'It's less than two days to St John's.'

'Easy,' soothed J.D., when Roberto tried to turn his head to see Kevin.

Mary said, 'The thing is, Roberto, we'll lose the ship. Now what I want to know is would you like us to try to sew you up here, and keep going?'

'Roberto,' Kevin called. 'I'll take you anywhere you want. I think you need a doctor more than a pig farm.'

'I don't want a pig farm.'

'Okay,' said Kevin. 'We'll get you to a hospital. J.D., lock up that engine. Finish the job dockside. Let's see if we can tape that brow.'

'No,' said Roberto.

'Gotta tape you.'

'No,' Roberto whispered. 'I want a restaurant.'

Mary looked at Kevin. 'What did you say, Roberto? A restaurant?'

'I'm not a farmer. I'm a cook. I want a restaurant in Manila. I'm going to name it *Bowery Queen*. Is okay with you?'

'No problem, Roberto, *Bowery Queen* would be great.'

'You sew me.'

Leo leaned in. 'I sew you, Roberto. I done it once off Java. Real easy, like sewing turkey.'

Mary sagged with relief. But Roberto said, 'No. Mary sew me.'

'I'll help Leo,' she offered.

'No.'

'What if we found a fishing boat?' said Mary. 'The big processing ships have doctors.'

Kevin shook his head. 'You don't want a Russian fishing doctor sewing you, Roberto.'

They rigged a hammock against the movement of the boat, but it didn't work because Roberto swung while Mary struggled to stand on the deck. Finally, she climbed on top of him, straddling his chest, and swaying with him.

J.D., who had kept a big hand on his shoulder throughout the application of ice and Novocain to the edges of the wound, chuckled. 'Well, hell, amigo, soon as she's done with you I'm going to go bash *my* head on something. That looks like fun.'

Roberto's eyes locked on the needle.

Mary could not figure where to start on the broad, blue-edged cut that had ripped his forehead from temple to temple. She looked away, helplessly. Her mind was suddenly whirling with fears of causing Roberto pain or infection or going on while he was badly injured. 'I can't.'

'Sure you can,' rumbled J.D. 'Hell, compared to Roberto, you got the easy job.'

'I can't . . .' She took a deep breath. 'I can't. Let's take him to the hospital. This is crazy.'

For a moment, no one spoke and the only movement in the galley was Roberto's eyes blinking from face to face. Then Leo spoke to Roberto in Tagalog, apparently asking if he could sew him. Roberto shook his head vehemently and the action caused his brow to slip and he cried out.

At last Kevin said, 'Leo, you want to help J.D. finish up that power pack?'

He replaced J.D.'s hand on Roberto's shoulder with his own when they left, and looked at Mary. 'Come on. Let's do it.'

'I can't.'

'I'll help you.'

'Why?' she demanded. 'Why are you suddenly on my side?'

'Because I know why you're crying.'

'I'm scared.'

'Not really. You're crying because you don't like what you're doing. You don't like leaning on Roberto like this.'

'How do you know?'

'Happened to me once.'

'What were you doing?'

'Sharpening a boathook with a file.'

'What are you talking about?'

'A gang of kids from Port Richmond found the place I was sleeping and trashed my stuff. I knew they were coming back . . . I had to protect myself.'

'Well, I'm scared, too. That's why I'm crying.' She wiped her eyes with her sleeve.

'I was scared. But that was not why I was crying. I was crying because I didn't want to fight. I'd seen plenty violence around the house and I didn't want it. I don't want it. But I didn't want to get hurt, either, and they were going to do me.'

'But you did it. You did what you had to do.'

'No. I got lucky. Your old man came along. That's when he found me. He was suddenly standing there on the barge, looking in where I was sharpening the boathook. I figured he was after me for stealing it, but he just stood there a minute and then he said, "Scared?"

'And I lied, No I wasn't scared.

' "So why you crying, Kid?"

'And I said, "Not 'cause I'm scared." Your old man stared and stared like he could look right through me. Then he said, "You hungry?"

'Shit, yeah, I was hungry. So he took me home to supper.'

'I remember.'

'Next day he went around to Port Richmond to see the fathers of some of those kids — I'll hold Roberto's head. You sew.'

'You don't owe my father, you know. He thinks you're even.'

'He never could count worth a damn.'

'*You* hold Roberto's head, *I'll* sew.'

130

ELEVEN

Hooking up the replacement power pack took three hours, and the job finally ended with Leo passing one last nut to J.D., a part so small it could have come from a typewriter.

They were deep into the night before J.D. completed his tests, pre-lubed the turbocharger, checked the fuel filters, and cranked the engine to life. When it was warm and rumbling to his satisfaction, he telephoned the wheelhouse.

The port engine shuddered into gear and built to 750 rpms, at which speed the bent shaft resumed its familiar vibration.

Mary said, 'Thank you, J.D. Thank you very much.'

J.D. plodded over to the bleed valve and washed his hands in fuel oil. 'Think I'll get in the rain locker.'

She left him to his shower — and any drink he thought he deserved — and dragged herself up to the wheelhouse. She was dead on her feet, but it was important to enter a full account of the repair into the log. It was money in the bank, with no embellishments needed to impress the salvage arbitrator of the sheer guts of the crew of the *Bowery Queen*.

She looked in on Roberto, whose head was wrapped in an enormous bandage that covered the thirty stitches she had taken in his brow. He was whimpering while he slept. She held him until he stopped. Then she fell on to her own bunk, fully clothed, and into a dreamless sleep that ended too soon when Kevin Patrick woke her for her watch with a mug of coffee that smelled of diesel and a radio-telephone report from her father that the *Noorde Titan* was closing in on the last position reported by *Der Schmetterling*'s lifeboat.

*

The powerful Dutch salvage tug gave nothing away on the radio. Her signals to Noorde's Rotterdam office were sent in code. But a US Coast Guard buddy of Mary's father had relayed the news that British Royal Navy long-range search planes had sighted the *Titan* before weather had ended the air search.

'Can't help praying,' J.D. remarked to the others in the galley, 'that the Good Lord helps the *Titan* save them poor sailors, slowly.'

The chief mate nodded agreement, and Kevin said he felt like a ghoul: 'But as soon as they find the lifeboat, they'll go after the ship, at which point we are fucked.'

'Figure she'll do twenty knots, Kev?'

'Easy. Even in these seas.'

'We're doing twelve?'

'Not when you subtract going up and down and yawing sideways. More like ten. I'm figuring two hundred and forty miles a day. Two-fifty, tops.'

Mary coaxed a wan attempt at a smile from Roberto as she finished changing his bandage. The stitches seemed to be holding, but he was dead white from pain. 'We're closer to the ship,' Mary said. 'And they have to find the lifeboat, first.'

No one answered. A look at the combers rocketing past the porthole showed that they had strayed into the territory of ships like the *Noorde Titan* where 'closer' meant little to an overgrown harbour tug like the *Bowery Queen*.

Newfoundland's shallow fishing banks were behind them now. The sea bottom had plummeted from a few score fathoms to thousands. Harried by an Arctic wind that had lost the rich stink of fish and weed, the *Bowery Queen* was roller-coasting on seas that tumbled after her like avalanches.

Mary clung to her original hope that the abandoned freighter had kept going on autopilot. 'It doesn't matter,' she said doggedly. 'We're here first.'

'If the ship kept going,' said Kevin.

'If she didn't sink,' said J.D.

'If she stayed on course,' said Leo.

Mary stood up. *They* were getting paid, while the *Queen* gobbled fuel enough to run a large town. 'I'll be in the wheelhouse if anyone else comes up with something to worry about.'

'What's got into her?' asked Kevin as she went through the door. 'In my limited experience,' said J.D., 'gals tend to get that way. It's a quirk of the species. Probably why we don't usually keep 'em aboard – Hey, Roberto? Amigo. If your head don't ache too fierce, why don't you run her up a slab of your chocolate cake? . . . Hell, while you're slicing, I'll have some too. How about you, Kev?'

'I'll carry it up.' He found Mary bent over the log, writing furiously. 'J.D. thought you might want some dessert.'

'God, no. I've been eating like a pig. You have it.'

'Naw . . . Listen, what's the problem?'

'No problem. Just tired and worried and scared. Does it show?'

Kevin looked over at Boags, who was shuttling between the autopilot and the radar, and lowered his voice. 'The guys need a little encouragement. You know?'

'The *guys* are getting paid. I'm spending two thousand dollars a day I don't have on fuel.'

'That's a little out of their league. They're just guys. They're working for a living. They don't know from two thousand dollars a day. All they know is what they see from the boat and the captain. And this case, from the owner, 'cause she's aboard.'

'Am I making them unhappy?'

'They like you. Sort of. But you're not one of them.'

'I know I'm a woman. Not to mention head nurse and volunteer surgeon.'

'You're first an owner. You gotta act like a boss.'

'It's your job to tell them what to do. You're the captain, as you've seen fit to remind me several times.' She flipped the log back to the first day where he had noted her presence with his willing permission.

'Damn right you don't tell them what to do. But you *show* 'em what to do.'

'*Inspire* them?'

'If I were alone I could do it alone. But you're here and they see you and they know you're my boss. So what they see you do determines how they act.'

'I don't see anybody sloughing off.'

'The tug's running pretty good,' Kevin agreed. 'But we're going to be asking them to do a lot more than run a tug once we start a search pattern. And if we find that ship, God help us, we're going to ask them to do stuff they never dreamed of. Now, you did good getting J.D. to change out that power pack. I don't know what you said to him. I know he didn't want to do it and I didn't blame him, but you got him to try. But a simple problem like that's easier. Searching takes total concentration. You won't get that unless they believe they can find that ship.'

Mary ran a hand through her hair and regretted it instantly. It felt oily and dirty, coated in diesel smoke, like everything else on the boat.

'So why were you telling them we're fucked if the *Noorde Titan* finds the lifeboat?'

'My mistake. But you should have saved me, instead of storming out on them. Soon as I said it I knew I'd blown it. I can show 'em I believe. But you've got to show them you believe.'

'But I do believe. I believe that ship kept going. Don't you?'

Kevin shook his head, checked that Boags wasn't listening, and said, 'No. I wish I did, but goddammit, Mary, I don't. And —'

'Captain Kevin?'

'What is it, Boags?'

'There's something on the radar.'

Kevin beat her to the multi-coloured display screen. When Fulton got the Okimitsu contract, he had told her father he would rather swim to Nova Scotia than take a tow without a decent radar. Gone was the old rubber-cupped scope they used to press their faces to. Mike had scared up a top-of-the-line Furama — second-hand — with clutter suppressors, collision warning, range and bearing microprocessor, and a bright, steady twelve-inch screen several people could watch at once.

The Filipino seamen liked all the lines and numbers glowing like a video game. Kevin switched them off, crossed his arms, and eyed the blank screen. 'Where? I don't see it?'

'On the top. All the way. Twenty-four miles.'

'*Twenty-four miles?* Wha'd you find, Boags, a city?'

'When we get on top the wave you'll see . . . Here he come . . .'

Staring at the screen, willing a target to appear, Kevin felt the swell overtake and slowly lift the boat. The computer-enhanced screen was supposed to show the track of an echo temporarily interrupted by clutter, but whatever Boags had seen had vanished. The *Queen* rose higher. The sea spread before her, grey and white in the dimming of the day.

'Here he come — there!' Boags stabbed the screen with his finger. A square green light formed up at the top, nearly dead ahead, a few degrees north of their course. Kevin watched it until the boat lumbered down the back of the wave, into the trough. The light held for several revolutions of the spinning scanner, enhanced by the microprocessor, then faded.

Mary seemed afraid to breathe. 'Jesus,' she whispered. 'Is that it?'

'Too soon . . . Probably just a passing ship. Stick on it, Boags. Get his course. See which way he's heading. Maybe when he gets closer we can raise him on the VHF. Ask if he's spotted *Der Schmetterling*.'

Boags looked crestfallen. Mary said, 'How long have you seen him, Boags?'

'Couple of minutes. I didn't want to say till I was sure.'

'Is he moving?'

The boy glanced shyly at Kevin. 'I don't think so, Mary.'

'Well, nice going. Maybe you got something. We'll see soon.'

Kevin looked at her.

'Inspiring,' said Mary.

'Yeah?'

'Seeing a ship after being alone so long.'

'Captain Kevin? Can I go up on the monkey island with the glasses?'

'Kind of long range for binoculars, isn't it Boags? Okay, I'll take your watch. Go on. You got good eyes. But put something warm on and for Crissake don't fall off. All I need is to lose my best seaman and my good binoculars.'

Boags threw on a parka, grabbed the glasses from their case on the dashboard, and scampered up the ladder outside the back door.

'Getting dark soon,' Kevin remarked. 'He hasn't a hope in hell of seeing it.'

'It's back on the screen.'

Kevin shook his head. 'I don't believe it. But that 'sucker isn't moving.'

'No, it's not. You mind if I play with the radar?'

'Go right ahead.'

Mary got the instruction manual. She set it to the extreme range scale and moved the variable range marker to the echo target. The readout on the right side of the screen said it was thirty-one miles away.

'No way,' said Kevin. 'Unless it's three hundred feet high.'

'Supertanker?'

'Yeah, two of them. One on top of the other. Something's screwed up. See, now it's gone.'

'But something's out there.'

'Maybe.'

'And it still isn't moving.'

'Probably not.'

'And it really couldn't be more than twenty-four miles away, right?'

Kevin opened up Bowditch and they confirmed the

radar range tables. 'Right, figuring our height above the water and a hundred feet for its height above the water.'

'So we'll know in two hours.'

Kevin shook his head, mildly baffled. He opened the rear door, admitting a roar of engine exhaust, and yelled up to Boags. 'See any smoke?' He came back in, dogged the door, and shivered. 'No smoke . . . Very weird, Mary.'

'It's our ship.' She had abandoned the radar for the chart again. 'It got a few hundred miles closer than we thought. Half a day at twenty knots?'

'Very weird.'

'It's our ship!' she cried. 'We've got it, we've got it. We've got it.' She ran below and came back up in her parka.

'Where you going?'

'Up with Boags. I gotta see this.'

'Six thousand dollar radar and you gotta stand in the cold.'

'Can we board tonight?'

'It just fell off the screen again.'

Mary went out of the door, carefully timing the tug's roll so the heavy door wouldn't crush her hand. The wind was from behind, diminished by the tug's speed, but it was cold and the exhaust smoke was choking. Hand over hand, she went up the ladder. Boags had one arm wrapped around the stubby steel mast which carried the radio antennas and the radar scanner. His eyes were pressed to the binoculars, but he wasn't looking ahead. He was looking off to the right, to the south of their easterly course.

'What are you doing? The ship's ahead.'

'I saw a sail.'

'A *sail*? Out here?'

'A little sailboat. It came up on the wave for a second.'

Mary shielded her eyes and scanned the marching combers. 'Where?'

'Two miles off the beam.'

Mary searched. The Atlantic seemed to roam for ever,

an endless bowl of rolling water capped by a low sky as grey as itself. 'Which way was it going?'

'I don't know,' said Boags. 'It was there and then it wasn't. Maybe it never was.'

'What about the ship?'

'Nothing. No smoke.' He handed her the glasses. She found the horizon and focused on a point slightly north of the bow. She knew Kevin was right. Twenty-four miles was an impossible range with binoculars, even on a clear day like this. But it felt great to look, as if the eye could make the radar picture true. A darkening ahead showed it would be night too soon.

She and Boags stayed in the cold an hour. It became an unspoken contest to see who would give up first, as the *Bowery Queen* halved the distance to the target and the dark descended from the sky. Finally there was no horizon ahead, only a blackness that obscured half the water and half the sky.

'Let's see the radar,' she said, and a violently shivering Boags said, 'Good idea.' As they turned to go down the ladder, the yellow remnants of the sunset hung in the south-west. Mary looked again for a lonely sail, but it would be miles behind them now, if it ever was.

Leo had joined Kevin in the wheelhouse and the two were puzzling over the radar target, which, when it wasn't fading out, had hardened into a big rectangle. The screen described it as fifteen miles away and moving east at a single knot.

'Funny,' said Kevin. 'You'd think the wind would move her faster.'

Leo brought him the pilot chart and pointed at the green arrow which represented the Labrador Current setting south-west at half a knot. Kevin nodded.

'Yeah, maybe the Lab slipped down that far. That would slow her. But I kinda thought the current would be a little north of here . . . Well, we had a lot of north wind. Jesus, I don't know, Leo.'

'Big ship,' said Leo. 'Lot of windage.'

'Yeah, she's got a lot of house on her. And a mountain of containers.'

'Four hundred and eighty feet,' said Mary. 'Twenty thousand tons. Five hundred containers.'

'This guy looks bigger. Or the radar's screwy.' He winked at Leo. 'Hey, Mary, maybe we can salvage two ships.'

'Command decision, Cap.'

Kevin said, 'Listen, Boags, you better get something to eat. It's gonna be a long one. Tell J.D. I wouldn't mind seeing him in the near future . . . Leo, we got to find out what shape she's in first.'

'How you want to go aboard?'

Kevin gave him a thin smile. 'Haven't figured that out yet. Let's see how she lays.'

'Once when I was seaman, I swam.'

'If it comes to that, we'll ask Mary. You swim, don't you, Mary?'

'I'm afraid I strained a tendon sewing Roberto.'

'Well, maybe we'll get lucky and the sea'll come down and we'll just putter alongside and step aboard. You know when the *Titanic* sank out here, the sea was so calm they just walked off the deck.'

But Leo wasn't kidding. 'I don't know if I could still swim, maybe Boags. I show him how.'

'Well, if he wants to, you can show him how, but let's not start tossing guys overboard yet. First, we got to find this baby and see what's wrong with her. Damn, she's tall. You think maybe she's half sunk, ass in the air?'

'Saw a tanker sink like that in the Gulf, once,' said Leo. 'Maybe.'

'Well, look, go get Roberto squared away in the galley. We're going to need all hands. And let's check out the work lights.' Leo hurried down the stairway.

Kevin told Mary, 'The little guys are crazy, you know. I worked with some in Indonesia. They'll do anything. If you asked Leo to drive you to hell he'd only wait long enough to bunker.'

Mary was staring at the radar again. The target was nearing the twelve-mile range line, one hour away.

'Why's it so big?'

'Why's it keep disappearing from the screen?' Kevin countered. 'You want to take over? I gotta go below a sec.'

Mary moved to the autopilot, gazed through the dark windows at the black night, stealing glances every few seconds at the radar. The bright ranging lines and numbers were impeding her night vision. She switched them off. Now the screen was black, but for the intermittent glow of the target ahead, and otherwise eerily empty. She strained to see a light through the window, but the night was dark. At ten miles, she reached for the VHF mike and broadcast on Channel 16.

'Tug *Bowery Queen*, heading east at twelve knots, fifty-one degrees North, forty degrees four minutes West. I've got you ten miles ahead on the radar. Do you see me?'

The radio hissed a steady, empty noise.

She tried again, but whatever was out there was not talking. She was relieved. Any answer at all would have meant it was not *Der Schmetterling*, not abandoned, not ripe for salvage.

Kevin came back. 'J.D. thinks it's a whale. See any lights?'

'Nothing. Nothing on the radio, either.'

'Yeah. I tried before.' He took the mike and called again.

When the radar target was five miles away, Kevin sent Boags up on the monkey island with a walkie-talkie, and posted Leo on the forward fiddley deck. At three miles, Leo came back in.

'Smoke,' he said.

'She's running?'

'No, no, no. Sea smoke. Fog.'

'What?'

Kevin switched on the big searchlight. The beam drove out a quarter-mile, then mirrored back softly from a white bank of fog. 'Where the hell did that come from?'

'Wind's dropping.'

Kevin looked at the radar. They were approaching the fog fast. 'New target.'

The radar showed another smaller target to the side of the first. Mary thought of the sailboat Boags swore he had seen, but it would be thirty miles astern.

'What the hell is that?'

'Got me,' said Kevin, throttling both engines back to three hundred. As far as he was concerned, the radar was now a liar and not to be trusted. 'Leo, I'd like Roberto on the bow, with a sharp eye.'

'Better I go,' said Leo. 'Roberto's head is killing him.'

The tug slowed and began to wallow a little. Kevin switched off the autopilot and manned the starboard steering stick. Mary put on her parka and climbed up to the monkey island. The fog was cold and penetrating. She tightened her hood. Suddenly Boags tore his own hood off and listened intently.

'What?' asked Mary.

'You hear?'

'What?'

She threw her hood back. The cold seeped through her scalp. She strained to hear over the muffled thunder of the engines. She took Boags's radio and said, 'Hey, Kev. You want to stop the engines? We hear something.'

Kevin throttled back. The EMDs growled quietly to themselves.

'My God,' Mary said. It was a muffled boom, a sound that made the hairs stand on the back of her neck.

'No,' whispered Boags. 'It can't be.'

Mary thumbed the walkie-talkie. 'Kevin, get ready to stop. You're not going to believe this. We hear surf.'

The hollow boom, the hiss and slide of receding water were unmistakably crashing waves. But crashing on what in the middle of the ocean? The Queen's search beam stabbed fog; the suspect radar showed the ship nearly stationary, less than two miles away. The smaller target had disappeared from the screen. Another cropped up on

141

the opposite side, only to slide like the first behind the giant rectangle dead ahead.

'Okay,' said Kevin. 'Enough bullshit. We're going in. Leo, sharp eye. Give a shout.'

'What if you run aground?'

'The chart shows there's two thousand two hundred and sixty fucking fathoms of water. That's two and a half *miles* deep. We're not running aground. Unless they had a volcano this afternoon.'

He slid the throttles into gear, forward to two hundred rpms, and lowered his window. Wet, cold air poured into the wheelhouse; it smelled, vaguely, of land.

'Hear that?' Mary breathed.

'I smell it, too,' he answered, mystified.

'Could waves be hitting the ship?'

'Nope. The ship moves with the water.'

He twirled the overhead wheel that turned the searchlight. Mary followed the beam bouncing on the smoky fog. Suddenly it penetrated, and shot through an alley between two banks. The steering stick hissed. The tug nosed between the drifting walls.

'Breakers!' Boags yelled from the monkey island. 'Breakers dead ahead.'

'I see them! I see the waves!' Mary cried.

'Son of a bitch.' Kevin stopped the engines.

The fog was falling away, allowing the searchlight more play. Mary stared, mesmerized by the impossible sight of breakers smashing white froth against a hard shore.

J.D. huffed up the stairs, peering nearsightedly. 'The ship?'

Above the surf line a high crystalline bluff scattered the search beam like a mountain of prisms.

'Iceberg.'

Kevin Patrick named the iceberg *Boags' Berg* and, as the *Bowery Queen* left it in her wake, reported the 600-foot-long, 300-foot-high monster to the US Coast Guard, which ran the International Ice Patrol. The radio link was tenuous, patched through a Newfoundland high seas station, and he lost the signal without getting any new information on the whereabouts of *Der Schmetterling*.

'They had a problem believing we're out here – Hey, cheer up.'

Mary was bitterly disappointed. For a few hours it had seemed so easy. Now they were back where they had started, ploughing eastward against the track she presumed, or guessed, or hoped, the abandoned ship would have steamed. And when Boags' Berg disappeared astern, the Atlantic looked emptier than ever and twice as enormous.

'It's a big ocean,' said Kevin. He was positively buoyant, by contrast, and she began to understand that he preferred driving a harbour tug because he liked the constant action. He had surged to life as soon as they had something on the radar, and had seemed thoroughly to enjoy every moment of hunt and discovery.

By midmorning the next day, however, with the ocean as bleak and featureless as the iron-coloured sky and nothing ahead but a line on the chart, Kevin was down again, and so pessimistic that Mary worried he would infect the crew with his doubts. Her own spirit had begun to rally and she had awakened from a short sleep fired up and ready to go again. She spent the morning with the pilot chart, weather reports and a calculator, projecting possible courses and drift *Der Schmetterling* might have followed since the Mersk sighting.

Finally, 150 miles past Boags' Berg, she showed Kevin her figures and asked him when he thought they should start to search. Kevin stared at the chart and shook his head.

'I think maybe we veer a little south. Current's setting south-east and the wind's been north and west. Ship's drifting south . . . What do you think?'

Both captain and owner knew they were on the edge of a fateful decision, gambling everything on the Mersk liner sighting. Once committed to a ladder search, the

143

Bowery Queen would advance in rectangular increments covered by its radar, broadening the sea spread it could investigate, but severely limiting her forward advance. If *Der Schmetterling* had stopped earlier, they would never reach it.

'Might as well flip a coin,' said Kevin.

'Let's start.'

TWELVE

The idea of Alison Knight's thirty-nine-foot *Twice a Knight*
beating into a North Atlantic gale would have chilled the
blood of the yacht broker who had sold it second-hand for
a pittance – and hints of gratitude that somehow never
materialized into a roll in the kip – for the little yacht had
left the factory a mass-produced, ultra-light racing sloop,
built to sail the amiable waters of Long Island Sound for
ten weekends a year, followed by a snug winter's refit in
a suburban boatyard. The actual sight of it battling up the
wintry swells and skidding down their backsides would be
reassuring, though confusing, for Alison had so radically
re-rigged and altered *Twice a Knight* that even the broker
would not have recognized the sailboat.

The Englishwoman had replaced the mast in a back-
water Antiguan shipyard, exchanging the tall, flimsy light
air aluminium spar for a shorter, sturdier one made of
wood. The new pole – heavily stayed and cutter-rigged for
smaller foresails a woman could handle alone – was strong
enough for a Southern Oceans passage and, not incidentally, invisible to radar.

A sail loft on the French side of St Martin had re-built
Twice a Knight's sails for the new rig, and punched in spider
grommets so she could change jibs singlehandedly. And a
Barbados ship carpenter had extended back from the cabin
a protective doghouse that shielded the cockpit from most
of the cold spray that *Twice a Knight* was banging out of
the Atlantic rollers. The Barbadian had done his work so
neatly that the join was seamless and the sloop, even on
close inspection, looked like one of the many idiosyncratic
ocean-passage one-off designs seen briefly moored around
the world at the scruffier fishing docks and grottier

marinas. Dockside, *Twice a Knight* appeared capable of avoiding trouble; but the re-fit had not been totally successful, and at sea, she moved like a skittish cat.

Characteristically, Alison did not blame *Twice a Knight*'s shortcomings on the boat's designer, but faulted herself for not anticipating them and was constantly dreaming up improvements. The boat heeled over too far sailing to windward. Alison felt the sails spilling the wind and she took the loss personally. She wanted a heavy lead bulb on the keel to stiffen her up. Better yet would be water-ballast tanks, which would allow her to transfer weight from side to side. Right now she could do with a bit of extra weight on the port side to make her stand taller.

Another problem she kicked herself for was the rudder. *Twice a Knight* tended to veer off the track thanks to a minuscule free-hanging spade rudder. Alison had been leery when she snorkelled for a look and saw it dangling with all the authority of a butter knife. It overworked the auto-pilot and rendered the self-steering gear near useless, which forced her to spend long stretches at the helm in the cold and wet. What *Twice a Knight* needed to steer better was some sort of skeg to both seat the rudder more solidly and to help hold the boat on course. She should have walked away the instant she saw the rudder, but the price had been right and time short.

Beating into gales for the past week, pounding north-eastward on a close port reach, *Twice a Knight* slammed mercilessly into the steep choppy waves that shifting winds had riled in the troughs between the rollers. Only on the crests of the rollers did she find respite, and that was brief, so that Alison's days and nights had been a blur of short naps snatched from endless rounds of sail trimming, course correction, and repairs. Despite radically strengthening the boat and sails and rigging, gear chafed, rubbed and pounded itself to destruction. She was deep in one of those repairs — trying to thread a bolt into a new shackle on the boom vang — when she heard the shrill electronic beeping of the radio alarm. Manfred.

Cramming tools and the new shackle and pin into her foul weather jacket, she scrambled below into the comparative warmth and quiet of the cabin. Hans was reading in his bunk, deaf to everything but the Walkman grafted to his head. He looked up with a grin, probably thinking she had come down to cook him dinner.

His grin faded when she sat down at the single sideband high frequency radio and he watched suspiciously as she started her diesel generator to feed the power-hungry transmitter. He had already thrown her satellite telephone overboard in Bermuda, yelling that their position could be detected from its signal.

'It's Manfred again,' she explained. She untangled the headset wire.

'Put it on the speaker.'

'It's harder to hear.'

'Do it.'

She did as he ordered and fine-tuned to the signal that had tripped the alarm. Then she waited, towelling her salt-matted hair, listening to the radio's hollow, empty hissing, and trying to ignore Hans's eyes on her. Exactly five minutes after the alarm, Manfred's voice filled the cabin, rich despite the thin signal and the distance between them.

'*Come in R-O-O-K. Come in R-O-O-K. Romeo-Oscar-Oscar-Kilo.*'

Alison signalled the 'Go Ahead' by switching her transmitter on and off.

'*Where are you?*'

She sent her position, subtracting ten degrees from latitude and twenty-five from longitude. Manfred responded with his coded position, and demanded, '*How much longer?*'

'Are you sure of your position?' she asked. His drift was phenomenal. The wind was blowing the dead ship at nearly half the speed she was sailing.

'*Yes, goddammit.*'

'Sorry.'

How long? She had sacrificed speed re-rigging for strength. And the January pilot chart promised more high

147

seas and gale force headwinds. She had had a tougher than
expected sail from Bermuda, just to reach the rendezvous,
but that had seemed a piece of cake compared to the passage to her present position. Hans was useless, and she was
wearing down.

'Three more days,' she radioed back. 'At least. I'm sorry.'

Manfred's transmitter clicked off. Hans staggered across
the rolling deck, holding a ceiling grip as the boat lurched.

'He's in for a shock if he thinks this is any better.'

'Next time charter the *QE2*.' She pulled up her hood.

'Where you going?'

'I'm going to try more headsail, goose some speed out
of the bitch.'

'But you said we're sailing as fast as we can.'

'The wind's blowing Manfred away from us; we've got
to take chances.'

'Just don't get us drowned.'

'Don't worry, Hans. We're in the same boat. Why don't
you heat up something to eat?'

'I think I lie down again.'

Alison hurried up on deck.

She was worried about the crew of Manfred's ship.
When Manfred first radioed about the breakdown, she had
been afraid to ask what had happened to them. Had 'I am
stopped' meant he was alone on the ship? Or was it just
his egocentric German syntax where 'I', a freighter, and
her entire crew, were one and the same?

North Atlantic radio chatter had cleared that up. A lifeboat from the German freighter *Der Schmetterling* had sent
some garbled Maydays. Royal Navy planes and a Dutch
tug were calling to each other as they searched a storm-
swept area half as big as France.

Manfred had not violated security by telling her the
name of the ship that carried his container. All she had
known when she set out was where on the ocean to meet
him. Even now, with Manfred's stopped ship and the
abandoned *Der Schmetterling* so obviously the same vessel,
paranoid Hans still pretended not to know.

It didn't matter any more. Just as it didn't matter what had gone wrong, though obviously the crew had found him and he had forced them to abandon ship. Thank God he hadn't killed them. That she allowed herself to admit he could have, frightened her, and she pushed it from her mind with generous explanations. Manfred was Manfred, after all, not a monster like Hans. This was not to excuse Manfred's crimes, but she had always seen him as a victim of circumstance.

'Alison,' her exasperated mother used to complain, 'you think too much.'

It was a private failing well hidden behind a ready smile and can-do attitude. Whatever the whizzings around her head, what people saw was an eager-to-please, cheerful woman – a bit too strikingly blonde and blue-eyed to be credited with intelligence – who would probably wind up making an older husband happy. Daughter of a disappointed Royal Navy submariner whom budget cuts had beached young, and a woman whose own father had retired a famous admiral, Alison had fled a house of disappointments to race sailing boats, starting in dinghies, then demonstrating a great aptitude in the difficult Soling class.

Those who had followed her career wondered why she had not stayed the Olympic course. She had possessed the superb sense of speed and distance and the first-rate boat handling skills to be a winner. But something had gone wrong. Somehow her competitive drive had tapered off, and she had drifted away from the sport. She had dropped out of sight for a while. And when she had re-surfaced, people were surprised to hear that Alison Knight had been hiring out as a fifty-dollar-a-day yacht captain, or was delivering boats between the Canaries and the Caribbean, or, as one story went, had bought a second-hand sloop and was trying to make a go of chartering to the holiday trade.

She just didn't seem like the sort of woman to have secrets.

Manfred Echtheit was primary among them. They had met at seventeen in Denmark, at a Royal Danish Yacht Club regatta, racing Solings for the 1980 Olympic Trials. The handsome East German had become her first lover and, Manfred's boasts notwithstanding, she was reasonably sure that she had been his first, too. They had discovered they shared surprisingly similar experiences for two children from such ostensibly different worlds. Manfred enjoyed, in fact, as privileged a life in Communist East Germany as Alison's in England; each knew the pleasures of birth to the Establishment.

For years they met at races around Europe, both rising to prominence in 1984, though both failed to make their national teams for the Summer Games. Racing gossip deemed Manfred too casual in his training. But Alison had looked like a skipper moving into her prime. And yet, by 1988, she had ceased to compete.

What had happened had occurred two years earlier in 1986. An uncle, one of her mother's brothers she had known all her life, had invited her down to London for lunch. The scene at his club had seemed straight out of Len Deighton. (Uncle Richard was too cheery a soul for a Le Carré spy.) He told her how Manfred's family belonged to the oligarchy that ruled East Germany under the banner of 'Democratic Socialism'.

Alison had been thinking that Uncle Richard's spreading baldness made him look incongruously sexy when he started the Manfred tack. 'I'm not sure why you're telling me this.'

Uncle Richard chuckled, enjoying the moment as he had enjoyed everything from sherry in the reading room to the poached salmon entrée. 'The point is, your friend's relations run East Germany like a closely held private corporation.'

'But —'

Chuckling some more, Uncle Richard had made obscure reference to the Belgian King Leopold's maniacal stewardship of the African Congo, and another to Monty Python:

150

'The point is, the boy is heir to everything — "What, the curtains?" — which is where you come in.'

She would have thought him drunk by now if he had had more than that one sherry in the reading room. 'He's hardly a boy, Uncle Richard.'

'Just as you're no longer a girl.'

'I beg your pardon?'

'Duty calls, m'dear. It's as simple as that. Your friend is on the fast track, as the Americans say, career-wise. The Stasi beckons. You do know what the East German Stasi is? State Ministry of Security. Hmmm?'

'Secret police.'

'Bit more than that. Sort of the elite of the elite when it comes to running things and spying on your neighbours, not to mention bedevilling the civilized world with their terrorist clients . . . Now, your friend, as befits his station, has been admitted to the exalted ranks of the Stasi. They have big plans for him. He is genuinely talented, it seems, as well as high-born — isn't that a marvellous picture, a high-born Communist? And certain sources indicate that he is as deliciously amoral — spell that corruptible — as any we've come across in a long time.'

'We?'

'The Foreign Office . . .' Alison grew aware that Uncle Richard had stopped chuckling to gauge her reactions. He seemed pleased. 'Obviously, one is not so open with every candidate, but you're one of us, dear.'

Alison interrupted again; dealing with her sponsors, companies that manufactured sailing gear, she had learned to get clear on details early on. 'Candidate for what?'

'Recruitment, of course. Look here, young lady, Queen and Country need you. Your friend —' Uncle Richard rarely called him anything but that '— strikes us as ripe to pass the odd secret.'

'Why?'

'He wants money he can spend outside his gilded cage. We caught wind of a second-hand car smuggling scheme he started, selling clapped-out junkers to the Russians.

There's been a drug deal or two, and hints here and there that he doesn't give a hang about much other than himself.'

'What sort of East German secrets are you looking for? Isn't it all a bit passé?' she asked.

This was 1986 and no one, particularly Uncle Richard, imagined the Berlin Wall collapsing overnight in '89. His chuckle turned worldly. 'East Germany is the most important Warsaw Pact nation, by far. One does not advance in the Russian army without major postings to group command in East Germany. The Stasi works hand in glove with the Red Army. Your friend has been selected for a post liaising with their Soviet masters. And we would like very much to learn the odd bit about Red Army intentions . . . In order to do that, to keep your friend happy and productive and as loyal as money can make him, we need one of our own to take care of him, minister to his needs while directing him towards the information we want. This person, this agent, if you will, or spymaster, will be doing her country a great service while advancing rapidly in a boundless career . . .'

The funny thing was, she was flattered. Uncle Richard laid it out and she listened almost with delight. It sounded exciting; she would get to see plenty of Manfred. She'd be serving her country as her family always had. And it couldn't have come along at a better time because the racing wasn't going all that well, though this last she did not admit openly to herself. The fact was, however, she was losing her drive. She was better, more skilled and shrewd than she had ever been, but a little voice had been asking regularly, so what? What was so great about sailing fast around a bunch of buoys? Not a winner's question.

'But why should Manfred be given such important duty as liaising with the Red Army for his first job?'

'First job?' Uncle Richard looked incredulous. 'First job? My dear, he's been Stasi since he was a cadet . . . He never told you?' Uncle Richard was suddenly all solicitous innocence.

'No, he did not.'

'Not to worry — first lesson learned without blood on the walls. You won't be fooled again. Will you?'

Alison took the cigarette Uncle Richard offered, Senior Service of course, and accepted a light. 'What about his brother?'

'Hans?' Uncle Richard's smile vanished and his mouth set hard. 'Steer clear of Hans. Rather a lethal fellow, Hans.'

'You're not serious. Hans is just a teacher.'

'Hans teaches Libyans, Palestinians, Syrians and Irishmen how to be terrorists.'

'Hans? Little Hans?'

'A dreary little academic?' Uncle Richard asked wryly.

'Not that dreary, but he's no spy or policeman. I simply can't see Hans selling secrets. Or even knowing any.'

'Hans knows plenty, but he'll sell nothing. Hans is a believer — a dedicated believer in Marxist Germany, unlike your friend. He'd cut his heart out for the cause. Or yours. Steer clear of Hans, dear. Put your "trust" in Manfred.'

She would always remember Uncle Richard at that moment, happily lunching in a panelled dining room at the Reform Club, doing well what he was so good at, without an inkling that the forty-year Cold War would end as suddenly as it had, or that he would have to find a new place in the new order. As for her, when the Wall collapsed and Manfred disappeared, she had found herself twenty-six years old, on the beach. And while not a fugitive like poor Manfred, she was just as unemployable.

Her quiet branch of the Foreign Office wasn't exactly declaring people redundant. They didn't have to. Frustration and impotence scythed them down as agents and spymasters quickly ran short of operations worth risking life or reputation for. In the summer of 1990 she was wondering what to do, when a yard manager at Cowes asked her to deliver a ketch to Spain.

'Good idea,' said a subdued Uncle Richard. 'Keep in touch.'

In Spain she met an American doctor who wanted his Swan 41 moved to Antigua for the winter. She had kicked around the Caribbean for a couple of years, then sailed some big boats with crew to Wilmington, Delaware, then delivered a grand old wooden Bermuda yawl to Newport, nearly drowning in the process when its seams opened up in Buzzard's Bay. An elderly Hyannis couple who wanted to 'cross the pond' before they were too old, hired Alison to come along in case they had cut it too close. She had flown home from Ireland and had just started drinking more than she meant to when Manfred, who had vanished like a coin in the ocean, suddenly surfaced in London with a suite at the Park Lane, an excellent forged passport and a plan to change their lives.

Or as Manfred, who could really turn a pontifical phrase, particularly when Hans inspired him, put it: 'A plot to take our place in the new order.'

He usually chose the wrong English word to make a point, but in this case a plot was exactly what he had in mind. A plot to smuggle valuable paintings, he said — Impressionists the Nazis had stolen from the French and the Communists had stolen from the Nazis. Alison had seen some of them in Hans's Berlin flat. And she had been forced to admit he had worked it out rather well; there was little she could add but sail the boat. Still, she had stalled Manfred with several moral questions: who owned the paintings? Manfred and Hans, who had inherited them from their father, and hidden them from a righteously vengeful East German people in 1989? Their father, recently dead, who had inherited them from his father? Grandfather, who had taken them at gunpoint from Nazis caught between victorious British, American, and Russian armies? The Nazi occupation officers who had stolen them from the French forty-five years ago? Or the French men and women who had displayed them in their Paris drawing rooms and country châteaux?

Alison had argued that it looked fairly good for the French owners. Manfred turned almost violent on the subject. The Picassos, Pissarros, Cézannes and Manets had been Echtheit property for forty-five years.

'During which years the Echtheits were citizens of a Socialist state that banned private property,' she had reminded him.

'We held the paintings in trust for the state. Now that the state is collapsed, the paintings are ours.'

'Oh, Manfred, that's totally self-serving.'

'What would the French do with them, stick them in some museum? Alison, they're our ticket to a new life.'

'A ticket we have not paid for.'

'Easy for you to say. Hans and I paid with everything we owned.'

'No, no, no. You didn't pay. People took back what was theirs.'

'People revolted.'

'What did you expect them to do when the Red Army left?'

'They did what they wanted and now I am doing what I want. And I am inviting you to come do it with me.'

By this point in the conversation he was whispering in her ear, with one hand firmly between her thighs and the other cupping her bottom. They had been lovers for ten years and their appetite for each other was still growing. He shouldn't have been a good lover, self-absorbed as he was, but he was in fact wonderful, the only man Alison Knight had ever known who was a better person in bed than out. Others brought their disappointments with them like pioneers looking for a new life on the frontier. Maybe Manfred had no disappointments, but for whatever reason, all that was rotten about him remained in the bastard's realm outside the blanket. He played, he teased, he growled and yelled and laughed. It was hard to hate a man who laughed in bed, harder yet to fear him.

Even now, shivering in the cockpit, sea-weary and exhausted, she conjured him in fantasy. She was alone in her bunk. Hans had fallen overboard. Manfred appeared in the cabin, shucking off his jumper and stepping out of his blue jeans. The blankets flew. His eyes raked her. Soon he was lowering his powerful body on to hers, pinning her arms, sliding between her legs, slowly tasting her mouth . . .

His big hands exploring – that night in London – Manfred had reminded her that art moves west. Wealthy Japanese and Taiwanese collectors would be the logical beneficiaries, while she and he took up residence in free-wheeling Hong Kong.

Alison raised a second moral argument about scamming off to Hong Kong: did cold war loyalties end with peace? Manfred demolished it easily: a few short years ago she had taken her life in her hands crossing into East Germany to debrief and pay him. They could both have been tortured and shot for what they were doing, he reminded her, she as a foreign spy, he for treason. Today their nations debated the merits of Common Market butter subsidies.

But that led Alison to a third and deeper dilemma: Manfred's nation, while displaying no interest or knowledge that he had spied for the British, was determined to try him for crimes against his fellow citizens. What exactly had her spy and lover done to make him one of a dozen or so out of forty thousand former officers they wanted to imprison? Who had been imprisoned unfairly because of him, or by him? Who had been tortured, who had been murdered?

Manfred only smiled, 'You know me, dear,' and she said she did. But what about Hans?

The German State Prosecutor *was* seeking Hans, Manfred admitted, but his indictment was as unfair as Manfred's. The brothers had caught an unfair share of blame for others' depredations. Their father was dead, their grandfather dying in an old folks' home, which left the sons as the only target in the Echtheit clan to satisfy the prosecutors.

'*You* know *I* couldn't do such terrible things, and I know Hans couldn't, but do they? They're out for blood. They want to make examples of us.'

In that moment, in Manfred's arms, Alison had known with blinding clarity that she had been less a spymaster or spy controller than a simple courier – a warm body to keep Manfred happy, pay him off, and carry his secrets home to Uncle Richard – for she knew she hadn't a clue whether he was telling the truth or pulling the wool over her eyes with one hand while he caressed her with the other. One thing was sure, she wanted to believe him.

'Does Hans know about us?'

'Only that I'm a slave to your breasts and thighs, and nuts for your lovely mouth. He wouldn't understand the other thing.'

On the contrary, Alison feared, Hans would understand his brother's spying only too well. Over the years she had got to know Hans. He was ferociously intelligent. She suspected he knew. The question was, would he forget the past, or at least forgive?

'Where is Hans?'

'Hiding in Germany.'

'With the paintings?'

'Of course. We hid them together. We've tapped some old colleagues to help move them to a seaport, blackmailed others who've got jobs with the new government. The whole point of the plan is to ship the entire freight container with the paintings inside. Nobody inspects containers. How do you think they ship cocaine and heroin?'

'Is that what's really in your container?' Alison asked bluntly.

Manfred returned a superior smirk. 'Where would I get heroin and cocaine in East Germany?'

'You could get anything you wanted in East Germany. You know damned well the Stasi moved drugs.'

'Drugs, bombs, terrorists,' Manfred admitted. 'But as you know, I was not involved in those operations. I was liaison to the Russian army, which had its own drug problem in Afghanistan.'

'Was Hans in those operations?'

157

'Absolutely not. Hans was a glorified baby sitter, not nearly as important as me. He's just a teacher — a cog in a rusty machine. Since the "Fall" I've really had to take care of him.'

'I'm asking you straight out: are there drugs in your freight container?'

'Only aspirin.'

Alison stared, as if she could see the lie in his eyes if there was one. 'Do you swear you're only smuggling paintings? Nothing else? Only paintings?'

Manfred laughed at her. 'Do you see me risking a drug deal in Asia?'

'No,' she admitted. 'You're not a fool.'

'Thank you for that vote of confidence.' He squeezed her thigh, hard. It hurt. 'Do I have to watch my back?'

'What do you mean? Let go of me.'

His hand clamped tighter. 'What I mean is, are you going to turn me in?'

'No, I am not going to turn you in. Now let go of my leg.'

He hurt her a moment longer, then bowed his head and kissed the burning red marks, one by one. 'I came to you because I love you. I don't want to start my new life alone. Nor with anyone else. So I ask you, please, come with me.'

Cradling his head, running her fingers through his golden hair, pressing against his lips, she finally whispered, 'What do you want me to do?'

A month later, she was back in the Caribbean, sailing the newly purchased *Twice a Knight* from island to island, altering its appearance at each stop. A retired MI5 forger sold her documents for the boat and a passport. She sailed out of the past and into Bermuda as a single-handed circumnavigator from South Africa — a fair-haired girl on a funny little boat who had chosen the oceans of the world over a perilous homeland. She had anchored in St George's only long enough to take on food and water and pick up Hans, who had flown in as a tourist with a Norwegian passport — trusting, friendly Hans, who had immediately thrown her hideously expensive satellite telephone into the harbour.

Poor Manfred. Two days short of their rendezvous his luck had deserted him. Right now they should be sailing together, with this wind at their backs, south into warmer and gentler seas. Alison shrugged the thought away. So they would wait a few more days. She had the boat in hand, no major breakdowns, no injuries. The barometer was falling, but that was to be assumed out here this time of year when the low pressure Atlantic depression dominated the weather. And there was certainly nothing to be gained by complaining about it. A cup of tea would go nicely now, and maybe some melted cheese on bread. Stoke the furnace, that was the main thing. Keep going. And that meant nurture the body as well as the boat . . . She set the autopilot, and when she was reasonably certain it would hold the course for fifteen minutes, she darted below and lit the stove.

Hans watched her through slitted eyes. 'What's happening?'

'I was just going to toast some bread and cheese. Like some?'

He nodded. She made enough for both of them and passed him his. He took her arm.

'Manfred won't like it, Hans.'

'Manfred won't know.'

She waited for *Twice a Knight*'s next lurch to throw him off balance and pulled away. 'I'm a one-man woman,' she said lightly. 'Always have been.'

'People change.' He eyed her closely. He had been seasick the first week. Now these little grabs were coming more often, and he watched her all the time. But he didn't fool her. Hans didn't give a damn about sex. He was testing her, his advances an act, a bit of theatre to test her loyalty to Manfred. She half-suspected that if he could sail the boat himself he would slit her throat while she slept.

'I haven't changed.' She backed into the galley and finished eating standing braced against the sink. Whenever

159

the boat straightened up she would get a brief glimpse out of the leeward port of the seas rampaging past.

'What are you smiling about?' Hans demanded.

Alison shook her head. 'Nothing.' She had recalled the advice of her Great-uncle Quentin, a polar explorer, on the subject of walking across Antarctica: 'Live it. As if it's all you do in your life.'

Back up on deck, warm and full and smiling at another memory of Uncle Quentin — who, suffering as he did from haemorrhoids and accustomed to travelling everywhere with a folding tub, claimed to be the only man on earth who had bathed at both the North and South Poles — she saw that the wind had stopped shifting west to north and was blowing hard and steady from the west. Initially, the change made *Twice a Knight*'s passage easier as the violent chop between the seas had begun to subside. But after several hours, the price of this newfound comfort became apparent each time the sloop crested a roller. The sea was rising, dramatically. The troughs between the rollers were lengthening, and the rollers themselves were getting taller, growing into enormous cliffs of water, high as the spreaders on her wooden mast.

It was going to be a long night. With a full gale blowing astern, *Twice a Knight* was a bitch to steer. She steered until dark, forcing more speed out of the boat, then put it briefly in the care of the autopilot and went below to warm up and eat something. Chewing a peanut butter sandwich, she sat at the nav station and turned on the HF scanner.

'What are you doing?'

'Listening.'

'To what?'

'I want to hear if they've found *Der Schmetterling*'s lifeboat.'

'Fuck 'em.'

'They're innocent victims.'

Hans snorted contempt. 'I've seen it happen a dozen times. An operation is going perfectly, till some ordinary citizen fucks it up. There are no innocent victims.'

Glorified baby sitter, thought Alison. She tore the latest broadcast off the weather fax, staring at the sheet, praying for a better report.

THIRTEEN

Two hundred miles ahead of *Bowery Queen*, a fast-moving depression rocketed down from Greenland and engulfed *Der Schmetterling* in towering seas. The dead ship rolled in great arcs, which were powered by the waves and extended by the wind, and began wheeling from beam end to beam end. Manfred — riding the storm out in his hammock, terrified each time the ship lay on its side — suddenly felt something enormous rumbling inside the ship.

He lay in the swaying hammock in the dark waiting to feel it again, praying he would not, knowing he would. Finally, with a groan of self-pity born of cold, hunger and seasickness, he struggled into his boots. He felt it again, a rumble, followed by a deep thunder that shook the container.

Cargo was shifting in the hold.

The wind blew the door out of his hands. Cold rain sluiced across the container tops, drenching him, as he battled the door shut and climbed down the web of restraining chains to the main deck. He hurried down the alley, avoiding glimpses of the rainswept boiling sea. The containers grumbled as they rocked and shifted against each other. What if one of them broke loose? Would they tumble overboard like dominoes, taking his with them, his treasure and all he owned? He had read an account of a rich American yachtsman designing a sloop to survive a collision with a submerged container — so such things happened. Might he not come up from the hold to find the deck swept clear as a soccer field, Tannenbergs and all? The grinding rumbled underfoot again.

At the house, he undogged the door, timing his entry

with the roll of the ship. In the second she hung on her side, he lifted the door against the heel, braced his back and slipped inside. It got away from him anyhow, and slammed, almost crushing his fingers. Breathing hard, he dogged it shut.

The upper house was dimly lit by portholes, but it was pitch black belowdecks. He trundled down a stair, following the point of his penlight, conserving his big halogen light for later. He clung to railings at every step and was still smashed against the bulkheads.

Descending to a catwalk that overlooked the upper deck of the main hold, he turned on his halogen flashlight. A fleet of Mercedes limousines were rocking side to side and nose to back with the movement of the ship. It looked as if the Black Forest engineers had packed them in egg cartons. Each car was so meticulously chained that though they bobbed on their springs, not one touched another.

The ship fell on its side again. Hollow thunder exploded below and the limousines shivered from the unseen impact.

Manfred retreated to the stairs and hurried down. The next deck contained machinery in crates the size of refrigerators. He shone the light at a loud noise. A smaller wooden crate was tumbling over the others as the ship rolled one way, and bouncing back when it rolled the other. Manfred climbed down to the crates and started across them, eyeing the fast-travelling crate, which suddenly smashed into a pillar, shedding splinters and split planks and its contents — a slew of metal parts that flew every which way and fell harmlessly through the cracks between the bigger crates. He backed away, disappointed. The prospect of action had focused his energy. He headed down to the next deck.

The sight that greeted him in the cavernous main hold shortened his breath. He stared in disbelief, overwhelmed. A huge, bright orange machine on caterpillar tracks — it looked as big as a Soviet tank — was sliding across the deck, bearing down on a twelve-foot pile of twisted metal and shredded tyres. The rubble Manfred recognized as the remains of several medium-sized farm tractors.

The orange machine crashed into the scrap heap, driving it into the side of the ship with a deafening *boom*. It nuzzled hard against the wreckage until the ship began to straighten up. There it stood. Then the ship rolled the other way.

Fascinated – like a jack-lighted deer – he watched the orange monster disconnect from the tractors and slide the other way, gaining speed as it skidded the breadth of the ship. He shone the light ahead of it to see what it would hit, and his blood ran cold.

There was no wreckage on that side of the hold to absorb the impact, merely the hull. And not just the hull, he realized with terror in his heart, but a massive set of barn doors cut in the side of the ship for loading. The machine gathered speed, the treads screeching over steel. Manfred wondered why it didn't turn over and tumble.

The ship heeled farther. The machine accelerated and smashed into the doors, which seemed to buckle like cardboard. Sea water geysered in. For a second, Manfred expected to see the machine blast right through the door and disappear as the sea poured in. The ship would sink long before he could find his way back on deck.

But *Der Schmetterling* swung back like a pendulum. The spraying stopped, as the ship lifted its side out of the water and the orange machine headed back across the hold to deal the tractors another blow.

It was, Manfred realized, some sort of bulldozer, squat and broad, with a massive blade in front, and a backhoe behind that arched like the tail of a scorpion. He could not imagine what it weighed. It dragged chains it had snapped like guitar strings. They rattled behind as it screeched across the deck.

He had to stop it, somehow, before it blasted a twenty-foot hole in the side of the ship. There was no waiting for Alison on this one. It would pulverize the weakened door at any moment. It crashed into the wrecked tractors and

164

started sliding back, gaining speed as *Der Schmetterling* shifted sides again.

Darting his beam about the hold, he spotted the steel tiedowns the beast had been chained to, bent off the deck like paper clips. A pair of mooring bollards flanked the barn door. He saw his chance. The ship was going way over; the bulldozer picked up speed as it crossed the centre line and bore down on the weakened door. Manfred dropped down the ladder to the deck and raced after it. The ship always held on its side a moment — a heart-stoppingly long moment — and he could use that moment to wrap the loose chains around the bollards.

Running full tilt in the path of his flashlight, his feet suddenly flew out from under him. That, he thought, as he lofted through the dark, smashed to the deck, and slid after the bulldozer, was why the monster didn't turn over: the deck was slick with hydraulic fluid from the wrecked tractors. The bulldozer boomed into the doors and an instant later Manfred crashed into its caterpillar treads.

He tucked in his arms and legs, to protect his head. Knees and elbows took the brunt of the collision. Pain shot up his legs and down his arms. Blood poured into his eye. Stunned, he realized he had torn his brow. Icy water blasted under the bulldozer, soaking him. The cold shocked him to awareness that the massive machine would not stay put.

The ship was rising again.

He tried to crawl along the machine, but he couldn't get purchase on the oily deck, which tilted so sharply that he was as much on the bulldozer as he was on the deck. He scrambled along it, still gripping his flashlight, banging knees and knuckles on cold steel. He imagined himself spreadeagled to the side of the machine as it raced across the hold to its rendezvous with the opposite side.

It was tilting back.

The machine shivered alive under him, like a wounded horse trying to stand. Manfred scrambled to the front of it and leaped off the blade as it began to slide away. He spied a trailing chain, grabbed it and dragged the massive links toward the mooring post. The bulldozer yanked it out of his hands. His boots slipped and he started sliding after it, saving himself with a desperate lurch at the mooring bollard, which he embraced with both arms as the bulldozer disappeared across the hold like an elevator plunging down a shaft.

It hit with an impact that shook the ship, and started back. Manfred watched it grow enormous in his vision, bearing down on him like a landslide. He cowered behind the mooring bitt, though he knew in his heart that if it hit the post it would snap and crush him.

Screeching, throwing sparks, it hit the barn doors five feet from where he crouched. He hurled himself on a chain and dragged it around the bollard, wrapping it twice before the bulldozer tried to travel again. It slid to the end of the chain, yawing sharply as it fetched up, hung there an instant, then snapped the chain and roared on.

The broken chain whizzed back at him and smashed a deep dent in the bulkhead. Aching in a dozen places, gripped by terror, Manfred racked his brain for another way. He probed the rest of the hold with his light. Fore and aft of the bulldozer's oil-smeared track were tractors, delivery trucks, and a row of steamrollers parked like baby elephants.

Manfred jumped into the nearest truck and fastened the seat belt. He could hear the bulldozer building to speed again, screeching metal to greased metal. He found the key in the starter. The cold engine balked, fired. He raced it, slammed it in gear, popped the clutch. The truck jerked forward and stalled, held in place, he had forgotten in his panic, by the same restraints that kept it from rolling around the hold. He jumped down with his light: the bumpers were cabled with quick-release come-alongs for fast off-loading.

He loosed the cables, started the truck, switched on the headlights, fastened the seat belt, and drove, slipping and sliding on the hydraulic fluid, straight at the bulldozer,

166

which was pinned against the opposite side. The speedometer read twenty-five when they hit. He had braced against the wheel and the belt helped. The whole front of the truck crumpled, wedged between the caterpillar tread and the blade.

Manfred leaped down and ran to another truck, released the holddown, and coaxed it to start. The bulldozer began to slide back at the barn door, pushing the smashed truck ahead of it. Manfred roared at the rear. Skidding on the hydraulic fluid, he caromed off the tread, nearly decapitating himself as he smashed under the scorpion-tail backhoe.

He ran for another truck, shaking shattered glass from his hair. The bulldozer ploughed into the barn doors again and Manfred saw daylight where the impact bent it open. Flooring the accelerator, he raced down the slippery slope into the bulldozer. The truck wedged under the tread and now as the ship heeled the other way and the bulldozer began its retreat from the door, it slid more slowly.

He loosened another, waited for the bulldozer to crash into the pile of tractors, and ran into it. The wreckage stayed put, even as the ship heeled back again. Manfred crashed a fifth truck into the mess, and a sixth for good measure. Then he re-parked more trucks into two bumper-to-bumper lines that extended from the wreckage on one side to the mooring posts by the door. He gathered the holddown cables and cabled them all.

Night had fallen when he finally ascended to the main deck. He stumbled up the alley by the dying light of his flashlight, cold, exhausted, and triumphant. It felt like coming back to the lodge from a long day of stag hunting, soaked to the skin and looking forward to schnapps, a hot tub, and a girl or two from the gymnastics team. No gymnasts tonight, no hot tub, but he would settle for dry clothes and the schnapps.

He thought back to earlier triumphs – before the Stasi hunting lodges – back to sailboat racing, cold and wet, after a day of trails, looking forward to the pub with Alison

Knight. Drinking and hoping tonight would be the night
. . . seventeen years old and so patient.

He climbed the chains that held the containers. The
rolling had eased a bit, and with luck would soon stop
dipping the damaged barn door underwater. On top of the
containers, he paused to shine his weak beam on the sea.
If the waves had subsided somewhat it was still frothy,
hurling scud on the wind.

He had drowned a CIA man looking for the missiles on
a night like this. The agent was on the bottom of the Baltic,
cocooned like a spider's dinner in ten metres of anchor
chain.

'Fuck you!' he said to the sea, and shoved through the
container door, timing it perfectly.

His radio alarm was shrilling.

He paused to light his stove, towel dry, and don a warm
polypropylene jumpsuit. Finally he returned the radio signal, checking, as he did, his position on the sat nav. The
drift was phenomenal. *Der Schmetterling* was being blown
by the wind at near four knots. Alison sounded close, but
he was disappointed that she was still two hundred and
fifty miles away. She wasn't sailing much faster in the
heavy seas than he was drifting.

'At this rate I'll be back in Germany,' he wanted
to say.

Alison, however, departed from the code drill, asking
twice how he was, and then whether he had been listening
to the radio.

'No.'

'Channel seventeen hundred.'

He signed off and tuned in on 1700. It was alive with
Dutch chatter. Like any German, he could understand
Dutch, but these were broadcasting either in code or simply
heavily guarded language, which probably meant they
were salvors. He shivered, and thought, Thank God for the
weather. What the hell would he do if some big Dutch
salvage tug took him under tow?

Be towed right to Rotterdam, he thought miserably.

168

That is what he would do. Maybe they were looking for the lifeboat. But if they found it, the game was lost.

Suddenly a crisp English voice broke in on the conversation. It was a Royal Navy search plane, with the best news Manfred had heard in a week.

'*Sorry*, Noorde Titan, *we're packing it in again. Can't see the bloody front of the airplane, and the wind's trying to pull the wings off. We'll be back when it quiets down. Good hunting.*'

Noorde Titan. He had seen the name on the helicopter's tail. Manfred sighed with relief and climbed into his hammock. The storm which nearly sank his ship had moved east, back where he had left the lifeboat. It had ended the air search. Maybe it would drive the *Noorde Titan* back to Holland as well. And maybe, just maybe, it would sink the lifeboat, if it hadn't sunk already. He couldn't feel pity for the crew. He had already written them off when he drove them overboard.

Warm in his hammock, he sucked on a leatherbound flask he used to carry hunting. The liquor burned deliciously. He was drifting off, half-drunk and surprisingly happy, when it occurred to him that instead of crashing the trucks into the bulldozer he should have tried to drive the machine itself . . . Next time . . .

Then he remembered that Alison had twice asked him how he was. He thought upon that, debating whether he should try to raise her on the radio.

He had learned, after many years of Alison Knight, that she was constitutionally incapable of complaining about a personal ailment. The only way it ever came out was she would ask him how *he* was, repeatedly, until finally, he might ask how she was, at which point she might or might not admit she had a problem.

She had told him she was pregnant in that manner, once, admitting it only when he pressed her, and assuring him in a rush of words that she would take care of the problem. As well she should. Now he wondered: was her boat damaged? No, that she would have told him. Thinking it over, he concluded she had injured herself and was in pain.

He hoped, as he fell asleep, that it wasn't serious enough to slow her down.

Five hundred miles east of the drifting freighter dawn broke unseen by the sailors huddled in *Der Schmetterling*'s lifeboat. Sick and exhausted by endless days and nights of tossing on the sea, all but one slept on. That one moved purposefully over the sprawled forms of his shipmates and opened a hatch in the fibreglass canopy. During the long cold night he had dreamed up another idea, his third, how to erect a makeshift radio antenna to send another Mayday.

'Shut it!' someone growled behind him as spray poured in like ice pellets. The crew had divided sharply between the lethargic majority who were content to sleep in their own vomit, and a restless minority, consisting of the captain, the wounded bosun, and himself, who were determined to survive.

He was Frank Grandzau, a scrappy twenty-year-old Berliner, branded a troublemaker by his former Democratic Republic schoolmasters. Liberation from the Soviet whores and their Stasi towel boys had come too late to salvage his education; by then he had drifted into the merchant marine.

His head still throbbed where the madman in the ski mask had creased it when he tried to shoot the bastard with the flare gun, but his vision was improving. When he peeked out of the hatch, the red fog that had floated before his eyes had dissipated somewhat.

He opened the hatch wider and raised his head.

The sight drilled fear to the pit of his stomach. He had never seen seas as big or as violent. They towered like the snow-capped Hindu Kush in the Afghan war movies the Russians had shown at school. One of the mountains skidded toward the lifeboat, collapsing on itself. He lost his courage and banged the hatch shut. The canopy resonated under exploding spray.

But when the boat rose on the next crest, he opened up again, ignoring the complaints in the dark, and pushed out of the hatch, straining to see whether what he had remembered in the night was real or illusion. The madman had shot away the antenna fitting, but not the antenna, which Grandzau had managed to retrieve. He had rigged the wire on an oar and the captain had broadcast several Maydays before the sea carried it away.

Last night he had remembered that the boat had trailed a gripe line – used to keep it from swinging when it launched – and that it might be made of steel wire instead of fibre.

There – it was a wire – not an antenna wire, but maybe it could work as such. All he had to do was get out of the hatch, inch along the canopy and work it loose from whatever it was tangled on. He waited until the little boat, which had fallen into a frothy pit, had risen on another wave. Then he started climbing out.

Someone grabbed his leg. He kicked free, and they closed the hatch behind him. The fresh air was exhilarating after days inside the fetid canopy. He braced his feet on the gunwales, held tight to the hand rails and worked his way aft. The wire was trailing from the pointed stern. He hauled it in and his heart rose. It was six metres long at least. All they had to do was lash together three oars and stand them up, and use the well-stocked repair locker to solder the wire to the old radio he had found. With six metres of wire, they could probably call Berlin. He dragged it to the hatch and knocked.

Nothing happened.

He knocked hard. 'Hey. I got the antenna wire. Let me in.'

He heard shouting inside. That stopped abruptly. A body slammed hard, shaking the hull. More shouting. Then silence. He feared that the concussion that shook the boat was the captain falling. That left only the wounded bosun, who was in no shape to defend himself, and him, Grandzau, out here alone. Stunned by the betrayal, he clung to the boat, his mind useless, until he began to realize that the sky was changing, blackening. The morning sun was gone. Clouds towered. They were in for another blow.

He got frightened, then angry. He was doing this for them, too, not just himself, but they would let him die out here, rather than risk opening the hatch for a second. They were not up to trying. So fuck him.

The hatches all dogged down from the inside, but they had forgotten the weak spot the stowaway's bullets had bored beside the antenna mount. They had stuffed rags into the hole to keep the water out. Dragging his wire, he inched aft, braced both hands on the grips, lifted his big foot and stamped down. His boot went right through. They yelled. Something thumped on the fibreglass but he had already extracted his foot, which he drove down again.

They were screaming murder at him. Fuck them.

He stamped and kicked. Holding the grips, he lifted both feet off the gunwale, jumped high, and came down with all his weight on the weak spot. He fell through in a blur of motion and found himself inside the boat, on the floor. A storm of kicks and punches rained down on his body. He saw the captain in a bloody heap, and the bosun sprawled unconscious. The rest were kicking him. He kicked back, struggling to gain his feet.

A huge boot flew at his face, smashed his nose, and rose to kick again. Suddenly it stopped, hung there. Everything stopped. All the men circled about him, stopped, and they cocked their heads. They looked funny, like a pack of dogs hearing a lion roar. *Helicopter*, he thought. A gigantic helicopter, thundering down to their rescue. The light above the hole turned grey and the boat moved lazily on to its side. The roar grew louder, the sky blacker.

A sailor thrust his head through the hole, then pulled it in, his face a death mask.

'The sea,' he whispered.

Ton upon ton of water crashed down. It jetted through

172

the hole and filled the boat with such force that the pressure popped the canopy off the hull. Grandzau opened his mouth, but the cold paralysed his chest and he and his shipmates vanished in silence.

Six of the *Noorde Titan*'s youngest seamen with the keenest vision stood two-hour watches from her highest points, augmenting her state-of-the-art radar and the wiser, if somewhat older, eyes of her officers. But it was Captain van Pelt himself who spied the wind blowing the faded orange canopy across the wavetops like a feather.

'Blind men,' he crowed. 'Two points starboard.'

'Two points, Captain,' the helmsman repeated, swinging the great ship effortlessly on to its new course downwind of the wreckage.

A strapping bosun led the recovery. Three hands neatly speared the blowing canopy with their boathooks and hauled it on to the towing deck.

Van Pelt hurried down to investigate. It looked like a break at last in a search that had already cost him his helicopter.

'*Der Schmetterling*'s canopy,' said the bosun, pointing out the stencilled name, and then voicing the obvious fact that no open boat could survive these seas. 'They're lost.'

The *Noorde Titan*'s Indonesian Catholic seamen crossed themselves and looked towards heaven, while their taller, blockier Dutch Calvinist shipmates glowered at the cold Atlantic, which had confirmed, again, their grimmest expectations. First their pilots, now the German sailors. Who was next in God's mind?

Captain van Pelt removed a glove and stroked the wet fibreglass. It was all the proof he needed to show that he had done his duty to *Der Schmetterling*'s sailors and obeyed the law of the sea. Now their ship was his.

'Stow this.'

He could barely contain his glee. If it was unseemly to rate a salvage fee over the lives of the sailors lost, he forgave himself because the prize was the fate of his own ship

173

more than the actual money. The accountants had come within one season laying up the most powerful tug in the world. Now, with this piece of luck, *Noorde Titan* would be allowed to earn her keep and again stand on Atlantic station in the winter months. Back on the bridge, he issued new orders to the helmsman, settled into his comfortable leather armchair in the radio room, and raised the Noorde office in Rotterdam.

His enemies behind their desks fought back, so desperately that they dropped the code and whined and protested in clear.

'We've no firm proof the ship is afloat. Besides, there's already an American tug in the area.'

Van Pelt laughed. 'Have you ever *seen* a New York harbour tug?'

'Well, no,' came the prissy reply, *'but I know what fuel costs and —'*

'Have you ever seen the *Bowery*, for that matter?' A joke lost on the desk sailors.

FOURTEEN

'Kind of like driving around Staten Island looking for a restaurant that might be in Queens,' said Kevin.

The slow-moving *Bowery Queen* had radar-swept five thousand square miles of ocean in the first eighteen hours of her search. But instead of driving two hundred miles east along a radar path twenty-five miles wide — effective radar range being twelve miles or so to either side — they had committed to a ladder pattern that simultaneously broadened and shortened their search to a path a hundred miles wide, but only fifty long.

Even those numbers were optimistic, Mary knew, because their radar range plummeted in the sea troughs, and the five thousand square miles to which she had irrevocably committed was minuscule compared to the million square miles of Atlantic hiding the abandoned ship.

Worse was a radio report that lifeboat wreckage had been discovered and the search for *Der Schmetterling*'s crew called off. Fifteen men dead. And now the salvage tug *Noorde Titan* was free to search for the freighter. Mary was disconsolate. The big Dutch ship was nearly twice as fast, while her greater height and better electronics gave her a much wider radar range. 'Probably patched into satellite trackers, too,' J.D. had observed unhappily.

'Sky's clearing, at least,' said Mary.

'Making room for the next storm to catch up. The wind's backing north again.'

'How soon?'

'Day, day and a half. You see how fast the weather moves out here.'

Mary nodded. The fronts sped through like freight trains. The sea was lumpy this afternoon, cross-seas riled by gales that had swept the area during the night. But despite Kevin's gloomy forecast, the ceiling was lifting, the horizons widening. Patches of blue sky began elbowing the clouds aside, the first blue the *Queen* had sailed under since Nova Scotia — since New York, Mary corrected, a week and a day ago that seemed a year. Low in the south, the sun burst through, glinting on the water, which changed colour under the crisp new sky. The broad, flat slick of wake flung from the depths by the *Bowery Queen*'s big propellers emerged a tropical turquoise.

Boags went out with a squeegee and wiped the salt from the speckled windows. The sun felt almost warm on Mary's cheek, the fresh light magnificent after days of gloom. She ran below a second to wash her face, comb her hair and change into her cleanest sweater, and raced back up the stairs. The sea had turned deep blue in her absence, and had spread to the limits of her vision. There it stopped, abruptly, at the circling edge of the sky.

Boags was fine-focusing the binoculars.

Kevin's face was taut, the fine planes chiselled with excitement. He nodded at the radar. A square green light bloomed ahead of the starboard bow. There was no fading as there had been with the iceberg, no fuzzy edges, just a sharp green light that looked as though it had been stamped on the screen at the factory.

Mary flung open the aft door and scrambled up the ladder to the monkey island. A tiny dot perched on the hard blue rim of the horizon. She could not tell whether it was stopped or moving. But it was a ship.

The wind scythed through her, bitter and stinking of diesel smoke, and the engine noise was thunderous, but she stood her ground, shielding her eyes. The *Bowery Queen* cut the distance and the ship grew. It looked empty, riding high, or stacked high with containers. Or maybe the low angle of the sun, which painted it yellowish grey, made the ship seem taller than it was.

Unable to tell whether it was moving, she descended to the wheelhouse to see what the radar knew.

Kevin was staring at the screen. 'I don't think he's moving.'

'I think no smoke,' said Boags.

'*Noorde Titan*?'

'Too big. Besides, he's still to hell and gone east of here, unless the Dutch put wings on her . . . I don't see smoke, Boags. Let Mary look.'

Boags surrendered the glasses. Mary focused, scarcely daring to breathe. The ship was light-coloured. *Der Schmetterling* was supposed to be light grey. 'Could be, could . . . be . . .'

'*Ship ahoy, ship ahoy*,' rattled the VHF. '*This is* Galveston Girl *on channel sixteen.*'

'Son of a bitch!'

Kevin seized the mike. 'Yeah, *Galveston Girl*; tug *Bowery Queen*. We've got you. We're proceeding east at twelve knots. What's your course, Cap?'

'*Hello* Bowery Queen. *Hello* Bowery Queen. *Yeah, we're sitting here changing out an oil pump. Be moving in a minute, south-west, heading Virgin Rocks to Cape Hatteras. Gonna miss you by a country mile. Where you going,* Bowery Queen?'

'We're looking for *Der Schmetterling*, twenty-thousand-ton German container ship.'

'*Thought she sank,* Bowery Queen.'

'I didn't hear that, *Galveston Girl*.'

Mary grabbed Kevin's arm. 'Oh, no.'

'*Well, I didn't either, but her crew's drowned – did you say tug?*'

Kevin winked gloomily at Mary. 'Should I offer him a tow? . . . Yeah, we're a tug.'

'*Where you from?*'

'New York.'

'*New York? What the fuck are you doing out here?*'

'Hoping,' said Kevin, with another gloomy wink at Mary. 'Take care, *Galveston Girl*. Out.' He hung up, asking Boags to watch the autopilot, and went below.

Mary entered the meeting in the log, rubbed her eyes, and went back to looking out of the windows. By late afternoon, with the light leaking from the sky and the radar spinning empty circles, she wondered how much longer she could convince herself they would find the ship.

When the sun had faded to a pale yellow ball in the extreme south-west, Mary put on her parka and climbed up to the monkey island for one last look. She had never doubted they would find the abandoned ship. But now, having committed to a tiny patch of ocean, she knew she was going to have to get used to the idea of heading home light. What a way to lose it all, she thought, dragging broke and with no prospects into New York Harbour where Fulton men had flourished long ago.

She turned her back on the sun and stared ahead.

A single cloud had formed up in the east, quite abruptly, like a balloon tethered to the horizon. It was fat and dark and she wondered what sort of weather it meant, though the weather had been coming from behind them all along. The cloud floated up to the zenith, flattening and growing longer.

She scanned the horizon again, hoping, praying, and when she looked up again, in defeat, she saw the cloud had taken on a shape like a giant ship. Yeah, right, she thought. Why not hallucinate? It was so real she could almost touch it, a big, blocky cloud ship with a pointed bow and rounded stern and a deck cargo mounded up around a house at the back. Even a smokestack over the house. The only thing missing from the image of a ship in the sky was smoke pouring from the stack. Instead, it hung as dead and still as the abandoned *Der Schmetterling* must be, floating somewhere out there.

'Oh, my God.'

She raced down the ladder, flung open the heavy wheelhouse door, stumbled over the high sill, and dived for the book rack above the chart table where they kept the *Sailing Directions for the North Atlantic*.

'Do you see that cloud?' she yelled at Boags.

178

'I see it, Mary.'

'Head for it.'

She tore open the *Sailing Directions*, found the entry opposite the ice article Kevin had so diligently underlined.

'It's a mirage. The ship is under it.'

Kevin came up, shaking his head.

'Look at it,' Mary insisted. 'Does it look like a ship?'

'Sort of.'

'Read the article.'

'I read it.'

'So?'

'Boags,' he said, shaking his head some more, 'head for the cloud. What do we got to lose?'

J.D. clumped up after him, and squinted at it.

'What do you think?' Kevin asked.

'Well, if we can get a wire aboard, we can tow her to Disneyland.'

In an hour they got no closer. Night was blacking the sea and the sky. The cloud never lost its hard edges, but it began to simply disappear in the dark.

'We're bearing eighty degrees,' said Mary, as it faded away. 'Just keep going at eighty.'

'How long?'

'The book doesn't say how far. I guess we just keep going.'

They steamed into the night.

Leo's watch ended at eight. Mary stood until midnight, but would not leave the wheelhouse. Kevin took over after some sleep. Mary tried to radio her father, but could raise neither him nor any AT&T High Seas stations.

Doubts were crowding in from the dark and she would have given anything for a dose of Mike Fulton's optimism. Kevin apparently felt the same way. She awakened stiff from a nap in the port steering stool to hear him hailing the High Seas operator, with the same lack of success. It was nearly 7 AM, still dark as night, the radar empty.

'Lousy atmospherics,' he muttered, shutting down the transmitter. 'Just wanted to hear his voice.'

'Me too . . . Kevin, I'm sorry about some of the stuff I said the other night.'

'Sewing Roberto? Yeah, I'm sorry, too.'

'I felt I was doing this alone, the other night. The guys are with me, I suppose, but you . . .'

'I don't want to lose anybody else. My guys are worth more than my ten per cent of your five per cent of twenty million bucks.'

'You are so full of romantic bullshit, Kevin. That whole story about my father rescuing you – and you accusing me of not feeling anything for Jimmy. You're using your "sensitivity" like a club.'

'Why would I do that?'

'I think you're afraid of me.'

She turned away and her eye fell on the radar screen. Dark as stone. It was easy to look down at the deck and imagine the water under the hull, and miles below it the sea bottom waiting for their bones. She was afraid to stop talking. He had clammed up, so she changed the subject to shop talk. How, if they found the ship, they would bunker the tug, the food supply, and J.D.'s drinking – but it seemed more like another night for secrets.

'When we were kids, why'd you always treat me like I was ugly?'

'You're not ugly.'

'I know that – now – but I didn't when we were kids. You used to look right through me as if I were ugly. Or were you just fighting me for my father's attention? I told myself that was it.'

'I was not fighting you.'

Mary laughed. 'Hey, I paid an L.A. shrink a lot of hard-earned money to learn you had every right and need to compete for my father's attention. But I never could figure out why you treated me as if I were ugly.'

'You're not ugly,' he repeated.

'Then why'd you turn off? Why didn't you ask me out? Why didn't you even look at me? Why didn't you make a pass or say something stupid? You just ignored me.'

'Your favourite Uncle Ed took me out behind the engine shed. Said he would break my head if I laid a hand on you.'

'He was worried about me. I was fifteen years old. My mother was dead. My father was a heartbroken wreck. And you were . . .'

'A bum.'

'I was going to say a very sexy-looking boy.'

'Thanks for the compliment, if it was one, but all I wanted was a place to stay. But your family acted like I was there to hit on you.'

Mary was silent. Kevin listened to the soft whine of the turbochargers, remembering her hulking cousins, who despite their size always braced him in threes, a little awed by a kid their age who didn't sleep home nights.

'Hey, Kevin?'

'What?'

'You mean you didn't want to hit on me?'

In the dark he couldn't see if she was smiling and didn't care. 'I just wanted a place,' he said bleakly.

'Lighten up. You're romanticizing again. And tell me the truth. We were kids on the boat and then in the house nearly three years before I split. I don't believe that anybody scared you so much you wouldn't look at me in three years. Unless you thought I was ugly.'

'Maybe I thought Mike would have been mad.'

'So?'

'I owed him.'

'You're still lying . . . What would you have done if I just grabbed you?'

'Grabbed back, I guess.'

Mary shook her head. 'You would have run like a jack rabbit. God, you must be a mess in bed. I guess I'm lucky we almost sank the other night.'

'If you're looking for testimonials.'

'Not from the bimbos I've seen you with. Jesus, Kevin. You got to trust yourself a little more.'

'How much did you pay that shrink?'

181

'There I was, fifteen, sixteen, seventeen, flushed with emotion and sex and — God help me, love — and you're lunking around like my father's pet dog. Boy did you blow it.'

Kevin laughed. 'Sounds like I did, when you put it that way.'

'Or were you just afraid of getting tied down by me — God, that's it, isn't it? That's what you meant about owing my father — you couldn't just drop me like your other girls.'

'Wait a minute.'

'You just wanted to be free to run around, and here I am dreaming up all these theories . . .' She realized, then, with a shock, how much she too had longed for a romantic explanation, one that would also promise some hope of something from him. 'I feel like a total jerk,' she said, deeply embarrassed. 'I'm sorry I said any of this. I really am . . . You know something? I've been thinking about what you said about what's driving me? It's what's driving any woman.'

'What's driving any woman? I'd love to know.'

'I'll give you the secret to all women, Kev. You can use it any way your conscience lets you, if you have one.'

'What's driving you, Mary?'

'I just want to make up for all the stupid times I gave in.'

'That's it?'

'We surrender. Early and often. Until, when we get older and have nothing left to surrender, we regret what we've lost. But by then, the guys around us — guys we love — are used to it and if we try to save our lives, they think we're wrecking theirs. And the sad thing is, all we have to do to make them happy is give in again.'

'That's it?' Kevin scratched his head. He had a feeling he was missing a great lesson in Mary Fulton's confession. 'You say "gave in". But if that's so, why'd you walk out on your old man?'

'I didn't walk out on him.'

'The hell you didn't. You ran away.'

'For God's sake, Kevin, I had a right to my own life. I was eighteen.'

She had 'run away' from an industrial outback of oil and mud, sinking piers, rusted cranes, dying trees and burnt-out bars – too young to admire the unique rough and personal style of an old-fashioned family business, and too eager to live her own life to devote herself to prolonging the end of an era.

'Seventeen.'

'I'd already given up my chance to go to college. I was slaving away in the office, and he was not pulling his weight. It was all slipping away. It was too damned depressing. Just everything slipping away. The tugs getting old, the business changing, our contacts dying. I wanted a fresh start.'

'So was that when you stopped giving in?'

Mary sighed. 'It turned out not to be a magic formula. I gave in on my new job out in California. I gave in with guys who wanted an equal partner, as long as she didn't want her own life. I helped one guy with the marina, and another start a sail loft. I was always in the back room. Now I'm home again, in the back room, while my father puts his feet on his desk and lets it slip away – *Jesus*.'

There was a light on the radar screen. At the extreme top. Twenty miles, dead on eighty degrees. Twenty miles. Less than two hours. For a second she thought she would cry.

Kevin hit some buttons: 'He's moving south-east at four knots.'

She stood in front of the radar, eyes glued to the screen. J.D., Leo, Boags and Roberto were grouped behind her, dead silent, as if a spoken word would chase the image away. Kevin gripped the starboard steering stick, eyes intent on the dark beyond the glass.

Dawn materialized as a pencil line of grey light that glimmered between sky and sea. It spread in a semicircle, ahead

183

and either side of the boat, a greyish dome upon the black water. Then the water absorbed greyish hues, too, streaked white here and there as seas curled alongside or the tug attained a crest.

Kevin raised the glasses. Boags moved behind him, watching over his shoulder. Mary looked from the radar to the softening morning and back to the lighted screen.

'That ship is definitely not steaming.'

No one answered her. The men seemed to subscribe to a collective fear that even one ill-chosen word could derail the train of events that had led them to the ship at last. She stared through the window, blinking when her eyes misted over.

'May I have the binoculars, Kevin?'

'I don't see it.'

'I do.'

Her eye had fixed on a dot between the air and the water. In the glasses it was longer than it was tall, possibly a silver rectangle, broadside to the wind. Mary held her breath to steady the glasses.

'No smoke,' she said, handing them back to Kevin.

'Beam to the wind,' he announced. 'Just drifting. I don't believe it. I think we found her.'

He passed the glasses to Leo, who confirmed Mary's observation, 'No smoke.'

Boags had a look, then helped Roberto, who passed the glasses quickly to J.D. The radar said it was seven miles away. It was drifting fast. The *Bowery Queen* took three-quarters of an hour to close within a mile. It was blowing east, its bow pointed south, its stern north — presenting the tug with its starboard side.

They could see hundreds of steel freight containers stacked on deck, an unbroken wall from the flared bow back to the square house, and more behind the house. It was enormous, blotting sky and horizon as the tug drew near, a slab-sided grey ghost plunging on the swell, rolling ponderously, totally out of control, yet strangely untouched.

The house had rows and rows of dark portholes. In some, curtains swayed behind the glass. Kevin had the eerie thought that they had discovered an ancient city whose citizens had fled for reasons no one would ever know.

'Don't see no sign of fire,' said J.D.

'Window busted on the bridge.'

'Look at her roll . . . Don't appear to be much of a list on her.'

The ship was showing its bottom plates each time she rolled to port. When a sea fell out from under the stern, Leo said, 'Rudder's still there, Captain Kev.'

'Good.' A functioning rudder might help in towing her.

The tip of a propeller broke the surface when the stern rose. 'She's still got her wheel,' J.D. sang out. Better and better. If J.D. could get her engine going, she could tow *them* home.

Kevin spotted a tangle of ropes and pulleys hanging down the hull into the water: the lifeboat falls with which the abandoning crew had lowered the boat. His men fell silent, imagining the long descent down the side of the ship, the smack of the lifeboat hitting the water, and pulling away with the thin-skinned hull flexing on the waves.

J.D. loosed a triumphant blast of the *Bowery Queen*'s airhorn. 'Found the 'sucker!' he whooped, plucking Boags off the deck in a one-armed bear hug and spattering a hairy wet kiss on Mary Fulton's cheek. 'We gonna have farms fulla piggies and chicken on Sunday — SOOOOOOOO-WEEE!'

Levelling his grenade launcher at the tugboat's wheelhouse, Manfred Echtheit could see the crew pressed to the dirty windows. He lay prone, tracking them through a scupper — one of the narrow drain slits in the bulwark surrounding the main deck.

It was an odd duck of a little vessel, broad and squat, with a long, low stern, a jaunty bow and a pair of business-like smokestacks — quite old judging by its rounded lines

— streaming rust, draped helter-skelter with truck tyres for fenders, and so small. It was really less a ship than a boat. *Der Schmetterling* stood over it like a giant. The freighter's main deck, fifty feet above the water line, was protected by bulwarks taller than a man, whereas the tug's sides were barely waist high, so that the seas splashed over them. The tug's wheelhouse was lower than *Der Schmetterling*'s main deck; the stacked containers towered over it.

No need to waste another Tannenberg. His grenade launcher would do the job. The wheelhouse first — take out the captain, the controls and, most important, the radio before they revealed his position. Stop her. Silence her. Then blast the watertight doors off her house and let the sea, curling over her low sides, do the rest.

PART TWO

FIFTEEN

'SOOOOOOOOOOOOOOOO-WEE!'

Boags banged the tug's bell. Kevin thundered the air-horn. The bandaged Roberto pounded out a shaky rhythm on the chart table that set dividers and pencils dancing in their cup. And Mary Fulton knew the joy of a pirate with a rich East Indiaman in her spyglass. The slabsided treasure ship was alone on the empty ocean, and it, and everything in it, was theirs.

Five hundred containers gleaming in the morning sun were theirs. Holds overflowing with Mercedes Benzes, tractors, and trucks were theirs. The ship's engine, generators, Scotch boiler, air compressors, electronic wonders, fuel oil, stores, ropes, lines, cables, chains, winches and blocks, all theirs.

Euphoria denied law and custom. Screw Lloyd's of London. Forget salvage arbitration. To hell with the German owners. *Der Schmetterling* – the rust-streaked, wallowing, beautiful butterfly – belonged to the *Bowery Queen*.

She hugged Leo. The chief mate returned a smile. He was studying the freighter's stern, which was plunging up and down like a demented elevator.

'Well, Cap,' she asked Kevin, 'how you planning to board her?'

Kevin removed his cigar from behind his ear, popped it in his mouth, and chewed reflectively. 'Catapult. Cluster the little guys on a seesaw and jump J.D. on the high end.'

'Those lines,' volunteered Boags. He pointed at the falls swinging from the arms of *Der Schmetterling*'s lifeboat-launching davits. Alternately slapping the hull and skimming the water as the container ship rolled from side to side, they danced about as if the ship was teasing a cat

189

with a tangle of twine. Every second or third roll, the cat won, snaring the ropes with a claw of wave.

'You want I climb them, Captain Kevin?'

Kevin traced the ascent with his eye. A seventy-foot climb to the davit arm, then crawl a dozen feet inboard on the steel arm and drop to the boat deck, which was tucked in the side of the house, one level above the main deck. Only problem was, he'd have to approach from windward. 'Wrong side, Boags. Seas'll slam us against her hull.'

'I could swim in a wetsuit.'

Kevin raised his glasses and chewed harder on his unlit cigar.

Boags started to volunteer again; Leo growled, and the young seaman fell silent. J.D. nudged him with a confidential whisper: 'Captain's problem is *not* how to put an agile eighteen-year-old able-bodied seaman aboard that ship, Boags. Captain's problem is how to *hoist* a thirty-eight-year-old, three-hundred-pound chief engineer aboard that ship . . . Hey, Kev? If the boy here could shinny up there and lower the Jacob's ladder, I think maybe I could climb it.'

'And if you fall off, I pick you out of the water and get suspended for violating the whaling limits.'

J.D. started down the stairs. 'You'll think of something. I'm going to say goodbye to my engines.'

'I'll think of something,' Kevin growled to himself. 'Only thing is, what? Look at that 'sucker roll.'

Steering stick held loosely in one hand, Kevin looked, Mary thought, like a pool player gauging the effect of his last shot. He steered a couple of hundred yards away, lined up with the derelict's bow, and stopped to calculate the drift. The *Bowery Queen*'s deeply wetted hull, low freeboard and narrow house presented little target to the wind, but the ship and containers flung up a five-hundred-foot face nearly a hundred feet high, and Kevin had to engage the tugboat's propellers to keep up.

'Your old man hit it on the nose; she's making four knots.'

Mary entered this information in the log, along with their position and the sea conditions. Then she got her camera and shot a roll of film to illustrate the violent motion of the ship. If only she had a videocamera.

Kevin moved closer to the plunging bow, which slashed the water like a broad axe. He slid down a window and stuck his head out in the cold and studied the ship's anchors, massive twin-fluke affairs tucked into hawsepipes fifty feet above the water line. With her tumble home sides and pyramidal house, the New York tug was designed to press alongside a moving ship. But in harbours the forces stemmed from fairly predictable forward impetus. Here in the ocean, if he got too close, the rolling ship could smash the *Queen*'s wheelhouse, knock the tug on its side, and drive her under.

The seas were roughest, as he had observed, on the windward side. In the ship's lee, a smoother triangular slick spread to a point six or seven hundred feet downwind of the hull. He moved the *Bowery Queen* into this calmer shadow of the ship. Definitely the better side to board from, despite the lifeboat falls dangling to windward. But heaving a grappling hook as high as *Der Schmetterling*'s main deck wasn't easy. The *Queen* had an old line-throwing gun somewhere. Of course it hadn't been used in years and might blow up in their hands.

'Too bad they didn't launch that boat,' Mary said, indicating *Der Schmetterling*'s other lifeboat still nestled in the portside boat deck. Its falls would be hanging on the proper side to board.

Kevin ran the *Queen* slowly around the ship, past the stern and out of the lee. The full force of the wind and waves hit them again.

'Look at that door!' There was a bulge midships in the hull where a huge loading door had been battered partly out of its track.

'Cargo shifting,' said Leo.

'Wonderful,' said Kevin. As they watched, the damaged area dipped below the waves. God knew how much water

191

poured in. They'd need pumps. Kevin shook his head. He didn't even know how to get J.D. aboard, much less a ton of pump. Ahead of the barn door was a smaller accommodation hatch. It was conveniently low to the waterline; he could back right up to it if it weren't on the dangerous windward side.

He turned the tug into the waves and inspected *Der Schmetterling*'s stern. Plunging and rising, it exposed the rudder, flapping loose, and two massive blades of the propeller. Kevin watched them slash the water for a sober minute.

He looked up at the ship, shaking his head. The sun was rising higher, the day racing along. The only good news was that the west wind had begun regaining control of the water, building longer, evenly-spaced rollers and flattening the lumpy cross-seas. *Der Schmetterling*'s rush downwind seemed a little less chaotic.

The radio speaker squawked.

They had set the long-range HF scanner skipping along the green lights of the channels. Its stops were few, weather broadcasts and the occasional ship-to-shore transmission. Now it stopped at 1841. Mary reached over, locked on and turned up the volume. The Dutch salvors were going at it in code — a terse exchange between the *Noorde Titan* and her Rotterdam office, over in ten seconds.

'Guess they haven't sunk yet,' said Mary, which was all they knew for sure. The *Noorde Titan* might be searching five hundred miles to the east, or could be steaming over the horizon, tracking *Der Schmetterling* on radar.

Kevin tossed his cigar out the window. 'Leo, you got a cigarette?'

Leo produced Marlboros and matches. 'Back in New York you said don't give you one, if you asked.'

'We're not in New York . . . Thanks.' He exhaled smoke and stared down the length of the ship, the falls on the windward side, the slick in the lee.

'Captain Kevin?'

'What, Boags?'

'You want I swim?'

'Yeah, sure. Why don't you swim to Holland and rent us a real salvage tug. And a full crew.' Tired and pale, his eye cocked against the smoke of his cigarette, Kevin suddenly looked fourteen, Mary thought. A baffled kid. The baffled kid her father had brought into their home — though not so cocky at the moment.

'Why not,' she ventured, 'back in on the leeward side and throw a grappling line?'

Kevin glanced through her like a pane of glass. 'We could use some coffee up here, Mary.'

The others looked away, silent, and she knew she had stepped across a line none of them wanted her to. Baffled or not, Kevin was their captain. Boags had volunteered to risk his body. But Mary had offered a challenge. She unhooked the thermos and started down the stairs.

'Okay,' Kevin said. 'We're going to move closer and see how the hulls react to each other. Boags, might as well put on a wetsuit; one way or another you're going to get wet . . . Wish to *hell* they'd launched the other boat.'

'Hey, Kevin,' Mary called from the stairs. 'You just gave me an idea.'

'Coffee!'

'It's ours. The whole ship is ours.'

'Until we get a wire aboard it's anybody's, especially the Flying Dutchmen.'

'It's ours,' she repeated. 'Why don't we lower *our* boat?'

'Launching the inflatable in this wind is not my idea of a good time.'

'Our *other* boat.'

'Would you get the —' he stopped, genuinely puzzled. 'What other boat?'

'The other lifeboat. The one on the leeward side they didn't launch.'

Kevin got it at last and, though he looked annoyed for not thinking of it himself, said, 'That's a slick idea, Mary. Not bad at all. Boags, we'll get you up there somehow and you'll lower the lifeboat for J.D . . . And Mary.'

'Me? You putting *me* aboard the ship?'

'I need Leo on the tug,' he said flatly. 'And Roberto's head's a mess. At least here we got heat and hot water for him — Okay, guys, we're going to pass close, see how they get along . . . Mary, I want that coffee.'

The Soviets made the best grenade launcher in the world. And Manfred Echtheit had won medals at the Red Army's All-Arms Army Camp where he had received his weapons training. But it was not an easy shot, down at the tug. The little boat was bobbing like a cork. If it happened to drop into a sea trough just as he fired, the grenade would sail right over its roof. A near-miss would send them scurrying out of range, where they would radio for a warship.

The hunter in him waited with an icy patience for the *Bowery Queen* to come closer. And while he waited, the sailor in him read the water ahead of the tug's high, blunt bow. Somewhere in the turmoil was forming a crest that would pick the tug up and hold it still for a fatal instant.

Just at the extreme edge of close range one did, but before he could fire *Der Schmetterling* rolled the wrong way and all he could see from his scupper was sky. When the ship finally rolled back, the tugboat had slid into a trough. But it was closer now, and as he watched it turned and started driving for the side of the ship. The falls, he realized. It was heading for the lifeboat lines that trailed down from the boat deck beside the house. They would board there.

Manfred raced down the narrow aisle beside the bulwark. Fifty feet from the house he threw himself flat again and peered through another scupper. Perfect. The little tug was angling in, so close he could practically lob a brick through the window the captain slid open to see better. He found the man's curly black hair in the sight and curled his finger to the trigger.

Suddenly, the tug veered, black smoke billowing from its stacks, engines thudding urgently. Manfred thought they had seen the weapon extending through the slit of the scupper. But it wasn't him. A massive sea was bearing

194

down on the tug, threatening to fling it against the ship. Gushing smoke, it wheeled smartly, stern skidding within yards of the ship, and careened to safety on a boiling wake.

The windows at the back of the wheelhouse presented an unmissable target. Manfred started to fire. Then he saw the tug's name and port in white letters on her stern:

BOWERY QUEEN
NEW YORK

He had assumed that the tug was European, the Dutch tug that had been searching for *Der Schmetterling*'s lifeboat. But New York . . . New York was west. West towards Alison. They would stop his terrible drift to the east. And when it came time to part company, its scruffy little crew would be much easier to deal with than twenty Dutch salvage men.

Mary had brewed fresh coffee and had been filling the thermos while the engines raced and the clutches whined. The boat surged along, rocking side to side. The galley port offered quick glimpses of sea or sky, and suddenly the rust-stained wall of the ship. When she felt the starboard engine come out of gear and slow to reverse, she braced herself. The *Queen* heeled much harder than she expected, tossing her and the thermos across the galley on to the table.

She mopped up, ran cold water on her burnt hand, and struggled up to the wheelhouse.

'You missed the fun. Ship just tried to eat our stern . . .'

The *Bowery Queen* approached the dead ship again, warily, like a terrier picking a fight with a mastiff. Leo and Boags were on the foredeck, Boags in a lifejacket and bright orange diver's wetsuit. The gap between the two hulls narrowed. Kevin drove in until *Der Schmetterling*'s lifeboat falls dangled down on the foredeck.

Boags and Leo grabbed for the ropes, trying to untangle

195

one Boags could climb. Suddenly a big sea shoved the tug like a great hand.

'Let go!' Kevin yelled, reversing his starboard engine and turning his rudders hard left. The *Queen* tried to pivot away. Her bow swung wide, but her stern hit the ship with a bang that shook the wheelhouse. Mary watched in disbelief as twenty feet of towing deck disappeared under the ship. Kevin slammed the port throttle full ahead. The bow rose, the deck slanted sharply, and the stern sank lower. For several eternal seconds the ship held her down. Then the starboard engine finally engaged and both propellers bit.

The back of the tugboat broke from the water, towing deck awash. The tug rolled heavily under the weight of the water she had shipped. Kevin leaned out the window. 'Boags and Leo – *where the hell's Boags?*'

Leo pointed.

An orange speck was ascending the side of the freighter like a patch of rust come to life. When the ship rolled away, Boags held off with his feet and walked up the steep incline. When it rolled back, he dangled over the water further and further, until the return roll carried him swiftly back. Fending off with his feet, he stopped his rush and resumed climbing, hand over hand, until the ship swung him outboard again.

'Looks,' J.D. observed, 'like some mean little kid's got him on a yo-yo.'

Higher and higher Boags rose, gaining speed as he ascended and the fetch in the ropes grew shorter. He climbed another fifteen feet in a rush, but instead of ascending to the davit arm he suddenly slithered through a scupper and disappeared. Moments later, he popped up behind the bulwark, with his arms flung high in victory.

Kevin thumbed on the walkie-talkie. 'Nice going, Boags. Okay. Why don't you get in the lifeboat and see if you can launch it?'

The tug circled the ship and waited in its lee while Boags made his way to *Der Schmetterling*'s other boat.

196

'*Hello Leo?*'

Kevin passed the handset to the chief mate. A rapid-fire exchange of Tagalog ensued. 'Sounds,' J.D. muttered to Mary, 'like a couple of Martians exchanging impressions of an elephant.'

Leo reported to Kevin. 'There's no power to the davits.'

''Fraid of that.'

'Boags says he can lower the boat . . .'

'And then we power it up with our winch?' Kevin shook his head. 'End up killing somebody. No way I can hold the tug in place so long . . .' He probably could, in fact, but lifting the lifeboat with the tug's winch would involve a maniacal cat's cradle of rigging; and any mistake that parted a hoisting line would be fatal to the people inching up the side . . . Better if Boags could scrounge up some cargo nets.

'J.D.? Think you can climb a cargo net?'

'More to hang on to than a Jacob's ladder.'

'How about you, Mary? You in as good shape as you look?'

'Better.' She was itching to get going. It had been years since she had worked on a tug and she had forgotten how long it took to get anything done.

Boags's search for cargo nets ate up a half hour. He spent another lashing them together, and draping the orange mesh down the side of the ship.

Mary put on her warmest clothes and helped Roberto pack food and thermoses of soup and coffee, freshly charged flashlights and walkie-talkie radios. Then she changed his dressing – noted that the saw-toothed stitches showed no infection – and made him promise to keep taking his penicillin and let Leo change the bandage regularly.

'When do my stitches come out?'

'I had them once. It was about a week.'

'But you won't be here.'

'I'll do it with Leo by radio. Okay?'

She returned to the wheelhouse to say goodbye to Kevin.

'Get your stuff down on the towing deck with Leo and J.D.'

'Already there.'

'And try not to get killed climbing the net. Your old man would be really pissed at me.'

'You got it, Cap.'

'J.D.'s boss over there, but he's going to have his hands full in the engine room. Boags'll clear her anchor chain. You help whoever needs help, after you make a fast survey to make sure she isn't going to sink on us. Check out that door.'

'The main thing is we have to get a wire aboard before the Dutchmen get here.'

'The main things *are*, nobody gets hurt and the ship don't sink.'

'You worry too much, Cap.'

'I only worry about things I can't control. That riding crew that drowned? Our two-thousand-foot tow wire could have been two thousand *miles* for all we could help them when the weather made up.'

'Later.' She started for the stairs.

'One other thing. Little Boagsie's got a crush on his lady boss.'

'Don't worry, we won't elope.'

'I'm serious. You're the only woman aboard and you treat him nice.'

'That's flattering. For a second there I thought the boy might find me attractive.'

'Don't let him kill himself trying to impress you.'

'Okay. I get it.'

'Mary?'

'Now what?'

'I'm not afraid of you.'

'Yes you are. You can't even say goodbye without cranking out orders.'

'It's like I raise you up on a pedestal. Like I make you into a Madonna — Not that Madonna. The real one. The original.'

'I think I'd be happier as the new one — Kevin, we have work to do.'

Kevin grabbed her shoulders and tried to kiss her. She turned her face.

'What is going on with you? First you banish me to the riding crew. Now you want to get all sentimental?'

Kevin backed off, grinning his black Irish grin. 'Probably just confusing love and lust.'

'I'm glad you're afraid,' said Mary. She plunged down the stairs, wondering if it meant she could have him and keep him too.

J.D. and Leo were waiting just inside the towing deck hatch, their eyes intent on the freighter which loomed like a cliff. Kevin began backing the tug toward it. The orange net slapped the ship's hull as *Der Schmetterling* rolled up, and dipped into the water when she careened back down.

Mary zipped up her windbreaker and shrugged into her knapsack of thermoses, sandwiches and flashlights. J.D. and Leo picked up tightly packed seabags. 'Okay, let's do it.'

The wind funnelled over the top of the ship and straight down on the backing tug. Inky whirlwinds of diesel smoke blasted the towing deck. Mary, J.D. and Leo ran to the stern, choking on the smoke, deafened by the engines, slipping in the icy seas that tumbled over the low sides.

Leo forged ahead. He climbed on to the stern bulwark and raised his arm to guide Kevin the last few feet.

'*Mary.*'

She scrambled on to the bulwark. The bulge of the tug's rubber stern fender held the net a scary four feet away. The tug rose on the swell. The net dipped in the water. Kevin smacked the stern against the hull and Mary jumped. She got one gloved hand and one rubber boot in the mesh. Her other boot skidded and she felt the knapsack pull her backwards into the gap of water that opened again between the net and the tug. She got a grip with her other hand, caught an awful glimpse of the ship leaning over her like a five-storey townhouse, found another foothold, and climbed up the rough mesh.

The net swung away from the hull as the ship rolled. She climbed as fast as she could find footholds. 'Hold on,' J.D. yelled below her. 'She's coming back.' As the ship rolled the other way, the net lurched toward it, gathering speed. Mary felt her stomach drop. The net rocketed into the ship. She held tight, turning her face, crumpling into a ball as it smashed her against the hull. When it swung away she climbed higher until her shoulders burned and her hands were raw through her gloves. 'Swinging back.' She made the mistake of looking down. The *Bowery Queen* lay forty feet below on a boiling sea.

'Here!' called Boags, leaning over the bulwark. He grabbed her knapsack and pulled Mary over the bulwark, catching her in his arms as they fell seven feet to the deck. Up instantly, Boags reached for J.D., who came over the top bellowing, '*Gangway!*'

Boags heaved a line to Leo, who caught it as the tug backed in again and bent it around one of the seabags. They hauled it up and lowered it again. The instant the last bag was aboard, J.D. took his tools and vanished into the house, heading for *Der Schmetterling*'s engine room.

'*Everybody okay?*' Kevin radioed. The tug stood a hundred yards off.

Boags had clipped his radio to his chest so he could hit the transmit switch with his chin. 'No problem, Captain Kevin.'

'*Okay. Boags, we got to clear a hawsepipe. Deep-six the starboard anchor. Mary, check out that door and the bilges. Then give Boags a hand getting rid of the anchor. Let's go. It's getting late.*'

The young seaman hurried forward through a canyon-like corridor between stacked containers. Mary opened a heavy watertight door in the house and stepped over a high sill into a foyer lit by round ports. It was cold in the still air, colder somehow than the wind whipping the deck.

She flipped a light switch. Nothing. The bulkheads were

neatly hung with hard hats, fire extinguishers, foul-weather jackets, hand tools, and walkie-talkies and flashlights in their chargers. She tried a light and, finding the beam strong, left her own in her knapsack and took it, along with a coil of lightweight heaving line which she draped over her shoulder like a naval attaché's anguillettes.

The foyer emptied on to an open stairway beside an elevator. She could see up five or six decks in the grey light. Down, the stairs disappeared into spooky darkness. Reluctantly, she headed below. Two decks down she found an elevator stuck between floors with the door jammed open.

She pressed the transmit button on her radio. 'J.D.?'

Static hissed. Around her metal clanged as objects rolled and doors banged. Two more decks down, her imagination started running wild with hands reaching out of the dark.

'J.D.?'

He didn't answer. She cupped her hands and yelled, 'J.D.?'

Metal creaked and groaned and clanked as hundreds of small collisions were set off by the rolling ship. She shivered, thrust the light ahead of her, and continued down. The beam struck a watertight door with a sign:

LADERAUM A

It opened on a long, low-ceilinged hold that smelled like a Beverly Hills parking garage. A field of cars reflected her light back at her. They rocked on their springs, nose to tail in long rows. Mary laughed. Mercedes Benzes as far as the eye could see. She thumbed the radio again and called J.D. No answer. Then the radio spoke back. It was Kevin's voice, thin through the metal walls of the ship. *'How you doing?'*

'I found a million Mercedes.'

'How's that buckled door?'

'I think I'm still above that deck.'

'Find it,' Kevin fired back. *'Before she sinks.'*

201

She backed out of the Mercedes hold, dogged shut the door and continued down the stairs. *Laderaum B* contained more Mercedes.

In trying to figure where she was, she pictured the ship like a high-rise building — bridge on the roof and engine room in the cellar — behind a suburban mall of cargo holds. The damaged loading door was in the suburbs, near the water line, several decks down and halfway to the bow.

She started down again, skipping *Laderaum C*.

Laderaum D looked like a dinosaurs' boneyard. It was a cavernous space, two decks high. The double-height ceiling accommodated heavy machinery — trucks, tractors and earth-movers. Her darting light played shadows on backhoes, buckets, blades and ploughs.

Daylight gleamed in the distance and water flowed.

Mary hurried towards it, down a narrow alley between the machines, which tugged and pulled at their chains. The water sound stopped abruptly. Emerging between two square delivery trucks on to an open space lit by daylight, she saw a tangle of wrecked trucks and tractors sprawled across the width of the hold. On one side, the side nearest her, an enormous bulldozer was pressed against the hull, against the door they had seen from outside. Daylight poured in both sides of the door and under the bottom, where the bulldozer had shoved it off its track. As she studied the destruction, the ship commenced its stately roll, dipping that side. Water poured through the twenty-foot rent.

She ran back to the stairs, and raced down them, in terror of what she would find on the bottom. Expecting water sloshing up the steps, she found only steel deck and an open door marked MOTOR RAUM.

'J.D.?' she yelled into the radio.

He waved his light. She stumbled over the doorsill into a gigantic space that stank of smoke, burnt rubber and scorched paint. Daylight leaked down through a grating eighty feet overhead. She saw pipes and uptakes soaring to the top of the ship. J.D.'s face loomed in the backglow

202

of his flashlight like a Hallowe'en pumpkin with eyeglasses and moustache. He had donned a yellow *Der Schmetterling* hard hat over his Volunteer Fire Department cap.

'Have you seen any water? It's pouring through that door.'

'I hear it sloshing down in the bilge. Go look for a sounding pipe — tube going down with a measuring rod?'

He turned back to what he had been doing and Mary went looking. She found no sounding pipe but she did discover a ladder, and descending it, found deep water slick with oil, and a measuring rod lashed to the ladder.

'Three metres,' she called.

'Tell Kevin.'

She radioed the tug, moving around the engine room until she found a spot where she could get a clear signal. Kevin groaned. *'Ten feet. Christ on a crutch. Tell J.D. we'll need pumps.'*

'I *know* that,' J.D. called over his shoulder. 'Only thing is, they had themselves a little fire in here.'

'How bad a fire?'

'He wants to know how bad was the fire?'

'About as bad as he'd expect from burning fuel oil. She popped a feed line. Only reason she didn't burn to hell is somebody shut it down.' J.D. shone his light on a valve wheel.

Mary relayed this. Kevin said, *'Mary, you better get busy plugging that leak in the door.'*

'I can't get to all of it. It's blocked by a huge mess of cargo.'

'Plug what you can. We'll finish up once we're underway. I heard the Flying Dutchmen on the radio again. We gotta move.'

A big motor ground over and started roaring.

'Mare, haul on that.' J.D. pointed his light at a red knife switch. It shot a fat spark. Mary jumped and the ship's engine room was suddenly bathed in dim yellow light. 'Emergency generator!' J.D. yelled in her ear. 'Unfortunately, the main generator runs off the main engine.'

They turned a slow circle, surveying the damage. Flames

had rampaged everywhere, melting wires and insulation, breaking glass and twisting steel pipes. Mary followed J.D. to the remains of a large instrument display – broken glass and blackened wiring that looked as though a bomb had hit it.

'Can you start the engine?'

'In a year or so.'

'Can't we bypass all this?'

J.D. led her round the eighty-foot-long, three-storey-high main engine to a bulkhead laced with scorched and twisted piping. 'This used to be the air compressor. Those tanks were the air reserve till the fire burnt their seals. I need compressed air to start the main engine, even if I could "bypass all this".'

'So we have to tow her.'

J.D. nodded. 'She's dead. I can route power for emergency steering, I think, for which Old Kev's gonna be mighty grateful when the tow takes it in mind to sheer.'

'But we need power on the bow, first, to haul the tow wire aboard.'

'Not right off,' J.D. shook his head. His breath puffed cloudy in the frigid air. 'Fire fried the cables.'

Mary's heart sank. Two men and a woman could not muscle the *Bowery Queen*'s two-and-a-half-inch steel towing wire from the tug to the ship. 'What should I tell Kevin?'

'We gotta use the tug's power.' J.D. fished his radio from an overall pocket and thumbed it on. 'Kev, you hear me?'

'*Barely. What's happening?*'

'Captain, what we have here is an opportunity to exercise your famous boat-handling skills.'

SIXTEEN

The day was racing by. Alone in the *Queen*'s wheelhouse, holding the tug in the downwind lee of the ship, Kevin observed that the sea had already taken on a silvery hue as the sun glinted through the clouds at a lowering angle, and weighed his few options. His priorities, as he had kept reminding Mary, were the safety of his crew, the fate of his tug – although out here these first two were synonymous – then keeping the ship afloat, getting a wire aboard, and controlling the ship's rudder. He could not wait for J.D. to jury-rig electrical power to the capstan on the ship's bow. Not with weather cooking in the west, the winter daylight waning fast, and the *Noorde Titan* on the prowl.

'J.D.,' he said, 'get her pumps going. Mary, go help Boags on the bow. Boagsie, you there?'

'Yes, Captain Kevin.'

'Ready to let go that anchor?'

Boags's heart soared when he heard Captain Kevin order Mary to join him on the bow. He radioed Leo for help in releasing the anchor to clear the hawsepipe. The chief mate rehearsed him, step by step, just as earlier he had advised how to disconnect its chain. When Mary arrived with her glossy black hair cascading from her hood and her eyes sparkling bluer than the Sulu Sea, he was ready with a heavy maul.

'Mary. Watch.' He motioned her to the bulwark, where she could climb and stand on a crossbar to see over the starboard side. 'Ready?'

The anchor was bigger than a Jeep, tons of solid steel tucked snug in the hawsepipe. The disconnected end of its massive chain lay on the deck like a dragon's backbone.

'Ready,' she called.

Boags waited until the ship rolled starboard, so the anchor wouldn't hit the hull as it fell.

'Tugboat out of way?'

'He's away.'

Boags rose on his toes, swung the maul high over his head and whipped it down on the brake. A steel pin flew. The anchor dropped fifty feet from the hawsepipe and vanished into the sea with a sullen boom that splashed water to the sky.

'*Good going, Boags. Now find yourself a big snatch block and secure it to something solid. Mary, get down from there and give him a hand.*'

The storeroom behind *Der Schmetterling*'s chain locker, where Boags had already found his maul and punch, reeked of oil and tar. Coils of rope and wire and massive blocks swayed with the motion of the ship. Boags's light landed on a big snatch block – a pulley that hinged open to fit a loop of line around the wheel.

They dragged the snatch block up the ladder to the foredeck. With wire rope, they secured it to a mooring bitt, a massive steel post anchored to *Der Schmetterling*'s frame.

The *Bowery Queen* circled out of the downwind slick and butted into the rolling seas on a course that put her to windward of the drifting ship. Diesel smoke streamed over her house, as Kevin got his stern pointed directly into the wind. Then, slowly, the tug caught up, aiming for a near-miss with *Der Schmetterling*'s plunging bow.

A tiny figure in a flapping yellow slicker edged on to her towing deck – Leo, with coiled heaving line in his left hand, a monkey fist of knotted rope twirling from his right. A big sea broke over the stern, sluiced along the flat deck, and tore at his knees. Mary and Boags heard Kevin on their walkie-talkies, '*Okay, Leo. Here we go.*'

Leo centred himself, letting line slip through his fingers as he widened the spinning circle of knotted rope. The *Queen* drew close.

'*Boags. Mary. You ready?*'

'Ready, Captain Kevin.'

Der Schmetterling's foredeck was fully fifty feet above the waves — seventy above the *Bowery Queen* when the ship rose and the tug dropped. Leo waited. Kevin slowed more, running a risk that the rolling seas would push the tug around and slam it sideways. The freighter settled into a trough, mashing the sea out from under its bow into a hump of water that lifted the tug. Leo stepped and slung hard. The monkey fist raced skyward, the light heaving line whistling out of his fingers.

It came hard and fast, rising out of the smoke and spray like a major-league strike. Mary and Boags reached over the top of the bulwark. But the monkey fist lost speed and drifted downward, thunking against the hull two feet below Mary's outstretched hands.

Kevin had read its failure early and the *Queen*'s engines were already thundering to put distance between her propellers and the heaving line. The tug wheeled away, the line streaming behind it. Leo reeled it in, coiling and re-coiling the dripping rope, while Kevin put the tug in a broad turn and circled around for another try.

His voice came reassuring over the radio, *'Don't worry, Leo,'* he laughed. *'Mary dropped it.'*

Boags radioed, *'No she didn't, Captain Kevin.'*

'It's a joke, Boagsie — Okay, Leo. Three balls, two strikes, bottom of the ninth . . .'

The red tug closed again, tight from windward, and Mary saw that Kevin was trying to give Leo an even better shot than last time. She held her breath. The *Queen* was on a collision course, Kevin slowing just to steerage, and timing his pass to climb a sea that was erupting from under the ship. From her vantage point she could see more than Kevin: other waves were converging on the freighter's bow; if he was off by one second, the ship would cut the tug in half.

'Okay, Leo!'

Leo stepped forward again, swinging a wide loop, his face lifted intently to the towering ship. He burst into a running start and slung the whirling monkey fist. It arced out of the smoke high above Mary and Boags's out-stretched arms, and soared over the bow.

The line snapped down on the bulwark and started slid-ing toward the stem. Mary and Boags sprawled on the deck with it under a tangle of arms and legs. Grabbing madly as it pulled away, Boags pawed it against Mary, then jerked his hands off her chest as if he had been burned. His face went as red as the *Queen*'s wheelhouse, and the line started to slither away.

Mary rolled on to it again, pinning the thin line under her and batting at it with her heavy gloves. She twirled it around her wrist, and before she saw her mistake the line fetched up and dragged her across the deck. Boags pounced on it and heaved with all his wiry strength.

'Slack! Give me slack!' Mary yelled into the radio.

Scrambling about the foredeck, they couldn't see the tug over the high bulwark. Its engines growled and rumbled as Kevin played the throttles to hold her in place. Hauling in slack, they led the line outside the bulwark and pulled it back in through the empty hawsepipe with a boathook.

'Messenger.'

Down on the *Bowery Queen*'s towing deck, Leo bent his end of the heaving line around the middle of a much heavier messenger line, and motioned Roberto to help. His fresh white bandage looked grotesque, as if the chief mate had shanghaied a hospital patient, or the *Bowery Queen* had inadvertently gone to war. But he shambled gamely after Leo.

'*Heave away!*'

Boags and Mary hauled on the heaving line, lifting the loop of the doubled messenger off the deck of the tug.

Inch by inch they raised the double line while Kevin fought to maintain position twenty yards from *Der Schmetterling*'s lethal bow. Leo and Roberto fed them slack while trying to keep it from getting doused in the waves.

Mary paused to catch her breath.

'*Heave!*' Kevin yelled. '*Don't let that goddamned thing get wet – it'll weigh a ton.*'

Fighting for every foot, she and Boags pulled the doubled line through the hawsepipe, looped it over the snatch block pulley, and shut the block. When Leo and Roberto looped their end around a winch drum on the tug, the two vessels were connected by a moveable double rope, like a backyard clothesline on a pulley.

It was a frail connection on the running sea. Kevin used every trick he knew to hold the *Queen* in position – and several new ones he dreamed up for the occasion. His hands flew between the two engine throttles and the steering sticks, backing and filling with the propellers and walking her sideways with his flanking rudders, while Leo and Roberto struggled on the rolling deck to attach a second, stronger messenger line to the first and winch it up to the ship. By the time the new messenger had travelled up through *Der Schmetterling*'s hawsepipe, around the snatch-block, and back down to the tug, the chief mate was white from exhaustion and blood was streaming from the little cook's bandage.

They tied the new messenger line to the eye of the *Queen*'s tow wire. Then Leo manned the towing winch, releasing the wire from the drum, and Roberto powered it up to the ship.

'*Coming at you, Boags. All set to shackle on to the anchor chain?*'

The eye of the towing wire clanged through the hawsepipe. Boags worked it over the shackle link at the end of *Der Schmetterling*'s anchor chain, closed the shackle, and hammered in the pin that locked it.

'All secure, Captain Kevin.'

'*Release the chain stopper and the windlass.*'

Mary and Boags stood clear. The wire fetched up as Leo reeled in a few feet on the *Queen*'s towing winch, dragging the chain. The shackle slid out of the hawsepipe and the chain rattled after it. Leo winched some more. The anchor chain rumbled up from its deep locker, over the free-wheeling windlass, across the deck, and slid bumping and banging down the hawsepipe.

'*There should be a white painted link every fifteen fathoms,*' Kevin radioed. '*Tell me when we got thirty fathoms.*'

The *Queen* moved slowly out of the sheltered slick and into the windblown seas, dragging *Der Schmetterling*'s anchor chain out of the ship. The heavy links roared.

'Thirty fathoms, Kevin.'

'*I'm going to take another fifteen.*'

The tug engines slowed. '*Okay, get ready to lock it up, Boags. Stopper and winch.*'

'Forty-five fathoms.'

'*Brakes.*' Boags leaned on the windlass's friction brake. The chain stopped. Conferring with Leo, he locked the windlass and the chain stopper. Two hundred and seventy feet of heavy chain sagged ahead of *Der Schmetterling* like a giant spring.

The *Bowery Queen* jetted black smoke and began letting out her towing wire. The tug ran out two thousand feet, the weight and length of the wire adding a second shock-absorbing catenary sag deep in the water.

The tug diminished to a row-boat-sized dot in the distance. The ship was still dead, still blowing to leeward and rolling its stately roll. The anchor chain dipped into the water and disappeared a couple of hundred feet ahead of the bow. The tug was too far away to make out where the wire eventually re-emerged from the ocean.

Black smoke billowed again.

Gradually the ship came alive, as the chain straightened and set the foredeck rattling with a minute vibration. It was like taking someone's pulse, Mary thought, or resting your ear on his chest. Through the chain, through the deck, she could feel the *Bowery Queen*'s engines beating.

With the vibration came at last a sensation of forward motion. Leaning way over the bulkhead, she looked down at the bow. A little ripple was spreading on the sea.

'*Security call. Security call. This is the tug* Bowery Queen, *Echo-Lima-Mike-X-ray, towing the dead container ship* Der Schmetterling *on a long wire in position latitude forty-nine degrees ten minutes North, longitude thirty-five degrees fifty minutes West. We are steering to course 270, making two knots through the water and are restricted in our ability to manoeuvre.'*

The security call, vital in case some express freighter came roaring through the high latitudes, was sure to attract sharks like *Noorde Titan*. It was also the most satisfying Kevin Patrick had ever sent. It felt so good, he sent it again. He wanted to call Mike and tell him the news personally, but raising the High Seas operator took time and energy he couldn't spare.

Leo was shambling around the towing deck with Roberto, raising the Norman pins and rigging the wire with a chafing sleeve and a gob line to keep it from jumping the pins. As soon as the mate signalled the go-ahead, Kevin drained his cold coffee, lit another Marlboro, and began coaxing the *Queen* into a long turn west.

The ship fought him.

To avoid breaking the wire, he took the turn in increments, five degrees at a time, babying its bow into the wind and the waves. For a long while it stopped dead, it seemed, then, gradually, it came around, sheering and yawing side to side. When he finally had it headed west, fishtailing at a stately one knot, and looked at the chronometer to log the event, he saw the ninety degree turn had taken an hour.

In the next hour Leo and Roberto shifted the chafing gear four times as Kevin let out and took in wire to relieve strain by getting the ship and the tug to ride the ocean crests in unison. He finally ordered them inside to warm up and eat something hot. Properly, there should be a man on deck watching the wire every second. If something went wrong, it would go wrong fast. But Roberto was close to collapsing from pain and cold, and a totally exhausted Leo, experienced as he was, was still only one mistake from getting killed.

Der Schmetterling started yawing as their speed increased. Kevin stared blearily back at her in the dying light of the day. Her top row of containers, bridge and radio mast were yellowed by the sun, which had dropped below the horizon.

A third of a mile astern, she still looked enormous, a huge box that promised a cabal with the wind and another with the waves.

He wished he could call Mike.

He thought, suddenly and unexpectedly, of his father. 'Your Old Man,' his mother used to call him. Never 'my husband', or even 'the guy who knocked me up'.

He knew why he had thought of him. 'Your Old Man' had been a seaman and kicked around the world on second-rate rust buckets like *Der Schmetterling*, when he wasn't in jail or de-tox. Watching ships sail, when Kevin first started decking for Mike Fulton, he would see the sailors staring glumly over the side, and wonder where his father was. Then Mike would throw a big arm around his skinny shoulder and sometimes let him steer the *Queen* to the next job. The last Kevin had heard, 'Your Old Man' had slugged a nurse at Smithers and run out of the door.

The wind increased and the sea began to make up, but the *Queen*'s knot meter climbed slowly towards three. She was doing what she did best, pulling hard. Her big propellers were sucking rivers of seawater through her Kort nozzles and jetting them astern in a hard, flat wake. Dark smoke thundered from her stacks, darker than Kevin liked. He had hoped the strain on her engines would ease a little once she got some way on her, but the ship was fighting her and the seas were marching head on.

The sun glow vanished behind thickening clouds that stretched over the tow and blotted out the stars.

'*Running lights rigged,*' Mary radioed. '*Oil lanterns, till J.D. splices electric lines.*'

Kevin lit three white lights on the tug's mast – the international signal that he had a big tow on a long wire, and broadcast another security call.

'*Security call. Security call. This is the tug* Bowery Queen, *towing the dead container vessel* Der Schmetterling *on a long wire in position latitude forty-nine degrees ten minutes North, longitude thirty-five degrees fifty-one minutes West. We are*

*steering course 270 making three knots through the water and
are restricted in our ability to manoeuvre.'*

The wire started jerking hard.

Kevin cranked the communicator. 'Leo, come up and
drive. I got to pay out some wire. The crests are spreading
apart.'

'I'll do it, Captain.'

'Up here,' he said harshly, the only way to deal with
misguided heroics. Leo had been in the cold all day and
was ashen with fatigue.

'She's sheering, Captain. Look out the wire don't throw
you.'

'Can Roberto help?'

Leo shook his head. The injured cook had passed out
on his bunk. 'Safer by yourself. You sure –'

'I'm sure.' Kevin lit the work lights and went down to
the towing deck in his foul weather parka, sea boots and
heavy gloves.

Green seas were crashing inboard, and the wet deck
glistened like Broadway in the rain. The wire was sliding
side to side on the oval stern, dragging the chafing gear
between the Norman pins in fits and starts. Suddenly it
stiffened, sabre-slashing out of the water. A third of a mile
astern, the ship had hung up on a crest; the tug staggered.

Leo lost the rudders for a second. The boat turned, causing the wire to slip across the stern and hard against the
Norman pin. Kevin waited until it was straight behind
again, then winched in forty feet. Bare wire rode the stern,
snapping sparks through the wet.

He approached the chafing gear in a low crouch, got a
yard-long wrench around the bolts and threw his weight
against them. Returning to the winch, he paid out wire
until the tug and the ship, which he couldn't see in the
dark, were rising and falling in unison again.

He stopped the winch, tightened the chafing sleeve's
forward bolt and was tightening the rear when the wire
shifted suddenly. Caught off guard, he gripped the wrench,
which levered him fifteen feet across the towing deck on

to the portside bulwark, where he landed with his feet inboard and his head over the side. A curling sea doused his head and threw him back on the deck.

Coughing and spitting salt water, dragging the wrench he had never let go, he finished securing the chafing sleeve, then let the wire out until it was riding over the stern again. He staggered into the warm galley, poured some burnt coffee and sat until he stopped shaking. Then he went up to the wheelhouse.

'Almost got yourself a promotion, Leo.'

The chief mate did not smile. 'Captain Kevin, if you were a seaman, I'd kick your ass for not watching the wire.'

Kevin was in no mood for a lecture, especially from an older, wiser chief mate. 'Get some sleep,' he said curtly. 'Relieve me in three hours.'

Leo went below, and Kevin had smoked three cigarettes when he became gradually aware of a dim green light catching up on the port side. He gaped in confusion, wondering who the hell that was, before the truth dawned on him: *Der Schmetterling* was sheering alongside, the way the *Okimitsu Enterprise* had tried to sink the *Queen* in the Ambrose Channel.

He slowed the engines and radioed J.D. If the wire jumped the Norman pins there would be no happy ending out here, alone. 'How we doing on that steering, Chief?' When he got no reply, he called Mary. 'Where's J.D.?'

'*Down in the rudder well rigging power to the emergency steering.*'

'You and Boags patching that door?'

'*Trying to.*'

'One of you run back and tell J.D. I need that steering soon as he can. Tell him to lock the rudder amidships. Tell him after he's rested up, it would help if you guys could steer from the bridge.'

'*I'll tell him, but you ought to know, Cap, J.D. found the engineer's stash.*'

'Say again.'

'*Schnapps,*' she said. '*I swear he even knew where to look for it.*'

'Shit. Is he drunk?'

'*He's working on it.*'

'Tell him to call me on the walkie-talkie soon as he climbs out of the rudder well. Goddammit.'

He signed off, telling himself that it took a lot of booze to get J.D. drunk, and returned his attention to the tug. He had throttled way down to get the ship back on course and they were barely making two knots. Any slower and he would lose tug steerage. The ship was trailing behind him again, a fat rectangle on the radar screen, the red and green oil lamps occasionally visible to the eye when they crested together and the spray settled down for a second.

The tow wire was his main concern. The sea, while regular, was not entirely regular; cross-seas suddenly sprang up and troughs inexplicably doubled or shortened, and when that happened, *Der Schmetterling* and the *Bowery Queen* made every effort to go in opposite directions. But he had sprung the wire well with the anchor chain. It rarely jerked hard enough to threaten parting. When it did, though, it was a heart-stopping reminder that the tug-to-ship connection was whisker-thin.

It might be his imagination, or his sleep-starved brain adrift, but after a while it seemed that the sudden jerks were occurring more often. He shone the spotlight far ahead, and got a sobering view of the North Atlantic making up before a gale. Seas marched out of the west, high as houses with steep white roofs.

'*Kev?*' J.D. on the walkie-talkie. Kevin couldn't tell whether he was high or just plain exhausted. '*Got the rudder wired below and locked amidships. Which way do you want me to point her?*'

'Can you hear me down there on the radio?'

'*Too much steel. I'm getting mostly static.*'

'I'll get Mary to relay my directions . . . J.D., she can't hear me either. You get her.' He waited ten minutes until

215

J.D. found Mary and Boags stuffing canvas in the buckled barn door, and set Mary in a place where her walkie-talkie could receive Kevin's signals. Slowly, he throttled ahead. At three and a half knots, the ship sheered to the left.

'Mary. Tell J.D. five degrees right rudder.'

'*Five degrees right rudder.*'

Kevin waited, watching the ship's lights and its image on the radar. Suddenly, it raced behind the tug.

'Midships!'

'*Midships!*'

Long before she reached J.D. with the correction, *Der Schmetterling* was careening alongside, overtaking the tug like an attacking destroyer.

'Left! Left two degrees.'

'*Left. Two degrees.*' She was gasping for breath.

'No. Wait. Mary come back. This won't work.' He slowed the *Queen*'s engines. 'Tell J.D. to set the rudder amidships and don't touch it again until we can steer from the bridge. Got that? Midships and lock it. Tell him to call me, and you get back to the door.'

'*Midships and locked.*'

Even when J.D. restored control from the bridge, Kevin decided, he would decree to all watches that trying to steer the ship out of a sheer would be a last and final resort. And only after he had been called to the tug's wheelhouse.

The walkie-talkie crackled. '*Locked amidships, Kev.*'

'Leave it there. How long to get steering on the bridge?'

'*'Fraid I better stretch out a minute before I fall on my face.*'

'Where's Boags and Mary?'

'*Curled up in the officers' lounge like a pair of puppies. I told 'em to take an hour.*'

Manfred moved easily in the dark.

The rolling had eased markedly since the tug took *Der Schmetterling* into tow. He made his way into the house. Noise didn't matter with the creaking and banging of shifting steel and the distant mutter of the generator below. He watched for the shooting beams of their flashlights.

Only three had come aboard — two small seamen and the giant who had gone straight to the engine room.

He climbed to the bridge and paused in the doorway between the chart room and the wheelhouse. Through the big windows he could see the tug's three vertical white lights far ahead. The bridge was empty, but he sensed a presence and waited patiently as his ears distinguished the faint hissing of static on their walkie-talkies. Scanning the dark, he decided the noise was not here, but below. He started down again. There. The door was open to the captain's cabin and there on the bed was the giant engineer, sleeping in his eyeglasses on his back with the radio clutched to his chest. He caught a whiff of schnapps. Excellent. He eased down the stairs, hunting the seamen. On the next level down was the shabby officers' lounge. They were sprawled on couches and sleeping so deeply that as the ship rolled, their heads lolled like dead bodies. Manfred stepped through the door. One was Asian, more boy than man. He looked at the other, who was even smaller. *Der Schmetterling* pitched forward and the sailor's hood slipped.

Manfred broke into a slow, pleasured smile. He moved closer. Her hair was salt-matted, her face grease-stained. But she was perfectly delicious, with lovely little ears and a pretty mouth. Eight days had elapsed since he had had the ship's stewardess, and under any other circumstances he would have beaten in the Asian boy's skull and tied this one to the nearest bed.

He backed out of the room and, unable to resist a macabre little joke, found a blanket in another cabin, crept back into the lounge, and draped it over her. Then he backed out again, smiling over the thought that if tomorrow night, as they neared Alison's yacht, he had to eliminate the three American sailors, the order of elimination was his to choose.

Kevin lit another cigarette, punched up their position on the sat nav, and drew it on the chart, confirming what he already knew: the tug was badly outmatched by the North

Atlantic; in the six hours since the *Bowery Queen* had begun pulling in earnest, she had rarely exceeded three knots. At this rate, battling thirty-knot headwinds and the endless ranks of rollers the winds had spawned, she would pull *Der Schmetterling* less than seventy miles in a day.

Nor was the ocean her only opponent.

Even with her rudder amidships, *Der Schmetterling* was no butterfly. Immediately after Kevin logged his satellite position, it swung wide left as if some ghost at the helm had suddenly decided to spend the winter in the Azores.

Flaunting its twenty thousand tons, it dragged hard on the wire. The tug heeled as the tow line crept forward and nudged the Norman pin. At the same time, the sheer jerked up the slack. Hundreds of yards of wire sliced up out of the water behind the tug. Kevin shone the spot astern and saw the ship's chain jump, too. It looked as if a giant sabre and cutlass were exchanging thrusts and parries under water. Kevin slowed his engines, begging *Der Schmetterling* to behave, but it surged ahead on its momentum, running alongside a quarter-mile off, still threatening to rake the wire past the Norman pin and yank the *Queen* on her side.

He was trying to steer out of it, when Mary woke up and radioed, '*If I don't do something soon, Cap, we'll be in New York ahead of you.*'

'Don't touch that rudder!'

The radio crackled again, but it wasn't Mary this time. Nor was it the VHF, but the long-range HF single sideband: '*Bowery Queen. Bowery Queen. Echo-Lima-Mike-X-ray. Echo-Lima-Mike-X-ray. This is* Noorde Titan *Hotel-Yankee-Lima-Romeo calling the* Bowery Queen *on eighteen-forty-two.*'

'Roberto!' Kevin yelled into the communicator. 'Get up here.'

The cook shambled up the steps holding his head. 'Get on eighteen-forty-two and find out what they want.'

'My English not good, Captain Kevin.'

'Neither is theirs. You're calling *Noorde Titan*. Hotel-Yankee-Lima-Romeo.'

Roberto went hesitantly to the radio, while Kevin tried

to get the wire back in the water and the ship behind him again. The Dutch sounded close. *'Good evening, Bowery Queen. What is your current position?'*

Roberto looked panicked. Mary had gone on and on about radio silence while they were hunting the ship. But now that they had the ship Kevin was glad of anyone nearby in case any one of thirty possible things went wrong.

'Tell them,' he called over his shoulder to Roberto. 'Read it from the sat nav.'

Roberto transmitted their position.

'Now find out where they are.'

Roberto asked.

The *Noorde Titan's* answer was circumspect, though to the point. The salvage vessel did not give its position. It merely said, *'We'll be there zero-nine hundred tomorrow morning.'*

Kevin, still trying to steer a course that would mollify the rampaging *Der Schmetterling*, did the numbers quickly in his head. Twelve hours. Twenty knots. Two hundred and fifty miles. Close. Very close. The *Bowery Queen* had found the ship just in time.

'Roberto. Take the helm. Steady as she goes. I'll tell you when to turn.' He stepped back to the radio and picked up the mike, with one eye on the ship, which was finally dropping back, and the other on the wire slacking into the water.

'*Noorde Titan?* Let me talk to the captain.'

'This is Captain van Pelt. And who are you?'

'Captain Patrick.' He waited a moment, not expecting van Pelt to remember him or acknowledge him, and he was not surprised.

'What help will you require, Captain Patrick?'

'Well, Cap, we're doing fine, for the moment.'

'Are you moving?'

'We're moving.'

'It would be best if you were just to hold her to the wind until we get there.'

'Ten degrees right, Roberto. Yeah, that's good.' He looked at the wire and then back at the ship again.

'*It will take us longer to catch you up,*' van Pelt explained sternly.

'Yeah, Cap, I think we're just going to keep going like she's going.'

'*Surely you don't intend to tow a twenty-thousand tonner across the North Atlantic in winter?*'

Good question. At seventy miles a day, fuel was going to be a headache sooner rather than later. If they didn't burn up the engines first. Mary had assured him that she could hire a Canadian oiler to meet them at sea with twenty-five thousand dollars' worth of diesel fuel – which was, Kevin thought, the sort of selective optimism with which her father had lost thirteen tugs in twelve years.

'*What are you making?*' van Pelt asked. '*Three knots?*'

The Dutchman knew his business. 'On the nose,' Kevin admitted. 'Home in twenty-four days.'

'*You'll burn up your engines. We can have her in Rotterdam in one week.*'

Kevin had plenty of his own reservations; no one but he knew how hard the *Queen* was struggling, and the next twenty-four days held endless possibilities for mayhem, starting with the *Queen*'s worn-out machinery and escalating to the weather.

But van Pelt's blithe accusation provoked in him a little twinge that felt like patriotism. 'They're General Motors EMDs, Captain. They'll take a lot of punishment.'

'*And your crew? Five men? How much more punishment can they take? . . . My condolences, incidentally, for the sailor you lost,*' van Pelt added, a brutal reminder of the intelligence network real salvage companies maintained.

'Appreciate your concern, Cap . . . Ten degrees back, Roberto.'

Van Pelt heard. '*She's sheering, isn't she?*'

'She's a deep-laden ship. What do you expect?'

'*I'd expect to put several of my best helmsmen aboard,*' van

220

Pelt snapped back. *'Before she tripped my tug. She'll sink you, young man.'*

'Yeah, well, we're a little short of helmsmen.'

'Precisely why I am bringing help in the morning.' Van Pelt crowed in triumph.

SEVENTEEN

One hundred and seventy miles west of the tow, *Twice a Knight* was kiting along under a bra-and-panties rig of storm staysail and triple-reefed main. The wind was northerly, threatening to back west again as the advance squalls of a huge depression gathered behind her.

Alison, having finally worked up a sail balance the auto-pilot could control, had gone below to warm up, just in time to catch the tug's conversation on the HF. The cabin resonated with the steady rattle of water passing the hull and the occasional grinding of the auto-pilot correcting the rudder, sounds that seemed louder after the salvage captains stopped fencing and the radio fell silent.

Hans took the news that they had lost the ship to the salvors calmly. He sat at the nav station, studying the chart.

Alison collapsed on her bunk, her back to the nav station, to hide the relief on her face. God bless the *Bowery Queen*. And God bless the Dutch chasing her. Her only problem now was how to get Hans away from the radio long enough to send Uncle Richard the news that the ship under tow was the one carrying the Tannenberg missiles.

'Alison.'

'Yes, Hans.'

If only the little shit hadn't deep-sixed her satellite telephone she could dial home in a flash from the privacy of the foredeck. But hailing a High Seas operator on the HF was a cumbersome, noisy and often long-drawn-out procedure. Still, she had time — days if the Dutchman took the ship, weeks if the Americans kept it — time enough for Uncle Richard to wangle a Royal Navy frigate to remove the missiles at sea. Time for a quiet end to an elegant operation.

'Alison, I'm talking to you.'

'Yes, Hans?' The thought of Hans being marched off in handcuffs by half a dozen broad-shouldered SAS types had sustained her for a week.

'How much longer to get there?'

'One tugboat already has the ship in tow,' she reminded him. 'The second will catch up at dawn. Twenty men in their crews, maybe more. What can we do in a sailboat?'

'Make for the ship,' he ordered.

'What's the point? We can't very well sail up and say, "Excuse us while we remove some valuable paintings."'

'It's not the paintings, you silly bitch.'

For a second she thought he would admit to the Tannenbergs, but he caught himself, saying, 'He's my brother. We have to rescue him.'

'Your brother is the slickest customer in Europe. He can take care of himself. It's an enormous ship. They'll never find him. We'll get the paintings, somehow, once they tow her into port. No one knows he's aboard. The crew's dead, remember.'

'We will press on,' said Hans. 'With any luck the Dutch tug will go away. The American captain did not sound inclined to share his prize. What is Manfred's position?'

Alison heaved her aching body off her bunk and pointed to the chart where she had marked the coordinates of the American's last security call. To her astonishment, Hans reached up and punched the numbers into the satellite navigator. He hit the proper buttons to display the bearing from *Twice a Knight* and pointed at the screen. 'There's your course. Stick to it.'

'I didn't know you could navigate.'

'The head of my university had a yacht in the Baltic.'

'You know how to *sail*?'

'It was a motor yacht. They're really quite simple. And these electronics make navigating much easier than a sextant, though, of course, shooting planets with the sextant is far more satisfying.' He looked up with a reptilian smile, and Alison knew there was no way she could accidentally miss the rendezvous. She was surer than ever that Hans knew, or guessed, her reason for joining Manfred. The sooner she radioed Uncle Richard the better, even if she had to knock Hans on the head while he slept. As if he could read her mind, he took a pill bottle from his shirt pocket, swallowed two red ones, dry, and offered the bottle to her.

'They'll keep you awake two days, more than enough. Then we'll sleep while Manfred steers.'

Alison declined. 'One of us had better keep our head on straight.' God willing, the Dutch salvage tug would seize *Der Schmetterling* and tow it east faster than she could sail. But if it didn't, she still had one more trick up her sleeve. Uncle Richard's plan to slip coded messages into the weather fax hadn't worked at all, but hidden on deck was an Argos position transmitter. If she tripped the distress signal, Uncle Richard still had enough clout to scramble an RAF plane to investigate. But the distress signal alone wouldn't tell a high-flying jet fighter much unless she was next to the actual ship that had the missiles.

'Captain Kevin . . . Captain Kevin?' Leo shook his shoulder. 'J.D. on the radio.'

Kevin was dreaming that the tug was bearing down on an iceberg. The steering sticks were falling off in his hands. 'J.D. on the radio, Captain.'

He swung his feet to the deck and sat up. His voice wouldn't work when he tried to ask the time. Leo shoved a mug of coffee into one hand, and a radio into the other.

'Kev, you there?'

The tug felt as though they'd picked up some speed. He pushed his sweater off his watch: seven-thirty. Dark as a pit outside his porthole. Three full hours' sleep. He swigged the coffee. His stomach rolled over and his brain lurched into gear.

'Yeah. How's that helm?'

'There's something weird going down.'

'What kind of weird?'

'I'm up on the bridge. Looks like they had a war. It's all shot to shit.'

'Guns?'

'The standard means of shooting something to shit,' J.D. replied. *'The bridge is wrecked, Kev. Busted glass all over. They had themselves a firefight up here.'*

'Any bodies?'

'Not that I've seen . . . Hey, Boags, Mary?'

'Yeah, J.D.?' Thin with static, deep in the hold.

Kevin cut in. *'Mary. Get up to the bridge with J.D. Boags, you go with her, stick close. Hear me?'*

'We're scrounging more canvas to stuff in the door tracks,' Mary's voice came back irritably.

'Get the fuck up there with Boags,' Kevin yelled. *'And don't give me any lip!'* He instantly regretted yelling at Mary on the radio. Everyone had heard and a crew didn't trust a man who got excited. But he felt helpless, trapped on the tug while God knew what roamed the ship.

His first instinct was to turn round and take them off, but manoeuvring alongside a tow on a running sea with an exhausted crew would be suicidal in the dark. He thought of the drowned riding crew on the tug that sank. This was the same thing all over again, except worse, because this time *he* was captain, responsible for three lives he was powerless to protect, two thousand feet astern. He wished to God he had kept Mary with him.

'J.D.?'

'Yeah, Kev.'

'Any guns lying around?'

'Found an old Luger in the captain's office.'

'J.D.? You sure you're alone back there?'

'Haven't seen hide nor hair. I suppose we ought to look around.'

'Yeah, well, don't shoot Mary and Boags by mistake.'

'Shoot? This thing would blow up in my hand . . . Make a fair club, though.'

Kevin thought he heard J.D. swallow. *'You drinking?'*

'Nope. Just finished.'

Kevin's head swam. No two tows were ever the same? Mike should see this one. Leo tapped his shoulder and pointed out his porthole. *Der Schmetterling*'s lights.

'Shit. She's sheering alongside me. Search the ship, fast as you can. Soon as you're sure no one's there, get busy rigging the helm.'

He signed off, pulled his sneakers on, and climbed up to the wheelhouse. The sheering, at least, was a problem he could deal with.

J.D. broke down the old Luger, swabbed the pieces with one of the oily rags dangling from his pockets, reassembled it, and led the way. Boags carried a fire axe, and Mary a sack of spare flashlights, with the vague intent to brain someone with the heavy lights if she were attacked. It was a little scary flinging open the first of the cabin doors and wondering what would jump out, but their reflection in a mirror almost made her laugh: God help the poor soul who ran into them! Three-hundred-pound J.D. holding a pistol as though he knew how to use it; the swarthy Boags, a Malay pirate wielding a boarding axe as though he *wanted* to use it; and even her, bundled to the chin in a filthy insulated boiler suit, greasy watchcap over greasier hair, black smudges on her face, toolbelt clanking from her hips.

By the time they had searched six levels down to the main deck it all seemed a little unreal – a theoretical problem far from the very real problems of pumping and steering the dead ship – and a waste of their failing strength.

Mary hadn't slept twenty minutes in twenty-four hours and was shambling with exhaustion. Boags had lost a little of the coltish spring in his legs. Only J.D. seemed relatively unaffected by the lack of sleep, the physical battles they had already fought, and the constant motion of the ship. He was sucking on a flask when he thought she wasn't looking, but the liquor seemed to act like fuel.

Kevin stood at the starboard steering sticks, staring out at the sea, wishing he had kept Mary on the tug. It was one thing having her along as crew. Cool as ice and reliable at the helm, she pulled her weight. But with violence hovering over the tow there was no getting away from the fact that she was a woman. And Mike's daughter. And making him crazy.

He couldn't shake off the aura of violence at the end of the wire. His father floated into memory again, the violence among men at sea. Mutinies and hijackings or whatever had driven *Der Schmetterling*'s crew overboard were not common because the violence was almost never organized. It usually just exploded when a quiet sailor picked up an axe and started swinging. One of the things he preferred about tugs was that the boats were so small and the crews so busy, that the crazies usually waited till they hit the beach to cut loose.

An hour crept by. When he couldn't stand waiting any longer, Kevin radioed, 'What's happening?'

Mary answered. *'We're just finishing up.'*

'What did you find?'

'Absolutely nothing. We checked every cabin. The only shooting we can see was on the bridge and in the captain's cabin.'

'No blood? No bodies?'

'I think I would have mentioned blood and bodies, Kevin. Can we get back to work?'

'What about where they launched the lifeboat?'

'Hana on.'

'Take Boags with you.'

'Aye, aye, sir.'

It was bitter cold on *Der Schmetterling*'s boatdeck. With the tug holding the ship's nose to the waves and pulling it at four knots, the wind slammed past, drumming Mary's parka hood so loudly that she could only exchange hand signals with Boags. They shone flashlights in the space where the lifeboat had hung. The falls Boags had climbed dangled down to the dark. He swept the side of the house and stopped the light abruptly on something he had not noticed in the scramble to board. Mary saw it too, a black scorch mark in the paint. Movement caught her eye, a spark reflected in the dark. She crouched beside a yard-long metal cylinder rolling back and forth in the gutter at the aft end of the deck. It was pocked with bullet holes. She had seen enough on the bridge to recognize them. Boags leaned close and shouted in her ear.

'Emergency beacon.'

She recognized it now. An Emergency Position Indicating Radio Beacon, of the type the KLM flight had picked up signals from five hundred miles east of here. Not from this one. It was riddled. Her radio squawked. She took one last look around and motioned Boags back inside, where, out of the wind, she said, 'What's up, Kevin?'

'What did you find?'

'I don't know. They did some shooting here, too, but there's nobody around. Boags thinks they shot a flare that hit the bulkhead. Kevin, can we get back to work?'

'You're sure you're alone?'

'Positive.'

'Listen. If there was a fight, there must have been winners and losers. No one stayed behind?'

'Maybe the winners threw the losers overboard.'

'And then abandoned ship?'

'I don't know, Kevin. There was a fire, remember?'

'What if the losers abandoned ship and the winners stayed aboard?'

'How could the losers launch a boat if the winners had the guns? How could the losers have escaped?'

'Maybe you should keep looking.'

'Oh no,' Mary groaned. They had searched the house, but not the enormous holds. 'We're chasing ghosts, Kev. Besides, there's no way we could find someone who doesn't want to be found.'

A new voice boomed on the VHF channel. 'Bowery Queen. Bowery Queen. *We have got you on the radar.*'

'Kevin, who the hell is that?'

'Noorde Titan. *Eight miles astern.*'

Mary ran from the boatdeck to the bridge. Boags loped after her. Dawn was silvering the east, lighting the jagged collisions of western rollers and storm-driven waves from the south-west. She spotted a hard shape on the saw-toothed horizon and snatched up her radio.

'Kevin, what the hell is going on?'

'*He picked up our security call last night and said he was coming to help.*'

'Why didn't you tell me?'

'*It wasn't debatable and I had my hands full. He said help was on the way. What was I supposed to do, say no?*'

'We don't need help.'

'*I wasn't so sure about that last night. What we want may not be debatable either. If he wants to help, it might be tough to tell him no.*'

'This ship is ours.'

The shape on the horizon was getting harder fast, and sharper, like a spearhead hurtling through a mist. The mist, it soon became apparent, was actually sheets of spray hurled left and right by an enormous, speeding hull. 'I see them,' she said.

'*Captain's calling me,*' said Kevin. '*I'll keep you posted.*'

'Kevin?'

'*What?*'

'You can talk to his captain all you want. I'll talk to his owner.'

'*Mary, do we have to go through this again? The safety —*'

'— of the *Bowery Queen* and her crew is your responsibility, but the decision to share a salvage fee is mine.'

'*Gut morgen,*' a cold voice broke in. '*I am Captain van Pelt of* den Noorde Titan. *We are prepared to assist you. Are you there, Captain Patrick?*'

'*Yeah, Cap. I'm here. We've got a third party on the line, the owner's —*'

'Mary Fulton, the owner,' Mary cut in. 'Good morning, Captain van Pelt.'

'*Gut morgen. I'm surprised there's room for a young lady on such a small boat.*'

Kevin finally fell in place. '*Ms Fulton's with the riding crew, Cap.*'

'Now, young man, let's get down to business. We should put a wire aboard, now, for safety sake, while the owners work out the details, don't you agree?'

'Well, Cap, that's going to be a lot of trouble for something we may end up casting off in an hour.'

'No problem. I'll send some hands over by breeches buoy and make short work of it.'

Mary picked up her glasses. The *Noorde Titan* was big on the horizon, coming straight at them. The black hull had a graceful, flared bow. It looked as big as a freighter and carved a bow wave like a destroyer. It was coming fast, resonating authority, like van Pelt's voice on the radio. She half-expected a puff of smoke and a loud boom announcing a shot across her tugboat's bow.

'I don't know that we're ready for any hands on the tow, Cap. But thanks. We'll keep it in mind.'

Van Pelt was obviously prepared to discuss it all day and Kevin got an uncertain note in his voice when the Dutch captain started throwing around legal terms from the Lloyd's Open Form No Cure-No Pay Salvage Agreement.

'Cap, I think that's more up to the lawyers than you and me.'

Manfred studied the *Noorde Titan* from a hole he had bored in the side of his container. It was closing fast. Compared to the *Bowery Queen* struggling in the distance, it looked like the *QE2*, moving as if it could meet the sea on its own terms.

He had a wild, though not entirely improbable idea. The helicopter shot had proved he could hit his target. If he landed a Tannenberg on the salvage tug's bridge, would the nerve gas wipe out her crew? Would the tug then stop? Could he somehow board it? He already had a raft in the forward storeroom by the accommodation door. He had seen an outboard motor there. Could he rig it and power across to the tug? Or simply don his own wetsuit and swim? How long would it take the gas to dissipate? What would the *Bowery Queen*'s crew do? The questions mounted in number and complexity. His head began to whirl. Some of the gas would stay trapped in the interior, lethal for days. Would the Dutch get off a radio distress signal before they all died?

J.D. lumbered on to *Der Schmetterling*'s bridge with his tool box. 'What's up, Mare – son of a gun, look at that ship go. *Noorde Titan*?'

'They want to board us.'

J.D.'s jaw set. 'I don't imagine that would prove particularly beneficial to our salvage award.'

'You backing me?'

'Believe it.'

Mary turned on her VHF handset. 'Excuse me, Captain Patrick. Captain van Pelt. Captain Patrick has his hands full at the moment. You may negotiate with me while he goes about his business. Bye, Kev.'

'*Negotiate. I hardly –*'

'You're not welcome aboard, Captain. We're doing fine. We don't need your wire or your help. We appreciate your coming by, but Captain Patrick has things under control.'

The *Noorde Titan* slid alongside the freighter. At least a dozen seamen were out in the cold, watching. There was a flurry of activity on the main deck as they readied a line-throwing gun.

Van Pelt rattled papers by his radio: '*May I draw your attention, Ms Fulton, to Article Eight of the Montreal Salvage Convention, adopted in London, 1989, Clause One (a and d) "The salvor shall owe a duty to the owner of the vessel or other property in danger: (a) to carry out the salvage operations with due care; (d) to accept the intervention of other salvors when reasonably requested to do so by the owner or master of the vessel . . ."*'

'But you're not the owner or the master, Captain van Pelt.'

'*I can assure you,*' came the cold reply, '*that the owner of the vessel is discussing this matter with my office even as we*

231

speak. Now let's not delay any further. You need help. It's your responsibility to accept it because you will never bring that ship in alone.'

'You've got me at a disadvantage, Captain. I don't have a copy of that thing you just read me.'

'That's because you did not sign a Lloyd's Open Form with the owner.'

He had her there, she thought, feeling suddenly overwhelmed by van Pelt's assuredness and the sheer size of the modern-looking salvage tug pacing them like a mastiff waiting orders to spring.

Stupid Kevin should have warned her the *Noorde Titan* was coming. She could have been ready. Could have signed the form . . . 'Wait a minute.'

'We've waited quite —'

'I didn't sign any form because there's no one here to sign one with. What are you telling me? I have no claim because I didn't sign a piece of paper? I have a claim. Every man on my boat has a claim. It's a two-and-a-half-inch wire they put aboard.'

'Actually,' the Dutch captain interrupted, *'your father Captain Fulton did sign one with the owner's New York agent. So you are bound by its provisions, including Article Eight. You must accept my help.'*

Mary raked the *Titan*'s bridge with her glasses. It was spacious, gleaming with electronics, and filled with busy officers who looked as though they had started the day with a hot shower, fresh clothing, and breakfast on china. Through a window behind the wheelhouse, she spotted van Pelt in the radio room — a fit-looking middle-aged blond gazing back at her with hawk eyes and an arrogant smile. He waved.

'Shall I describe for you the conversation taking place right now between Der Schmetterling*'s owners and my company?'*

'I don't care about their conversation.' What she needed desperately, so she could defend the *Bowery Queen*'s claim, was a look at the Lloyd's Open Form or a talk with a lawyer.

232

'It will go something like this. ''Ah, Mr German Shipowner, there's been a slight problem. Your valuable ship and cargo have been waylaid by some unqualified Americans on some sort of a little tugboat. They're doing remarkably well, considering they are amateurs, but they are going to lose your ship when the next storm hits, which storms tend to do, as you know, Mr German Shipowner, about every three days in the North Atlantic in the winter. We strongly recommend that you and your insurers and the owners of your cargo sign a Lloyd's Open Form with us before these rank amateurs damage your ship further –'''

'There's no damage!' Mary yelled.

'''Oh, yes,''' van Pelt went on mimicking the meeting. '''Our Captain van Pelt – a veteran salvor of forty years at sea – reports massive damage to a loading door near the water line. Apparently they've let the cargo shift. The vessel is in danger of sinking, unless we board it and secure the cargo immediately.'''

'It was like that when we got here,' said Mary.

'Is that so?'

'We patched it. It's in my log.'

'Tell it to the Lloyd's arbitrator, Ms Fulton. Maybe the case will go to a long appeal. Three or four years to get your share of our fee.'

'Screw you, Mr Lawyer.'

'I'm not a lawyer. Just a simple sailor. But I can assure you that the Noorde company has plenty of lawyers ... Now, I calculate your fuel costs from Nova Scotia to this point and back to New York, running light, of nineteen thousand dollars. You've a very small crew. I believe I could persuade my directors to pay you a one-time fee of twenty-five thousand dollars for your time, fuel, and trouble.'

'You son of a bitch ...'

'That is if you cast off now. Just drop your wire, take your men off, and go.'

J.D. said, 'Excuse my French, Mare, but tell him to fuck himself.'

'Captain van Pelt?'

'Yes, Der Schmetterling.'

'Does that line gun work?'

'Of course.'

'I'd like to see a copy of your Lloyd's Form, please. Just the form. No hands. No equipment. You are not invited aboard my ship.'

She sent Boags scrambling to the top of the containers. He ran forward to where the heaving line could be shot without tangling in the radio masts on the house. The gun boomed. A light line gleamed against the sky and Boags retrieved it, and hand over hand hauled a package across the water. He ran into the wheelhouse with an envelope. Inside were Captain van Pelt's business card and a Xerox copy of a fax of a Lloyd's Open Form signed hours ago in Rostock and Rotterdam, with a note cancelling the previous LOF agreement with Fulton Towing of New York.

Mary turned directly to Article Eight and read it twice.

'*As you see, the document is in order and properly signed by the parties. Satisfied?*'

Mary laughed. 'I didn't have my own copy, Captain. I've never seen one. I think you left out some important words in Article Eight, Clause (d) about me having to accept the intervention of other salvors, namely you? at the request of the owner?'

Van Pelt's excellent English became less so as he replied cautiously, '*Yes, I am reading copy, too.*'

'It says here, "the amount of my reward shall not be prejudiced should it be found that such a request was unreasonable."'

'*But it is reasonable,*' van Pelt countered. '*The ship is in danger in mid-ocean.*'

Mary changed channels. 'Kevin?'

'*Yeah?*'

'Would you please send another security call?'

'*What for? We're the only three vessels for a thousand miles.*'

'Just do it, please, and leave your mike open so I can hear.'

'*Security call. Security call. This is the tug* Bowery Queen, *towing the dead container vessel* Der Schmetterling *on a long wire in position latitude forty-seven degrees forty-one minutes*

234

North, longitude thirty-nine degrees West. We are steering course 270 making four and a half knots through the water and are restricted in our ability to manoeuvre . . . How's that?'

'Sounds good to me. How about you, Captain van Pelt?'

'I'm not sure I understand.'

'Oh, you do. You understand that every ship on the North Atlantic, and all the Coast Guards, and every ship agent and every maritime lawyer has heard again that the master of a seagoing tug has his tow in charge and that any demand to surrender her is unreasonable. So if you want to hang out at — what does the *Titan* cost to run, Captain? ten-fifteen thousand dollars a day? — you're welcome. You can even breeches buoy over and join us for lunch. But you've no reasonable claim on my fee, I don't care how many lawyers you stall me with, you still won't get a thing.'

'You refuse my help,' van Pelt said stiffly. *'You need nothing.'* It rang of a setup. He was suddenly talking as if establishing a legal record to absolve himself — or give him grounds to try later.

'J.D. What kind of fuel does he burn?'

'Heavy oil, I'd reckon. Like this ship. You know, with a pre-heater.'

'Can we burn it in our engines?'

'Hell no. It's thick as tar. Why?'

'Just for the record, I want him to refuse me something.' She thumbed Transmit. 'Actually, Captain van Pelt, there is one thing you could do for me.'

'Ja?' came the guarded reply.

'I'm getting low on fuel. Less than three weeks steaming. I can't burn *Der Schmetterling*'s heavy oil. I'll arrange a lighter, but we'd be grateful to top up now, just in case.'

'No. We, too, burn heavy oil. Not your light diesel.'

'Maybe you've got some light diesel for your generators?'

'Not enough.'

'Thanks anyway. Goodbye, *Noorde Titan*.'

Captain van Pelt finally lost his cool. *'You'd never get*

away with this ten years ago. There used to be salvage tugs always on Atlantic station. Dutchmen off Brest. Newfounders and Nova Scotians on the Canadian coast. The salvage business is wrecked.'

'Well, sir, the *Bowery Queen* is reviving it.'

The *Noorde Titan* swept off to the east, hurling angry black smoke and a stupendous wake.

'Probably just as well they didn't have a cannon,' said J.D. 'All right, let's rig some steering and secure the hull. Mare, you and me gonna run some juice to the helm. Boags, amigo, hop down to D hold and finish stuffin' that door. And see to it that 'dozer don't take it in mind to start moving again.'

'What about stowaways?'

'Captain says we're gonna see some weather tomorrow. We'll rig steering and secure the hull. Then we'll worry about stowaways. You gonna be alone down there, so you take the gun. Run into a stowaway offer him a job. If he don't want to help, shoot the sumbitch. Here.' He made sure the safety was on and handed it butt first to the seaman.

Boags smiled at Mary and leaped off the deck. Spinning like a figure skater, he turned around in the air, kicking backwards. His boot blurred between them. The Luger flew from J.D.'s hand. Boags caught it, landed lightly as a blue-jay, and handed it back, butt first. 'No thank you, J.D.'

'Well I'll be,' rumbled J.D.

Mary said, 'Wow.'

Boags blushed, mumbled he hoped he hadn't hurt J.D.'s hand, and ran below, boots echoing in the stairwell as he bounded from *Der Schmetterling*'s bridge to the deepest hold four steps at a time.

Seconds after the *Noorde Titan* disappeared over the horizon, to Manfred's enormous relief, the renegade Stasi officer heard Alison's *click-click* on his HF radio. Hans himself spoke. There were too many radios around on the *Bowery Queen* and the *Noorde Titan* to risk a conversation. Hans spoke one word, vibrating with excitement: 'Tonight.'

That was Manfred's signal to switch on a homing beacon and shift their treasure from the container to the hold. He had already gathered the Tannenberg missiles into five separate bundles of four missiles each. As each missile was cushioned in bubble wrap inside a length of six-inch PVC pipe, the bundles were a foot square, with rounded edges. Four and a half feet long, they weighed one hundred and sixty pounds — heavy, but not impossible, while smaller bundles would mean risking extra trips to the hold. Manfred himself weighed two-forty; lazy in the extreme, he had done little to sustain his superb physique until the last year hiding in Hong Kong, where he worked as an executive health club instructor, a job suited to his good looks, fine build and natural arrogance. He shackled a bundle to a mountain-pack harness modified to seat it firmly and slung it on his back.

The tug was nearly a half-mile ahead, small in the distance, and partially obscured in black smoke and spray from the mountainous waves. Still, he studied it intently with his high-powered Zeisses, until he was content that no one on the tugboat was watching with binoculars. Out of the container door with his first bundle, hunched under the weight, he climbed down to the main deck where, hidden under a canopy of containers, he headed for the house.

Hans popped another red pill to celebrate; Alison declined again, despite a long night of little sleep. A look out of a porthole suggested celebration was premature.

The sea was grey and white, spindrift whipping along the surface. It looked like a dense fog down in the troughs, but it was blowing water, not fog, which became obvious as *Twice a Knight* shimmied to the top of a towering sea. The midday sky was clad in hard-edged high cloud, a cold-looking overcast, beneath which she could see for miles.

The barometer was down, down a lot. And the wind was still backing, swinging counterclockwise to the south, which meant that the big depression to the south and west had intensified.

A shadow darkened the skylight. Alison, brewing a quick tea before going up again, glanced blearily across the cabin. The starboard ports – three oval lights facing south – had turned black. A faraway sizzling noise grew loud. Hans looked up.

'What is this?'

Line storm, she thought, the sky blotted by a racing wall of wind-boiled sea and snow. Her body – light-years ahead of her brain – scrambled to take in the sails. She had one arm into her cold, wet, foul-weather jacket when hail drummed on the cabin roof and the first gust smashed the boat.

Twice a Knight fell on her side, tumbling Alison across the cabin into the nav station. Hans hurtled out of his bunk on the starboard side and fell into hers on the port side. The boat stayed down, down so long that Alison feared it would never come back. Then a sail – the main, she guessed by the explosion directly overhead – blew out with a bang and the miserable little keel finally straightened her up, rolling drunkenly. Another gust banged into the remaining sail. *Twice a Knight* heeled sharply, and flew.

The compass card – the only glow of light in the suddenly pitch dark cabin – spun mad circles until the autopilot, making the best of a bad bargain, chose a course due north.

Alison turned on the lights and battled into her jacket and boots. The boat banged from sea to sea, hurling her around the cabin. She hauled herself up the companionway and flung open the main hatch. A wave broke over the washboards, a freezing torrent that caught her full in the face and knocked her down the steps. She landed hard on her back, stunned, the wind knocked out of her. Hans yelled. A second wave poured in. She got up and closed the hatch; then, donning the safety harness she had forgotten, she reminded herself not to get washed overboard while trying to keep *Twice a Knight* from sinking.

She went up the companionway again and reached cautiously for the hatch. Before she could open it, *Twice a Knight* careened. Alison locked the hatch and clung to the steps, her legs dangling on to the nav station, her feet banging the chart table. Then she was standing on the books in the bookshelf above the radio. A tremendous wave, solid as concrete, slammed the hull. She lost her grip and fell on the ceiling, a fact she could not quite believe until the floorboards started raining down on her.

Something heavy hit her in the face and something sharp jabbed her ribs. She slid along the ceiling, forward to where the mast foot entered the cabin, then suddenly back to the top of the companionway, then forward again, on to the Lexan skylight, which was bulging inward from the weight of the yacht pressing upside down in the water.

Hans was yelling at her to do something.

Keel in the air, mast pointing to the bottom of the ocean, *Twice a Knight* hung upside down. Icy seawater sprayed into the cabin through ventilators, the stove chimney, around the mast, and two of the oval side ports.

'Turn over, you bitch!' Alison screamed.

A sailboat couldn't hang upside down in the water. The weight of the keel and the ballast had to pull her upright. But the yacht would not budge. A moment ago Alison's biggest fear was that the mast had broken; now she feared she would die trapped in the cabin. The mast and rigging and sails were acting like a second keel. She cursed the light ballast and the bulbless keel and promised God that if she ever got out of this she would never sail a light displacement boat again.

A deep grinding shivered the yacht. She looked up at the sound. The companionway stairs had hinged away, revealing the engine compartment. She saw to her horror that the engine was moving. It had sheared the bolts that held it to the hull and was threatening to break loose and drop through the ceiling.

A heavy sea crashed into the upside-down hull. The boat shuddered and started to roll. As it did, the engine moved again. The drive shaft bent, then snapped with a loud *bang*.

Twice a Knight whooshed upright in a swirl of water and a flapping of wet lines and sails. Alison landed on the floor, darted up the companionway, leaped into the cockpit and slammed the hatch shut in one motion. She clipped her safety harness to a padeye in the cockpit and turned, heart in her throat, to see if she still had a mast.

By a miracle she had, a mast and a hard-working staysail which was already driving the boat at eight knots. Strips of dacron were tangled around the tiller – remnants of the main – the steering vane had gone by the board, and the engine was a goner, but she still had a mast.

She cleared the shredded main, wadded the sailcloth into a hole where the sea had plucked out a ventilator, and checked that the dummy hatch that concealed the Argos hadn't been washed away. Then she ran below for a new mainsail and to get Hans to help her rig her spare steering vane. She found him crumpled up, out cold on the cabin sole, a huge egg on his forehead. Immediately, she hit the generator switch to energize the HF radio. The generator rumbled. Hans stirred only slightly. She turned on the HF, but the generator made a high-pitched screech and stopped. Alison threw back the companionway to look into the engine compartment. The dislodged engine had knocked the generator askew. Judging by the acrid smell, something had burned up inside. She sat at the HF and tried to get a signal out to a High Seas operator. She got through briefly to New Jersey, but before they could lock in their moveable antennas, her batteries, already over-burdened by the autopilot, gave up the ghost; Uncle Richard, his RAF fighter and his Royal Navy frigate might as well have been on Neptune.

Three hours after the *Noorde Titan* left the *Bowery Queen* to her prize – while Leo stood watch and Kevin and Roberto slept – the tugboat's three-thousand-horsepower port engine coughed twice and stopped.

Kevin snapped awake, thanking God for twin engines. He jammed on his sneakers and raced to the engine room in time to hear the starboard V-16 gasp once and fall silent, like a man shot.

The generator was still roaring, powering lights and blowers. And the engine alarms were shrieking like a riot. But to Kevin's disbelieving ears, the engine room was gripped by a silence so deep it seemed to echo.

He plunged down the greasy metal stairs to the control panel and tried the main port engine's starter. The behemoth ground over and over with no effect. Starboard. Dead metal grinding dead metal. With J.D. stuck on the tow.

He shut the fuel and oil pumps, silencing the alarms, and ran for the wheelhouse. At this moment, the question of why the ancient engines had stopped was less important than the fact that *Der Schmetterling*'s greater weight and momentum would carry her along for miles. He had to get the *Bowery Queen* out of the way before the ship ran them down.

Already it looked much closer.

Leo was at the helm, attempting to steer out of its path. The tug was losing way rapidly, slowed by the running seas and the drag of the towline, so the rudders had little purchase on the water.

'Keep her head up,' said Kevin. If the wind got behind her, it would blow the *Bowery Queen* straight back at *Der Schmetterling*.

'Yes, Captain Kevin.' The warning had been unnecessary. The mate was playing the steering stick like a violin bow.

Kevin reached for the radio. 'What happened? They just stop?'

'Just stopped. No warning.'

'J.D., J.D. You there? The fuckers quit dead.'

'I know, Kev. I felt it. Better shut down the fuel pumps.'

'I did.'

'That's fine. Now what the hell did you do to my engines?'

241

Kevin took a deep breath, controlled the impulse to yell at J.D. to quit screwing around, and said, calmly and judiciously, 'You tell me, J.D.'

'*They quit together?*' the engineer asked. '*Both the same time?*'

'Damn near.'

'*Are they smoking?*'

'Smoking? They're cold as icebergs.'

'*Well, now . . .*'

'Ship slowing down any, Leo?'

'A little,' the mate answered. He had managed to walk the tug south a little and was now, Kevin noted with admiration, letting the wind, which had shifted slightly north, blow it to the edge of the freighter's track.

'*It's a new one in my experience,*' J.D. mused aloud.

'Yeah, well, I'm thinking maybe I'll go down there and you can talk me through it.'

'*We get any closer,*' J.D. replied, '*I'll just hop down myself.*'

'We get any closer, we'll join you 'cause this baby's going under.' Kevin looked out of the back window. *Der Schmetterling* had halved the distance between the vessels.

'Leo. Wake Roberto. Tell him to lay out survival suits.'

Leo cranked the communicator.

Kevin went out on deck for a better look. It was eerily quiet. He could hear waves slushing past. The ship loomed and he saw white where the knife bow parted the waves. Still moving forward. But now, for a moment at least, the wind was his friend, blowing the tug towards temporary safety.

At last, *Der Schmetterling* began to fall off, turning broadside, drifting broadside to the wind as it had when they first found the ship, yesterday.

'Okay, J.D. I'll call you from the engine room.'

He went below, noting that about five hundred feet of water separated the two vessels. The freighter's greater windage would make it drift faster so that soon it would be dragging the *Queen*, backwards, bow to the waves. That might steady the tug, making working on the engines easier if they could figure out what had gone wrong.

Conversing by radio from the engine room, he acted as J.D.'s eyes and ears and hands. They started with the alarms and automatic shutoffs, testing circuits for shorts that might have tripped the shutoffs accidentally. When all that checked out, J.D. fell silent a moment. Then he said, *'I am presuming you shifted fuel to the day tanks as I instructed.'*

'Yup.'

'You want to check the fuel level in the day tanks anyway?'

Kevin sounded the tank, thinking he would gladly feel like an idiot for screwing up if that were the simple solution. Half full.

'It's not the day tank.'

'Okay, there's one thing we ought to check, though I don't want to. Make sure the oil pumps are working. They didn't burn up, did they?'

'Nope. I looked at the temperature. They didn't burn up.'

He turned on the oil pumps at J.D.'s request and reported that pressure was normal. The engines had not overheated. Kevin glared at them, sitting there, getting cold. He went through the start procedure, pre-lubing the turbochargers and cranking the port engine and then starboard.

'They won't catch, J.D. They're coughing like a couple of old rummies.'

'They getting air?'

Kevin checked all the intakes and all the air filters, which were dirty but not clogged.

The communicator shrilled. 'Yeah, Leo.'

'Better come up, Captain Kevin.'

'Right back, J.D.' He ran up the steps two at a time. In the wheelhouse, Leo was pointing out of the back window. *Der Schmetterling* was much closer.

'Christ,' said Kevin. 'What the hell . . .' The starboard side bulked huge against the sky, looming over the tug. Mary spoke on the radio.

'We're getting close, Leo.'

The towing wire drooped straight down from the *Bowery Queen's* stern. The ship's chain hung straight from the bow. 'The wire's sinking.' Its weight was pulling the two vessels together.

'Leo, let out more wire.'

'Not much left, Captain.'

'When you get to the end, bend on the nylon messenger and anything else we've got. If that don't work, we'll have to drop it.'

Leo had left the transmitter on and Mary heard.

'Don't drop the wire.'

'Get off the radio. I'm talking to J.D.'

'But what if it takes a day to fix the engine? The wind could blow the ship a hundred miles. You'll never find us.'

'I'm trying to talk to J.D.'

'But why not pull the wire in if it's dragging us together? Why can't we reel it up and take the weight on the winch?'

'Because winching it in will *also* pull us together.'

'It's like a couple with a past,' J.D. interrupted in a slurry voice. *"lesh one cuts loose, it's going to pull them both down — which ain't necessarily a bad thing. For a couple.'*

Mary sounded crushed. 'I can't believe this is happening,' she whispered.

'Madre!' Leo swore. He pointed down at the towing deck. Little Roberto was staggering around in his bulky rubber survival suit, gazing up in terror at the plunging wall of the ship.

Kevin laughed.

Leo stared at him as if he had lost his mind. Mary gasped on the radio. J.D. rumbled, *'You okay, Kev?'*

'Wonderful. My engines are dead. My owner's in tears. My poor cook's losing his marbles. My tow's been in a gun battle. And my chief engineer's drunk.' Shit happens? Mike Fulton didn't know the half of it.

'I'm not in tears.'

'I ain't drunk.'

Kevin took a deep breath. Ageing ten years in a minute

felt pretty good. 'It's okay, everybody. Leo, go help Roberto. Tell him everything's going to be fine when you bend on that messenger. J.D., drop the jug. I need your head on straight for the rest of the tow. Mary, go make him some coffee. *Drop it*, J.D.!'

'. . . *Okay. It's dropped.*'

'There's got to be *something* wrong with the fuckers. EMDs don't just stop for no reason.'

'*I know . . . Hell, maybe we ought to take a look at the fuel filters.*'

'The fuel filters?'

'*I would have suggested them earlier, only I just changed them out the other day in Sheep Harbour. Maybe bouncing around the ocean stirred up a mess of sludge in the tanks . . . And if that don't work, Captain, I recommend we call them Flying Dutchmen back.*'

Hans woke up on the cabin sole saying, 'What's that smell?'

'The generator burned up. Batteries are dead. I can't run the autopilot or the pumps.'

Hans sat up, groaned, clutched his head, leaned over and vomited. Alison handed him a towel. He wiped his mouth and cast off the blanket she had draped over him. 'What happened?'

'The boat turned turtle. You went flying. The engine and generator are shot. The mast's okay.'

'How long was I unconscious?'

'Not long.'

'*How* long?'

'I don't know. I've been pumping. We shipped a ton of water.'

Hans struggled into his bunk. He cocked his ear to the water and looked out of a port. 'We're moving.'

'Not fast enough. We lost a lot of time.'

'How long to the ship?'

Alison hesitated. 'I don't know.' She had been weighing options when he woke up. She had recovered from the first shock of turning over, buoyed by survival she supposed, but was still struggling with the second, more numbing shock that she couldn't signal Uncle Richard. 'I don't even know if we have enough battery power to run the homing beacon receiver. Otherwise, all I've got is one VHF handset.'

'Then get us close enough to see him,' Hans snarled.

She would have thought that a three-sixty rollover would inspire a little more humility, but it wasn't Hans who worried her now, it was Manfred. She was re-thinking how Manfred would react when she didn't show. Impatient, impulsive, there were limits to how long he would wait, particularly if he felt abandoned. He had probably been tempted to fire a Tannenberg at the Dutch salvage tug. How long before he turned one on the Americans, or lured their tug alongside the ship and tried to take it over?

But could she make it to the ship by tonight? For her it was tonight or never with the storm in the west catching up. The tug would probably hold her head to it, but *Twice a Knight*, even heaved to, would be blown far to the east. Too far east ever to beat back against the prevailing westerlies.

She crawled into the sail bin in the forepeak.

'Where are you going?' asked Hans.

Alison came out dragging an enormous spinnaker bag, which she pulled through the cabin and up the companionway, where, pausing to open the hatch, she said, 'What I'm going to need from you is plenty of hot food, hot tea, hot soup. Whenever I bang on the hatch, you bring it up straightaway.'

'What are you doing?'

'Give us a push.' She dragged the sail through the hatch into the cold, wet cockpit and slammed the hatch shut. What she was going to do was lay *Twice a Knight* alongside *Der Schmetterling* and trip the distress lever on her Argos transmitter to pinpoint the missiles for Uncle Richard. If she could reach the ship in time.

There were really only two ways to sail very fast: fly the best sails for the conditions, which she was already doing; or take chances you would not take if all you cared about was staying alive. The yacht was already flying at its limit of hull speed under reefed main and storm jib. A spinnaker would plane her on a surf ride and damn near double velocity. But the wind was blowing too hard for a spinnaker.

Even if she could somehow set the huge sail in this wind, it would take every skill she possessed to keep the boat from broaching, or rolling on to her side, or even pitchpoling, if *Twice a Knight* drove her nose into a sea.

She dragged the light nylon spinnaker forward to the bow, where she secured it to the lifelines so it wouldn't wash overboard while she hooked one end of the heavy spinnaker pole to its track on the mast and ran a spider web of sheets and guys to the cockpit. She moved carefully on the wet, pitching deck, gradually losing herself in the routine and the joint-tearing, muscle-burning spurts of effort to lift the pole.

Much bigger than the mainsail and the storm jib combined, the spinnaker was encased in a long sock to keep it from filling before she was ready. She clipped a halyard to its head and hoisted it up the mast, where it hung down like a giant sausage. When she opened the sock, the spinnaker boomed open and filled the sky in front of the boat, dark as a blue thunderhead.

Twice a Knight leaped like a dog kicked from sleep, rolling and yawing until Alison got control of the helm. Then the boat skittered across a broad ocean trough, eagerly climbed the back of a swell, burst over the top, and planed like a surfboard down the front.

Alison caressed the helm, steering by instincts developed as a child sailing dinghies. Numbers flickered like elevator floors on the digital speedometer. Ten, twelve, thirteen knots. At fourteen knots, *Twice a Knight*'s little rudder grew so responsive that the slightest miscalculation could hurl the boat into chaos. Fear threatened to overwhelm her, just as the wind would overwhelm the flying yacht. But fear channelled actually sharpened her senses: she began to believe she could predict the wind shifts in advance, and how the water would lie on the far side of the crests.

On the cabin roof ahead of the cockpit was the Argos with its own electrical supply — solar panels under the dummy Lexan hatch cover. The second she spotted *Der Schmetterling* she would reach in and move the distress lever.

The *Bowery Queen*'s heavy tow wire sank a thousand feet, drawing the stricken tugboat closer and closer to *Der Schmetterling*. While Kevin Patrick tore down and cleaned her fuel filters, Leo and little Roberto battled the thick nylon messenger line on to the end of the tow wire. Then they released it from the winch and eased it over the stern, buying a little time before the plunging hulls crashed together. The wire dragged the messenger after it. When it ran out, they bent on a floating polypropylene hawser and attached floats to it. The towline dragged them under like a snapping turtle drowning ducks.

Leo sent Roberto in to rest, while he went up to the wheelhouse and stood with his hand on the useless steering stick, watching the ship grow taller on the sky. Up there, he knew, J.D. was trying to figure out how the filters had got clogged, so it wouldn't happen again.

'Leo?'

'Yes, J.D.'

'Something's wrong with Kev's radio. You want to run him down another and tell him I think I know what happened. We been drawing on the Number Seven bunker and I think a mess a sludge got riled up in these seas and we drew down a little too far. So, we got to drain the day tank back into Seven and forget that fucker. Then tap Eight and Nine and not draw down so deep. That ought to do it. Only thing is, it's going to reduce our running time by a week or so.'

Leo relayed the message. Kevin drained the day tank.

While he was waiting for clean fuel to pump into it, he came up for air and a cigarette and radioed J.D. He was getting about as tired as he had been the night of the ice. 'You want to run me through the start procedure?'

J.D. started to explain how to blow out the cylinders.

'Fuck that. The ship's going to eat us. Tell me how to fire one up fast.'

By the time Kevin had pre-lubed the turbocharger and established he had oil pressure, the sinking tow wire had pulled the tug within twenty yards of the drifting ship. The air starter screamed. The port engine turned over, heavily. Kevin hit the starter again. And again. He radioed J.D.

'It won't start.'

'*Okay. You know the control panel?*'

'Yeah?'

'*Down on the lower left, you'll see a dent where it looks like somebody kicked the sumbitch?*'

'Yeah? I see it.'

'*Kick it there.*'

'J.D., for Chrissake, we're about to hit.'

'*Kick it. Don't ask me. Just kick it.*'

Mary cut in on her radio. '*It's true, Kevin. Uncle Charlie used to kick it there.*'

Kevin slammed his sneaker into the control panel. The starter screamed. The engine turned over once and rumbled, whistled and wheezed to life.

Black smoke issued from the port stack.

Kevin rang up the wheelhouse. 'Leo. Go.'

Leo blew the whistle and eased the motor into forward. Down at the stern Roberto leaned over the bulwark, trying to hold the floating line away from the propeller with a boathook. The cook waved the 'all clear'. Leo gave her some throttle and the *Bowery Queen* pulled slowly away from the ship. Kevin ran into the wheelhouse, breathing hard. 'Okay, I got her. Let's get the wire back.'

Leo and Roberto hauled the polypropylene line aboard with the capstan, shucking off the floats as they came, and hauled up the nylon hawser until the end of the wire came over the stern. They led it forward with a messenger to the main winch, got it started around the barrel and winched in two hundred feet. Finally, they attached the chafing gear and worked it over the stern.

Pulling at one-third power, Kevin turned the helm over to Leo and went down to the engine room to start the starboard engine. When he got back to the wheelhouse, the sky was dark in the east. High altitude winds were shredding the cloud cover, revealing glimmers of a waning moon, as if the gathering storm was clearing the stage for a special performance. In the south-west, where the storm would make its entrance, the sun set in sombre black and yellow.

Roberto had collapsed in one of the captain's chairs. Leo looked like a man about to die on his feet. Kevin reached for the steering stick. Leo stopped him. 'You better get some rest, Captain.'

Kevin was surprised to see his hands shaking. He could barely speak. 'Okay. An hour. Call me if anything goes wrong.' He started down the steps. 'At this point, it's a little hard to imagine anything more going wrong.'

Leo knocked the wooden ceiling and Roberto woke up to cross himself.

'Boags? Is that you on the containers?'

For one crazy second, Mary thought she was hallucinating when she saw a man run across the containers. Alone on *Der Schmetterling*'s bridge as night closed, she had been staring ahead, over the four hundred feet of stacked containers between her and *Der Schmetterling*'s bow. The *Queen* was pulling proudly now – a full five knots – and she was watching to warn the tug if the ship sheered off on one of its sudden yaws. Every few minutes she tried Boags on the walkie-talkie, but he was working far below.

The light was spooky. Broken clouds scudded across the sky, backlit by a shard of old moon. The beams that streamed between them scattered moving patterns over black troughs and white crests. Ahead of the ship, on a shifting sea of shadows, flickered the *Bowery Queen*'s three white towing lights and, now and then, a red spark from her stacks.

The shadow had passed between her and the *Bowery Queen*'s towing lights. They seemed to vanish for a second, exactly as if a man had darted across the top of the containers.

Mary shivered and gripped the locked helm, and stared long and hard at the moon-dappled sea. Her uncles used to swap stories of seamen hallucinating on night watch. Next she would spy a galleon in the moonlight with the Flying Dutchman at the helm.

She picked up the binoculars and scanned the moonlit container tops; then she went out on the bridge wing and stared aft. There was little to see of the ship, other than the containers. The wind was bitter cold. She scanned the ocean: nothing but an endless waste dotted with a million white caps under a shifting sky.

What if, after the gunfight, a crewman *had* stayed aboard when the rest abandoned ship? Some poor soul, wounded and hiding in terror after the shooting, only to wake up to the sight of her and J.D. and Boags clambering aboard like pirates? What if — God help her — the *captain* had stayed aboard? Was the ship even legally abandoned? What if — this was too crazy — but what if, as they passed under the Verrazano Bridge, having towed the ship eighteen hundred miles to New York, the captain popped out of hiding and said to the lawyers, 'I never signed a Lloyd's Open Form.'

Crazy? The lawyers would wallow: the captain was frightened; the captain was intimidated; gunfire; mutiny. Thank you, *Bowery Queen*; here's tug time for your trouble.

'Boags?' she called again, and when the seaman didn't answer, she radioed Kevin on the tug, not entirely sure she wanted to share her thinking with him if it meant he would insist on taking them off the ship.

'Yeah, Mary.'

'Oh, Christ!'

'What's wrong?' Kevin yanked his feet off the dash and whirled round to check the tow. The lights were holding position. Then he heard a siren over the radio. J.D. had hooked up *Der Schmetterling*'s bridge alarms so the watch could rouse the sleeping hands. Mary had tripped it.

'What's wrong, Mary?'

'*Something's crashing around the hold. I —*'

At that her radio died.

Kevin called. 'Mary. Mary? . . . J.D.? . . . Boags. You there, Boagsie?'

'*I'm here, Kev*,' said J.D. '*Generator blew. We'll talk to you on the handsets.*'

'Can you fix it?'

'*Not before we tie down what got loose in the hold.*'

EIGHTEEN

The end came suddenly.

Alison Knight had kept the spinnaker up, and *Twice a Knight* afloat, hours longer than she had any right to hope. The wind had risen after dark and snow squalls were savaging the moonlit horizon, sending out fierce gusts that caused the yacht to develop a peculiar roll. Suddenly dipping the spinnaker pole into the water, the sail backed, then filled and dragged her over. Alison steered out of it, icily avoiding the over-correction which would careen the boat too far to the other side.

A vicious cross sea knocked the boat's head up. The sail collapsed on top and started to twist into an hourglass shape. Invincible, she steered out of it, and *Twice a Knight* rewarded her by planing along with a burst of speed – an incredible eighteen knots – the fastest the yacht had ever gone.

Hans flung open the hatch, his eyes shining. He waved the homing receiver. 'Manfred's close. It's beeping.' Not a moment too soon. She rose to douse the spinnaker.

Something – her greatly heightened awareness, or a cold breath on her cheek – made her look back in the moonlight. The water was ruffled by a powerful gust chasing after her. The gust caught up and banged into the fully-bellied sail. *Twice a Knight* surged, hydroplaned like a racing dinghy. Skimming the surface, she tried to rise out of the water. Alison kept her dead even. To dip the pole at this speed would be catastrophic. Nineteen knots.

A tremendous explosion shook the yacht. Alison blinked in disbelief. There was an enormous spread of moonlit sky where the spinnaker had been. Staggered off its plane by the sudden power loss, the boat fell into the solid arms of the water.

The spinnaker had failed at the masthead. As it fell, it blew ahead of the boat, flapping like a giant blanket aired by a vigorous chambermaid. The water snared it. Alison tried to turn, but the boat skidded sideways and broached to a rising sea that lifted it high, then dropped it hard, smack on top of the sail.

'What happened?' Hans yelled.

She shone a light over the side into the cold black water. *Twice a Knight* was stopped dead with a thousand square feet of nylon tangled around her keel.

'There!' Hans screamed. 'There he is!'

Square as a biscuit tin, heaped with cargo boxes, *Der Schmetterling* had materialized in a patch of ocean vacated by one of the squalls. Alison felt the racing sailor's thrill at finally sighting a competitor, and the familiar tightening she got in her throat whenever Manfred was near. Hans was clumsily focusing night glasses on the ship. She climbed past him on to the cabin, made a show of stowing the spinnaker poles, and reached under the dummy hatch to trip the Argos distress lever.

Pain like a bee sting shot up her finger. She pulled it out, bleeding, and shone her flashlight inside. The Argos looked as though someone had driven a lorry over it – or, more likely, jabbed it with a boathook while she was sleeping.

Hans was watching her. 'Sail,' he said. 'The ship is getting away.'

The freighter was moving into the teeth of the wind, the tugboat dragging it away, while *Twice a Knight* might as well be anchored to the ocean floor, for all the sailing it would do before she cut the spinnaker free.

'Sail,' said Hans.

She sucked the blood from her finger. Killing, Uncle Richard had once said in his cups, was quite simple once one had made one's mind up. Focus on a simple thought – him or me. And if you're still too gentle, try right or wrong.

254

'I can't sail,' she said. 'We're stuck. The spinnaker's wrapped around the keel.'

'Fix it.'

The question still was, what would Manfred do if she didn't show? The likeliest answer: his worst.

She went below, pulled on a rubber diving suit — a wetsuit intended for nothing colder than a chilly day in the Caribbean — sharpened her rigging knife, and came up with a twenty-pound mushroom anchor which she shackled to one of the spinnaker sheets and dropped overboard.

'Hurry,' yelled Hans. The tugboat's lights were pinpricks on the horizon.

She rigged a ladder, tied a line around her waist, and plunged with rigging knife and diving light feet first into the sea. The inch of skin between her gloves and her wetsuit sleeves, and parts of her face not covered by the balaclava hood, burned as if the cold water was fire. The hull pounded up and down on a frothy bed of bubbles. Probing with the diving light, she tried to get her bearings and distinguish the rudder and the keel. She ran out of air before she could, broke surface, and dived deeper.

A huge dark shadow reached for her. She kicked away in terror, the flippers carrying her fast and far before she recognized the blue spinnaker billowing in the swell. She went back with the light and groaned through the snorkel. It looked as though a practical joker in scuba gear had spent an hour knotting the sail between keel and rudder.

The rudder, slashing up and down, would be the hardest, so she went there first, after surfacing for another gulp of air. It still looked like a butter knife, a lethal, plunging butter knife. Clinging to it with one glove, she tugged the sail with the other. One end had tangled around the useless propeller. She slashed it with her rigging knife, surfaced twice for air, and dived again to attack the keel. Freed, the sail streamed down, dragged to oblivion by the anchor.

Twice a Knight started sailing suddenly, pushed hard by the wind on her bare mast. Alison's diving line jerked up and dragged her behind the boat. She kicked her flippers and pulled herself hand over hand to the ladder, fighting the wake. The stern looked twenty feet high. Exhausted by the repeated dives, she clung to the bottom rung, trailing behind the boat, waiting for the strength to return to her arms.

'Hans,' she called. 'Help me.'

Hans leaned over the lifeline, smirking, 'It's a trick.' He produced a small, ugly pistol and aimed down at her. 'Get in the boat.'

'I can't. And you can't sail.' At this statement of the obvious, Hans hesitated. 'Put on my safety harness, slip it onto the padeye – that's the stainless steel circle in the cockpit . . . Okay, you're safe. Now give me a hand up.'

Clipped to the boat, he leaned over and tried to help her, but he couldn't reach far enough and she fell back into the water. She came up gasping, clutching at the ladder. 'Listen to me. Unclip from the padeye and clip on to the stanchion here so you can reach me. Hurry, Manfred's getting away.'

Hans did as she said, leaned over the lifeline and pulled her up with both hands. When she had one foot firmly on deck, she gasped 'Thanks,' swung her other leg over the lifeline, and yanked Hans through the ladder opening. His surprised scream cut short when his head went underwater. Pulled along by his harness, he flailed at the bottom rung of the ladder until Alison took her rigging knife from her boot and cut the nylon tether.

He held on, cursing her, threatening, then begging, 'I didn't mean any harm.' The cold sapped his strength. In two minutes he was gone.

She dragged herself, shaking violently, into the cockpit. *Der Schmetterling* had vanished. She unfurled her jib, sheeted in the main, and began beating to windward. When she looked back, there was no sign of Hans.

Manfred's homing signal was a crude guide, supposedly

beeping louder to indicate proximity. It sounded to her as though the battery was running down. She tacked repeatedly, sailing as close to the wind as *Twice a Knight* would allow.

Blinded by the moonlight shifting on the rolling sea, she was on the verge of giving up when she thought she smelled the stink of diesel on the wind. The swell dropped her into a trough where she saw nothing. The next lifted her high. Confused and disoriented, she scanned the desolation: breaking crests in the moonlight; shadowy planes in between. A cloud streamed across the moon and in its shadow she saw the bright column of the tugboat's towing lights.

It was off her port bow, half a mile ahead and a mile to her left. She had blundered alongside the dark ship. She saw it now, shadowed against the moonlit clouds, and then a tiny opening in the hull, marked by a dim yellow square of light, low on the waterline.

Wheeling a welding outfit, a carbide saw and a portable generator, the salvors headed forward through D Hold guided by the screech of tortured metal and the rhythmic boom of the bulldozer pulverizing *Der Schmetterling*'s hull.

An acrid odour stung Mary's nostrils. Fire, she thought, dragging the generator between rows of trucks, but it wasn't fire. A familiar odour that made no sense.

'What's that smell?'

J.D. and Boags had forged ahead and now stood at the edge of a vast deck slick with oil. 'Look out!' said J.D. He threw up his arm, pushing Mary back into the tethered trucks. A steam roller whizzed by, caroming against the trucks, freeing one with a bang of broken steel.

'Do you smell that?'

'Diesel exhaust. If I didn't know better I'd say some son of a bitch started up those trucks and busted them loose. Maybe that generator didn't stop by itself, either — Look out, Boags! That sumbitch'll squash you.'

The steam roller came back the other way, tore loose

257

the truck they were sheltering behind, and crashed on. They started the portable generator and were aiming work lights on the moving wreckage, when with a resounding *BOOM* the bulldozer rocked hard against the barn door that Boags and Mary had spent the day caulking with canvas. Water rushed gleaming under bent steel.

'Mary, run up where you can radio Kev. Tell him maybe we got a crazy aboard and shit sliding all over the place. Tell him to slow down to two knots and head into the wind so she'll roll a little less till we hogtie that machine. Here's the gun. Safety's off. Shoot the first son of a bitch you see and shoot him again. Can you do that?'

Mary nodded, thinking that after what they'd been through for *Der Schmetterling* she could shoot her own father if he got in the way.

J.D. looked at her hard. Satisfied, he said, 'Then get your tail right back down here. We gotta shore up the door soon as we get everything settled down.' As he spoke the bulldozer came sliding slowly back at the door, now protected by a van from which Boags was exiting hurriedly. J.D. sauntered towards it, put on a burst of speed, and vaulted on to the treads and into the cab. Mary ran to the stairs and as she headed up to the bridge to radio Kevin, she heard its engine roar to life.

Her radio was running down and she had to climb all the way to the bridge before Kevin answered her signal. 'J.D. says slow down. The bulldozer got loose again.'

'*How the hell did that happen?*'

'We . . .' she hesitated. 'We might have that stowaway.'

'*Jesus Christ. I'm coming around and taking all three of you off right now.*'

'No.'

Kevin weighed the threat posed by a stowaway against the danger of disembarking three people from a dead ship in the dark. If the gunman who had shot up *Der Schmetterling*'s bridge started shooting again, then his riding crew was lost at the end of a two-thousand-foot wire. But they could end up equally dead crushed between two hulls at

258

ight. At least he should wait for dawn. Except the clouds
scudding past the moon looked like the depression roaring
after them would soon kick up seas that would make disembarking impossible. It was a boat handling job, after all,
and the *Bowery Queen*'s crew was safer with him than some
crazy with a gun.

'Okay. Get together with J.D. and Boags, right now. Don't
separate. While I'm slowing down, you finish shoring up that
door. Soon as I can stop the tow, I'll swing around and take you
off. We'll lower the lifeboat. Figure a half-hour before I can get
her stopped. Fifteen, twenty minutes turning around. I'll have
you off in an hour.'

Perfect, thought Manfred, who had listened in on his own
radio since the salvors first boarded. The ship would stand
like a five-hundred-foot-long, eighty-foot-high wall
between him and the salvors struggling to board the tug
on the other side while he launched his raft and waited
for Alison.

'But we can't leave him,' the woman protested. 'He
sabotaged the barn door.'

'Why the hell would he sabotage the ship he's on?'

'Maybe he's a nut. But the ship —'

The captain cut her off. 'He's got guns, for Crissake. I'll
call the Coast Guard to board her.'

'That will take days. Weeks. It could sink.'

'My crew is coming the fuck off. You've got one hour to seal
that door and abandon ship!'

The captain clicked off his radio, punctuating his command, but the woman didn't notice as she shouted back
in a voice afire with eagerness and rage. 'There's one of
him and three of us. I'm not letting the son of a bitch take my
ship.'

'*Hündin*,' Manfred cursed. Mary would wreck everything. He ran to *Laderaum C*, pausing in the corridor to
open his trousers and piss on the deck, and stepping in the
puddle.

*

259

Mary ran down the stairs. Kevin was right about one thing: they were safer together. But when she passed the door to C Hold, she skidded to a stop.

The watertight door was open. The first thing they had done was shut every door they found open. She never went through one without sealing it behind her. Scalp pricking, she edged closer and peered down the corridor that connected the stairwell to the hold. The interior door was open, too, and wet bootprints gleamed in the light.

'Boags, J.D.'

She could hear the carbide saw howling on the deck below.

The gun, cold and heavy, made her brave. She pushed through the door, down the corridor, and shone her flashlight over the sea of bobbing Mercedes. Nothing moved. Shielding her light with her fingers, she crept through the interior door into C Hold itself. Steel clinked in the dark. She turned off her light, backed against a cold bulkhead, and peered, blinking until her eyes adjusted. The cars whispered and sighed on their springs. The ship creaked.

'J.D.' she breathed into the radio.

A ribbon of light flickered between rows two hundred feet ahead. Mary eased among the cars, gun in one hand, radio on Transmit in the other. The light moved, further into the dark. She followed, silent in her rubber boots, scarcely breathing. It was pitch black. She cocked her elbow and let it bump along the cars as she followed the light down the narrow corridor. She counted cars as she went, her rubberized jacket squeaking on metal. Twenty feet per car? Ten cars brought her close to the point where she had first seen the light. Far ahead, it went out.

She turned away to muffle her whispered, 'J.D.'

J.D. answered in a voice that began like thunder as she tried to screw down the volume control while juggling gun and light and radio. '*WHERE THE Hell are you, gal?*'

'Right above you,' she whispered. 'In C Hold.'

'*Say again — Boags, stop that infernal racket! Say again, Mare?*'

'I'm in C Hold.'

The light flickered again, further ahead, and she glided after it. 'I found the stowaway,' she whispered. Metal banged heavily in the dark. 'I think he just opened a manhole to the storeroom ahead of D . . . Oh, Christ, there's a door down there! Hurry!'

She ran. When they had surveyed the ship after boarding she had found a twelve-by-eight accommodation door in the hull. It was right on the water line, for loading from lighters, and the fear was careening through her head that a guy crazy enough to release the cargo would open it to let the sea in.

Light bloomed through an open manhole. She crept closer, knelt in utter silence. Stretching out prone on the deck, she inched towards the rim of the manhole. A steel ladder descended to the storeroom.

She saw a flashlight rolling on the deck below, and by its moving beam a rectangular opening in the hull. The sea rushed by, waves breaking on the sill. Then the ship careened. A foot of water poured over the sill and spilled through the grating and gurgled down to the bilges. She saw an orange four-man canopy life raft beside the accommodation door. Next to the raft lay three rectangular bundles of some sort of tubing. A fourth bundle had apparently fallen through the manhole, bursting its bindings, scattering four tubes. One − a length of six-inch plastic pipe − had shattered. And spilling from the broken end was something that anyone who had ever seen 'coming attractions' for a technothriller would recognize as a weapon.

Sealed in clear plastic bubble wrap, it appeared to be a launching tube with a handle and trigger, a telescope sight, and a fat warhead protruding from the barrel. Mary stood up in astonishment. *Der Schmetterling*'s stowaway was no crazy. He was a man with a plan. The weapons, the raft, the open door all meant that the stowaway had sabotaged the tow to slow it down so that he could get off.

'Let him,' she thought, backing away from the manhole.

'Good riddance. The sooner the better.' Poised to turn and run, she suddenly recalled the stricken expressions on the faces of the *Bowery Queen*'s crew when they heard *Der Schmetterling*'s lifeboat had foundered. Leo had muttered in Tagalog, and pressed for a translation had said, 'When a seaman dies we all die.'

Despite herself she leaned forward again and counted nineteen tubes. They must be extraordinarily deadly for someone to smuggle nineteen missile launchers in a world full of weapons ... Just beyond the open door the sea rushed by, two thousand fathoms deep. Twelve thousand feet. Two and a half miles straight down, far beyond the reach of a man who would send fifteen sailors to their death.

Steel clinked behind her. Before she could move, something moaned out of the dark. A length of chain wrapped, stinging, around her calves, and fetched up with a tremendous yank. Her feet were jerked out from under her and she fell head first through the manhole.

Flailing wildly as she fell, Mary jammed her left arm between the ladder rungs. Her body pivoted around her shoulder. She heard something tear inside her and screamed with the ferocity of the pain that shot from fingertips to skull. Her feet crashed to the deck. Kicking the chain from her legs, she tripped and lost her balance on the flashlight the stowaway had tossed through the manhole to trick her into thinking he was already there.

He came down the ladder fast, a six-foot-four-inch guy in his thirties, with a hard mouth and eyes like ice. He held the chain in one hand, twirling a knot tied in the links. Mary dived for the captain's Luger that she had dropped. He snapped it off the deck and threw it out of the accommodation door. Then he pulled a pistol from his coat, pointed it at her face, and said in a heavy German accent, 'Tell J.D. you're on the boat deck.'

He scooped Mary's radio off the deck and tossed it to her. To her whirling brain, stunned by the fall and rattled with pain, everything he did seemed fast. But of everything going on and every question roaring in her mind, one thing was frighteningly clear. He had listened in on their walkie-talkies since they had boarded. He knew who was aboard, who was on the tug. Directing J.D. and Boags to the boat deck would be the end of her.

She feigned confusion, closed her eyes and shook her head. A stinging blow snapped her head, knocked her down and flipped her eyes open.

'Tell him you're on the boat deck. Tell him Kevin is turning back to take you off.'

Movement on the ladder caught her eye, and before she could stop herself she betrayed Boags, who swung through the manhole like a monkey. The German exploded into motion as if her face were a mirror reflecting Boags as big as life. He whirled on the boy, tucking the gun in close to his body, swinging the chain.

Boags landed lightly, ducked the whizzing chain, spun completely around on one foot and kicked backward. The German's gun twinkled out of his hand, sailed through the accommodation door and vanished in the sea. Boags continued spinning. His other foot flew from the deck, blurred through the air in a perfect circle and arced into the German's elbow.

The stowaway sucked in his breath. His big hand convulsed and the chain clanked to the deck. Boags, still whirling, launched a third kick at the man's throat. His foot connected with a wet thud that flung the German hard against the bulkhead. His eyes glazed. Boags danced, left, right, left, right, lining up another shot. The German shook his head, blearily tracking him. Boags feinted. The German lunged and the boy launched a kick to the face that dropped the bigger man to his knees.

'Run, Mary.'

She tried to rise. Boags feinted again, whirled in the air, and sunk his boot into the German's chest. The German fell backwards. He rose with an effort of sheer willpower, but his arms hung at his sides, and his massive frame seemed to sag. Boags went straight at him – no longer bothering to feint as he gathered his body and spirit for a final killing blow.

Mary saw Boags's mistake before he did, saw the gleam of triumph in the German's eyes. She cried a warning, but Boags was already in motion, tricked into thinking the German was defenceless. The stowaway slipped the kick like a boxer slipping a punch. Boags's foot banged harmlessly on his shoulder and the next instant it was seized and jerked higher. He landed hard on his back.

Still holding Boags's foot, the stowaway kicked him in the head with a force that shook the boy's body. Mary lunged to her feet and swung the flashlight. A knitted watchcap flew, revealing a bright shock of white-blond hair. The stowaway knocked her down with a backhanded slap.

He stood back and kicked again. Mary dragged Boags towards the shelter of the ladder. The stowaway followed them, kicking. Boags struck back. The attacker brushed his hands aside, ripped the boy out of Mary's arms and carried him to the open door.

'No,' she screamed. Boags wrapped his arms around the stowaway's head and gouged his eyes. The stowaway broke his fingers with a snap and flung him through the door.

'No,' Mary screamed again. She stared at the black hole of the sea in disbelief. One second he was here, the next gone, in pain and cold and fear. She heard him cry once, 'Mary,' but distant already, far from help. And now the stowaway was coming for her. He knocked the flashlight out of her hand, seized the loose folds of her boiler suit, yanked her to the door and set his legs to heave.

She went limp in his hands — a last-ditch trick her women's defence instructor had taught the class. Then, as he lifted her, she used his grip as a base and levered both heels hard as she could into his knee. He gave a furious gasp, let go and punched her. She scrambled to the ladder, with hot salt spurting in her mouth.

'*Manfred.*' A walkie-talkie, thin on its last batteries.

Stunned by the punch, head reeling, Mary looked for hers, but it was Manfred who pulled a radio from his coat and snapped, 'Where are you?'

A woman's voice. '*Starboard. I see a light. Is that you? Where's the raft?*'

'Fuck the raft. Come alongside!'

He peered out into the dark. Mary climbed the ladder. Two rungs. Three. Shoulders through the manhole. Manfred pounced, and dragged her down kicking and screaming to the door. A wave broke over the sill, soaking her to the waist. He shook her like a rag and lifted her.

An access hatch from D Hold slammed open with a steel *boom*. J.D. filled the opening. 'Just put the little lady back where you found her.'

'Look out,' Mary screamed. 'He killed Boags.'

The Mississippian moved a lot faster than she would have guessed possible. The stowaway shoved Mary at him, kicking her legs out from under her so that she sprawled on the deck in his path. J.D. nimbly side-stepped, but he had been set up. The stowaway took a quick step forward and punched the still-moving J.D. in the side of his head with a sound like steel hitting wood. J.D.'s glasses flew.

The German darted in again, swinging hard lefts and rights. J.D. turned ponderously, raising his big forearms to meet a hail of punches. Several skidded between them, reddening his face, opening a cut on his cheek.

Mary had attended enough prize fights with her father to recognize a trained boxer. Though the German weighed fifty pounds less than J.D., he began to cut the engineer down, blow by well-aimed blow. She looked for a weapon.

J.D. bellowed. A fist had caught him full on the nose and blood gushed. Mary gathered her strength and crawled to a coil of wire rope. It was too big. She couldn't lift it. She found a flashlight and swung at Manfred's leg. He kicked her aside and turned again on J.D.

The giant pulled a broken tooth from his mouth and tossed it contemptuously in Manfred's face. 'Trouble with rastling a feller who's learned a mite of boxing is, you got to take a little pain to figure out his moves.' He spat blood, raised his big hands and moved towards Manfred. 'Tell you this, I've seen better.'

He kept his hands open, batting at Manfred the way black kids street-jived. The German swung hard, scored on J.D.'s cheek. But when he swung again, his arm disappeared as J.D. let the punch slide past his head, grabbed his shoulder and drew him close.

The German gave a startled shout which turned to a groan as J.D. squeezed him in his arms. He levered a knee into J.D.'s groin. The engineer's legs buckled and he fell, still holding the stowaway, who landed on top and squirmed free. Leaping up, he kicked J.D.

He bellowed shock. J.D. had him again, pinning his legs, drawing him in as he stood, lifting him, squeezing like a python. Growling with effort, J.D. lifted him chest-high, turned him in the air, and slammed him down on the deck. And sunk his engineer boots into Manfred's ribs. When the German stopped struggling, J.D. then picked him up, whirled him overhead and hurled him against the steel bulkhead. Manfred slid to the deck, and lay still.

'You all right, Mare?' J.D. knelt beside her, breath rasping through his bloody nose and broken teeth. 'Here, I'll get something to cover you.'

'Look out,' she whispered.

J.D. had already caught motion in the corner of his eye. Puzzled, he rose to do battle again. The stowaway was something else. Bear-hugged, stomped and slung against the bulkhead, he was getting up and coming back for more. And judging from the crazy grin on his face, the dude was enjoying himself. J.D. figured this time he was just going to have to throw him a little farther.

He never saw the chain.

The knotted links smacked him behind the ear like a steel fist. He saw a blinding flash of what he could only call black light. He had been kicked almost as hard, once, by an ornery mule. The difficulty that time had been the animal's desire to finish the job by trampling him into the mud. There'd be no trampling this time. He was flying through the open door, as if he had sprouted wings, and God had no mules in His ocean.

The icy sea water cleared J.D.'s head like the first beer of the morning. Thirty degrees Fahrenheit. Three minutes to get out before he froze to death. The ship slid by, the lighted storeroom accommodation door far from reach. His heavy boots were dragging him down. He kicked them off. Everything was fuzzy-looking; he had lost his glasses.

Then he thought he had lost his mind because he saw something that looked very much like the pointed bow of a boat bearing down on him. He tried to wave with a leaden arm. The cold had sucked up his strength. A holler for help came out a croak. In an instant the boat had gone the way of the ship.

Where it had come from — and where it was going — would be a mystery he would carry to an early grave.

Der Schmetterling's wake broke over his head. He thought of his wife and their passel of kids. Funny how in his memory's eye even the grown ones looked like children, and his wife like a girl. A strange feeling tightened his guts and squeezed his heart. He turned it over slowly in his mind. Maybe it was the cold, but it bore a strong similarity to what he had heard about fear.

The wind gusted crazily beside the ship, crackling *Twice a Knight*'s sails like gunfire as Alison tried to turn the boat round. The rudder wouldn't bite. The wind was everywhere. The moving ship exerted a tidal pull on her hull, drawing her to the open door.

Flashlights rolling around on the deck inside flickered on a big orange survival raft and bundles of tubes, which had to be the Tannenberg missiles. As she drew closer, she saw some had broken loose. Suddenly Manfred was there in all his splendour. Moonlight fell across his chiselled face and golden crown of hair and he looked like a Viking prince on a raid as he leaned out of the door, legs braced around a mooring bollard, swinging a chain.

The chain sang through the air and tangled around the wire shrouds that guyed the mast. Manfred wrapped his end around the bollard and *Twice a Knight* stopped short, crashing sideways against the ship with a bang that shook her keel.

His eyes were hot with action. She had seen him many times like this, at the helm, shooting stag, and always in bed. He offered his hand with an ironic smile — their traditional *Hello again* at regattas. Alison took it and stepped on to the ship, with a long shot in her heart.

'I know about the Tannenbergs. Leave them. I can save us.'

His smile vanished. 'Hans said you — Where is he?'

'Overboard. It's just us: I love you. Come.' She searched his face for something soft. But there were no tears for his brother. Nor joy in her love.

'You silly bitch. How do we sell the missiles without Hans?'

Twice a Knight fetched into the ship with a sickening crack of fibreglass against steel. Manfred upended the rubber raft and dropped it between the crashing hulls like an enormous fender.

'Load the boat!'

He seized two of the bundles, grunting with effort, and slung them down to the cockpit. 'Get those!' he pointed at the loose tubes, swinging the third bundle aboard the sailboat.

'Look out! He killed them.'

Alison saw a frightened young woman struggling to climb a ladder towards a manhole in the ceiling. Her face was rigid with pain and horror. One arm dangled like a rope. She had stopped climbing to warn Alison, assuming — Alison realized with a sinking heart — that no woman could possibly be partner to Manfred's crimes.

Manfred slapped her. 'Load the boat. I didn't kill anybody. He fell overboard trying to kill me.'

The blow stung, the contempt twisting his face cut deeper. There was no love in his abuse, nor even perverse pleasure, merely expediency. He had hit her to make her do what he wanted. Like driving an animal through a gate.

Disgusted with her weakness and her clumsy hopes, she bent to release the chain and cast *Twice a Knight* adrift with the Tannenbergs. Before she could, Manfred hit her again, a backhand blow that slammed her against the door frame. With an athlete's economy of motion, she drew her rigging knife from the sheath in her boot and slashed up at his throat. Against anyone but Manfred Echtheit the razor edge would have severed arteries. Faster than flame in the wind, he recoiled. Her blade caught the bone of his chin and slid over it, up his cheek, opening a deep white line which spouted blood.

Manfred screamed, but he was already moving. The blood distracted her long enough to roundhouse a fist into the softness of her body. She flew toward the ladder in a crumpled heap, retching and gasping for air.

Ignoring his wound, Manfred scooped up the loose tubes of missiles. He leaped on to *Twice a Knight*'s cabin, flung off the chain, jumped into the cockpit, grabbed the tiller and hit the engine start. Alison always took good care of equipment. He expected the engine to crank ferociously and fire, but the batteries were dead.

He had to sail her off.

The wind was funnelling down the side of the ship. He let the jib sheets loose, ran forward and backed the sail way out by hand. It filled, reluctantly, and began pulling the boat. The motion was sluggish. She wouldn't answer the tiller.

He found himself sailing, after a fashion, alongside the ship at a shallow angle. When he tried simply to stop and let the freighter pass, the ship sucked him back. He filled the jib again and made her sail, slowly drawing ahead, creeping up on the bow. Once there, he could sheer off and be gone on a broad reach before the tug crew knew what had happened.

Mary slid down the ladder. The Englishwoman was retching like a dying animal. The sailboat was pulling away, sails ghostly in the cloud-spattered moonlight.

'What are those missiles?'

'Nerve gas. Stop him.'

Mary crawled around the deck, feeling for her radio.

'Kevin?'

'*We're slowing down*,' Kevin answered from the quiet of the *Bowery Queen*'s wheelhouse. '*I'll commence swinging back in five minutes*.'

'Listen to me,' she cut him off. She was crying, gasping air in shuddering breaths. 'The stowaway is escaping along the starboard side in a sailboat.'

'*What?*'

'He's smuggling missiles. Nerve gas. He killed Boags and J.D. Get him!'

'Killed J.D.?' She sounded hysterical, except for her steely 'Get him!'

Kevin switched on the spotlight, tore off the drip rag, and beamed it back at the ship. '*I don't see a sailboat . . . Are you okay — Jesus! There he is.*'

The sails were brilliant triangles in the light, the brightest, cleanest things he had seen on the ocean since Nova Scotia. Boat and sails, white as Boags' Iceberg.

'*Get him!*' she cried again.

He switched on the work lights to confirm that the Norman pins were up, opened his throttles, and moved the steering stick. The *Bowery Queen* slithered into a broad turn. The heavy wire dragged hard against the starboard pin, heeling the tug at a steep angle.

He had known J.D. two years and found it impossible to imagine the giant dead. Boags he had known two weeks. The kid was like a candle in the wind and as long as Kevin lived he would never forget him spidering up the lifeboat falls.

Leo ran up the steps.

'Where'd that sailboat come from?' It was veering away from the ship and pulling ahead as it found the wind.

'Watch him close. Tell me if he moves his sails and tries to turn.' The tach needles shivered past 750. The port tail shaft started rattling. Kevin gave the engines more fuel. The stern shook. The turbochargers howled.

'That sailboat's going to hit the wire, Captain Kevin.'

'I hope so. He killed J.D. and Boags.'

Leo started, as if someone had slipped a knife in his chest. 'You serious?'

'Guy was stowed away on *Der Schmetterling*.'

'Where'd he get the sailboat?'

'Mary'll know.'

The chief mate raised the binoculars and studied the sailboat's course. Then he fixed its bearing on the radar. It was clearing the bow of the ship veering north. 'A little more starboard, Captain.'

Manfred Echtheit closed one eye against the glare of the tugboat's searchlight, clamped his slashed face with his left hand, steered with the right. The little yacht was picking up speed as it cleared the ship's suction, and an unbridled wind filled the sails. He pulled abreast of where the tow line's shock chain entered the water. Two more minutes and he could swing back behind the ship, out of the light and invisible to radar.

He watched the light, waiting for the slow, cumbersome tug to commit to a course. It was swinging north. Manfred tacked and headed south, racing between the ship and the tug. Most of the towing wire was deep underwater and he aimed for what would be the lowest point in the catenary sag.

The tug turned west.

'You want to play?' Manfred locked the tiller between his knees and stripped the bubble wrap from the Tannenberg that had burst its storage tube.

The sight worked by image memory, snapping a picture

271

of the target, imprinting it on the missile's brain, permitting the operator to lock crosshairs on the precise point he wished to strike. Manfred found the spotlight in the sight, scored the dark outline of the tug, and zeroed in on the wheelhouse windows. The sea dropped him down in a trough before he could lock on. He waited, blood running down his neck, ducked his head underwater when the boat heeled, and screamed as the brine cauterized the wound. The next roller gathered, lifting him towards the line of sight.

He heard a distant tearing sound — a noise like ripping cloth. The tug was still turning west. The search beam locked on him, laying down a broad white trail like a second moon on the waves.

He saw something dark split the trail.

It moved towards him, rising from the water, gleaming like silver. It closed swiftly, the source of the ripping noise. Then he heard the same sound to his left.

Sliding the crosshairs towards the wheelhouse, he glanced back at the ship. Dark motion rose out of the water from that direction too. It looked, even sounded, as if twin shark fins, cutting the water, were converging at great speed. He trained the missile on the tug. The thing was closer, tearing the water. The one from the ship was closer, too. They were going to meet under him.

'Hit the deck, Leo!'

Kevin hauled back on both throttles, reversing engines to take way off the tug. The wire was scything up out of the water. All he could do was try to protect the *Bowery Queen*.

The chief mate threw himself flat, covering his head in his arms. Kevin knew he should, too. You only had to see a wire part once to believe the backlash could tear the top off the wheelhouse.

Transfixed by the tow wire ripping after the sailboat, Kevin estimated four seconds to impact: one second to acknowledge that he was willing to execute a man on Mary's word, another to embrace the chance to avenge

272

his crew, a third to pray he hadn't miscalculated the angles.

A thousand feet astern, the stowaway's golden hair gleamed in the spotlight. Through Kevin's binoculars, he looked close enough to shake hands. A weapon lay easy on his shoulder.

The tug slammed to a stop. Kevin fell against the dashboard. Black water broke over the bow, climbed to the wheelhouse, and buried the towing deck.

The wire sprang from the sea — a rigid two-thousand-three-hundred-foot horizontal steel rod that picked up the sailboat. For a second it seemed to balance on its stubby keel. Then the wire cut it in two. The entire front end of the boat, cabin, mast and sails, fell on its side.

Kevin gaped in disbelief. Cushioned by *Der Schmetterling*'s anchor chain and the impact with the sailboat, the wire had not broken. And when the stern half of the boat splashed into the water, the stowaway was still standing in the cockpit, aiming his weapon.

Then the wire slashed down like a razor from the sky.

The stowaway still stood tall, still aiming, until the split halves of his body fell to either side.

Der Schmetterling yawed when the tow wire fetched up, broadside to the seas which thundered through the store-room door. The icy water that revived Alison swept her towards the opening. She crashed into the injured Mary, who was mewing with pain as she set her shoulder to the door, trying to slide it shut.

'Hang on.' Alison ducked the next wave and swam through its backwash to help. Her body ached to the core where Manfred had hit her. She couldn't stand. On hands and knees, she pushed from the bottom of the door while Mary pushed the top. Together they forced it along its tracks until the water stopped pouring in and the sea pounded angrily against it.

Mary collapsed against the bulkhead, shivering; the pain raging up and down her arm began spreading throughout her body.

'Who are you?' she asked.

'Alison Knight.' The Englishwoman extended her hand and Mary took it, thinking that if there was a woman in the world in more pain, or more tired than she was, it was Alison Knight.

'Mary Fulton. Tell me you were just sailing by and —'

'*Kev?*' Her handset crackled.

'Yeah, J.D.,' Kevin answered. '— Jesus Christ! Where *are* you?'

Mary cried, '*I hear J.D. on the radio!*'

'Get off the channel — J.D., where are you?' Kevin knew this was impossible. No one could live five minutes in the cold water. Had he crawled on to the wrecked sailboat? Impossible.

'*Kev?*'

'J.D., I'm here. Where are you?'

'*Kev, can you hear me? . . . Sumbitch!*'

'Where are you?' Kevin yelled.

Mary broke in. '*The stowaway had a raft.*'

Kevin blasted the *Bowery Queen*'s whistle until Leo came running up from the towing deck where he'd gone to look for damage.

'Drop the wire. J.D.'s out there on a raft.'

'Boags?'

'I don't know . . . Drop the wire. We got to search.'

'What kind of raft?'

'I don't know. He's transmitting, but he can't receive. Drop the fucking wire, Leo.'

The Filipino raised both hands, palms out, in a calming gesture. 'The ship is drifting nearly two knots. J.D. is a heavy man. The raft sits low in the water — not drifting so fast. He's ahead of us. Not behind.'

Kevin was trying to cram this into his exhausted brain, when Leo leaned past him for the searchlight wheel. 'Excuse me, Captain.' The beam swept the sea surface ahead.

'I don't see anything.'

The chief mate began sweeping the beam over the bow into the sky. Kevin started to order him to drop the wire, when he finally realized what Leo was doing.

'Kev,' J.D. radioed, 'I think I see your light . . . Kev? . . . It occurs to me you hear me but I can't hear you. I've managed to crawl into a canopy raft. She's International Orange and leaking like a sieve. So if you can point that light around, maybe we can figure where each other is . . . You want to blink, yes?'

Kevin switched off the searchlight, waited ten seconds, and turned it on.

The radio resonated with J.D.'s sigh. 'There's a preacher, down home, going to be flabbergasted by a certain convert to his persuasion.'

J.D. credited 'anti-freeze' as much as body fat for keeping him alive long enough to climb into the stowaway's raft that came drifting down on him. He was, however, in much worse shape than he sounded, too far weakened by hypothermia to climb out of the raft. While Kevin manoeuvred alongside, fighting the wire, and Leo manipulated the deck crane, Roberto hung from its fall to hook on to the raft's lifting eye. They hoisted the raft to the towing deck, then Leo and Roberto dragged J.D. down to the ninety-degree engine room to thaw him out.

Wrapped in blankets on the grating over the starboard EMD, he motioned Leo to lean close so he could raise his ear muff and whisper hoarsely, 'I'm real sorry about Boags, amigo. You should inform his folks that he saved Mary's life before that son of a bitch got him.'

Roberto hovered with a warm gruel of oatmeal and honey.

Leo moved aside. The *Queen*, he noticed, was unusually quiet. Her engines were idling, the propellers barely turning in their nozzles. He left the engine room, peered into Boags's empty cabin for a few minutes, then rolled up the boy's blankets and went up to the wheelhouse. The tug and tow were drifting backwards, the autopilot holding the *Queen*'s head to the seas while Kevin Patrick swept the water with his binoculars.

Dawn had broken, grudgingly. Grey light seeped through the clouds, which were stacked in deepening layers. The wind had accelerated after a few hours of relative calm, and gusts were starting to whip spray off the waves. It looked to Leo as if the big depression was coming fast and that they would remember this sullen morning as the best part of the day.

'Weather's making up.'

Kevin continued scanning the water with the binoculars.

Leo said, 'The pieces would have sunk by now.'

'I'm not looking for the sailboat.'

'I know.'

Kevin checked the autopilot, went out without a word, and climbed the ladder to the monkey island.

Leo waited half an hour. He tuned in a weather report, plotted it on the chart, and confirmed what he already knew. They would do well to head north fast. He went up and joined Kevin on top of the wheelhouse. The wind was bitter. The captain was standing with his legs braced against the railing, scanning the ocean in slow circles.

'Captain Kevin?'

'Yeah, Leo.'

'Boags is gone. There's nothing for us here.'

Kevin looked at the chief mate, took in the grey cast of exhaustion on his face, and the silver threads in his shiny jet hair, and stopped trying to hide his tears from a man old enough to be his father.

'You been at sea a lot longer than me, Leo. You've seen guys die, right?'

'Of course.'

'So why's Boags so special?'

'They're all special,' said Leo. 'You know that. You have to know that to lead them.'

'Poor Jimmy Sanborn was one thing. He was a damn

fool. But Boags was mine. He – I ran around like him when I was decking.'

Leo almost smiled. 'You haven't been a captain very long.'

Kevin shook his head. 'You look after guys. You stop 'em from doing stupid things that might get 'em killed. And then something like this happens.'

He snatched up his glasses, and tried to dry the eyepieces with his glove. 'Fucking guy. He was like a mini-superman . . . Leo, maybe I'm crazy, but it's like I can *feel* Boags still swimming – I know he can't be – but I can feel him. How can I leave here?'

'He's still swimming, Captain Kevin. But not in this sea.'

NINETEEN

Twenty-one days later, red-topped at daybreak, the twin towers of the World Trade Center rose on the horizon like a double thumbs up.

'"New York City,"' said Kevin Patrick, chain-lighting a Marlboro, and quoting Stevie Wonder. '"Just like I pitchered it."'

At 1100, Mary logged 'Ambrose Light', and showed him the numbers: in three weeks the *Bowery Queen* had towed the dead ship sixteen hundred miles at an average speed of three knots. The *Queen* had often bettered three knots, but they had lost a full day east of the Georges Bank waiting for a Canadian oiler to bunker them with fifty thousand gallons of diesel fuel, then two days in a storm that drove them backwards while she pulled her heart out.

And they had lost most of last night stopped off Montauk while J.D. and Kevin tried to fashion a makeshift seal for the port stern tube gland, which the bent tail shaft had finally popped. Seawater was still fountaining into the engine room. The pumps were grinding. And J.D. was looking grim.

'If we don't sink,' said Kevin, 'I'm going to drink brandy tonight. A lot of brandy.'

'Brandy and a bath.'

The *Mary Fulton* and the *Sally Fulton* hove into view, carrying a Sandy Hook pilot and a pickup crew of seamen for *Der Schmetterling*. Kevin and Mary shortened up the wire. The *Sally* got a line on the freighter's stern, and little *Mary* came alongside the *Queen* to deposit a beaming Mike.

Mary greeted him on the towing deck. Mike hugged her. 'Missed you.'

'Missed you, too, Dad. Missed you a lot and many times.'

'You done good. You done real good.'

'Come on up. Kev's in the wheelhouse.'

She helped him, wheezing and coughing, up the stairs. Her father had lost more weight. She could feel his ribs under his coat and his jowls were sagging, and yet something vital about the cock of his head gave her hope that he might make it through the winter.

With a hand draped casually over the steering sticks, Kevin had been working hard at the image of a man who regularly towed twenty-thousand-ton dead ships across the Atlantic. But he stood eagerly off the stool when Mike appeared.

'Hey, Cap.'

Mike Fulton observed him for a long moment under the guise of catching his breath at the top of the stairs. 'You done good, Kid.'

'Mary did it. I just drove.'

Mary patted Kevin's shoulder. 'He drove great. You should have seen it, Dad. He stood off the bow for an hour, in twenty-foot seas while we winched the wire aboard. He held her so steady you could have done brain surgery on the towing deck.'

Mike grinned at the hand Mary had forgotten to remove from Kevin's shoulder. 'Looks like you both done good. So how come the tug's listing?'

'The stern tube gland went, like I warned you.'

'Hey, if you told me you was going to do four thousand miles in the ocean, I would have fixed it.' He reached for the VHF. '*Mary*? You want to hip up, port side? Better use wire. She's sinking. Kevin fucked up a tail shaft.'

Little *Mary* huffed alongside. Mike directed the crew securing her to the *Queen*. He tossed Kevin the radio. 'There. Any other problems?'

'Yeah. Here comes the Coast Guard.'

'They want to survey the ship, make sure she won't sink in the channel. By the way, they scheduled a hearing for that stunt you pulled with the Okimitsu barge. Mary, there's lawyers coming for your log. And I put the ship agent aboard the freighter. He's going to check out the cargo. When she gets to Quarantine the insurers'll have a look, too.'

Mary had arranged most of this in the past week by radio-telephone. 'What's the word on a settlement?'

Mike looked worried. '*Der Schmetterling*'s lawyers are saying it was a piece of cake.'

'Relax,' said Kevin. 'Mary read a piece of her log to the Changs' lawyer. We could hear dollar signs rattling on the radio. "Tale a woe," he kept saying. "Tale a woe".'

'Bowery Queen?' boomed the VHF. '*This is Coast Guard Captain Frye on twenty-two-A.*'

'Jimmy Frye,' said Mike. 'A real ball buster.'

'*Welcome home, Captain Patrick. Where's this English broad?*'

'She kind of disappeared.'

'*Captain Patrick, we want to talk to her. So do Customs. So do Immigration. So do the Justice Department. So if you would just get to the point. Where the hell is she?*'

'She was with us until we bunkered. When the oiler was gone, so was she.'

'*What oiler?*'

'Canadian vessel out of Halifax.' Kevin looked at Mary, shaking his head. 'I told you this would come down on me.'

'I wouldn't piss these people off, if I had a hearing coming up,' Mike chuckled. 'Wha'd you do, let her go?'

'She went,' said Mary.

'Oiler captain sure as hell looked happy,' Kevin said.

'Good-looking broad?' Mike winked.

'Never saw her. Mary kept her under wraps back on the tow.' He pressed Transmit. 'Talk to you later, Captain Frye. I got my hands full here.'

The *Bowery Queen* unshackled her towing wire from *Der Schmetterling*'s anchor chain and secured the freighter to a mooring at Quarantine. Then, hipped up to little *Mary* on one side and *Sally* on the other, the listing tug proceeded up the Upper Bay and into the Kill van Kull.

J.D. ran up the wheelhouse steps. His overalls were wet to the knees. 'How much further, Kev?'

'About eighty yards.'

The Fulton dock was a decaying coffee barge, tied end on to the shore to form a long, narrow slip on either side.

'Isn't one of them slips silted up?'

'We'll dredge it soon,' Mike promised.

'Kev, if I were you, I'd aim for the shallow one.'

'Cheques!' Mary announced, striding into the galley in a skirt and blouse and high heels. 'Lloyd's of London cheques – good as gold.' She skidded on the deck, which slanted, marking the angle at which the *Bowery Queen* had come to rest in the mud two weeks ago.

J.D. caught her arm. 'Easy there, little lady. My, don't you smell good.'

'Where's Kev?'

'I think he's working the *Mary*,' J.D. answered.

'He's not on the *Mary*.'

J.D. gave her a sympathetic shrug.

Kevin had disappeared immediately after they landed. J.D. had predicted a two-week 'tomcattin'', during which the locals were advised to lock up their daughters. But he had returned in only three days, sombre and remote, and persuaded her father to put him to work running *Mary*, aboard which he had remained until last night.

'Well, we'd better not wait. You'll miss your plane.'

She fanned the cheques in her hand, and plucked them out one by one.

'Leo. And Roberto.'

'Thank you, Mary . . . So much?'

'My father and I thank you, and we probably should all thank our lawyer, who convinced *Der Schmetterling*'s insurers to be, if not quite generous, at least reasonable.'

The Filipinos were dressed in brand-new identical

sharkskin suits with a sheen like silver. Roberto sported a plastic surgeon's neat bandage from temple to temple, and a restaurateur's vivid Italian necktie. Leo's tie was a sober red, as befitted the owner of a Luzon piggery that J.D. had estimated would rival the size of Rhode Island. Suitcases and bags of gifts were heaped at their feet.

Mary handed Leo another cheque for Boags's mother. Her father was delivering Jimmy's to his mother. '. . . J.D.'

J.D. reached, with a sound of seams splitting. Leo and Roberto had taken him shopping with them, and had stuffed him into a double-breasted brass-buttoned blue blazer. Mary stroked the broadcloth as she handed the engineer his cheque. 'You sure about those chickens, J.D.? You're dressed like a man who raises racehorses.'

'I'm only wearin' it to give my old lady a thrill. Figure she can turn it into slipcovers for the davenport. Thank you, Mare. Thank you kindly.'

A taxi bounced down the rutted drive, blowing its horn. J.D., Leo and Roberto grabbed their bags. 'Hey, there's Kevin.'

Behind the taxi, bottoming on shot springs, a rusty, faded, flame-red Camaro skidded to a stop. Kevin jumped out, trailed by a tall blonde in boots, orange Lycra tights, and a rabbit coat. She gave him a big hug and kiss, waved to the crew and drove away.

J.D. patted Mary awkwardly on the shoulder. 'I thought he was hooked, but he sure ain't in the skillet yet . . .' He clumped on to the pier. 'You might be wise to throw him back . . . Well, you take care, now.'

Kevin helped load their bags into the taxi. 'Any of you guys ever need to work for a living, call me first.' He shook hands around. 'Mary aboard?'

'She's got your cheque.'

Kevin squared his shoulders and boarded the *Queen*. He found Mary in the wheelhouse, slouched in the battered port captain's stool with her feet on the dash and her skirt trailing down from her knees.

'Hi.' He knew what he wanted to say to her. All he had to do was form the first sentence.

Silently, she passed his cheque over her shoulder.

Kevin read it. It was ten times the biggest cheque he'd ever held. He slipped it carefully into his wallet. 'Thanks.'

'Thank *you*, Cap.'

'Listen, we gotta talk.'

'Oh yeah?'

Kevin took the starboard stool and propped his feet on the dash. Their toes almost touched over the radar. Mary brushed cookie crumbs off Mr Takashi's lacquer tray and studied 'The Breaking Wave off Kanagawa' in the fading light.

Kevin was still ordering his thoughts when she came back at him from an entirely different tack.

'What are you going to do with your money, Kev?'

'What? – Buy a tugboat.'

'You're not going to buy much of a tug for a hundred thousand bucks.'

'I can get bank money with this down payment. Or I can go in with somebody. I know some people running their own little boats. In fact I know a couple who run a little oil tanker up and down the Hudson. Guy and girl and little baby and a dog named Buster.'

'Are you looking for a tugboat or a family?'

'Never had much of a family. Except Mike. And you. What I'm trying to say –'

'You want to buy in to the *Queen*?'

'Sure. Depending on what it'll cost to raise her. Treat her right, keep her in shape, people notice. She's not that old, and we've sure as hell given her a reputation.'

'You'd dump your whole share into this boat?' she asked, sidetracking him again.

'I'd want my name on her.'

'You want to name the boat "Kevin"?'

'Let go of my chain. If I was investing my money in a company, I'd want my name in it.'

'Like Fulton & Patrick?'

'Why not? I've worked for Fulton Towing since I was fifteen. Listen Mary –'

'You realize *Sally*'s on her last legs and little *Mary* needs an engine before she kills somebody.'

'Sell them and put everything into the *Queen* is my vote.'

'One tugboat is not exactly a towing company any more.'

'Your great-great-great-whatever grandfather started with one. You had the right idea with the Okimitsu contract. Offshore's where it's at. We gotta baffle her stacks and engine room vents to keep the water out, but otherwise she's a hell of a tug.'

'What would I do under such an arrangement? We wouldn't need an office for one boat.'

'Go to school. Or open your plant shop. Or –' he looked at her, '– or you could study for your master's ticket, and I could sit for my Cape Cod and Sandy Hook pilot licences.'

'Where'd you go when we landed?'

At last, thought Kevin. 'I went out to get laid. Instead, I got drunk.'

'Maybe after you got drunk you got laid, but don't remember.'

'I'm sure – that's what I want to talk to you about. We can talk boats later. The thing is, I'm kind of in love. With you. I mean, we get along pretty good. Very good. Three weeks rockin' and rollin' out there I'm still glad to see your face. And now, cleaned up and dressed and all, you look good enough to eat. And I was just wondering, do we have a shot at making something work?'

'Who's the bimbo in the Camaro?'

Kevin took a deep breath. All he had to do was lie and he would be a free man for the rest of his life. But thanks to Mary Fulton, chasing women who wanted to get caught wasn't that much fun any more.

'That was no bimbo,' he told her. 'That was my mother.'

'*What?*'

Mary's feet hit the deck and she skidded off her stool. Kevin caught her.

'I went to see my mom. First time in ten years.'

'Oh my god, Kevin. What's she like?'

'She's okay, I guess. She hit me up for money. I wasn't surprised. I didn't expect her to be much different. I mean, it's me I'm trying to change.'

'Trying? Sounds to me like you've already changed and don't know it.'

'So what do you say?'

'Do you want me or my tug?'

'I went for a blood test. Passed.'

'All this and safe sex too?'

'Well, I wouldn't go that far. Last time we almost sank the boat.'

The Shipkiller
Justin Scott

The riveting story of a supertanker, sea-monster, killer.

When *Leviathan* – the largest moving object on the face of the earth, 1,800 feet of arrogance and power – bears down on Peter and Carolyn Hardin's ketch *Siren*, the smaller boat is brushed aside, crushed out of existence. Carolyn, ripped from Peter's frantic grasp, is lost; Peter is left battered, half-dead but vowing vengeance. Obsessed by the awful might of the technological giant, Hardin becomes the shipkiller, stalking his murderous prey across the raging seas and oceans to a final, apocalyptic confrontation in the snake-filled waters of the Persian Gulf.

'A marvellously taut, brilliantly told story of revenge, and the sea and the dark forces that can shape the human condition'
Robert Ludlum

'The biggest sea-hunt since Ahab . . . a first-rate tale of suspense' *Publishers Weekly*

'As heady as Francis Chichester's narrative, with a draught of Melville' *Time*

ISBN 0 586 04861 8

The Cossack's Bride
Justin Scott

A towering story of love and espionage.

Combining glamour and ruthlessness, Natalie and Wallace Nevsky were both respected and feared throughout the sophisticated, dangerous world of the fur trade. Having just launched their latest and most spectacular range to an ecstatic reception, the Nevskys were the toast of the fashion industry. Suddenly, amid the flashing of cameras and the excited buzz of the post-show celebrations, came a sound like the popping of a champagne cork. Wallace spun around and, with an astonished look on his face, fell to the ground. The party was over . . .

With the brutal killing of her husband comes Natalie's shocking discovery that their life together was not as it seemed. Back in his native Russia, Nevsky had been playing a deadly game of espionage – and his one mistake had cost him his life. Now, thrust into a dark and seedy world of spying and murder, Natalie must learn to walk a tightrope of survival – and she cannot afford to put one foot wrong . . .

'With elegance, intelligence and pluck, Natalie outwits. Like a female James Bond'   *Publishers Weekly*

ISBN 0 586 06969 0